Dancing
with
David

Karen,

I hope you enjoy
the Dance with David!

Shalom,

Sieg

Dancing with David

SIEGFRIED JOHNSON

atmosphere press

Dancing with David is premised on two actual events in the archaeological history of the Dead Sea: (1) the 1956 discovery in Cave 11 of the Great Psalms Scroll, which included a psalm often labeled Psalm 151 and described as David's only autobiographical song; (2) the 2017 excavation of Cave 53, a joint project of The Hebrew University of Jerusalem and Liberty University in Virginia, its lead archaeologists concluding that Cave 53 had once housed Dead Sea scrolls which were likely looted by locals and sold to antiquities dealers.

The Mount of Olives conclusion of *Dancing with David* centers on two 20th century architectural marvels built by the renowned Italian architect, Antonio Barluzzi: (1) The Church of All Nations, also known as the Basilica of the Agony, completed in 1924; (2) The Church of Dominus Flevit, meaning, "The Lord wept," completed in 1955.

Unless otherwise noted, quotations from Psalm 89 are from The Jerusalem Bible, General Editor Alexander Jones, Doubleday and Company, Inc., 1966. All other scripture references, unless specifically noted, are from The Holy Bible, New International Version, 1973, International Bible Society.

Dancing with David is dedicated to the many hundreds of friends who have since 1997 trusted me to guide their pilgrim journey to the Holy Land. We often describe the Holy Land experience as one's "Journey of a Lifetime." After writing *Dancing with David*, I shall prefer in the future to invite those considering travel to join me in the "Dance of a Lifetime," the Lands of the Bible our dance floor.

Hail, Queen of Heaven, the Ocean Star,
Guide of the wanderer here below,
Thrown on life's surge, we claim thy care,
Save us from peril and from woe.
Mother of Christ, Star of the Sea
Pray for the wanderer, pray for me.

(Marian hymn, Father John Lingard, 1771 – 1851)

MOUNT OF OLIVES, EAST JERUSALEM
SATURDAY, NOVEMBER 26, 2022

"I bring you glad tidings of great joy!"

Pastor Michael Tabash's proclamation, timed for precisely 3:39 p.m. and crafted to replicate the joy of the angels as they announced Jesus' birth to the shepherds in the fields of Bethlehem, reverberated over the still gathering crowd of some four hundred onlookers at the terraced pavilion built into the upper slope of the Mount of Olives. Offering a breathtaking overlook of Jerusalem's Old City, each day a steady stream of eager tourists emerges from their motor coaches to line up for their group photo, a must-have souvenir with the Dome of the Rock prominent in the background. That golden gleaming holy site of Islam has stood for over a thousand years on Jerusalem's Temple Mount where once, three thousand years ago, stood Solomon's Temple and then, in Jesus' time, the Second Temple, often called Herod's.

"I bring you glad tidings of great joy for all people!" my dear friend shouted again after the crowd's energetic response had subsided, "for unto you is born this day on the Mount of Olives – exactly twelve hours ago, at 3:39 a.m. – the child prophesied by the seventh tablet of David's last psalm, discovered only nine months ago not far down the Palm Sunday path from where we are standing. With joy I proclaim to you that Regina Malka Maris-Aaronson, resting now less than a mile away from this spot, at Augusta Victoria Hospital,

3

she now entering the 13th hour of her miraculous life, is the promised daughter of King David and his Star of the Sea."

As Michael paused his sermon in response to the crowd's surge of emotional energy upon hearing the good news of Regina's birth, I looked down at my newborn daughter, cradled softly against my chest with my left arm. She had been lightly fussy since I fed her an hour earlier, but seemed now, at Michael's calling of her name, to grow blissfully peaceful. My husband, sitting on the right side of my hospital bed nearer the window, was holding his phone at arm's length for us to watch the nearby celebration together. Seeing that Regina's fussing had stopped, he gripped my hand, our eyes connecting to convey utter joy and profound thanksgiving.

Our attention immediately came back to his phone as Michael shouted, "Maranatha Assembly, let us glorify God, who has answered our prayers for the peace of Jerusalem, sending Regina to join her holy brother, Jesus, the Son of David, to bring healing to the peoples of this Holy Land, in fulfillment of David's prophecy. God's promise is not only for the peoples of this Land. The seventh tablet declares that she has come to guide all nations. People of all races, colors, and creeds will be called out of their perilous wandering and into the safe harbor of peace."

Michael Tabash had founded his church, the rapidly growing Holy Land Maranatha Assembly of the Blessed Hope, only eight months earlier, on the day my husband, Hebrew University archaeologist David Aaronson, announced to the world that our quest to find the seventh tablet had been successful. At first comprised of only local Palestinian Christians who were neighbors and friends of the Tabash family, as news of the seventh tablet's message spread, the church quickly grew, evolving into a mosaic congregation of believers from a wide array of different backgrounds and

4

faiths. Whether Palestinian, Jew or other, all found unity in the belief that soon would be fulfilled King David's newly revealed prophecy that he would return in spirit to father a daughter with his beloved Star of the Sea, and that this miracle child would be for the healing of the nations.

Earlier this morning, after coming to greet our newborn at Augusta Victoria, Michael had texted his entire church, summoning them to the pavilion for his precisely timed proclamation, an assembly now being joined by curious tourists who, knowing little or nothing of the prophecy, were being drawn by the energy of the festival atmosphere.

Clustered around Michael on the road connecting the pavilion to my hospital room were thirty-nine children. Clad in brightly colored t-shirts of various hues, they were in constant motion, moving in a circle around him to create a kaleidoscope effect. These were the children who had, in a processional parade this morning, greeted Regina at our hospital window. Three by three by three they came as David and I stood and waved, holding our daughter up for these little magi triads to celebrate by laying small gifts, flowers and olive leaves outside our window.

David and I laughed, recognizing the sweet faces of many of the children as we watched the rally on his cell phone, Michael's wife, Tamara, having established a Facetime connection for us to see and hear the joy-filled gathering.

"This mountain has been a place of weeping," Michael preached. "Three thousand years ago King David wept on this mountain as he fled Jerusalem, his dynasty crippled by his own son's treachery, the evil Absalom. A thousand years later, Jesus, the Son of David, showered this mountain with his tears as he gazed over the city, prophesying that it would soon fall to the Romans. 'Jerusalem, Jerusalem,' he cried, 'how often I would have gathered you under my wings as a hen gathers her chicks, but you were not willing.'"

Michael paused to survey the crowd, breathing in waves of energy from their mounting enthusiasm. "Behold, my friends," he started again, "how God has answered our prayers! This mountain has been a place of weeping, but on this day all tears are wiped away. This Mount of Olives is today a mountain of rejoicing! Weeping may stay for the night, the psalmist wrote, but rejoicing comes in the morning. On this mountain, early this very morning, joy has arrived! Joy to the world! Joy to the world!"

I heard Tamara shout, "This is the day the Lord has made, let us rejoice and be glad in it!"

Michael, laughing, said, "Yes, my wife! *Shukran*, thank you! Indeed, this is the day that the Lord has made, so let us sing together!" David and I joined in as Michael led the crowd, singing "This Is the Day," a chorus sung thousands of times a day by pilgrim groups in the Holy Land, but I think never more exuberantly joyful than on this day of Regina's birth. As the crowd clapped and cheered, I gazed at our now sleeping daughter, then turned to offer a silent, contented smile to David.

Looking beyond David and out the window, my thoughts drifted from Michael's preaching to recall that on the road between the hospital and the pavilion sits the Chapel of the Ascension, a small dome from the Crusader era of a thousand years ago built over a strange rock they believed bore the last imprint of the feet of Jesus before he was taken up into heaven, as if the divine energy required for the ascension had actually scarred the rock upon which Jesus had been standing. For thirty-nine days Jesus had made post-resurrection appearances before, on the fortieth day, ascending to heaven. Since Jesus promised that he would return "in like manner" as they had seen him rise, Christian theologians have taught that Jesus' return to earth would be here, on the Mount of Olives, in a manifestation of power and glory.

But what if God planned something very different than centuries of professional theologians have imagined? What if God's next step in the redemptive plan is to send another baby, this time, a girl? Why, after all, should it be surprising if God's plan unfolds differently than long expected? Was not a virgin giving birth to a boy in a Bethlehem cave two thousand years ago drastically unlike long-held Jewish messianic expectations? Could it not happen again?

I believe that God has once again surprised his people. To help you understand what has brought us to this glorious day on the Mount of Olives, we must turn the clock back fifteen months, to September 2021, when I began to write my story of Dancing with David, inspired by my then-future husband's Dead Sea discovery of King David's last psalm.

That ancient song, the original Psalm 151, reminded me who I once was, and who I am yet Called to be.

Prologue

Maranatha Assembly of the Blessed Hope

FAYETTEVILLE, ARKANSAS

MONDAY, SEPTEMBER 27, 2021

My name is Stella Maris, and this is my story of Dancing with David. I don't mean with David Aaronson, my former professor and recently made famous archaeologist, though today I would leap at the opportunity, his stunning Dead Sea discovery nine months ago confirming the story I've told for thirty-three years that, bizarre as it sounds, I danced with Israel's greatest king, who called me his Star of the Sea.

Inspired by Dr. Aaronson's classes during 1988's fall semester, I experienced six dreams of being sent to David as his Muse. Though I came to regard these dream-wanderings as private, heaven-sent confirmation of my Call to ministry, I've always sensed they were more, a suspicion of the heart now buoyed by Dr. Aaronson's discovery of six inscribed limestone tablets scattered amid ancient human remains in Qumran's Cave 53.

I had at first shared my dreams only with my college fiancé, Jakob Rothman, who, hearing my descriptions, agreed that they had to be more than mere dreams. Long ago I gave up that claim. While through the years I've often shared the six visions with my congregation, my intent was to convey how God sent them to me as a gift to renew my then-fading sense of a Call, reclaiming me for service in his Kingdom. In my heart of hearts, though, I never relinquished my imagining that I had actually guided David at key moments in his life, beginning with his anointing by the prophet Samuel in Bethlehem.

Since reading Dr. Aaronson's English translation of the new Psalm 151 twenty-one days ago, utterly swept away is any vestige of doubt about the miraculous nature of my visions, especially when I read that David had dedicated his song to a woman whom he called his Star of the Sea. Reading those words in an *Israel Hayom* (Israel Today) online article three weeks ago resurrected the remembrance of my visions, recalling how the words Star of the Sea sounded in Hebrew as they fell from David's sweet lips, *Kochav Hayam*.

Readers versed in Latin may think my name proves my story a delusional fantasy and me a fraud, wondering if I took Stella Maris as a nom de plume only after reading the Aaronson translation. Stella Maris, you see, is Latin for Star of the Sea, one of the many names in Roman Catholic tradition assigned to Mary, the mother of Jesus.

In fact, though, my name has been Stella Maris since the day I was born in 1966 in Siloam Springs, Arkansas, thirty-nine miles from my present home in Fayetteville, where today I serve as Teaching Elder of the Maranatha Assembly of the Blessed Hope, a church emphasizing Bible prophecy, the triumphant return of Jesus to the Mount of Olives, our Blessed Hope.

Dr. Aaronson used to say that divine providence, like Hebrew letters, must be read backwards. It must be true, for how could my parents have known fifty-five years ago that the Hebrew equivalent of the name they had chosen for their newborn girl would one day surface in a Dead Sea text to validate their daughter's bizarre claims?

My name is no mystery, Stella Maris being my mom's married name, her maiden name Stella Jackson. My dad, Lt. Colonel Hans Maris, was a second generation American whose Scandinavian parents from Copenhagen, Hans and Ursa Maris, found it delightful that their soon-to-be daughter-in-law's name would become Stella Maris. Roman Catholics born and raised in Denmark before immigrating to the United States, they knew well their religion's veneration of the name as a title honoring the holy mother of Jesus.

Soon after mom became pregnant with me in the summer of 1965, my dad, a fighter pilot, redeployed to Vietnam. Already back in Asia when he received word that mom was pregnant, dad declared his wish to name their baby, if a girl, Stella Marie Maris, saying that he thought growing up as Marie Maris would be easier than Stella Maris.

Mom didn't go for it, though, protesting that she loved her married name and that her daughter would love it as well. Instead of Marie, she insisted that my middle name be that of dad's mother, Ursa, a Scandinavian name meaning, "Little She Bear."

At first dad objected, arguing that Ursa, an uncommon name even in Denmark, was unheard of in America. The argument ceased, though, dad giving in to mom's wishes one night after an intense nighttime sortie in Vietnam. It was Christmas Eve, mom nearly seven months pregnant. The fight over, he broke through high clouds and, just as he was breathing a prayer of thanks to have survived, witnessed an incredibly vivid Ursa Minor. He told mom that Polaris, the North Star, was shining with such an intensity that he took it as a divine sign that Ursa was God's intended name for their unborn daughter.

Dad often told me that story as a child, always ending with a bear hug as he declared his love for the little north star of his life, his then blond and still blue-eyed she-bear. He would often remind me, even up to the time he passed away three years ago, that my initials – S.U.M. – meant that I was the SUM, the fullness of his joy.

That's how I came to be named Stella Maris, the Star of the Sea so prominent in the recently discovered psalm from the Dead Sea, archaeology confirming my story of a time when I, a twenty-two-year-old college senior, experienced six dreams – visions would be the better word – of being sent to David as his Muse, aiding him in spiritual combat against a foe far more formidable than Goliath. David called this enemy *Hakol*, meaning, The Voice.

I had my own Muse voice, that of Professor David Aaronson. While for the last fifteen years he has taught on the faculty of The Hebrew University of Jerusalem, in 1988 he was a charming and charismatic thirty-two-year-old professor from Boston in his first year of teaching at Covenant Christian College in Memphis, a school students and faculty affection-ately called C-cube.

I kept a journal of my dreams, of course, each experienced after one of Dr. Aaronson's six classroom lectures on Psalm 89. While my precise memory of his classes and of my visions naturally faded a bit more with each passing year, I've managed to keep them alive by sharing them with the congregation I've served for twenty-seven years, since 1994, Fayetteville's Maranatha Assembly. In sermons and classes, I've many times told how extraordinarily intense those six dreams were, saying (smiling, of course, so they wouldn't think I actually believed) how I wished one day to see them proven real.

That day has come.

I've told many hundreds of people over the three decades of my teaching about the extraordinary gift I received in 1988, how with each awakening I was filled with gratitude to be the recipient of such an unsought miracle and undeserved gift.

But if a gift, who was the giver? Experiencing something this magical could only have been heaven-sent. How else could one's dreams open a portal into the biblical past, unless heaven intended to accomplish something extraordinary?

I find myself a bit ashamed now that, as powerful as my dreams had been, pulsating with aliveness in 1988, I came to use them only to sprinkle sentimental seasoning into my sermons. I wonder now, after Cave 53's six tablets have matched precisely my six dreams, how I could ever have come to regard these gifts as merely private.

That changed twenty-one days ago, Monday, September 6, with the *Israel Hayom* online report of their interview with archaeologist David Aaronson, he announcing the publication of his English translation of the newly discovered Psalm 151. It was Labor Day in America, so, with our church offices closed, I had plenty of time to download and study the Aaronson translation. With each line of text my dreams re-emerged with astonishing clarity, the newly discovered psalm brushing away the patina of the years.

Fascinating, I think, that Dr. Aaronson's announcement on September 6 happened to fall precisely on the thirty-third anniversary of the day we met. It had been on Tuesday, September 6, 1988, that I sat in the front row of his Hebrew Poetry class at C-cube and accepted his invitation to step onto the Star of David dance floor. I would receive my first vision that very night.

Before I take you back to 1988, I'll share with the reader that *Israel Hayom* article that rocked my world, a media conversation with the archaeologist who tripped upon the first Hebrew Dead Sea text discovered since 1956. Fitting I find it that, just as the first Dead Sea scrolls were discovered accidentally by Bedouin teenagers seeking lost sheep, so the last Dead Sea text was discovered accidentally, a professor-led field trip with no intention, nor even tools, for excavation. His post-earthquake, getting-away-from-covid-lockdown excursion out of Jerusalem with a couple of his own student "sheep" was intended only to give them space to breathe without a mask. Where better to do that than the vastness of the Judean Wilderness?

One last thing is necessary for the reader to understand before I take you back to 1988, perhaps the most important thing. I hear the new Psalm 151 as an invitation to return to the dance floor. The sixth tablet tells of a hidden seventh tablet on which are recorded the king's dying words, prophesying that it will one day be discovered by David's *Kochav Hayam* and the one whom she will call *Ishi* (my husband).

Though single, I am married. This is not a contradiction. I've been married for thirty-three years to the church, a decision I made on the morning after my sixth vision, immediately breaking off my engagement to Jakob. Now, reading the sixth tablet prophecy of the Star of David and her husband discovering the long-lost seventh tablet, my fifty-five-year-old body is infused with twenty-two-year-old energy, confident that my husband – the church – will support my Calling to find the seventh tablet.

The journey I invite the reader to embark upon, then, will be much more than a nostalgic thirty-three-year jaunt into the past, our Boston-bred Jewish professor skillfully weaving current events into his teaching – 1988 happenings in sports, film, politics, and more. Dr. Aaronson infused his teaching on ancient texts with current events in a way never diversionary. He called it the art of misdirection, claiming misdirection indispensable as a tool for teachers, just as it is for magicians. For David Aaronson – an admirer of David Copperfield, both born on the same day, September 16, 1956 – inspired teaching is magical.

His teaching was, indeed, magical. Students would wonder where he could possibly be headed, but always he led us to the "Aha!" moment, leading us to a deeper appreciation of Hebrew literature. That's what he wanted most, that his students fall in love with the stories of the Hebrew Bible.

Reader, I invite you to step into the past with me, then to join me on an adventure of discovery. We must first go back to 1988 and then further, to King David's 10th century BCE, before we embark upon our still unfolding adventure, our Holy Land quest for the seventh tablet of King David's last song.

Before our journey commences, here's that *Israel Hayom* online article from three weeks ago, proof that I danced with David.

And that I will again.

Cave 53's new Psalm 151: A Conversation with Archaeologist David Aaronson

ISRAEL HAYOM, ONLINE
MONDAY, SEPTEMBER 6, 2021

Dr. David Aaronson, a Hebrew University professor of biblical Hebrew and archaeology, announced this morning from his Mt. Scopus campus office, in a Zoom call joined by multiple media outlets, the publication of his English translation of the new Hebrew text version of Psalm 151, which he discovered eight months earlier in Qumran's Cave 53. Composed on six inscribed limestone tablets, the Aaronson translation compiles the text by placing each tablet's story in the sequence of events known from the biblical record.

Aaronson pointed out that while the collection of psalms in the Hebrew Bible concludes with Psalm 150, two ancient versions of a text known as Psalm 151 have been previously known: a Greek text in the Septuagint (LXX), and a Hebrew version of the same psalm discovered in 1956 in Cave 11.

Composed as an autobiographical song, in both previously existing versions David recounts only two events in his early life: the first his being selected and anointed by the prophet Samuel despite his small stature relative to his taller brothers; and the second being his vanquishing of the Philistine giant, Goliath.

For centuries, he noted, scholars supposed the unnumbered LXX text placed after Psalm 150 to be an original Greek composition, there being no known Hebrew text. That assumption was proven wrong in February 1956 with the discovery of The Great Psalms Scroll in Cave 11. Also known as 11Q5, the Great Psalms Scroll is housed in the Shrine of the Book wing of the Israel Museum and can also be found in the Leon Levy Dead Sea Scrolls Digital Library.

Aaronson pointed to the most obvious distinguishing feature of the new Psalm 151 as its length. While including both of the aforementioned early events in David's career, the new text's additions carry the ancient king's against-all-odds story further, incorporating three subsequent events known from the Hebrew Bible: (1) his sparing of Saul's life in the cave of Ein Gedi; (2) his being dissuaded by one of his future wives, Abigail, from killing her foolish husband, Nabal; (3) his lurid dancing while leading the Ark of the Covenant into Jerusalem.

Cave 53, originally discovered in 1993 during a jointly-sponsored archaeological survey known as Operation Scroll, had most recently been excavated in January/February 2017 by archaeologists Randall Price of Liberty University and Oren Gutfeld of The Hebrew University of Jerusalem. While yielding no new Dead Sea manuscripts, seven storage jars identical to those discovered in Caves 1–11 were found, leading the archaeologists to publish an article for The Society of Biblical Literature in their November 2017 issue, titled, "The Discovery of a New Dead Sea Scroll Cave at Qumran."

To discover more Dead Sea manuscripts, Aaronson noted, has been for decades the Holy Grail of archaeologists. All efforts since 1956 to discover Hebrew texts in the Dead Sea caves have proven futile until Aaronson's discovery in Cave 53. While the IAA (Israel Antiquities Authority) announced only six months ago, in March 2021, a new discovery of dozens of fragments of biblical text from Zechariah and Nahum in a cave known as the Cave of Horror (due to the dozens of skeletons found during the cave's initial exploration in the 1960s), those 1900-year-old texts were written in Greek, not Hebrew.

The first post-1950's Dead Sea text written in Hebrew was discovered when Aaronson's field trip to Cave 53 on January 18 revealed an adjacent cavity that, assumedly after an ancient collapse, was almost entirely filled in and completely sealed off from the portion of the cave excavated to the bedrock four years earlier.

Aaronson explained that the timing of his mission had been intentional, based on his speculation that the cave's structure might have been compromised in the aftermath of a swarm of twelve small-magnitude earthquakes impacting the area nine days earlier, on January 9. The largest of the quakes, its epicenter only three kilometers north of Qumran, registered 4.5, followed by smaller quakes rumbling south like a drum roll along the western edge of the Dead Sea. Throughout history, he noted, this region has experienced significant quake activity, Qumran sitting in the Great Syrian-African Rift, a tear in the earth's crust extending 3700 miles from northern Syria as far south as Mozambique.

After his post-quake discovery, Aaronson assigned a name to the January 9 earthquakes, *Ra'ash Shevi'it Katan* (the Minor Seventh Noise), January 9 having been Shabbat and resulting in a discovery sure to make noise throughout the scholarly world.

Asked why, if the discovery had been so significant, he would call the quake a minor noise, he explained that *Ra'ash Shevi'it* (the Seventh Noise) is a term often used to describe the vastly more devastating quake of January 18, 749 CE, largely destroying the cities of Tiberias, Beth Shean, and Hippos. His January 18 discovery, then, coincided with the anniversary of the *Ra'ash Shevi'it* quake.

Millions of tourists have visited the spectacular ruins of Beth Shean National Park, the only ancient Decapolis city situated west of the Jordan River. While that January 18 quake left Beth Shean with only a shadow of its glorious Roman past, tourists can today roam the once ornate, colonnaded streets, observe the workings of its opulent Roman bathhouse, and sit in its impressive amphitheater.

Not only does Shabbat punctuate each week, Aaronson reminded, but each seventh year punctuates Jewish life in what is called a Year of Release, known as a *Shmita* year, meaning "Release." The name *Ra'ash Shevi'it* was assigned to the devastating quake of 749 CE since that year was a seventh, *Shmita* Year of Release.

Aaronson said that when he set out on a field trip to poke around Cave 53, nine days after the January 9 quakes, he was hoping that the relatively minor Shabbat shaking on January 9 had been a noise sufficient to release yet more of Qumran's hidden secrets.

"We knew immediately that our hopes were realized," Dr. Aaronson said, "as upon entering the cave it was evident that a wall had fractured, creating a jagged opening, a crevice through which a small cavity was visible. Though not nearly large enough for a person to enter, we could plainly see skeletal remains, along with the cornered edges of what appeared to be stone tablets."

Asked about reports that he had become ill upon seeing

the bones and tablets, he laughed, "Yes, that is true. I became suddenly light-headed and passed out. I would like to blame it on wearing a mask, but we weren't wearing masks, our trip to the desert being an opportunity to ditch them for the day. Regaining consciousness after only a minute or two, I find it humorous that my students had all put their masks back on, thinking I must have been infected with covid. I wasn't, and can only conclude that my temporary illness was my body's response to the rush of excitement. We were a little concerned at first, wondering if the crevice might have released odorless toxic fumes. I quickly recovered, though, and was fine. Better than fine, actually. The adrenaline that kicked in on January 18 hasn't left me to this day."

After photographing the cavity, Aaronson explained, the images were sent to the IAA, whose subsequent exploration was able to exhume and examine the human remains, determining them to be those of a male approximately sixty-five years old and dating to the 10th century BCE, nearly a thousand years older than the Qumran community producing the Dead Sea Scrolls.

"While unexpected," he said, "this dating of the bones and stones is not entirely surprising, the 1993 initial survey of the cave having produced flint arrowheads identified as Neolithic, as well as blades appearing to be Canaanite, evidence of the cave's use by populations inhabiting the area long before the Dead Sea Scroll community of Qumran."

Recovered with the bones were six limestone tablets, each of rectangular cut and similar size, the largest measuring 30.54 x 23.27 cm. The tablets, all inscribed, were in good condition and bore a Paleo-Hebrew script identical to that of the famed Gezer Calendar discovered in 1908 in the Canaanite city of Gezer. A smaller limestone tablet by roughly a third (11.1 x 7.2 cm), the Gezer Calendar bore seven lines of text and was similarly dated to the 10th century BCE.

"The six tablets," Aaronson said, "were likely placed in Cave 53 in a funerary ritual, adding to the mystery of identifying the bones and generating speculation as to how the man came to be buried with King David's last poetic work."

Unveiling the tablets' significant additions to the previously known stories of Psalm 151, Aaronson stated that he long suspected the two previous versions of Psalm 151 to be incomplete.

"That the new Psalm 151 carries David's story further along the biblical trajectory of his life should not be surprising, the new Psalm 151 inviting the reader to join David through yet more significant moments of his monumental life, even dancing with him as he leads the Ark of the Covenant into *Yerushalayim*."

Pointing to the psalm's most intriguing mystery, Aaronson said, "Truly astonishing is the appearance of a woman previously unknown in biblical history. Appearing, evidently without aging, in each episode of his life, she is present in all six tablets. David describes her, not merely as a woman, but something more, his Angel, his Muse. So important is this woman that David, in the sixth tablet, dedicates his song to her."

Elaborating on the three names assigned to this mystery woman, Aaronson said, "David first calls her Eliana, meaning, 'My God has answered me,' affirming her sudden appearance in Bethlehem an answer to his prayers. Second, he calls her My Angel/Muse, my translation of the Hebrew *Malaki*. Third, and most fascinating, David calls her his *Kochav Hayam*, meaning, Star of the Sea. We can only hope that future discoveries will tell us more about this woman whose impact on Jewish history, unknown until now, was clearly profound."

Asked about the sixth tablet, Aaronson pointed to its

uniqueness in containing no subsequent story from David's life. "The sixth tablet serves as a footnote, extremely important, the author naming himself as Shemaiah ben Nethanel. This name is known from the Bible's story of David, a *sofer* (scribe) listed in 1 Chronicles 24:6 as a Levite active near the end of David's life, one privileged to work in the presence of the king."

Asked why the new Psalm 151 might end with David's entrance into Jerusalem, Aaronson said, "That is a very good question. While I am thankful we now have more of David's life in his song, I, too, wonder why the new Psalm 151 doesn't continue beyond his conquering of Jerusalem, his capital for the remaining thirty-three years of his life. Half of David's life is still missing. Why? It's a mystery, and the sixth tablet offers an even greater mystery, Shemaiah claiming that he hid a seventh tablet, and that David's *Kochav Hayam* will one day prove her identity by discovering the tablet with her husband. This prophecy of Shemaiah weights the song with apocalyptic overtones, similar to Revelation's description of the Lamb who alone is worthy to open the seventh seal."

Asked if there was a common denominator in the now five stories from David's life, Aaronson said, "Again, you ask a great question. Yes, a clear standard is evident. Each story emphasizes the smallness of David's stature, thus amplifying his legendary exploits. This theme is announced in the opening words of the psalm as recorded in now all three extant texts, reading, 'Smaller was I than my brothers.' Now, I'm an archaeologist and not a psychologist, but I think the new Psalm 151 provides a window into David's soul, so that we can observe his struggle to discern the voice of God over the voice of *Hakol*, his enemy, meaning, the Voice. This voice of *Hakol* was intent upon reminding David how small he was, and don't we all have such a voice with which we must contend? The story of *Hakol*, the Voice, who comes to us seeking harm, is as old as the serpent in Eden. Everyone struggles against the Voice."

Concluding, Aaronson said, "As exciting as the Cave 53 discovery is for what it has revealed, I confess to having hoped, when it first dawned on me that this was David's Psalm 151, that the song would bring David's life all the way to his deathbed. Only there do we read the story of his being nursed by Abishag the Shunamite, the beautiful young virgin described in 1 Kings 1 as having been brought in to warm the aging king. The text adds the awkward note that the king had no intercourse with her. So, while I am disappointed that Psalm 151 ends with his conquest of Jerusalem, I hold out hope that perhaps, on another day and in another cave, we will discover the seventh tablet, and that it will provide the final piece of the puzzle, the quintessential finale for this song celebrating King David."

Asked a final question, if he had any theories as to the identification of Cave 53's skeletal remains, Aaronson answered, "No, I don't. To determine with any confidence this man's identity seems an impossible dream. Perhaps these bones belonged to the person who hid David's song, perhaps Shemaiah himself in an act of ritual suicide. On the other hand, perhaps these bones simply belong to an ancient explorer, his tragic death claiming him as the cave collapsed at precisely the moment of his greatest discovery.

"Whose bones are these? For now, perhaps forever, this remains a mystery. However, let us have faith. After all, *Rosh Hashana*, the Jewish New Year, begins today, so that the next *Shmita* year – the Sabbatical 'Year of Release' – begins fully tomorrow, September 7, 2021, Year 5782 in our Jewish calendar. Could it be that, during this *Shmita* year, the noise of a new epiphany will be released to answer the triad of

mysteries posed by the Cave 53 discovery of Psalm 151:
Where is the seventh tablet?
Whose bones are these?
Who is David's Star of the Sea?"

Chapter 1

First Aaronson Lecture – The Star of David Dance Floor

COVENANT CHRISTIAN COLLEGE, MEMPHIS, TENNESSEE

TUESDAY, SEPTEMBER 6, 1988, 2:00 P.M.

"Here's an idea for a television series," Professor Aaronson announced, calling his class of fresh faces to attention. "Celebrities competing against each other in a dance competition, each paired with a professional dancer. America would love it, don't you think?"

Walking toward the television monitor near my front row desk, he said, "I think I'd call it Dancing with the Stars."

"Nobody would ever watch such a thing," I remember thinking. Obviously, as I share my story these thirty-three years later, I was wrong.

"In my six lecture series opening this semester's class in Hebrew Poetry, I'll invite you to dance with the brightest star

24

of Israel's ancient history, King David. Born 3,000 years ago in Bethlehem, David ben Jesse's star shines brightly still. On these Tuesdays and Thursdays of September, I'll be inviting you to dance with David, the Star of David our dance floor."

Bowing, he added, "And I am delighted, as C-cube's newest professor, to be your professional partner, your guide."

Taking a remote from atop his desk he aimed it at the monitor, which then lit up with a bright, multi-colored Star of David formed by six dancers appearing to be whirling dervishes. The bodies of all six emerged from the center of the star, so that each of the six points of the Star of David was formed by the extended right arm of the dervish.

"In this intriguing image, the points of the star's hexagon are formed by the outstretched arms of six synchronized dancers. Like Rumi's dervishes, each dancer's right arm is raised higher than the left, as if to receive the blessings of heaven, while each dancer's left arm is lowered into the center of the star, suggesting that divine blessing is to flow through the dancer to the world."

So began my first class with Professor David Aaronson, a unique figure at our small Christian college in Memphis. Not only was he the only Jewish professor on our faculty, he was also the only non-southerner, hailing from Boston. Having completed his doctorate in the spring of 1988 at the University of Michigan in Ann Arbor, Professor Aaronson came to Memphis eager to launch his teaching career in the most unlikely of places for a Jewish scholar – a small and thoroughly southern Christian college.

He quickly won the admiration of C-cube's students, an aura growing around him as his passion for ancient Hebrew literature shone through his teaching. His classes made the

Old Testament – the Hebrew Bible, as he playfully insisted we call it – come alive.

I would discover that semester that much more than the Hebrew Bible would come alive in me under his teaching. On each of the nights following his first six lectures I experienced an intense dream of being sent to the biblical past as Muse to David ben Jesse, Israel's greatest king. It is Dr. Aaronson's recent Dead Sea discovery that compels me now to share my visions from 1988, and the transformation those three weeks thirty-three years ago made in my life.

Dr. Aaronson's teaching seemed to me very much like a Holy Land guide. I had joined a guided tour of Israel with my parents in the summer of 1987, between my sophomore and junior years. While our Israeli guide had the advantage of a classroom in which the biblical landscape spread out in living color before our eyes, each classroom experience with Dr. Aaronson in Memphis brought my Holy Land memories back in vibrant color, despite our room being bordered by four walls with our only window looking out at the traffic on Poplar Avenue.

While it was no wonder that he quickly won over the students of C-cube (college students, like the ancient Athenians, seem always fascinated by the newest thing), it was a bit of a miracle that he seemed even to have won over those faculty members who had at first questioned our college president's out-of-the-box, controversial decision to invite a Jewish scholar onto the faculty of a Christian college.

Especially, I heard, our two Old Testament professors at first regarded his hiring an insult, as if the school's president and board were somehow declaring them unfit, inadequate to the students' educational expectations. The rumor I heard was that they penned an angry letter to President Farris, reminding him that our school's mission was to offer students a

Christ-centered environment for learning. How, then, they asked, can you justify hiring a Jewish professor?

Our president's terse response? "Jesus was a Jew."

Dr. Aaronson moved quickly, wisely, to befriend those two professors, reading the few articles they had published and offering them lavish praise when he arrived on campus. I don't mean to imply that he was insincere with his compliments. On the contrary, he seemed genuinely to appreciate the scholarship of all our C-cube professors, especially our Old Testament professors concentrating their study on the Hebrew text which he embraced with such intimacy.

It must have been supremely ironic for him that our Christian college on Poplar Avenue near downtown had been purchased from a Jewish congregation, Temple Anshe Emeth, after they had moved to a new location in the late 70s. A panorama of Jewish symbols was embedded in C-cube's architectural designs, in the woodwork and stained glass, including the Star of David. Scenes and symbols from ancient Hebrew life and modern Jewish faith surrounded us, as if embracing us as their offspring.

After being introduced to the student body in the fall semester's first weekly chapel service, Dr. Aaronson said, "Imagine my surprise, arriving at C-cube, to find in its architecture the stories and the art of my faith. How warmly welcoming!"

Pointing to a stained-glass window on the east wall of the chapel he said, "That beautiful stained-glass window of Jacob's Ladder tells the story of one of my Jewish ancestors, Jacob, whose vision was of a ladder connecting heaven and earth, with angels ascending and descending. Awakening from his dream, he said, 'How awesome is this place!' I must say that I think the same as I stand here today, proud to be C-cube's newest professor. How truly awesome is this place!"

I recall thinking, "Can he be serious? Surely this can't be his dream job, to land in Memphis at a small, conservative Christian college. Was nothing more prestigious available for this newly graduated Hebrew scholar?"

That his excitement was anything but insincere we students saw immediately, he quickly becoming the talk of the student body. Eagerly I enrolled for one of his classes, knowing it would be one of only two opportunities to sit under his teaching, I entering my senior year.

I chose his Hebrew Poetry class at the urging of Jakob Rothman, my boyfriend over the past three years who, spontaneously proposing to me after he felt the Holy Spirit speak through our pastor's June 5 Sunday sermon on love and marriage, became my fiancé. Jakob, a poet at heart, leapt at the opportunity to study the poetic books of the Hebrew Bible under Dr. Aaronson.

So there we sat, I on the front row and Jakob on the back row, on the first Tuesday of the 1988 Fall Semester, wondering how Hebrew might sound when spoken with a Bostonian accent. His Star of David introduction, the image of six variously colored whirling dancers forming the star, had more than sufficiently stirred my interest.

"Okay," I thought. "I'll get on this dance floor with David," meaning not so much the biblical David as David Aaronson himself. And why not? In a small Christian college of mostly aging professors, David Aaronson at 32 years old stood out, fresh from Michigan's Rackham Graduate School and its Department of Near Eastern Studies in Ann Arbor.

"From A-square to C-cube," he had quipped in that first chapel introduction.

Dancing with this David, I thought, might be a bit awkward. After all, he is my professor, even if only ten years older. Still, I found his ruddy features glowingly attractive, and his eyes – key to his communicative abilities – sparkling with alluring energy. There was no jadedness in him such as we had experienced in our other professors, a tired oozing of ennui.

Please don't read too much into my just confessed admiration and, if I am honest, attraction. This is not another "Me Too" story. I have nothing salacious to report concerning my former relationship with Dr. Aaronson, and certainly no abuse of power on his part as an authority figure. While true that, sitting under his teaching, I felt myself coming alive again, if his teaching of Hebrew poetry was to turn romantic for me in 1988, it would not be with my teacher, though I won't say anything just now about the other David in my story.

Sensual themes aside, what became quickly clear to me was that for this Arkansas girl whose sense of a Call to ministry was fading, David Aaronson's turning the classroom into a dance floor re-ignited a fire in me that had been thoroughly doused and left smoldering. A spiritual malaise had gradually spread over me during the two previous years of my studies. Once firmly committed to the path I had embarked upon when I entered C-cube, taking first steps toward ordained ministry, now I wasn't so sure. In fact, I had seriously considered leaving school over the recent summer break, ready to point my life in a new direction.

I might have quit had not Jakob dissuaded me, his argument merely a logical reminder that I was only a year away from my degree and that to quit at that point would waste three years of work. His was a sound case, and I decided to stay on course. Not because of any potential waste of time and money. My decision to stay was an acknowledgement of how serious my relationship with Jakob had become. Looking back, I remember the deep respect I had for both his academic abilities and his deep faith. What I don't recall, what I'm not at all sure of, is if I truly loved him.

I entered my senior year with a spiritual dis-ease that was suffocating my faith, close to turning my back on the church, and on faith itself. My college experience was not drawing me closer to God, as I had imagined it would. The God who had seemed so near three years ago now was depressingly distant.

"Where are you, God? Why are you hiding from me?" Those were my questions in my private moments. I had come, though, to expect no answer from a God I wasn't even sure, not anymore, existed. I was becoming an unbeliever. Despite my public appearance of being in step with the church, I knew myself more and more, and without the horror that would have accompanied such a thought three years earlier, to be entirely comfortable putting religion in the rearview mirror.

The thought of abandoning my journey of faith, at first chilling, now was growing warm with excitement, just as forbidden things are wont to do when one responds to their allurement, each flirtation another step toward completely giving oneself over to apostasy.

Why not give it all up? The world was changing, even in the 80s, though surely less so than in more recent decades, when values once regarded as fundamental to Christianity have been jettisoned by ever larger swaths of the church. In our day, some of the evangelical church's brightest stars, megachurch pastors, have declared themselves to have turned their back on their once loudly proclaimed faith. I came close, three decades ahead of them, to leading the way in that adventure of liberating apostasy.

As I look back on September 6, 1988, I can imagine that I must have been wondering, "Why?" Why was I still enrolled in a Christian college, pretending? Why enroll in a class of Hebrew poetry? Poetry! Surely, if my faith was to be revived, wouldn't it be in a class of Systematic Theology, compelling rational arguments overcoming my youthful fling with atheism? Or, perhaps a class on Spirituality, some shaft of unexpected light illumining a part of me growing dark?

Hebrew poetry? What elixir might exude from stichometric lines of verse? Little did I know then that the psalmist whom Professor Aaronson was about to introduce me to was asking the same questions, and just as frustrated with God's utter silence.

"Yahweh, how much longer will you hide? Forever?" Those were the psalmist's questions in Psalm 89, and Dr. Aaronson was about to take my hand and lead me onto the dance floor, allowing these questions intoxicatingly to swirl around me in a dance with a poetic text that would teach me how art can do theology better than theology can do theology.

"Our first six classes will focus on Psalm 89," Dr. Aaronson said. "Now, as you know, many of the 150 psalms of the Hebrew Bible are attributed to David. Not this one. Psalm 89's author is said to be one Ethan the Ezrahite. How then, we might ask, can we dance with David using a psalm not written by David?"

"I suppose," said a voice from behind me, "if he didn't write it, it must be because the psalm is about him?"

I didn't need to turn to see who spoke. It was Jakob. Why weren't we seated together? Simple. Jakob was a back of the class kind of guy. I've always been a front row student. Sitting in the back puts too many distractions in front of me.

"Precisely," Dr. Aaronson replied. "So sharp is the author's focus on David that his, David's, is the only name of an historical person found in Psalm 89. That only David's name appears – not Adam or Abraham, Isaac or Jacob, Moses or

Aaron – is remarkable enough. More remarkable still is that David's name is found not once, but four times."

Writing four Ds on the white board in a way to form a rectangle, each D placed at a corner, he said, "Moreover, I want to show you how these four Davids are strategically placed, evenly distributed through the psalm's fifty-one verses from beginning to end. David's name is found in verses 3, 20, 35, and 49; therefore, spaced out with 17, 15, and 14 verses between each mention of his name. Rather uniform, wouldn't you say? And, I should point out that there are only two verses before the first mention of his name in verse 3, and only two verses after the last mention of David in verse 49. How's that for symmetry?"

"Wait a minute," I countered, surprised at myself for speaking up. "In my Bible, there is a verse 52, so I count three verses after the last mention of David, not two."

"Are there now?" he said, feigning shock. "Why don't you read verse 52 for us, then?"

"Okay. Verse 52 reads, 'Blessed be Yahweh for ever. Amen. Amen!'"

"Ah, then you are right!" he said. "There is a verse 52, tilting my perfect scheme. I'm sorry, what is your name?"

"Stella," I replied. "Stella Maris."

It would be difficult for me to describe his expression upon first hearing my name. I sensed a flash of recognition from which he quickly recovered, as if hiding something. I had seen, though, what I'll describe as familiarity, as if he had wished to say, "Ah, there you are!"

Grinning, he said, "Roger that, Ms. Maris! I wondered who would be first to see it. You are right, a home run of an observation, if you catch my baseball reference to one of my least favorite players growing up, Roger Maris. Aware of the Christian institution for which I work, I will drop the four-letter adjective and say only that Roger Maris was a Yankee. Perhaps, being from Boston, you will imagine I am one myself, but I speak now only of baseball. I am a big fan of the game, you will come to learn."

Yes, we would indeed come to know his love for baseball and his Red Sox.

Dr. Aaronson wasn't finished with me. "So, a verse 52 would skew the symmetry I've outlined for you, an unacceptably awkward misstep, my big foot planted squarely on your little toe, so to speak, as we begin our dance."

Coming close, he pretended to stab at my toe with his foot then, stepping back, he beamed, "But, I am also right, Stella, despite the stellar point you've made. What you've read as verse 52 is actually a doxology placed at the end, not just of Psalm 89, but at the end of the entire third collection of psalms, known as Book Three. These are the psalms numbered 73 thru 89. There are five such collections in the Hebrew Bible and this section, ending with Psalm 89, offers the doxology you've so expertly read for us."

What he said next, describing the five divisions of the Bible's Book of Psalms, was the first time I had ever heard of the psalm destined to so profoundly change my life, Psalm 151.

"Class, before we look at Psalm 89, turn please to Psalm 72. As Psalm 89 concludes Book Three of the Hebrew Bible's collection, Psalm 72 concludes Book Two. Now, would someone please read its last verse for me, verse 20?"

"Yes sir," Jakob jumped at the opportunity. "It reads, 'This concludes the prayers of David, son of Jesse.'"

"It does?" Dr. Aaronson said, an intentional look of confusion on his face. "Concludes? David's psalms were ended? Are you sure it says that?"

"Yes sir. That's how it reads," Jakob answered.

"It does, in fact. Yet, we know that there are many more

psalms of David, nearly twenty of them placed between Psalms 73 and 150. Don't you think that such a note looks odd, stuck right in the middle, not quite halfway through the Bible's 150 psalms? Seems to me some ancient editor was trying to close something that wasn't closed, to draw down the curtain on a play not yet ended, its actors still offering their lines. Understand, then, students, that just as is the case with Psalm 89:52, which Stella read for us, this verse stuck at the end of Psalm 72 is not part of the psalm itself, but a doxology closing the entire division known as Book Two."

With a slight grin, he continued, "Now, turn please to Psalm 151."

A few started the search, but I didn't, knowing this had to be a joke. Most knew, and Dr. Aaronson had just confirmed that the Bible's psalms total 150. One of my professors once playfully asked us to turn to Hezekiah 33:3, amusing himself at how many students tried to find the non-existent biblical book. He was setting us up for a silly quotation, expertly offered in King James English, "Wheresoever the hen scratcheth, there shall the worm be also, unless some previous chicken hath plucked it asunder."

Ha, ha.

In the case of Psalm 151, though, that's not at all what Professor Aaronson was doing. This was no joke.

"Oh, you can't find it?" he said. "I should have been more precise. Will those of you who brought your Septuagint please turn to Psalm 151? Is anyone carrying the Septuagint?"

When no hands were raised, Dr. Aaronson lifted a book. "Not a problem. I have it right here. The Greek translation of the Hebrew Bible, made in Alexandria, Egypt before Jesus was born and known as the Septuagint, included a psalm after Psalm 150. Un-numbered, it was placed in the spot where a Psalm 151 would have been. Its fascination is that it reads like an autobiography, albeit partial, David recounting only two stories from early in his life: his anointing by Samuel and his defeat of Goliath. It's very short, so I want to read it in its entirety from the Sir Lancelot Brenton version, published only two years ago, in 1986:

> This psalm is a genuine one of David, though supernumerary,
> composed when he fought in single combat with Goliad:
> I was small among my brethren, and youngest in my father's house.
> I tended my father's sheep.
> My hands formed a musical instrument, and my fingers tuned a
> psaltery.
> And who shall tell my Lord?
> The Lord himself, he himself hears.
> He sent forth his angel and took me from my father's sheep,
> and he anointed me with the oil of his anointing.
> My brothers were handsome and tall; but the Lord did not take
> pleasure in them.
> I went forth to meet the Philistine; and he cursed me by his idols.
> But I drew his own sword, and beheaded him,
> and removed reproach from the children of Israel."

As he paused to let Psalm 151 sink in, I asked, "Is that it? Why would David write an incomplete autobiography?"

"Precisely," he replied. "Which is why I think that what we know of the psalms of David are, even now, not yet ended. Just as Psalm 72:20 claimed to close David's corpus of work prematurely, I think that what we know of Psalm 151 is also incomplete. It was only thirty-two years ago – in 1956, the year I was born – that Qumran's Cave 11 produced the underlying Hebrew text to the Septuagint's Greek version of Psalm 151. The Hebrew version was slightly longer, but still only told these same two stories. Students, behold the adventure of archaeology! Who knows what discoveries await us still? I think Psalm 151 must have originally been much longer, so that a significant portion of it remains missing. I can only hope that one day a longer version will be discovered that will tell us the full story of Israel's hero king, David. I will say more on that in my last lecture on Psalm 89, two weeks from now, when we take a dive into archaeology."

I formed a mental picture of Dr. Aaronson on an adventure to discover Psalm 151, my mind transforming him into a Harrison Ford look-a-like. "As Indiana Jones found the lost ark," I thought, "Boston Aaronson will one day discover David's long-lost psalm."

"Well, with that diversion," he said, drawing the curtain down on my imagining, "let's get back to Psalm 89 having, I think, adequately noted that verse 52 is an editorial insertion, not part of the psalm itself."

Seeing I was satisfied – though surely not seeing the extent of my fascination, envisioning him on a dashing archaeological adventure – he drew our attention back to the whiteboard.

"Can you see then, that if we map out Psalm 89 as a rectangle, a dance floor formed by the four Ds I've written on the board, the locations of the name David fall pretty nearly at the psalm's four corners. I find these four Davids to be foundational to the psalm's structure, load-bearing pillars, you might say. So, let's begin with the psalm's first David, in verse 3, at the lower left-hand corner of our rectangle, and proceed clockwise."

Looking back at me, he said, "By the way, Stella, you will know, perhaps, that your name is a Latin word meaning star, as in my stellar reference a moment ago? Did you pick up on that?"

"How could I have missed it?" I thought, though I responded to his question with only a slight nod, as nonexpressive as possible.

"And Maris is not just a baseball name," he said, "but also Latin, meaning sea. So, Ms. Stella Maris, you are our Star of the Sea."

I knew my name's meaning, of course, and that there were hospitals, colleges, detox centers, hospice care facilities, and more, all sharing my name. I wanted to speak up to say I did indeed know my name's meaning, and that I wasn't particularly fond of sharing it with so many institutions. I was a person, not an institution, and certainly no saint. I resented the thought that my name might have shaped me into a predetermined role in life. How does one live into one's name, anyway, especially a name shared with the mother of Jesus?

I wanted to say so, but I didn't reply. My lack of response and, no doubt, my surprised expression, led him, after only a moment, to look away.

"Think of it like this," he said, making a spreading motion with his hands. "Imagine that our author has spread David's entire life before our eyes, these four Davids being snapshots of Israel's hero at different stages of his life, each offering a different hue to color the newest version of the man."

Drawing a green circle around the D in the lower left-hand corner, he said, "Let's think of this first D as David the Shepherd, a lad in the Shepherds' Fields of Bethlehem, content with tending his father's sheep. Here he was discovered and anointed by Samuel. I choose green as the color of promise, a glorious future awaiting the young man, but only if seen by Samuel, only if anointed. This first mention of David, in verse 3 reads, 'I have made a covenant with my Chosen, I have given my servant David my sworn word.'"

Moving clockwise and circling in red the D in the upper left-hand corner, he said, "In the biblical story, David the shepherd becomes David the Warrior, whose unexpected defeat of the Philistine giant Goliath sent his popularity soaring, King Saul driven mad with envy as he overheard the women singing, 'Saul has slain his thousands and David his tens of thousands.' Think of this red as the warrior's blood, gushing from Goliath's neck as David beheads him. Verse 20 reads, 'I have selected my servant David and anointed him with my holy oil.' With those two stories of Samuel and Goliath, the autobiography of David in Psalm 151, at least the two versions we know from the LXX and Cave 11, is complete. Oh, but there must be so much more! David's life is only just beginning, so let's imagine it together."

Moving to the upper right-hand corner he circled the third D in purple. "Next, let's imagine David the King, conquering the Jebusite fortress of Jerusalem and dancing mightily, however thinly clad, in front of the Ark of the Covenant as he leads the sacred chest into his new City of David. With purple as the symbol of royalty, I've circled the third D. Verse 35 reads, 'I have sworn on my holiness, once for all, and cannot turn liar to David."

Circling the fourth and last D in black, taking his time to make the black circle thicker than the other colors, he said, "Finally – and make no mistake, this is the real point of Psalm 89 – the psalmist introduces us to David the Dead."

"What?" I thought to myself, the word 'dead' delivering the unexpected shock he no doubt intended. Or, had I actually voiced my surprise? Perhaps I had, since Dr. Aaronson's attention snapped back to me.

"The last mention of David's name whisks us over four hundred years into the future, when not only was David long dead, but the Davidic dynasty itself had fallen to the Babylonians. The temple, built four hundred years earlier by David's son, Solomon, lay now in ruins. Here the psalmist gets to his real point for writing, demanding that God answer his tough questions: 'Where are you, O God? Why are you hiding?' Think of black, then, as the color of disbelief, anger at a God who cannot be trusted to keep his promises. Verse 49 reads, 'Lord, where are those earlier signs of your love? You swore your oath to David on your faithfulness!'"

After allowing the class to absorb the four-colored David scheme, especially that fourth and final black-circled D and the harshness of David the Dead, he continued. "Obviously, the complaint of the author identifies the psalm as having been written after the collapse of the *Beit David*, the House of David, the temple destroyed by the Babylonians on the 9ᵗʰ of Av in the year 586 BCE. 'How could this have happened?' the psalmist wondered. God's covenant had been abundantly clear, promising that the Davidic dynasty would rule as long as sun and moon endure. The historical fact of the collapsed dynasty, then, led to the writing of Psalm 89, the best example of what is known as a Psalm of Royal Lament."

Pointing to the four colored D-clad rectangle, he said, "Now, for the Star of David to be complete we need a hexagon. We have four points already, two in the east and two in the west, forming a rectangle. We need now only two more points, one north and one south, one upper and one lower, and we shall have our Star of David dance floor."

The monitor again lit up with the image of the dervish-formed Star of David, this time the image actually revolving. "Students, are you ready to join me on the dance floor?"

I was more ready than I could possibly have imagined. Gazing at the whirling dervishes now spinning on the monitor, I could see that the four colors used by Dr. Aaronson for the four Davids were all there – green, red, purple, and black. The Star of David, though, was made by six dervishes, and I saw that the two other colors were blue and brown.

"I wonder what blue and brown will represent?" I thought.

Giving us a full minute of silence to look at the screen of whirling dervishes, he then asked, "Are you wondering by now about the blue and the brown dervishes?"

"Yes!" we said, in unison.

"Well, then, let's talk about that. Psalm 89's meter and cadence in the Hebrew text is a swirl of partners, shifting back and forth from what I'll call a 4-4 beat to a 3-3 beat. This obvious dissimilarity has led many scholars to suppose the psalm was not composed at once by any single author, but is a patchwork of cut and paste editing, a composite of pre-existing writings which the author blended into what we know as Psalm 89. That is possible, even logical. Still, I must say that I doubt it. Psalm 89, I believe, is the work of a single author, one who loved to dance!"

Taking a few dancelike steps to illustrate the point, he said, "I will show you how the sections of this psalm describing the historical David are marked by a 3-3 cadence, each line of the poem in Hebrew averaging six accented syllables. The rest of the psalm, sections I would describe as Heavenly rather than Terrestrial, are longer, averaging eight accented syllables per line in the Hebrew, resulting in a 4-4, march-like cadence. Psalm 89's shifting back and forth from the longer to the shorter lines, 4-4 to 3-3, generally follows the thematic shift from Heaven to Earth, from Cosmic to Historical. Evidently, dancing in heaven is an elegant four-step endeavor, while dancing on earth requires a skippy three-step."

"Your moves are smooth," Jakob laughed. "Which of the steps do you like best?"

"*Toda raba,*" he responded with a grin, slightly bowing.

Translating, he said, "*Toda raba* means, 'Thank you very much.' I've practiced my moves since early this morning, wishing to make an impression on my newest class. Your question is difficult to answer, since both cadences contribute to the psalm's balance and beauty. I do, however, especially like it that the author gives the historical David the livelier 3-3 step. Three, you see, is the divine number."

"Have you converted to the Christian Trinity?" I asked, not seriously.

"No," he sighed, again, not seriously. "I haven't yet converted, though I thank you for your prayers, which are ever welcome. I'm not referring to Father, Son, and Holy Spirit. I mean that with the number three we can be more than we are, that we can transcend our human experience of duality, of male and female, good and evil, black and white. Three, as Pythagoras noted with admiration, is the only number that is the sum of all the numbers preceding it, rendering three somehow divine. Baseball, which operates around the number three, must then be the divine game. In what other game do threes thrive, teeming in triads? Three strikes and you're out. Three outs and the side is retired."

I saw where he was going. At least, I thought I did, that he would next quote Susan Sarandon in one of the greatest sports movies of all time, released only a few months earlier, *Bull Durham*. Playing the role of a baseball groupie in Durham, North Carolina, Annie Savoi, she said, "I believe in the Church of Baseball. I've tried all the major religions, and most of the minor ones. I've worshipped Buddha, Allah, Brahma, Vishnu, Siva, trees, mushrooms, and Isadora Duncan. I know things. For instance, there are 108 beads in a Catholic rosary and there are 108 stitches in a baseball. When I learned that, I gave Jesus a chance. But it just didn't work out between us. The Lord laid too much guilt on me. I prefer metaphysics to theology. You see, there's no guilt in baseball, and it's never boring."

I was wrong. I guess Dr. Aaronson hadn't seen *Bull Durham*, since he passed right by that obvious opening to his divinity of baseball theme. He was just beginning, though, and enjoying it.

"Three by three by three we go through nine innings, like the Angelus bells guiding the prayers of the faithful. Those nine innings are matched by nine players on each team, uniformed Muses inspiring each other to victory. From their earliest days as T-ballers and Little Leaguers they learn to inspire each other, players in the field lifting their pitcher with chants of 'Hey, batter, batter, batter . . . swing!' Three swings and you're out! The opposing team has its own set of nine Muses, shouting encouragements to their batter. 'Good eye! Wait for your pitch!' So, what will it be? Will the batter in the box be the next runner on the bases, or the next out, heading to the dugout? To win, a team needs nine times three outs, a total of twenty-seven. Isn't it glorious! Threes and Nines, everywhere. Multiples of threes abound in baseball, its dance floor not a star, but a diamond."

"Wow!" someone in the back said, giving him a moment to catch his breath.

"Now, having waxed eloquent on baseball, I offer a doxology. Praise be to my Red Sox as in this, their 88th season of professional baseball in 1988, they close in on the American League pennant, led in the dance of the diamond by two stars, Wade Boggs on offense and Roger Clemens on defense. May the baseball gods shine upon you, in Fenway and away!"

They did, by the way, those baseball gods, shine upon Boston's Red Sox in 1988, as they would edge the defending champion Detroit Tigers by one game to win the American League East. While I was never much of a baseball fan, I know well that 1988 pennant race, Dr. Aaronson updating us on the Sox's chances with every class.

The screen now lit up with Israel's flag as he said, "But I digress. Leaving now the diamond of baseball to return to the Star of David, please note how the psalmist's 3-3 meter is perfect, the Star of David having six points formed by two overlapping triangles. The first triangle, which I will call the male, is upright. The second, the female, is inverted. Together, the overlapping triangles form a hexagram. Also known as the *Magen David*, meaning the Shield of David, it adorns Israel's flag, adopted on October 28, 1948, five months after the inception of the State of Israel. As we step onto the dance floor of Psalm 89, students, the Star of David will guide us in the dance, triangle laid upon triangle, male and female, three by three."

It was clear to me now, looking at Israel's flag and its Star of David, what Professor Aaronson had done with his four Ds, placed precisely to match the four east and west points of the Star of David. Drawing two horizontal lines on the board, one connecting the two upper Ds and the other the two lower Ds, he said, "Let's allow these two horizontal lines to become the base for both of the triangles forming the Star of David. From the bottom line we draw a triangle extending upward, the male; and from the top line we draw an inverted triangle, the female."

Completing the two triangles on the whiteboard, he stepped back and said, "Students, the dance partners are now paired, and I invite you to step onto the dance floor with me."

Stepping back to admire his creation on the whiteboard, he said, "Behold, the Star of David, in six colors!"

"Okay, but you still haven't told us why those last two points are blue and the brown," I said.

Glancing at his watch, Dr. Aaronson said, "I haven't, have I? Well, we're getting there, so bear with me. In the time we have remaining let's take a look at only the first four verses of the psalm, where we'll find the answer to your question. Think of these four verses as our dance rehearsal. This is where our author choreographs the two basics steps of his dance."

Walking back the board, he said, "Remember, Ethan's choreography takes us from heaven to earth, and those are the two points we need to complete our star – the upper and the lower. So, let's align heaven with the upper point of the star and earth with lower tip of the star. Blue for the heights of heaven. Brown for dust of the earth. Make sense?"

Circling those two points with the blue and brown markers, all six colors of the dervishes were now clear. Extending an open Hebrew Bible to the class, he said, "Psalm 89's superscription reads, 'A *Maskil* of Ethan the Ezrahite.'"

"What does '*maskil*' mean?" I asked.

"Great question. The word *maskil* is generally understood to designate the psalm as one of instruction. I prefer, staying with my analogy, to think of *maskil* as choreography. That's what instruction should do, right, choreograph our steps? As I lead this class, think of me as your choreographer, just the right word for our whirl through Psalm 89, our steps leading us to touch each of the star's six points."

His pointing to the six tips of the star reminded me of Tinker Bell in *The Wonderful World of Disney's* opening, using her wand to shower pixie dust over the castle in a spray of magic. I can't speak for the others, but it was working for me. Hebrew poetry, or at least Dr. Aaronson's teaching of Hebrew poetry, was magical.

"Professor David Aaronson, our choreographer," I said, smiling.

He nodded affirmation, returning my smile before he looked up to the entire class.

"Take your Bibles now and let's look at those first four verses. In verses 1 and 2 we are in heaven, dancing to a 4-4 step, the longer lines of text. This is the upper point of the star, circled in azure blue to represent heaven. Verses 3 and 4, on the other hand, are shorter, a 3-3 meter. We start in heaven, then come back to earth, planting our feet on terra firma. Blue for heaven. Brown for earth. In my course description I suggested the purchase of *The Jerusalem Bible,* published in 1966. I like this version while teaching the psalms because the English translation is presented on the page in a way clearly demonstrating the differences in the length of the Hebrew lines, long and short, eight accent and six accent lines. That is no small accomplishment in translation, but they pulled it off. *The Jerusalem Bible* makes this shift obvious to the casual eye."

I had purchased *The Jerusalem Bible,* and a quick glance confirmed his explanation.

"Let me speak just enough Hebrew for you to hear the eight accented syllables of the first line, a 4-4 cadence:

Has-DI ado-NAI o-LAM ashe-RAH
I will celebrate your love forever, Yahweh,
Le-dor ve-DOR 'oDAY-a' e-MUN-te-ka be-PI
Age after age my words shall proclaim your faithfulness."

"Nothing Bostonian in his Hebrew," I thought. Being a senior, I was one of those who had taken two semesters of Hebrew. My pronunciation was awful, to say the least, but I had heard enough Hebrew to hear his pronunciation as smooth and, to my ear, enchanting.

"That's verse one. Verse two follows the same 4-4 meter. In English:
For I claim that love is built to last forever;
And your faithfulness founded firmly in the heavens."

I could have translated "the heavens" into Hebrew myself, *ha-shemayim,* one of the first words in our Hebrew 101 vocabulary. His point was clear, that the first two verses are set in heaven, the azure blue upper point of the Star of David.

"With the heavens, *ha-shemayim* in Hebrew," he said, "it's clear in these first two verses that we're dealing with the Cosmic, God in his heavenly abode. This is where our Psalm 89 dance begins, at the upper tip of the Star of David."

Pointing next to the brown-circled lower tip of the star, he continued, "With the next two verses, three and four, Ethan brings us back to earth, the land."

"*Ha-'eretz*," I thought, just as he spoke it.

"*Ha-'eretz*," he said, "which means, the land. Here the lines shorten, averaging only six accented syllables per line instead of eight, thus, a 3-3 cadence.

> *Cara-TI be-RIT libhi-RAY*
> I have made a covenant with my Chosen."

He abandoned the Hebrew, saying, "Now, in the next line we encounter the first of the four load-bearing pillars, the first David:

I have given my servant David my sworn word."

Emphasizing the word sworn, he turned to the star and said, "So what is it that God swore to David? Verse four tells us emphatically:

> I have founded your dynasty to last forever,
> I have built you a throne to outlast all time."

As it was now just past 3:30, students began closing and stacking their books, readying to go home or to their last class of the day, but Professor Aaronson wasn't quite ready to release us. "Over the next three weeks we will see that God's sworn word to David, as least as it was understood by our psalmist, failed."

Glancing at the clock, he said, "Well, I see the time is precisely 3:33, perfect for my baseball analogy. I do apologize for keeping you three minutes late. For Thursday's class please familiarize yourself with the next section, verses 5-18, in which David will make no appearance at all, the scene entirely Cosmic. Ready yourselves, then, as on Thursday our dance will be a 4-4 waltz in heaven."

Grabbing the sportscoat he had hung over his chair, he sent us out. "March on, then, class! ONE, two, three, four; ONE, two, three, four; ONE, two, three, four! See you Thursday, and let the dance begin!"

Chapter 2

Dancing with David in the Shepherds' Fields of Bethlehem

WEDNESDAY, SEPTEMBER 7, 1988, 3:34 A.M.

"Ellie! Ellie!"

It was a male voice. Startled, I jolted up against my bed's headboard. The voice had been more than a mere fragment of a dream. It was clear, possessing unmistakable urgency.

"Who's Ellie?" I thought as my head began to clear. A glance at the clock showed that it was 3:34. Had I misheard? Both Ellie and Stella are replete with Ls. Had someone called my name and I simply misheard?

As awareness took hold, I heard a loud thunderclap. Walking to the kitchen for a sip of water, I listened to the rain falling outside as I stood silently at the sink, straining to hear again the voice that had awakened me. Spooked by the clarity of what I knew I had heard, I opted for my recliner rather than my pillow.

The clock's numbers, 3:34, were blazed in neon green in my head, stirring memories of Dr. Aaronson's afternoon lecture which had focused on those two numbers, the 3-3 and 4-4 alternating cadences of Psalm 89.

Class had ended twelve hours earlier with Dr. Aaronson pacing our steps like a drill sergeant. Now, here I was in the wee hours of the morning, threes and fours a-prance in my head, recalling how the Cosmic sections of the song beat to a 4-4 meter, then shift in the Historical sections to a livelier, 3-3 cadence, an artful mixing of heaven and earth, the upper blue and lower brown tips of our colorful Star of David dance floor.

It's that mix of heaven and earth that makes us interesting, I suppose. We exist in two realities, simultaneously. As a human being, I am duality. I Gemini, sharing light and dark, spirit and flesh, past and future. I am both three, tripping across the dance floor of human history; and four, stepping in accordance with an as-yet-undeclared divine plan.

It suddenly occurred to me that three and four are the month and day of my birthday, March 4. Strange, the meandering of a mind abruptly awakened by a voice calling through the storm. Am I hearing voices now? I thought of Mark David Chapman, the assassin who had ended John Lennon's life in New York City. He, too, heard voices.

Why would I think of Mark David Chapman? It must have been the thought of my birthday, March 4, 1966. That was the fateful day John Lennon made the statement that many say led to his assassination, his claim that The Beatles were more popular than Jesus. It hadn't caused much of a stir in Great Britain, not even the full quote, which was: "Christianity will go. It will vanish and shrink. I needn't argue about that; I'm right and I'll be proved right. We're more popular than Jesus now; I don't know which will go first – rock 'n' roll or

Christianity. Jesus was all right, but his disciples were thick and ordinary. It's them twisting it that ruins it for me."

"Twisting," Lennon had said. Now, there's a dance term from the sixties!

I was too young for that craze, but, thinking on it now, my journey of faith is totally in a twist. Three years earlier I would have thought Lennon's statement anathema. By 1988, not so much. Had college made me more British in my thinking? His words had barely caused a ripple at home, no big deal on a continent where the church was increasingly seen as a museum.

My faith was taking on museum status, I guess, something old to stare at. Real life is on the outside of the museum. At twenty-two, my cravings for real life were coming into full bloom.

When Lennon's words hit America, especially the Bible Belt, the reaction was massive, sparking bonfires of Beatle albums. Here in Memphis the Beatles performed at Mid-South Coliseum at the height of the disruption. Although the city council had voted to cancel the concert, the show must go on, right? It did, but people were nervous, and for good reason. During the show someone threw a firecracker onto the stage, causing panic, the band believing they were being targeted by gunfire. Chaos ensued, as you can imagine.

It would be fourteen years later, in 1980, that Mark David Chapman would fire five bullets at John Lennon, four finding their target.

How odd on this night to feel any kinship with Mark David Chapman, but I did. He was a born again Presbyterian who, like me, had been so filled with enthusiasm in his newfound faith that he instantly became a Good News evangelist, enthusiastically passing out religious tracts. He enrolled in – get this – Covenant Christian College.

No, not my own C-cube in Memphis, but Covenant Christian in Lookout Mountain, Georgia. He attended with his girlfriend for a semester before dropping out. And now, here I am at Covenant Christian, thinking of leaving not only college, but becoming a faith drop-out.

I was living in the three of human chaos, seeking four-square cosmic order. Three. Four. Those two numbers spinning in my head, on a whim I grabbed the Bible and looked up Genesis 3:4, which read, "'You will not surely die,' the serpent said to the woman."

Was the serpent's voice on this night speaking directly to me? "Taste the forbidden, my child, and fear not. You will not die!"

I felt sisterhood with Eve. I, as had she, was comprehending the unthinkable, my lips wetted to taste the forbidden fruit of apostasy. What to do, awakened at 3:34 in the morning and thinking such thoughts, but to listen, as had Eve, to the serpent. Was the serpent inviting me to dance?

I don't know how long I sat in the recliner before I drifted back to sleep, but this I recall vividly, a dream so intense as to feel the cool ground beneath my feet, the chill on my face a sudden contrast with my den's warm temperature, my apartment's air conditioner not nearly up to the task of combating the September heat of Memphis, Tennessee. Wherever I was now, it wasn't Memphis.

I saw a fire burning outside a tent-like shelter, perhaps twenty yards away from where I stood. Two men sat by the fire, talking. I walked softly toward the voices, unseen. One was a young man, perhaps seventeen or eighteen. I could tell that he was arguing, a bit timidly, with this other, an older man, beyond middle-aged. Drawing close enough to make out their words, I heard the young man say that he felt he should go, that he must go. He used a word I knew very well, saying he felt "Called."

Then I heard *Hakol*'s voice for the first time, though I didn't yet know his name. I couldn't see his face as he was turned away from me, the most distinguishable feature in his profile being a thick, jagged scar running the length of his face, temple to jaw bone down his left cheek.

"David," I heard him say with a deep staccato rasp, "they are coming now to fetch you. You must not go. Samuel's invitation is not your Calling. It is your test. I am sent to urge you toward your higher calling, to stay right where you are. Here, in the Shepherd's Fields, and nowhere else, is your destiny.

"How strange!" it suddenly occurred to me. I not only recognized they were speaking Hebrew, I could understand every word. How? My mere two semesters of Hebrew language had nothing to do with it, that's for sure.

I felt at that moment, and intensely, that I was two. An Other was present, sharing my dream-body. While this Other I did not know, I felt, eerily, that she knew me. Though two, we were one.

I, Gemini.

Aware now of the presence of my Other, my thoughts turned back to this young man, whose identity was without question. This was the teenage David, the Shepherd of Israel in a time before he had come to fame. I was in the Shepherd's Fields of Bethlehem. I'd been there only a year earlier, a place important to both Jewish and Christian history. Here it was that Boaz, a wealthy landowner, fell in love with an immigrant named Ruth who had come from Moab, some forty miles away beyond the Jordan River.

Knowing this, I felt Sent, just as I had heard *Hakol* declare himself to be. I was clear as to my mission, to extend to David a different Calling from that of this other claiming to have been sent, but bearing the opposite message. Was this to be a battle of the Muses?

As *Hakol* offered his arguments I thought about the history of this place. Several generations before David, Naomi had left Bethlehem in a time of drought with her husband, Elimelech, and their two boys. When all three men died in Moab, Naomi decided to come home. One of her daughters-in-law, Ruth, refused instructions to stay behind in Moab, saying, "Don't urge me to leave you or to turn back from you. Where you go, I will go, and where you stay, I will stay. Your people will be my people, and your God my God. Where you die, I will die, and there I will be buried."

"How unlike Ruth I am," I thought, "burned out already, and near empty."

I remembered the Bible's story, how upon her return to Bethlehem, a destitute Naomi told the Bethlehemites who had recognized her that they should no longer call her Naomi, a Hebrew name meaning pleasantness. Instead, they should call her Mara, meaning bitterness, since the Lord had dealt bitterly with her. Describing her journey away from and back to Bethlehem, she said, "I went out full and have come home again empty."

It would have been the perfect thing for me to say to my parents, had I left school to return home before my senior year. "Mom. Dad. I went out full, but have come home empty."

Things were soon to get better for Naomi and Ruth. Perhaps they will, also, for me.

The impoverished Ruth, left to glean in the fields, attracted the notice of Boaz, who ordered his reapers to leave the woman "handfuls on purpose," so that her physical needs, and those of her mother-in-law, would be met. Boaz had fallen in love with Ruth, and would soon declare himself her *go'el*, her kinsman redeemer, taking her in marriage. Their child would be Obed, the father of Jesse, who himself would become the father of eight children, the eighth being David, the shepherd boy I was watching now as he argued with *Hakol*.

"You must not go David," I heard *Hakol* say. "This is where you belong, with the sheep. Has not *Hashem* supplied all your needs? If you go to Samuel, kingship follows, holding with it untold danger and much death. Leaving these fields where you have come to know God, he will no longer speak to you as you now hear his voice, inspiring you to write songs of praise that will live forever. As king, you would be walking into the valley of *tzalmavet*, the shadow of death. Your life is much more valuable than that. It is here."

"Why then, do I feel Called to go?" David asked.

"As I told you, it is a test," the man said, turning slightly toward me as if, expecting me, he sensed my presence.

"And the test is not finished," he said, turning back to the boy shepherd. "Soon you will be visited by one whose beauty will make you imagine her the queen of heaven. Be not enchanted by her appearance, nor persuaded by her words. She is the queen of nothing but death."

As rain began to fall, I took a step toward the shelter of the tent and stumbled, the noise alerting David to my presence. *Hakol* turned toward me with what surely would have been a nasty sneer, but I never saw his face. It's not that he vanished. He simply slipped away into the darkness. Slithered is perhaps the better word, as if he, recognizing me, acknowledged that it was my turn to take the floor, as if I had tapped his shoulder to break in to the Muse-dance.

David was now staring at me, surely wondering if I was that queen of death *Hakol* had just warned him about.

"David," I said. "Why are you troubled?"

"I am avoiding Bethlehem, staying in my father's fields with his sheep. Samuel has come to anoint a king, and is at my father's house to choose one of my brothers."

"Are you not a brother?"

"I am the youngest, the smallest. This is my place."

"But, does not Samuel wish to see all of Jesse's sons?"

"*Hakol* . . ."

"Is that his name, the man who was here with you?"

"I don't know his name. *Hakol* is what I have called him, his voice cautious and, I think, wise."

I would learn with each dream that *Hakol's* presence would be constant, his urging of David to remain in the fields only the beginning of his attempts to disrupt the divine plan. For David to hide from Samuel would be hiding from destiny. My purpose, I knew now, was to lead David to the path God had ordained.

As a teenager I had read *Perelandra* by C. S. Lewis, the second in his sci-fi trilogy, Perelandra being Lewis' name for the planet Venus. The story is infused with deep theological dilemmas, recreating the Genesis story of the Fall by bringing two dueling professors from England. Dr. Elwin Ransom (the hero) and Dr. Edward Weston (the enemy) were engaged in a struggle of Muses, each offering contradictory advice to the Perelandrean equivalent of Eve, who was simply called, the Lady. Would the Lady, like Eve, fall to the serpent tempter, Dr. Weston? Or, would the Lady of Perelandra listen to Dr. Ransom, avoiding the deadly Fall of earth's first parents?

Hakol had exited the tent, but I felt myself part of a similar drama. I would play the role of Ransom, urging David in accordance with the divine will. *Hakol*, seeking to thwart providence by dissuading David, was playing the role of Weston, coaxing David toward a choice that would negate God's plan. I could not allow that to happen, for how would

Judeo-Christian history be written without David, King of Israel?

"Despite your fears, David," I said, "you must go to the prophet. I heard you say that you feel Called to go. Trust yourself. Go. Go for yourself."

"Are you sent from heaven to force me?"

"No, not from heaven, and not to coerce. I do feel sent, though, to inspire and to guide. But it must be your choice. Is it not wonderful that the sovereign of heaven seeks and waits for your consent?"

"And if I choose to stay here, in my father's fields?"

"Then, I think, you will have a beautiful life in these fields. You with your sheep, living an ordinary life, but never knowing what you missed. God's true plan for you, and for Israel, would be like a divine breath forever unbreathed."

Looking long at me, he asked, "Who are you?"

What would I say? My name is Stella, a name he would surely, not knowing Latin, hear as odd. What was the Hebrew word for Star? I recalled from one of my Old Testament classes on the Book of Esther, that the name Esther meant Star.

"How clever," I thought.

"I am Esther," I told him.

"Esther?" he said. "A beautiful name. It means . . ."

"Star," I said.

"No," he replied, wondering at my not knowing my own name. "It means, hidden."

I was confused. I was sure I was remembering correctly. Esther meant Star. I would check later, after my dream, and see that we both were right. Esther was indeed Star, as I had recalled, but only in Persian. He would have known no more of Persian than he would have known my Latin name, Stella. The Hebrew word for star is *kochav*. Esther, to him, would sound as if derived from the Hebrew *sether*, meaning hidden.

"I will not call you Esther," he said, "for in you the will of Adonai is not hidden, but revealed. I will call you, Eliana, meaning, 'My God has answered me.' Before *Hakol* came to me, I was playing my lyre and singing those words in my prayer, 'Answer me when I call to you, my righteous God.' I believe God answered my prayer, sending you. You, then, are Eliana, having brought to me the words of Adonai. My heart recognizes your words."

Eliana! It made sense now, the voice that had awakened me in the night, "Ellie! Ellie!" Had it been David's voice?

I followed as David walked toward Bethlehem, the timing perfect as servants were now coming from the house to fetch him. I lagged behind as he drew near the house, but close enough to watch David touch the mezuzah on the doorway and then kiss his fingers in reverence.

I had won. I knew, seeing him enter, that the first round of my bout with *Hakol* was won.

Approaching nearer, through the doorway I could see the prophet's face, creased with concern that his mission had failed. Samuel glowed with joy when at last he saw David, God revealing to him that this boy was the chosen one.

I heard someone say to Samuel, "But he's so small."

Samuel replied, "*Hashem* looks, not on one's stature, but on the heart."

Samuel was looking into David's heart. I saw him rise to his feet and command David to kneel. He anointed David with *shemen kadosh* (holy oil), not secretly, but in the presence of his undoubtedly jealous brothers.

I knew in an instant, watching liquid holiness stream in lanes down his face, that this oil of the anointing had changed David forever, a spirit of might and power entering him. For what seemed like a long time, David kept his head bowed. When at last he lifted his head and opened his eyes, he saw me in the doorway.

As the music of celebration began, he moved toward me, reaching out to take my hand and dance. I reached toward him, but, before we touched, my dream collapsed. I awakened in my recliner with my right arm extended, the oil's sweet scent lingering in my nostrils to confirm the magic of the night.

Leaning over the sink with toothbrush in hand, thrilled still at how sharp my memory of the dream was, I looked up and glanced into the mirror. At that moment, a flash of light illuminated my face, but it wasn't my face I saw. Instead of my blue eyes and light complexion, I saw a gorgeous woman of olive complexion, her dark eyes staring back at me. It was only a flash, vanished in a blink, but something deep within told me that I had just met my Other, the one who had shared my dream.

Wednesday was difficult. I've never been one to wake from sleep with much more than a vague recall of my dreams. This night, this dream, though, was different from all the rest. For thirty-three years it's been my personal *HaLaila HaZeh* moment. Meaning "this night," *HaLaila HaZeh* is the name for four special questions asked by the youngest present at the Seder, each asking, "Why is this night different from every other night?"

The answer, for me, is simple. This was my *HaLaila HaZeh* moment because this was the night I first danced with David. Almost.

All day Wednesday I relived the Shepherd's Field scene. My usual focus on my classwork, of course, was shot. Since Monday had been Labor Day, Wednesday was the first meeting of this semester's M-W-F classes. No matter what class I was sitting in, I couldn't get my mind off of Hebrew Poetry and the two Davids I had met a day earlier – David Aaronson and David ben Jesse.

I felt myself no longer a spectator observing a biblical story. I was now, however inexplicably, part of the story. I wanted to share my dream with somebody, but, how could I? It would sound crazy. Who would believe me? My mom? Jakob? Dr. Aaronson?

"Maybe I am crazy," I thought, a possibility keeping me silent all day on Wednesday, the longest Hump Day of my life.

Jakob noticed how distracted I was. It was our habit to attend Wednesday evening services together at Bellevue Baptist, a church adjacent to the C-cube campus. When I found him after my last class to let him know I wouldn't be able to attend, he was concerned, asking if I was okay. I lied, saying I was fine, just not quite feeling 100%.

In truth, I was feeling much, much better than 100%. My ordinary world last night had experienced an intrusion of unexpected meaning. Energized at being chosen to receive such an extraordinary gift, I wanted to tell Jakob, but it wasn't the right time. I needed to be alone with the gift for a while longer.

I spent Wednesday evening reading my class notes from Dr. Aaronson's first lecture, studying the section of Psalm 89 assigned for Thursday, verses 5-18. Trying to get a sense of the meter, I must have looked silly as I took Dr. Aaronson's dancing invitation literally, standing and gently swaying while reading the text aloud, allowing its sounds to wash over me. I read the words over and over, each time stressing the syllables in slightly different ways to alter its rhythm.

After a while I began to take steps while reading, able now to close my eyes, the hymn's phrases becoming committed to memory. Gliding back and forth across the room (I do not claim, gracefully), I imagined dancing not only with the text but with God, especially as I read of God's mighty right arm, imagining his right arm embracing me while his left arm led my steps.

What I most craved at that moment wasn't merely to be prepared for tomorrow's class, but to ready myself to experience again, this very night, a second dream. Dancing so intimately with the text was my invitation to God to enter my dreams in the same powerful way as last night. Already, after but a single dose, I was addicted. Unlike other addictions, though – food, cigarettes, or alcohol – there was nothing I could do, no price to pay, to satisfy my craving. To dance again with David, I must be invited onto the dance floor.

As I put the text away and prepared for bed, I remembered seeing David pause at the doorway to his father's house to touch the mezuzah with the tip of his fingers. I recalled how, on my trip to Israel, our guide had often pointed out the mezuzah attached to the gates and doorways, a ritual reminder of God in all of one's comings and goings.

My mom had purchased a mezuzah for me in one of the souvenir shops. While I never installed it at the doorway to my apartment, as I had intended, I remembered where I had placed it, in the drawer at my bedside. Taking the mezuzah out of its package, I laid it beside my bedside clock, wishing for it to become once again my doorway into David's world.

There, by my bed, my mezuzah has stayed, not only through those three weeks of 1988, but in every place I've made my home since, including hotels. It's always been with me, as I am always ready to respond to David's invitation to dance.

Though Wednesday night brought no new dream, my excitement in awakening was unabated. My first thought was Dr. Aaronson, filled with anticipation for his 2:00 class in

Hebrew Poetry.

After my 10:00 class I headed to the cafeteria, where Jakob and I had planned to meet for a quick lunch. After, we would walk together to the library to discuss the assigned section of Psalm 89, wanting it fresh on our minds for class.

Jakob had arrived before me and was sitting with our friend, Michael Caleb, his sparring partner in the much-debated theological conundrum of predestination versus free will. As I approached the table with my tray, I overheard Jakob saying, "But he was unplugged!"

Jakob stopped mid-sentence, seeing me.

"Unplugged?" I asked as I put down my tray next to Jakob. "Who was unplugged?"

"Zoltar," Jakob said. "When Josh's wish to be made big was granted, it had nothing to do with his free will. It wasn't about Josh. It was about his being chosen. Zoltar had chosen. If any other kid had asked to be made big, they would have found Zoltar silent and unresponsive. Zoltar would have remained unplugged, except for the chosen one. Except for Josh."

"Are you kidding?" I laughed. "Are you guys really debating theology based on *Big*?"

Zoltar was the robotic carnival fortuneteller from the Tom Hanks film released early that summer. Jakob and I, seniors now living in Memphis full time, had seen *Big* together at a matinee showing followed by dinner at Pancho's on Union Avenue, a locally adored Mexican restaurant which had begun across the Mississippi River in West Memphis, Arkansas in 1956 with a packed dirt floor, an indoor tree, and visits from celebrities. Even Elvis. What really launched its incredible success, though, was a new thing. Cheese dip.

Jakob's debate point had me remembering our date three

months earlier, eating cheese dip and talking about the amazing job we thought Hanks had done playing a thirteen-year-old inhabiting a thirty-year-old body.

Jakob knew I would not side with him, that I agreed with Michael's free will position on the question of divine election to salvation.

Michael said, "Well, Jakob, yes, Zoltar was unplugged. Josh, though, after his coin didn't work, did shake that booth with every ounce of energy he had."

"Your point?"

"That his shaking contributed to the miracle. His voice was calling Zoltar to act. Looks like free will to me."

"No, when that booth finally lit up and Zoltar said, 'Make your wish,' it had nothing to do with the force of Josh's shaking. Other kids could have shaken the booth just as hard, or even harder, and the booth would have remained dark. Josh was chosen. The choice was entirely Zoltar's. That's why, when Josh sees Zoltar is unplugged, he realizes a miracle has occurred."

As they argued, I played a portion of the film in my head, remembering how Josh woke up the next day, a child in an adult body. His magical experience was disorienting, of course. He had first to convince his friend Billy, naturally frightened when a thirty-year-old began to pretend to be his thirteen-year-old friend, that he wasn't a child molester. Director Penny Marshall found wonderful humor in that moment.

I thought how like Josh I am in this moment, having experienced a miracle having nothing to do with my seeking or my choosing. Jakob, I now knew, will be my Billy, the one I must first convince that my miracle was real.

Was I, like Josh, the chosen one? I had not wished to be David's Eliana. There was no free choice involved. I was chosen.

"What do you think, Stella?" Jakob asked, jarring my attention back to the debate.

"Sorry. I was thinking of our dinner at Pancho's on the day we saw *Big*. What do I think about what?"

"A great day that was!" Jakob said. "Since you abandoned me last night, maybe we ought to eat there tonight. Cheese dip sounds perfect."

"Yes, cheese dip," I said, deflecting. "It's a date. Now, what did you ask?"

"Stella, what's going on with you? You were distracted all day yesterday. I was asking your opinion about my argument from John 10:11 that Jesus gave his life only for the sheep, not the goats."

"Jakob, I don't understand how limited atonement is so appealing to you. Maybe Jesus, like David in the Old Testament, was ready to expand himself beyond the sheep under his care and head for wider pastures."

Jakob knew what my answer would be, this theological dilemma being a perennial favorite in all the public spaces of C-cube. Well-rehearsed were these conversations, in all their permutations. Jakob was a proud Calvinist. While I deeply respected his knowledge of the Bible, he knew I disagreed.

That his position on the subject was in the minority at C-cube made him prouder still. Jakob liked to stand out, and he did. Extremely intelligent with a nearly photographic memory, I marveled at the huge chunks of biblical text he seemed easily to commit to memory. His reddish hair was always laid in well-groomed flat waves, his speech flowing with equal precision and elegance. He was a committed disciple of Jesus Christ, seemingly unimpacted by the kind of doubts with which I was struggling. I saw in Jakob what Jesus saw in Nathaniel, "an Israelite indeed, in whom there is no guile."

Seeing I was unwilling to reengage the ancient debate, Jakob grinned as he turned back toward Michael. It was his poker player tell. Only three days into the new semester, I grimaced in knowing that already he was about to quote Romans 9.

"Remember, Michael," he said, "Paul's words, 'Jacob I loved, but Esau I hated.'"

Cringing, Michael replied, "Well, I'm sure God loves you, Jakob with a K. Since I don't know anybody named Esau, though, I'm happy imagining that God loves everybody, and that we all have a chance to accept his love. I agree with Stella. Maybe Jesus' love extends beyond the sheepfold."

Jakob loved that verse in Romans 9, using it for more than a defense of the sovereignty of God. Playfully, he would remind me that we were meant for each other, saying in moments when he felt a tinge of jealousy, "Stella, you must remind yourself, 'Jakob I have loved, all others I have loathed.'"

While I agreed theologically with Michael, I couldn't deny my realization that I had been chosen to receive the extraordinary gift of being sent to David, an unsought gift not of my own free will.

Michael stood to leave, saying he would see us in class but first needed to make a quick run to Lifeblood, the Mid-South Regional Blood Center on Madison Avenue where he worked part-time, only a few blocks from C-cube. He had left a book there last night, he said, while working until midnight, that he needed to retrieve before class.

As Jakob and I made our way to the library, I saw an opportunity to share my dream with him. "Jakob, I know you'll think I'm crazy, like Billy thought Josh was crazy when he first told him about his miracle, but I need to tell you that something has happened that makes me think I might have been chosen for something extraordinary."

"Chosen? Wow, I'll sure miss our debates! Does this revelation explain why your head has been somewhere else lately?"

"It will, I think. I'm going to share something with you, but I need you first to promise not to tell anyone else."

"What happened?"

"Promise?"

"Yes, of course, I promise."

"Nothing's wrong. In fact, I think something is right, righter than it's ever been."

Settling into a corner of the library, an area overlooking Poplar Avenue with a few comfortable chairs being, at the moment, deserted, I told him about my dream. Putting it in the context of *Big*, I searched for a way to tell him that I felt like Josh. I felt chosen.

"Psalm 89 is about David, chosen to be king despite being smaller than his brothers. Like Josh, he craved to be big. My dream landed me in the midst of David struggling with a decision of whether or not to present himself to Samuel. There was another there, a man he called *Hakol*. He told David that God had sent him to convince him to stay in the Shepherd's Fields, to hide and stay away from Samuel. I knew then that I was sent to convince David to step into his destiny, to go to Samuel."

Jakob's reaction surprised me, not going through the phases I'd expected, a progression from "You're joking!" to "You're nuts!" Evidently, *Big* had been the perfect platform to tell him about my dream. In his head and heart he might have been thinking me crazy, but, if so, he didn't say it. Fully engaged by my story, he asked so many questions that we never opened the passage Dr. Aaronson had assigned for class.

We talked only of my vision for the entire hour before class. I told him everything, beginning with being awakened at 3:34 by a voice calling "Ellie!" and how those numbers made me think of the cadences Dr. Aaronson had pointed out in Psalm 89. I told him about looking up Genesis 3:4, my birthday numbers of March 4, and how I felt oddly enticed by the serpent's words, "You will not surely die."

When at last we picked up our books to head to class, he joked, "Shall our steps be a 3-3 hop or a 4-4 march?"

"Let's just walk," I laughed, "one step at a time."

As we headed down the hallway, I said, "Oh, and one more thing about Tuesday night. One of my last thoughts before sleeping and dreaming was that March 4, 1966, my birthday, was the day John Lennon made his statement about The Beatles being more popular than Jesus, leading to his assassination by Mark David Chapman. I remembered how Chapman and I share something in common, both being students at Covenant Christian College. He attended the other C-cube, in Georgia."

I thought my observation about Chapman's collegiate days fascinating, but as we were arriving and entering the classroom, Jakob was clearly less impressed. Offering only a disinterested, "Huh, how about that?" he entered the room and our paths diverged, he heading toward the back row as I broke for the front.

We would discover, though, in the first few minutes of Dr. Aaronson's second lecture, that my dance with that David, Mark David Chapman, wasn't finished quite yet.

Since my six dreams align with the six tablets discovered in Cave 53, my dreams experienced in the precise order Dr. Aaronson placed them in his translation, I'll end each telling of my visions with the Aaronson translation, comparing it to the Septuagint and to The Great Psalms Scroll of Cave 11. The Aaronson English translation both transliterates several key words and translates them, providing the reader with some of the more familiar Hebrew wording.

Here, then, are the three extant texts describing my first dream:

David's anointing by Samuel
Psalm 151 – the Greek Septuagint

Superscription: This psalm is autobiographical,
ascribed to David (but outside the number),
after he fought with Goliath in single combat:

I was small among my brothers,
and the youngest in my father's house;
I tended my father's sheep.
My hands made a harp;
my fingers fashioned a lyre.
And who will tell my Lord?
The Lord Himself; it is He who hears.
It was He who sent His messenger
and took me from my father's sheep,
anointing me with His holy oil.
My brothers were handsome and tall,
but the LORD was not pleased with them.

David's anointing by Samuel
Psalm 151A – Qumran Cave 11

Superscription: Hallelujah! A Psalm of David, Son of Jesse:
Smaller was I than my brothers, and the youngest of my father's sons,
so he made me shepherd of his flock and ruler over his kid goats.
My hands fashioned a reed pipe, and my fingers a lyre;
and I gave glory to the LORD.
I said within my mind:
"The mountains cannot bear witness to him,
nor can the hills proclaim about him—
so cherish my words, you trees, and cherish my deeds, you flocks.
For who can announce, and who can tell, and who can recount my
deeds?"
The Lord of all has seen, the God of all—he has heard and has listened.
He sent his prophet to anoint me, Samuel to make me great.
My brothers went out to meet him,
so handsome of figure, tall in appearance,
So tall in stature, and beautiful with their hair—
yet the LORD God did not choose them.
But he sent and fetched me from behind the flock,
and anointed me with holy oil,
and he appointed me prince of his people
and ruler over the children of his covenant.

David's anointing by Samuel
Psalm 151 – Qumran Cave 53
Aaronson translation – Tablet 1

Superscription: A Psalm of David,
recounting the glories of Elohim's *Bachir* (chosen one).
Thanks be to *Hashem* (The LORD), *El Shaddai* (God Almighty)!

Hallelujah!

Smaller was I than all my *'achim* (brothers), youngest of the *bene*
(sons) of Jesse.

My father's *Ro'eh* (shepherd) was I, ruler of his Bethlehem flock.

There my hands fashioned a *kinor* (harp) and my fingers a lyre;

with these I gave glory to *Hashem*, thinking:

"The mountains cannot bear witness to *Hashem*,

nor can the hills proclaim his *kavod* (glory)—

Prize my words, you hills!

Prize my caring, you trees!

Prize my love, you flocks!

Give ear as I tell of my deeds!"

I am Elohim's instrument, I the *kinor* (harp)

For *HaShirrim* (the songs) of praise to God;

I, the *Ro'eh* (shepherd) of his *'am* (people), Israel.

When his *navi gadol* (great prophet) came to anoint me,

Samuel to lift me high.

My *'achim* (brothers) went first to meet him –

handsome and tall they were,

beautiful the locks of their hair,

yet *Hashem* did not *bachar* (choose) them.

Samuel sent and fetched me from the flock,

but *Hakol* (the Voice) urged me to stay in the fields,

my place of communion with Elohim's creation.

I sought *Hashem* for guidance, for direction I entreated,

and he answered my prayer, sending *Malaki* (my Angel/Muse),

whom I called, Eliana; for "My God has answered me."

Malaki (My Angel/Muse) spoke my name, "David!"

With a word, "*Lech lecha*" ("Go, go for yourself!")

she overcame my reluctance, courage filling my *lev* (heart).

I made haste to the prophet who,

looking upon my *lev* (heart) rather than my frame, *bachar* (chose) me,

and with *shemen kadosh* (holy oil) anointed me,

appointing me Prince of his people, Israel,

shepherd over the *bene b'rith* (children of the covenant).

"But what of Saul, my *Melech* (king)?" I asked.

"Is he not also *Bachir* (the chosen one) of *Hashem*?"

Chapter 3

Second Aaronson Lecture – The Dance of Terpsichore

COVENANT CHRISTIAN COLLEGE, MEMPHIS, TENNESSEE

THURSDAY, SEPTEMBER 8, 1988, 2:00 P.M.

"Good afternoon, class," Dr. Aaronson announced loudly just after the 2:00 bell, hushing our pre-class chatter. Oddly, he was speaking from outside the doorway, not yet having entered. What came next was more performance than entrance, something we would soon discover to be his modus operandi. With a whirling dervish imitation, he began to spin toward his desk, his body rotating with an unhurried, slow RPM, not as I had ever imagined a dervish dance. The very word dervish, to me, suggested a faster, even a furious, rotation.

The students' initial laughter subsided as it became clear that his dance was being offered with unmistakable seriousness. His right arm was raised with palm upward, as if open to receive heaven's gift. His left arm was lowered with palm downward, as if sharing what he was receiving. His head was tilted to the right, toward his raised arm, and his lips slightly moving, as if in conversation with God.

I found his moves oddly sensuous, reminding me of Johnny Castle dancing with Baby in the previous summer's film, *Dirty Dancing*. That summer, before my junior year, I had seen *Dirty Dancing* three times, once with Jakob and twice with my mom, both of those on the same day, mom having driven to Memphis without dad on an explicit mission to see *Dirty Dancing* with her daughter.

There was nothing dirty about Dr. Aaronson's dance, of course, only that it struck me as intimate, as if the dancer were in love with God which, I would discover, is the reason the dervish's head is tilted to the right, toward the arm raised to the heavens.

As he slowly moved in front of the class, I played in my head the melody and words of "Hungry Eyes," my favorite song from the soundtrack, fixing that tune in my head as a daylong earworm.

Dr. Aaronson's dance received precisely the reaction he was hoping for, all eyes now following him intently, eager to hear what he would say. When his slow spin ceased near his desk, he spoke softly, "As we continue our dance with David this afternoon, as your humble choreographer, I begin with a question. Who knows the name Terpsichore?"

No one immediately raised a hand to offer an answer. I thought I knew but wasn't sure. He allowed the silence to ride just long enough for me to speak up.

"Wasn't she one of the Muses?"

"Yes, Stella, very good. Now, a second question. Do you know how many Muses the Greeks revered?"

"Of course," I said, proud that my first answer had been on target. "Nine, the daughters of Zeus."

"Exactly! There were originally only three Muses, but by

the time of the classical Greek period, that triad had tripled to nine. Now, a third question. Since each of the Muses had their particular domain of inspiration, which domain was assigned to Terpsichore?"

None offered an answer, and I couldn't recall. I knew Erato was the Muse inspiring love poetry, an easy connection with the word erotic. I also recalled Clio as another of the Muses, but couldn't remember her specific domain. Something to do with writing, I thought.

"Dancing!" he said, re-enacting his dervish motion for three or four more rotations.

"Terpsichore, always seen with the lyre, was the Muse of dancing, of spinning and whirling. The c-h-o-r in Terpsichore is the same combination of letters in our word chorus, as well as in another word I've just used to describe my function in this class on Hebrew poetry."

"Choreographer!" Jakob nearly shouted from the back.

"Right! Choreographer. I told you on Tuesday that I am taking liberty to translate the Hebrew word *maskil*, found in the superscription of Psalm 89, 'A Maskil of Ethan,' as 'The Choreography of Ethan.'"

Bowing, he added, "Students, I am honored to be your Terpsichorean Muse as we continue our whirling upon the Star of David dance floor."

Allowing us a moment to reflect, he took a few steps away from us, toward the door. "So, nine is the number of the Muses. Now, in my first lecture I used, quite intentionally, the word Muse to describe another set of nine."

He halted, then spun back to look over the class.

"Do you recall?"

"Yes, sir," Michael said. Looking at his class notes, he said, "Three by three by three we go through nine innings with nine players on each team, nine uniformed Muses inspiring their teammates toward victory. I think that's how you said it."

"Indeed, it is!" Dr. Aaronson said, smiling broadly. "You take excellent notes, Michael. Perhaps you share my love of baseball?"

"I do, sir, but not your love for the Red Sox. I'm from St. Louis, a Cardinal fan."

"Oh, I'm so sorry," Dr. Aaronson said with mock compassion. "I see the Cardinals aren't having a great year."

Once again, as with his introduction, Dr. Aaronson had me in the palm of his hand. What he said next, though, shook me to the core.

"Now, thinking of my love for baseball's Red Sox, nine uniformed Muses dancing through nine innings, this afternoon I confess to you an equal passion for The Beatles, especially John Lennon, and for the same two reasons – the city of Boston and the number nine."

"What!" I thought. Could he have known that I, awakened from sleep the night after his first lecture, had been thinking about John Lennon? He couldn't have known. Could he have known? Surely this is just an eerie coincidence. Right? I had told Jakob but only a few minutes ago as we walked from the library.

I swiveled in my seat to look to the back of the class and made eye contact with Jakob, who responded with a quizzical look and a gesture of not knowing.

The coincidence was about to become even more eerie.

"John Lennon often spoke of how he thought the number nine had followed him as a Muse throughout his life. I became a Beatles fan when I was, believe it or not, nine years old, less than a month before my tenth birthday in 1966. My parents took me to Suffolk Downs Racetrack to see the Beatles. What a glorious night that was, spent with 25,000 Beatles' fans. The next day, the 19th of August, The Beatles flew right here to

Memphis, into the heart of the Bible Belt, for a concert at Mid-South Coliseum. Because of John Lennon's having said, earlier that year, that The Beatles were more popular than Jesus, the city was in an uproar."

"Right," I thought. Lennon's comparison of The Beatles to Jesus had happened on the day I was born. It was as if my private thoughts and his teaching were in sync, choreographed.

"Like many southern cities," he continued, "despite Lennon's apology, Memphis had witnessed album burnings and radio boycotts led by local pastors. During the concert that night, someone threw a firecracker onto the stage, causing panic. Video shows all the band members looking immediately at John to see if he had been shot. What happened here in Memphis, some think, was the reason The Beatles stopped touring."

Jakob, intrigued, gave our professor the cue to keep going. "Why did Lennon think the number nine was hounding him?"

"Hounding? Oh no, Jakob, the opposite. He regarded the number nine as a Muse, a source of inspiration choreographing his life."

"A number can be a Muse?" Jakob asked.

"Lennon thought so. He wrote three songs with nine in the title. Three with Nine. Remember that formula. Those three songs were: *Revolution 9. One after 909.* And, the third is the one I recall best, *#9 Dream* which, appropriately, peaked at number nine on the 1974 Billboard Top 100. Written after The Beatles had broken up, he claimed the words to have been inspired by a dream. It's a haunting song, spoken as if remembering a dream but wondering if it really had been only a dream."

"That's me right now," I thought, "wondering if my dream was only a dream."

"Many claim the song was autobiographical, a mysterious

description of his own death. In his dream, somebody calls out his name just as it begins to rain. The meeting of Lennon and this other is described as a dance, which is followed by a refrain that sounds like non-sensical gibberish. I don't remember the words, but I do remember the math – Three with Nine. Each line of the refrain had nine syllables and was repeated three times. Three lines. Nine syllables. Three with Nine. After the refrain, Lennon feels something that is at first warm, and then cold."

Pausing to choose carefully his words, he continued. "Many Beatles' fans regard Lennon's #9 Dream as a vision of his own death, despite being written six years prior to his assassination. Just before he started firing, Mark David Chapman called out his name, 'Mr. Lennon!' Could these be the two in his dream, twisting in a dance of death? Could the sensation of warmth followed by cold be his own warm blood, followed by death's chill? Students, do you think it possible Terpsichore visited Lennon in his dream, inviting him to dance with the death that would, six years later, twist itself around him?"

Had I heard Dr. Aaronson's commentary two days earlier it wouldn't have phased me. I would have found it interesting, but nothing more. Hearing those words today, though, brought back my dream in vivid detail. How could something that felt so real be only a dream?

Like Lennon, I had heard someone call out my name, at least, a name – Ellie – which was so like the name, Eliana, that David gave me in my dream. I remembered also, after hearing my name, a thunderclap, like a gunshot. Then rain began to fall. Was my dream like Lennon's #9 Dream?

I must have missed several of Dr. Aaronson's next comments, reflecting on the parallels between my dream and Lennon's. Catching him at a pause, I asked, "You said the refrain was gibberish. Might it have been a foreign language, having meaning?"

"According to Lennon," he answered, "who was asked that very question, it had absolutely no meaning. I don't recall the words precisely. I think something like cowagaba or, maybe, bowacaga. Sorry, I just don't recall, but I do know he claimed it to be simply a phrase that came to him in his dream."

Stepping to the whiteboard to write the numbers Three and Nine, he said, "Lennon took a deep dive into numerology before his death, fascinated by the number nine. He pointed out that he was born on October 9, and how his first home address was #9 Newcastle Road, Wavertree, Liverpool, pointing out that the three words – Newcastle, Wavertree, and Liverpool – all have nine letters. Three with Nine.

"He claimed to have met Yoko Ono on the 9th of November, only a few months after the Boston-Memphis concerts. He changed his own middle name from Winston to Ono, supplying another O so that John Ono Lennon and Yoko Ono Lennon would have a total of nine Os. Lennon believed those nine Os would be good fortune."

"Wow," Jakob said, "I never realized numerology could be this interesting."

"Oh, there's so much more," Dr. Aaronson said, ready to rattle off more dates.

"The Beatles appeared on *The Ed Sullivan Show* on February 9, 1964. He was shot in New York during the evening of December 8, but in his hometown of Liverpool, it was already the 9th. He was taken to Roosevelt Hospital on 9th Avenue and pronounced dead at 11:07 p.m., $1 + 1 + 7 = 9$."

By this time the class was gawking, partly in amazement at the nines in Lennon's life and partly at Dr. Aaronson's own fascination by his subject, his energy building as he sensed how intensely engaged the students were.

Though Dr. Aaronson was ready to change the subject, the mathematical, Three-Nine dance of Lennon's Muse has stayed with me always, each of my wanderings as David's Muse triggered by the numbers on my bedside clock, three finding as the trigger for each dream a different number with which to partner up and dance. No wonder, long after my six dreams in 1988, I would find sublime the words of Roman Payne, author of a book called *The Wanderess*, when he wrote, "The 'Muse' is not an artistic mystery, but a mathematical equation."

"Well, enough about John Lennon and his number nine, but I'm not finished just yet with baseball's nine. As I think of it, The Beatles can help me make seamless that shift, since their most famous American concert was at New York's Shea Stadium in 1965. Lennon said that concert took him to the top of the mountain. So, students, let's allow Shea Stadium to escort us back from the Star of David to the diamond."

Pointing to the whiteboard, he said, "Three and nine aren't the only numbers I stressed in Tuesday's class. Do you remember the other number featured in my first lecture?"

"Four," I said, without hesitation, the numbers having been with me since being jolted awake at 3:34 a.m.

"Correct, three and four. With the Red Sox in the pennant race, I am sad to report that, unfortunately, we lost last night to the lowly Baltimore Orioles by the score of 4 - 3. My boys just couldn't get that third out in the ninth. Alas, twenty-six outs will not win a baseball game, one short of the magical twenty-seven required, which is, of course," he paused, pointing to the board, "Three times nine."

Not yet finished with his post-game commentary, he said, "Let me tell you about last night's bottom of the ninth. We had a 3-2 lead, but those doggone Ripken brothers, Billy and Cal, were the last two batters, steering the Orioles to a come-from-behind victory as they scored two runs for the win. The last batter, Cal, barely beat out what could have been a double-play ball, allowing the winning run to score from third before we could chalk up that magical twenty-seventh out. I knew, I knew, I just knew, that if Mighty Cal could get to the plate, the Orioles would win."

Winking, he asked, "Did you catch my reference to baseball's greatest poem, Casey at the Bat? Can anyone quote the end of the poem?"

"Of course," Michael said. "There was no joy in Mudville that day, for Mighty Casey had struck out."

"Precisely! But last night, it was Mighty Cal at the bat, not Mighty Casey, and Mighty Cal did not strike out. He delivered the mighty blow, a dribbling ground ball. Sadly, there was complete joy Baltimore last night! Casey at the Bat, by the way, was written by Ernest Lawrence Thayer. Its subtitle is 'A Ballad of the Republic, Sung in the Year 1888,' exactly one hundred years ago. Speaking of the number nine, the poem begins:

The outlook wasn't brilliant for the Mudville nine that day;
The score stood four to two with but one inning more to play."

"Comeback stories can be inspiring," Jakob said, "unless you're on the losing team."

"Exactly right, Jakob. Let me tell you a comeback story. In my ninth year, my Red Sox were miserable, near the worst team in the league. Ah, but the following year, 1967, is known in Boston as the year of The Impossible Dream, led by Yaz. Hard to believe that was twenty-one years ago. Does anybody know who Yaz is?"

I had no idea, but Michael piped up, saying, "Of course, Carl Yastrzemski."

"Yes, Yastrzemski, one of Boston's most revered heroes. My Red Sox, led by Yaz in '67, came back to win the American League pennant. I turned eleven years old toward the end of that phenomenal season. My father that year promised to take me to Fenway to watch eleven games, a magical summer capped by allowing me to take ten friends with me on my eleventh birthday, September 16, 1967."

"Did the Red Sox win that day?" Jakob asked.

"No, unfortunately, we lost to the Orioles, thanks to Boog Powell's three run blast in the seventh. I'll never forget it, though. A Fenway birthday party with eleven kids on my eleventh birthday. It was unforgettable, in spite of losing."

"How can you remember all these games?" I asked.

"Because I've kept all the programs. My dad kept the box score of all games. Fans keeping score on the program is becoming an artifact these days, but, in those days, pencils were sold at the ballpark for a dime. The box of dad's programs that I've kept remind me of the year of The Impossible Dream. They've taught me to chase my dreams, to believe that the impossible is possible."

I thought this was the perfect moment to switch dance floors from the baseball diamond to the Star of David, a great segue into the impossible dream of a shepherd lad from Bethlehem becoming king. Dr. Aaronson had one more baseball lesson to offer, though, carefully framed to set the stage for Psalm 89's Cosmic Hymn.

"Let's say you're the manager of the Boston Red Sox, Joe Morgan. Thank God for Joe Morgan! He's brought Morgan Magic to Fenway this summer. After McNamara was fired in July during the All-Star break, Morgan led the Sox to 19 wins in his first 20 games, putting us back in the hunt for another

American League East pennant.

"Now, let's say you're the manager and you have a serious issue against the team's owner, the guy who pays your salary. You know he is wrong, and you know that he knows he is wrong. What do you do? At first you stay silent. Of course, you do! After all, he has the power to end your career. The issue, though, won't go away. It festers and eats at you until principle demands that you must say something, even if it means losing your job. How would you go about it?"

"Manager of the Red Sox? Making all that money? I wouldn't say a word," Michael said. "Some principles must be sacrificed at the altar of prosperity."

Jakob said, "No, I'd work my network of friends beneath the radar until I found another club to manage. Once my future was secure, I'd let the boss have it, guns blazing. Don't burn the bridge, though, until you know you're safe on the other side."

"Ah, such courage, such wisdom!" Dr. Aaronson said, grinning. "I love how you two boys stand your ground with integrity!"

It was clear to me now where he was going. "If I really felt it necessary to challenge the boss," I said, "I would remember that there was a great deal I admired about him in the first place, else I would never have taken the job. Knowing I had to confront him, I would, but I would begin by telling him how much I respected and admired him."

"Bingo!" Professor Aaronson said, pointing at me. "Obviously, Ms. Maris has done her homework, her course of action being precisely what Ethan has done in the section we focus on this afternoon, the Cosmic Hymn. As preamble to his bitter complaint, Ethan begins by lifting up all the glories of his sovereign boss."

Dr. Aaronson next introduced each of the five sections of

the Cosmic Hymn. "The first of these four-line clusters, verses five and six, begins with outright applause, acknowledging that no heavenly creature could compare with his God, that the God of Israel knows no rival:

> Yahweh, the assembly of the holy ones in heaven
> applaud the marvel of your faithfulness.
> Who in the skies can compare with Yahweh?
> Which of the heaven-born can rival him?"

"How's that for buttering up the boss?" he asked. "And he's only started. From there, his flattery flows in a stream of adulation throughout this hymn of praise. The next cluster of four lines reads:

> God, dreaded in the assembly of the holy ones,
> Great and terrible to all around him,
> Yahweh, God of Sabaoth, who is like you?
> Mighty Yahweh, clothed in your faithfulness!"

Pausing, he said in Hebrew, "*Mi khamocha.*"

"What?" Jakob laughed.

"*Mi khamocha* is the question Ethan asked in this section. It means, 'Who is like you?' I notice on our class roll that one of our students bears a Hebrew name meaning, literally, 'Who is like God?' Do you know who you are?"

None responded.

"Michael, did you know that your name, as well as your female counterpart, Michelle, means, 'Who is like God'?"

"I did not," Michael responded, "but I did know that El means God in Hebrew.

"Exactly right! The last two letters in your name – E and L – form the theophoric element, which is to say, God's name. El appears in many Hebrew names and places. Bethel means

82

'House (*Beth*) of God (*El*).' Simple, right? The name of the prophet Elijah means 'My God (*Eli*) is Yah (*jah*),' the shortened form of Yahweh. *Eli*, meaning 'My God,' is particularly interesting for Christians. It's used twice in Psalm 22 in a verse Jesus quoted as he died on the cross, '*Eli, Eli, lama sabachthani*,' meaning, 'My God (*Eli*), my God (*Eli*), why have you forsaken me?'"

Hearing Dr. Aaronson pronounce *Eli* stunned me. Spoken in Hebrew, *Eli* sounded, not like our English male name, Eli, but like the female name Ellie, the name that had awakened me two nights earlier. Could it be that I had heard what I only thought to be a name, when what I was actually hearing was someone crying out, "My God! My God!"

"Sir," I said, "are there any female names using that same theophoric element of El?"

"Of course. I've mentioned Michelle. Another example from Hebrew is easy for me to think of, my little sister's name being Eliana. In Eliana, the theophoric element – EL – is at the beginning of the name rather than the end, and its meaning is the exact opposite of what Jesus said on the cross. Instead of 'My God has forsaken me,' it means, 'My God has answered me.' My sister is ten years younger than I am, a college senior, as are most of you. After I was born, my parents wanted one more child, faithfully praying in the Jewish tradition of fixed hour prayer. Three times a day for nine years they prayed. Three with Nine again, right? They had almost given up hope when mom became pregnant. Born on the Ides of March in 1966, my parents named their miracle baby Eliana, an expression of gratitude to God for hearing their prayers."

"Eliana!" I thought, "That's it! That's the name David gave to me in my dream."

I'd been thinking about the name Eliana for two days. How could this be a mere coincidence? I wondered if I would ever meet Dr. Aaronson's sister, she only eleven days younger than I am. I would have to think on that later, though, as he was ready to move on.

"The third cluster of four lines reaches a pinnacle of praise, the psalmist declaring God's victory over his enemy Yam, a Hebrew name meaning 'sea.' Yam represents chaos. Listen as the psalmist describes God's victory over chaos:

> You control the pride of the ocean,
> When its waves ride high, you calm them;
> You split Rahab in two like a carcass
> And scattered your enemies with your mighty arm."

"Sounds like Jesus calming the Sea of Galilee," Jakob said.

"It does, very good, yes. Yam, God of the Rivers and Seas in Canaanite mythology, was the enemy of Baal. In Hebrew, El plays the role of Baal, the head of the pantheon with the power to calm Yam. So powerful is this image that we see it in the stories of Jesus, who calmed the waters of the Galilee."

"Dr. Aaronson," Michael contested, "you said David is the only name used in the psalm. Here is another, Rahab."

"No, what I said is that David is the only name of an historical person used in Psalm 89. This is not the Rahab of the book of Joshua, the prostitute who helped Joshua defeat Jericho. This Rahab is none other than the mythical sea-monster, Leviathan."

"Leviathan?" Michael said.

"Yes. You see, the ancient Hebrews regarded the sea with great fear, similar to those medieval European maps that labeled the blue sea with the words, *Hic sunt dracones!* Here be dragons! Why? Well, for one reason, from the sea came their ancient enemies, the Sea Peoples. The Sea Peoples came from the Aegean, perhaps from Crete. For nearly a century these maritime warriors wreaked havoc throughout the eastern Mediterranean seaboard, from Egypt in the south to Lebanon and Syria in the north. Interestingly, we know virtually nothing about them from their own writings, but only from their victims. Especially Egypt."

"Were the Philistines Sea Peoples?" Jakob asked.

"Unclear, but it's a great question. It does seem that the Philistines, the ancient enemies of Israel, were part of the coastal disruption during the Late Bronze Age. Archaeologists have shown that their early pottery bore traits of Mycenaean traditions before gradually developing a style that can be uniquely identified as Philistine. In addition, their script seems to have been Aegean, rather than Semitic. This, in my opinion, fits the Philistines within the definition of Sea Peoples."

"So, if the Philistines were Sea Peoples," Jakob pressed, "that makes Goliath a giant monster from the sea, like Rahab?"

"In a way, yes. David's victory over Goliath gave him, in the eyes of the people, something approaching divine status."

Dr. Aaronson was ready now to pick up the pace, moving to the next cluster. "Now, if the third set of four lines took us from east to west, from the Jordan River to the Mediterranean Sea (River and Sea being the two domains of Yam), the fourth takes us on a different axis, explicitly taking us from south to north by offering two more names – not of people, but of places – Tabor and Hermon. These are two prominent mountains in Israel, and to think of them is to think geographically. Hermon is in the far north, while Tabor is south, in the lower Galilee. These four lines read:

> The heavens are yours and the earth is yours,
> You founded the world and all it holds,
> You created north and south;
> Tabor and Hermon hail your name with joy."

Looking at his watch, he said, "Now, in the interest of time I'll skip for now the fifth and last quatrain of this section, only to say that it continues the groveling of Ethan, our choreographer, sashaying as he sets the table for offering up his bitter complaint to God, his accusation that God has lied to David."

Erasing the whiteboard, he asked, "Once again, what is the cadence of this section?"

"4-4," several answered.

"Precisely. So, let's focus on that number four and think of it as Cosmic Order, as Nature's Number. How many sets of four can you think of in the natural order of things?"

"Well, there are four seasons of the year," Michael said. "Is that what you mean?"

"Yes, the four seasons, and I don't mean Franke Vallie's Jersey boys."

"The four points of the compass," I added.

"Okay, good. Geography itself dances to the four step of nature. Psalm 89 has given us Israel's geographical landmarks for the four cardinal directions. East to west is the River to the Sea. North to south is Mount Hermon to Mount Tabor."

He had written "Four Seasons" and "Four Cardinal Directions." After a pause, he turned back to the board and wrote, "Four Elements."

"Most fascinating to me, however, is how the ancients regarded the cosmos as consisting of four essential elements: Earth, Wind, Fire, and Water."

Writing those four elements on the board, he said, "Now, to be sure, our modern periodic table has many other elements, but for thousands of years the educated classes regarded these four elements alone to be the essential make-up of the cosmos."

Circling the word Earth in brown, he said, "Earth is the

dust from which we are made and to which we will return, 'ashes to ashes, and dust to dust.'"

Taking the dark blue marker to circle the word Water, he said, "Water is the shapeless potential out of which creation emerged, able to quench, but also to kill."

Making the motions of circling the word Wind but actually leaving it without color, he said, "Wind, air, is the most difficult element, hard to pin down, so I've colored it with my magical, invisible marker. It's beyond our control, as Jesus said in John, 'the wind blows where it wishes.'"

Finally, circling the word Fire in red, he finished, "Fire is the element of transformation, the change element turning solids and liquids into gasses, not to mention our everyday kitchen experiences of turning what is raw and inedible into a delectable delight for the palate."

"Look at our Jewish professor, working Jesus into his lecture and then making him invisible," Jakob observed, clearly joking.

Ignoring Jakob with a sly smile, he continued, "I just mentioned Philistine pottery. Pottery styles help archaeologists identify civilizations. While pottery styles are distinct from one culture to another, the process of making pottery merges all civilizations, all peoples, all nations, into one. Each piece of pottery combines this divine quartet of elements."

"What do you mean?" I asked.

"Well, the entire quartet – earth, water, wind, and fire – contributes to the process of pottery making. The soft clay (the earth) is made wet (the water) and dried into shape in the open air (the wind) and hardened by the sun (the fire). Earth, water, wind, and fire."

Lifting his coffee cup, he drove home his point. "Behold in my hand the four essential elements of earth, water, wind, and fire. Behold the four-step dance of the Cosmos."

"That is so cool," Michael said. "Cosmic lessons from a cup of coffee."

"Class, in the creation story of Genesis this divine four-step is present. In the beginning the earth is watery, without form and void. Then, the *Ruach Elohim*, the Wind of God begins to change everything, moving over the face of the waters. The Hebrew word *marhephet* is translated 'moved,' but there are other ideas of what the divine Wind did. Did it move? Did it brood? Did it hover? All those translations stab at trying to define how the Spirit of God acted. I prefer a more energy-oriented word, that the Spirit 'sparked.' I suppose you could say that I see something electric in this word."

"Is this God, playing with fire?" I asked.

"Exactly, yes. With fire creation began its dance, spinning becoming its most natural movement. The Whirling Dervish is Rumi's sacred dance created eight hundred years ago to imitate the spiraling cosmos, the way things are in the natural order."

He began again his slow dervish spin, now heading back toward the door he had entered ninety minutes earlier.

"This spiral, students, is the way our world turns, from the double helix of our DNA to the spiraling arms of the Milky Way. With his cosmic hymn of praise, I think the psalmist wanted God to know that he had noticed, that he was paying attention, that he saw the divine order in the elegance of creation."

Ceasing his turning, he concluded, "But of course, that's not the end of Ethan's story. I look forward to seeing you next Tuesday."

As students were scattering, I lagged behind, as usual. Classmates, even Jakob, teased me incessantly, calling me a suck-up. Maybe, but I prefer to think I was an eager student, each class leaving me with more questions.

"I enjoyed your lecture very much, Dr. Aaronson," I said, once all students had exited. "Honestly, at first I wasn't too excited about Hebrew poetry, but now I admit I'm looking forward to each class."

"*Toda raba*," he said. "Stella, I've been most impressed by your participation. And, if you'll walk with me to my office, perhaps it will give me a chance to apologize."

"Apologize?"

"Yes. I felt bad about singling you out on Tuesday to talk about the Latin meaning of your name, Star of the Sea."

I started to assure him no apology was necessary, but he continued before I could form a word. "I've always loved etymology, especially of names. One of my professors in Ann Arbor, in our Akkadian class . . ."

"Akkadian?" I interrupted.

"Babylonian. His name was Peter, and he gently chided me, saying, 'David, etymology is the last recourse of scoundrels and fools.'"

"What did you say?" I asked.

"I told him, 'Well, if I can choose one, I'll take scoundrel over fool.' Still, I'm sorry if my first day enthusiasm embarrassed you."

"Oh, no sir, that's no problem. I actually think you helped me appreciate my name more. As a child I was sometimes reminded that Stella Maris was a title fit for the mother of Jesus. Who could measure up to that?"

"Well, I don't know about measuring up to the mother of Jesus, but I think you have very much to offer. The mystics of Judaism believe that all Hebrew letters possess a soul, each filled with a unique spirit. In Hebrew, the letter L is called *Lamed*. Your name, with two Lameds, invests you with double dose of that L-spirit."

"Yes, and two Ls also in Ellie," I thought.

"You've taken a class or two in Hebrew, right?"

"Yes sir, thinking I would follow college with seminary. I'm not so sure now, though."

"Really? Well, whether from pulpit or podium, I hope you'll follow through. I think you would be a great teacher. Have you studied enough Hebrew to know what the word *Lamed* means?"

Our walk from the classroom section had brought us out of the hallway to emerge into the cafeteria, a large circular-shaped room which was part of the original architecture of the Jewish temple. The classroom section from which we had walked was a newer addition, added sometime after C-cube purchased the temple.

The cafeteria was an atrium, the roof three stories above ground level. On the second and third levels of the structure, faculty offices circled the cafeteria in a ring. I think of my old college every time I enter an Embassy Suites, especially when I'm having breakfast on the ground floor, people watching as I look up at hotel guests entering and leaving their rooms. While dining, students often looked up to the offices overhead, joking how the professors hovered above us, spying.

Dr. Aaronson paused at the foot of the stairs, offering no invitation for me to ascend to his second floor office. I took his pause as a message that the foot of the stairs was as far as he would take me.

"Yes, sir," I replied, "I think I recall *Lamed* meaning, 'to learn.'"

"It does, well done. But *Lamed* also means, 'to teach.' You see, when learning is done right, it's a spiral, a circle like these offices circling the dining hall. Education, you see, is a spinning wormhole transporting a student not only to their own future, but impacting the future of others. One learns in order to give back. Like the dervish. One palm upward to receive. The other outward to share."

Stooping to lay his books on one of steps, he then stood erect, extending his right hand upward with palm up and reaching toward me with his left palm out. I suppose I should have felt uncomfortable, his hand nearing an invasion of my space, but I didn't. Resisting the urge to take a step back from his open palm, I found myself leaning ever so slightly toward him.

"*Lamed*, by the way," he said as he retrieved his books, "is the tallest of the Hebrew letters, sometimes called the Tower. I like that word since teaching and learning, learning and teaching, towers over everything else in life. Education is what separates humanity from the rest of creation, escorting generation after generation through the spiraling wormhole of time."

"Is that what happened to me Tuesday night?" I thought. "Had I been escorted three thousand years through the spiraling wormhole of time?"

"At the risk of sounding overly mystical," he said, snapping me back to our conversation, "do you hear the L-sound in the word, spiral? Can it be coincidence that so many words referring to the circle, the spiral, contain the L-sound? Circle and spiral, obviously. But also whirl, twirl, curl, coil, loop, reel, bowl, belt, roll, cylinder, elliptical."

Clearly having fun with his spilling of Ls, I added, "Yes, and how about Hallelujah, a triad of Ls for the Holy Rollers?"

"Hallelujah and Holy Rollers! A double triad of Ls! Thanks for playing, Stella."

Pausing, he continued with a more serious tone, "There's another Hebrew word whose basic meaning is 'circle,' which also has two Ls, *Galil*, meaning 'rolling' or 'cylinder.' From *Galil* we have the word Galilee, referring to the circular geographical area in northern Israel. In Galilee your rabbi, Jesus, began his ministry, and from the Galilee his teachings have spiraled through time, generation after generation."

He started up the steps, but thinking of my dream of dancing with David I had one more question. "Professor, do you think it's possible that the wormhole could also extend into the past, and not only the future? Can we be Muses to those coming before us, and not just to those coming after us?"

Laughing, he replied, "Surely not. Our journey is a one-way path, I'm afraid."

Now halfway up the stairs, I stopped him again. "I'm sorry, Dr. Aaronson, but one more quick question, if I may. When did it occur to you to mention the Beatles and Mark David Chapman in today's lecture?"

I wondered if he might say, "Well, I overheard you in the library speaking with Jakob."

Instead, with a perplexed look, he said, "Odd that you mention it. A teacher must always be open to the inspiration of the moment, to the Muse. Honestly, featuring Lennon's love for the number nine is something that came to me Tuesday night, awakened in the middle of the night. I was having a hard time sleeping, thinking how best to present the Cosmic Hymn which, honestly, to me is the least interesting segment of our psalm. Not wanting to lose the class before we reached the more interesting sections, I was looking for a way to make it memorable."

Nodding expressionless, trying to hide how much his answer stunned me, he disappeared into the constellation of faculty offices above. I thought of how Elisha had watched as his teacher, Elijah, ascend into heaven, recalling how he picked up his mentor's mantle and received a double portion of his spirit.

Dare I hope for such a double portion of the *Lamed*-spirit that I saw in David Aaronson?

Chapter 4

Dancing with David
in the Valley of Elah

FRIDAY, SEPTEMBER 9, 1988, 3:39 A.M.

"I wonder if John Lennon was trying to say cowabunga?" Jakob said after our server set the cheese dip on the table and headed to the kitchen to place our order.

"What?"

"You know, the refrain to his song, *#9 Dream*. Didn't Dr. Aaronson say the word was something like cowagaba?"

"And you heard cowabunga?"

"It's close."

"No," I laughed, digging in the chips. "Lennon never heard the word cowabunga. I doubt he ever heard of the Mutant Ninja Turtles."

"You're wrong. Cowabunga is much older. Surfers have used it for a long time to express amazement. Like you and me this afternoon, shocked when Dr. Aaronson mentioned The Beatles only a few minutes after you had told me your dream. When you turned around and looked at me, 'Cowabunga!'

would have been just the right word."

"I know! Wasn't that eerie? I thought he must have overheard us in the hallway, but I asked him after class and he said the idea had come to him Tuesday night, probably about the time I was dreaming. I didn't tell him about my dream that same night. You're the only one I've told, and you must keep it to yourself."

"C'mon, you know can trust me. I've not told anyone, and I won't tell anyone. I intend to spend the rest of my life with you. I'm not going to mess that up by breaking a promise."

Lowering his voice to a whisper as he held up an oddly shaped chip, he began to flirt a bit too suggestively for me. I reluctantly smiled, but was happy that our server was arriving at that moment with our food, ending the subject without my having to say, "Stop it."

I had never gone all the way with Jakob, though increasingly he was hinting that he wanted our relationship to grow more sexual than the kissing and making out that I had allowed. I won't deny my enjoyment of those intimate moments, nor that I wanted to go further, probably as much as Jakob did. I'm sure he mistook my commitment to my values as me lacking the urges he felt, but he would have been wrong.

I had to fight with my own *Hakol*, the Voice telling me that my commitment to those values was antiquated, that I was wrong to deny Jakob, and myself, the pleasure of being sexually active. I had made it clear to him, though, what my boundaries would be in the short term, and what my desires were in the long term. He knew that, for me, marriage must precede sex, and that after marriage I wanted to have many children. How many? Only the Lord knows.

Recognizing how irked I had been at his table behavior, Jakob apologized to me later, driving me home. Truth is, though, I felt I should apologize, not only for asking Jakob to be different than most college students our age, but for my undeniably growing attraction for David Aaronson. That, though, he must never know.

That night I couldn't get Dr. Aaronson's Three-Nine out of my head. Lennon's song was only one example of the triad of Three-Nine combos he had mentioned. Three outs through nine innings and three original Greek Muses growing to nine were the other two.

Climbing into bed, I recalled my dream from two nights before, how startled awake at 3:34, I couldn't get out of my head that Three-Four combination from the first lecture, looking up Genesis 3:4 before drifting back to sleep.

Would it work again, with the Three-Nine combo? Taking the Bible, I looked up Genesis 3:9 and read, "But the LORD God called to the man, 'Where are you?'" This was when Adam and Eve, having sinned and now knowing they were naked, hid from God when they heard his voice. I got out of bed to look at my Hebrew Bible and saw that the word "Voice" was *Kol*, the same as in *Ha-kol* (the Voice), David's enemy.

"The Lord has a *Kol*, a Voice, too," I thought, "so the question becomes, which Voice do I choose to follow?"

God was saying, in Genesis 3:9, "Where are you?" I've felt God saying that to me this past year, even as I was asking him the same. "God, where are you?"

This was the same question I had asked David in my dream, a boy tending his father's sheep and reluctant to be seen by Samuel, hiding in the Shepherd's Fields. I asked, "David, where are you? What are you doing out here with the sheep?" How differently Israel's history might have been written had David listened to *Hakol*, instead of to me.

Hungry for a second vision to open a portal into the past, I remembered asking Dr. Aaronson if he thought the Muse's wormhole might also extend to the past. His answer was immediate and certain. "No, it cannot," he had said.

After Tuesday night's dream, I knew differently.

"Ellie! Ellie!"

The clock's glow showed 3:39. Three-Nine. Cowabunga!

Two nights ago, startled by an urgent voice calling "Ellie!" I had spent some time awake. Tonight, I simply turned away from the clock, thinking only of David – the anointed David, not my professor.

Within minutes, I slept. My dream awakening (as I've come to call those moments, experienced with an abruptness unlike ordinary dreaming, as if "landing" in another time and place) was very unlike the first. I found myself, not in the cool and calm of the Shepherds' Fields, but in the hot midst of clamor and urgency. Troops were lining up for battle, commanders shouting orders barely audible over the din.

I heard a booming bass voice calling, "Where are you? Where are you, you little runt? Where the hell are you?"

It was the voice of Goliath mocking David who, in response, stepped out from the ranks toward the giant. David looked not much older or much different than when I had seen him in Bethlehem. Unlike the soldiers, he wore no armor. I had arrived at the scene too late to witness how that came about, but I knew the story well, David's refusal to wear Saul's gear.

Pausing at a stream on his way to meet the Philistine champion, he knelt, momentarily out of the view of Goliath.

"Where are you?" the giant bellowed again, tasting inevitable victory.

Nearing David, I saw that Other, *Hakol*, bowing to whisper in his ear. As in the Shepherd's Fields, I saw only his scarred profile. Slightly turning towards me, as if sensing my approach, *Hakol* turned quickly back to David. "I told you she is the queen of nothing but death. Your life is in peril. Do not listen to her, David, or she will bring you to death."

As I came closer, *Hakol* turned away to walk down the stream toward the Israelite encampment, vanishing quickly from sight. Obviously shaken by whatever *Hakol* had said, David continued to kneel, paralyzed, staring at the brook.

"David," I said.

Relief came over his face when he saw me, saying softly, "Eliana, where have you been? Many times I have prayed for you to come back to me. *Hakol* speaks to me constantly. Why do you not come more often?"

"I'm here now, David. Why do you hesitate?"

"*Hakol* urges me to let another do the fighting, warning me that my arrogance will be my destruction. Perhaps he is right. I am a shepherd and a musician, not trained for war. My victories with the sling over the lion and the bear, what are they against this giant? Hearing *Hakol*, this stream has become in my mind a roaring river I fear to cross."

Hakol's voice had created an illusion in David's mind, since the stream was gentle, barely moving. The danger facing David in Goliath was very real. The danger of crossing the brook was an illusion.

"David," I said, "Fear not, for Adonai Sabaoth (the Lord of hosts) walks with you this day into battle. Stand tall, David, and go forth! Goliath, your enemy, who now sees you as but a small stream to step across, will soon tremble before the roar of your terror-waves, crashing against him as a storm upon *Hayam Hagadol* (the Great Sea)."

Seeing a smooth stone glisten in the sunlight, I said, "Look, there is the stone you will bury into your enemy's forehead."

David reached down and picked up the stone, along with four others encircling it. Now equipped for battle, he stood while saying, "Eliana, *Malaki* (My Angel/Muse), on this day you have become my *Kochav Hayam* (Star of the Sea)."

It had been at that moment, as the brook's *Hakol*-inspired terror subsided, that David gave to me my name, *Kochav Hayam*.

The rest of the story is well known from the Bible. Goliath's taunting of David, thundering that he would soon offer David's flesh to the birds and the beasts. David's calm response of faith, proclaiming that he came not with a sword but with that which is more powerful than any weapon, the name of the LORD.

I watched as the stone to which I had directed David crashed against the giant's forehead with incredible velocity. I shall never forget the Philistine champion's wobbling, his dumbfounded expression, and the loud thud when his body hit the ground.

Most of all, though, I saw the blood. There is one biblical statement with which I must contend, that Goliath was dead when he hit the ground. No, for his heart was still pumping. When David beheaded the monster, his blood showered upward to drench us both, I now at David's side. His face gleamed in crimson glory as he looked up to me, a warrior face I hold forever in my heart.

As the crowd of Israel's soldiers rushed to David with shouts of victory, he reached out to me with his blood-soaked right hand, wishing for me to be his companion in his victory whirl. In that moment, though, I vanished from the Valley of Elah, awakening in my bed in Memphis. My dream had been so powerfully real that I instinctively felt the sheets to see if they were wet with the giant's blood dripping from my drenched clothes.

SIEGFRIED JOHNSON

"It was a 339?"

"Not just one. Three 339s were involved."

Never had a Sunday School class conversation so instantly seized my attention, the numbers 339 dancing in my head since Thursday night.

"What are they talking about?" I wondered, as Jakob and I searched for a seat in the crowded College and Careers class at Bellevue.

We had arrived a few minutes late, as usual, so were unaware of the topic the class was discussing. Our teacher was Corky Walker, a recent seminary graduate and the newest associate pastor at the megachurch. He insisted we call him Corky rather than Pastor Walker. If he was perturbed by our late arrival, he hid it well, acknowledging with a smile our whispered apologies and taking a moment to ask how we were doing.

"Very well," I said, "thank you. We're so sorry to be late. I was hoping you would still be in donut and coffee time."

"Would you like one?" Corky asked, pointing to the counter and saying there was still some coffee in the urn.

As Jakob headed for the coffee I said, "I'm a Diet Coke kind of girl, but I am very interested in what you were talking about when we came in. What 339s are you talking about?"

"Okay, then," Corky said, "Stella's ready to jump into our discussion. We're talking about the Ramstein Air Base tragedy."

"Oh, of course," I said.

The tragedy was all over the news. Two weeks earlier, on August 28, there had been a disaster at Ramstein Air Base in Germany, a military stunt flight team crashing while performing maneuvers in front of 300,000 spectators. Eventually the death toll reached seventy, with serious injuries to over three hundred others, one of the worst air show disasters in history.

"As you guys know," Corky said, "I entered ministry when I came out of the Air Force, so you could say military aircraft is my thing. I was saying, Stella, that the jets that crashed were three Italian Aermacchi MB-339 fighters."

"Is he doing a David Aaronson imitation?" I wondered, "using current events to get his point across? Good job, Corky! Let's see where you can take us."

"They were performing a maneuver called the Pierced Heart. The jets form a large heart shape in front of the audience. Then a solo jet, like an arrow, flies through the lower tip of the heart at only 135 feet above the crowd. When performed flawlessly, which it must be since there's practically zero margin for error, the stunt is exhilarating. Last week's tragedy occurred when the arrow came in too slow and too low."

"Tragic," Jakob said, taking his seat beside me with his coffee and a couple of donut holes. I took one as a perfect complement to my Diet Coke.

"It is," Corky said, "and our prayers are with all those impacted, both the injured and those who are grieving the loss of a loved one. Now, guys, the Bible talks about one important person whose heart was pierced with grief. Can anyone tell me who that is?"

"And here it is," I thought. This would be no random discussion of a news event. He had a reason for beginning class with the Pierced Heart airshow tragedy.

"I think I know the passage you mean," I said. "To me, it's one of the most haunting verses of the Bible, what Simeon says to Mary as she presents her baby at the temple."

"Yes, that's it," he said. "Simeon was an old man who had received a promise from the Lord not to die before he had seen the anointed one. Luke records the old man's prophecy, spoken after he took the infant into his arms. After blessing

Jesus, he told Mary that this child would cause the hearts of many to be revealed, and that a sword would pierce her own heart also."

"So," I asked, "Mary's pierced heart was the crushing grief of watching her son die, thirty-three years later?"

"Yes, but I believe Mary's heart was pierced long before her son's death. Imagine how she must have mourned when she discovered that the birth of her son had caused the death of the innocent children of Bethlehem. Herod was a monster. History has known many Herod's since then who have pierced many hearts."

"I've never thought of Mary's pierced heart like that, grieving over the lost children," I said, "but of course she would have suffered."

"Think of the many who are today sorrowing over last month's tragedy at Ramstein. So many the broken hearts. Now, let's take a second to look deeper at what Luke meant, saying that the hearts of many would be revealed. Here's my question: how does tragedy 'reveal' hearts?"

"Well," Jakob said, "My sister, Margie, was killed nine years ago in a horseback riding accident. She was seventeen and I was thirteen. Mom nearly decked a pastor at visitation before the funeral when he tried to offer comfort by saying, 'We have to trust the Lord, Sister Rothman. We don't know why this is the Lord's will, why he wanted Margaret with him in heaven.' When he said that, I saw mom's eyes and thought she was going to deck him. Instead, she just turned away, saying nothing. She told me later that she was furious at his suggestion that God wanted this tragic accident to happen, but understood that he was a young pastor, not experienced, and that he meant well."

"That's awful," Corky said. "Thank you for sharing that. I'm so sorry."

"I think our family's loss, the sword piercing our souls, did reveal hearts. It revealed the pastor's heart as young and inexperienced, not well equipped to comfort the grieving. It revealed my mother's good heart, withholding her anger and full of grace. It also revealed my heart, I'll admit. Despite mom's words, for a time I thought I would never have anything to do with a God who would kill my sister just to have her in heaven with him."

"These are all visceral reactions in the midst of grief," Corky said. "When tragedy strikes, we want to know why. We wonder where God is, and we wonder why God would allow this to happen. To prepare for this class, I reread parts of one of my favorite books dealing with these difficult questions, *When Bad Things Happen to Good People*, by Rabbi Harold Kushner. It came out when I was in seminary."

"I've heard of that book," someone said. "To me, it sounds like the rabbi's attempt to exonerate God for all the evil in the world."

"A nice summary," Corky said with a smile. "It's a thorny question with which theologians have grappled forever. The fancy term for it is theodicy, meaning 'the righteousness of God.' So, I ask you, is God righteous in allowing human suffering?"

"Yes, in allowing suffering, God can be righteous," someone said, "but surely not in causing it."

"Why not? He caused Job's suffering," Jakob said, playing devil's advocate.

"That's right, Jakob," Corky said. "Many are the Old Testament passages that mention God's active involvement in causing the suffering of, not just Job, but his own people. The prophets saw calamity as not just allowed by God, but caused by God as punishment for their sin. After the destruction of the temple in 586 B.C. by the Babylonians, Jeremiah laments by writing the Book of Lamentations."

"Lamentations!" I thought. Since Corky had begun with three 339s, I wondered what Lamentations 3:39 might say, quickly looking for it in my Bible. It was perfect for the discussion.

"You mentioned the 339s of the Ramstein disaster," I said. "With those numbers already on my mind from a lecture I heard this week, I looked up Lamentations 3:39."

"What does it say?" Corky asked.

"It reads, 'Why should any living man complain, when punished for his sins?'"

"Wow!" Corky said, looking up the passage in his Bible.

"And, look at the previous verse," he continued. "Verse 38 reads, 'Is it not from the mouth of the Most High that both calamities and good things come?'"

"But why serve such a God?" someone said. "Isn't this all just Old Testament thinking that Jesus rejected? Hasn't our relationship with God matured, no longer based on quid pro quo?"

"Some think so," Corky said. "That's one answer but, in my humble opinion, a wrong one. Have any of you heard of the book *J. B.?*

None had.

"One of my favorite lines in the book comes from a character named Nickles, who played the role of Satan. He sings:

> If God is God He is not good.
> If God is good He is not God,
> Take the even, take the odd."

"What kind of a book is that?" I asked.

"Thank you for asking," he replied with a wide grin. "*J. B.*

is the title of a Pulitzer Prize winning play written by Archibald MacLeish in 1956. It's meant to be a modern version of Job, set during the devastation of World War 2. Of course, J. B. is Job, the main character who loses everything and is left to wrestle with the same questions the biblical Job faced."

"Nickles is Satan, then?" I asked.

"Yes, the voice of the enemy. Satan challenged God to bring affliction on Job in order to test him, to see if he would remain faithful after God's blessings were removed. Nickles' point is that if God is sovereign, able always to accomplish his will, it must be his will that humans suffer. If so, God cannot be good, right? On the other hand, if God is good, wishing for humans not to suffer, God must not be powerful enough to enact his will. In that case, God cannot be God."

Corky was a wonderful teacher whose Sunday School class always left me with something to ponder. This Sunday was no different. I suppose I should have heard Nickles' song as blasphemous, but I didn't. Something in me understood the dilemma posed by his chant,

> If God is God He is not good.
> If God is good He is not God,
> Take the even, take the odd.

Here are the three extant versions of Psalm 151 as they tell the story of David and Goliath, the longest being the Aaronson translation of Tablet 2.

David's defeat of Goliath
Psalm 151 – Septuagint version

> I went out to meet the Philistine,
> and he cursed me by his idols.

But I drew his own sword;
I beheaded him,
and took away disgrace from the people of Israel.

David's defeat of Goliath
Psalm 151B – Qumran Cave 11

Superscription: The start of mighty d[ee]ds for [Davi]d,
after the prophet of God had anointed him:
Then I s[a]w a Philistine,
throwing out taunts from the r[anks of the enemy].
... I ... the...

David's defeat of Goliath
Psalm 151 – Qumran Cave 53
Aaronson translation of Tablet 2

At the Valley of Elah I came to my *Melech* (king) Saul,
my three eldest *ahim* (brothers) serving in his army.
Astounded by the Philistine's defiance,
offended by the absence of any valiant one to stand tall,
I determined to go forth as Israel's champion.
Rejecting the king's armor,
I went out to meet the Philistine alone.
Cursing me by the profane names of his idols,
He mocked and taunted me for my stature.
Crossing a wading brook, my dread rose as the tide,
the stream's ripples raging
like angry, storm-tossed waves of *Hayam Hagadol* (the Great Sea),
its spray drenching me with *mavet* (death).
Hakol whispered to my *lev* (heart), "Turn back, David,
Do not give yourself over to your foolish pride.

Let another more worthy than you take your place."

Then I heard Eliana speak my name, "David!"

Looking upon her beauty, unseen since the Shepherds' Fields,

my *nephesh* (soul) filled with Shalom.

"*Hinei!*" ("Behold!") she said, pointing to the brook,

"for as this small stream has become for you a furious *yam* (sea),

so shall you become in the eyes of Goliath of Gath."

With Eliana's words the waters grew calm,

smooth *ebenim* (stones) emerging from its shallows.

Stooping to choose *hamesh* (five), I said to her,

"Eliana, *Malaki* (My Angel/Muse), you are now my *Kochav Hayam!*
(Star of the Sea)

For your *'or* (light) has dispelled the *hoshek* (darkness) of *hayam*
(the sea)."

Rising, I felled Goliath with the sling,

its *eben* (stone) in flight singing sweetly as ever my *kinor* (harp)
has sounded.

The giant fallen, I drew his *chereb* (sword) and beheaded him,

blood-spray drenching me in *karmil* (crimson),

sounding forth the *kavod* (glory) of Saul, my *Melech* (king).

Looking up in victory, wearing the giant's blood,

my *Kochav Hayam* disappeared as I reached for her to dance.

Saul's army rushed to meet me with praise.

Chapter 5

Third Aaronson Lecture – Edgar Whisenant's Rapture Dance

COVENANT CHRISTIAN COLLEGE, MEMPHIS, TENNESSEE

TUESDAY, SEPTEMBER 13, 1988, 2:00 P.M.

C-cube didn't have a drama department but, had we, Dr. Aaronson would have been a natural to chair it. His classroom entrances were dramatic, a theme parade preparing the class for that day's focus. Many would no doubt think it childish, but we found the drama effective, in a Patch Adams kind of way.

On Thursday he had gracefully twirled into the classroom like a dervish, his dance introducing us to Terpsichore, Muse of the spinning ones. Today's entrance lacked any trace of such elegance. Today he entered cowering, back arched and arms crooked over him in a defensive posture, as if sheltering himself from imminent danger. Speechless, he maintained his frightened posture, crouching as he crossed in front of the class, then turning to continue his un-dance in and out of the rows of students.

At last, someone in the back cutely ended the awkward silence, asking, "Did Terpsichore choreograph these latest moves?"

"Haven't you heard?" he urgently whispered, still feigning panic.

"Heard what?" Jakob asked.

"That today is the End. Are you ready? Are you ready to meet Jesus? Are you prepared for the Apocalypse?"

Some will think this an entirely out-of-place remark for a Jewish professor in a Christian college, assuming that Dr. Aaronson's intent was to belittle an important Christian doctrine of Jesus' return in glory. But no, he was only mocking the latest date-setter prophecy of the rapture made by a former NASA engineer whose book led millions of fundamentalist Christians around the globe to expect the secret rapture of the church on Tuesday, September 13, 1988.

Reverting to his relaxed and scholarly self, having sufficiently dramatized his theme, he said, "Are you aware that today is the conclusion of the Jewish holiday of Rosh Hashana, the Jewish New Year, a three-day festival which began on September 11?"

"Happy New Year!" I offered.

His reply was a nod and a wink.

"Many Christians expect Jesus, during Rosh Hashana 1988, to come in the clouds to snatch the church out of this evil world. Rosh Hashana ends today, so if the prophecy is correct, we have only hours left, perhaps minutes."

We were all aware, of course, as the prophecy had been a much-talked-about topic on campus. While C-cube was conservative, fully affirming the doctrine of Christ's triumphant return, and while no doubt some were intrigued by the prophecy, no student or faculty member to my knowledge had been swayed to the point of urging others to prepare themselves, much less to the point of leaving school to gather in conclaves prepared to meet Jesus in the clouds.

"Former NASA engineer Edgar C. Whisenant," he said, "who hails from just down I-40 in Arkansas, has caused quite the religious fervor with his prediction that Christ will return by the conclusion of Rosh Hashana 1988. His little book, *88 Reasons Why the Rapture Could Be in 1988*, has sold a stunning four million copies. His fervent believers pooled enough financial resources to send hundreds of thousands of copies free to pastors around the world, hoping that they would believe and warn their congregations. I have a Christian friend from Ann Arbor, a youth pastor in one of the grad classes I taught, who mailed a copy to me only last week with a plea for me to consider its logic and convert, to ready myself, my family, and my friends for the Second Advent."

"He didn't convince you?" Jakob asked.

"No, I'm afraid I remain unconvinced. Still, it is an intriguing use of numbers, I must say, as is evidenced by the many who are today expecting to be transported to heaven. I saw an article in this morning's Memphis Commercial-Appeal about emotional gatherings of believers all around the world over these last three days."

I had seen a similar article on the cover of USA Today, glancing at the newsstand when I stopped for coffee at the 7-11. It showed a group of Christians praying, I think in Asia, readying themselves for the certain return of Jesus predicted in Whisenant's *88 Reasons*.

"His mathematical premise is simple," Dr. Aaronson said. "Playing on the number forty as a biblically symbolic period of time, which of course it is, Whisenant offers the number forty as the period of time representing a full generation. Forty years equals one generation. So, since Israel was re-constituted as a nation . . ."

"Forty years ago," I interjected.

"Yes, exactly. In 1948 the U.N. General Assembly's approval of Resolution 181 cleared the way for Israel to become a nation for the first time in two thousand years. The nation of Israel was founded on May 14, 1948. That is fact. Mr. Whisenant takes that fact and points to Jesus' Olivet Discourse in Matthew 24 – his last sermon spoken atop the Mount of Olives – claiming that Jesus premised his return to earth on the timing of Israel's reconstitution as a nation. 'When you see all these things,' Jesus said, 'you know that it is near, right at the door. I tell you the truth, THIS generation will certainly not pass away until all these things have happened.' So, how long is a generation?"

"Forty years," several replied.

"Right, and what is 1948 plus 40?"

"1988!" we replied in unison.

"So, there you have it," he said, "a prophecy built upon supposed mathematical certainty, divine providence as precise as clockwork."

"I don't believe it," Michael said. "It's just another opportunity to make money preying on the gullible, mesmerizing them with numbers to cloud their ability to think logically."

"I agree. Virtually all Christian scholars, of course, have rejected Whisenant's ideas, reminding believers that Jesus taught in that same sermon that no one knows the time of the end, not the angels of heaven nor even the Son, but only the Father. Prophecy, like Hebrew letters, is best read backwards. That way, you have 100% accuracy."

"Doesn't the Bible say, though," Michael said, "that Jesus will come in glory on the Mount of Olives to judge the nations?

As Christians, shouldn't we expect that?"

"Well, think of it like this. Your Messiah was born of a virgin in a Bethlehem cave, a scene radically different than long-held Jewish expectations of how the Messiah might appear. So, if God surprised Jewish expectations, might God also surprise Christian expectations? What if God's next act is to be completely unlike long-held Christian expectations?"

"In what way?" Jakob asked.

"Well, let's say that God's plan is not – or at least, not yet – a return of Jesus in power and glory upon the Mount of Olives to judge the nations but, instead, a second miraculous birth? What if there is work yet to be done, so that God sends another to help Jesus accomplish what is still unaccomplished?"

"And what if it's a girl this time?" I said, joking.

"Yes, what if? Point is, if the long-held expectations of Jews was upended by God's plan, might not the long-held expectations of Christians fall to the same fate?"

After pausing to allow the class to ponder his suggestion, he continued, "In my opinion, Whisenant's prediction is preposterous, merely another recipe for the Apocalypse du Jour. Predictions of the end are always on the menu. Make no mistake, there has always been a boom in doom because, truth be told, whether Jewish or Christian or anything else, even secular, we are all crystal ball gazers by nature. Which is why I predict Mr. Whisenant will, after today's disappointment, write another book claiming to re-calibrate his prediction, then a third, then a fourth. Remarkably, sadly, such lunacy will continue to sell and enrich those who wish to exploit the crystal ball gazing template of human nature."

Dr. Aaronson was half-right in his prediction. Mr. Whisenant did, just as predicted, revise his mathematical calculations and publish new books in both 1989 and 1990 but, to the credit of his once believers, his sales diminished with each of his revised predictions.

I say this despite today, as Teaching Elder of the Maranatha Assembly of the Blessed Hope, believing with all my heart that Christ will return. I draw the line, though, at setting dates. That, to me, is a racket, a manipulation of current events by so-called prophecy experts.

Making a playful pouty face, Dr. Aaronson re-directed the subject to lead us back to the text. "Also, in today's Commercial-Appeal, however, was something I found quite distressing, convincing me that today is, in fact, the end."

He had our attention.

"I refer, not to the end of the world, but to the end of something for which I have been fervently hoping, my own political blessed hope."

He paused, responding to our silence by pursing his lips in feigned sadness. "I'm talking about the election to the presidency of Michael Dukakis, governor of my home state of Massachusetts."

"I thought he was well ahead in the polls," Jakob said.

"He has been, and remains so. Alas, that, I predict, will soon end."

"Why?" Jakob pressed.

"Yesterday he was photographed sitting in an Abrams tank wearing a combat helmet, a photo-op intended to show his capacity to be Commander-in-Chief, despite his diminutive stature. The photo is an attempt to allow Americans to picture the governor in a Davidic frame, Dukakis the giant killer. I have no idea what dumb advisor led him to do such a thing, but whoever it was should be fired. That photo will, I fear, come across to Americans as inane."

"I saw that photo," I said. "It did look pretty silly."

"Silly is an understatement. My prediction? I agree with the assessment of a talk radio political commentator I've been listening to, his show having begun earlier this summer. His name is Rush Limbaugh. I don't agree with much that he has to say, but I agree with his prediction that this image of Governor Dukakis will doom his candidacy, despite his current double-digit lead in the polls over Vice President Bush. People, I think, will be laughing at him, exactly the opposite reaction of what the photo was intended to do. I will make another prediction, though. This Rush Limbaugh, a very talented man, and his political influence, will endure far beyond that of Governor Dukakis."

My last dream still fresh, standing with David at the brook in the Valley of Elah, I wanted to say, "Have faith in your little candidate, Dr. Aaronson. Remember, they laughed at David, too."

It was only a brief closing of my eyes to remember my being with David but, when I opened them to refocus, Dr. Aaronson was looking squarely at me. I felt uneasy, as if, somehow, he knew my thoughts and was, in some magical way, intruding on my vision.

He continued while still looking at me. "Or, perhaps I'm wrong. Perhaps my governor is more like the young man David than I give him credit for, a future victor over the GOP Goliath that is George Bush."

I was thankful at that moment for Jakob changing the subject.

"Another of your hopes, I would imagine, came crashing down this weekend," he said.

"And what would that be?" he asked, looking over the front rows toward Jakob in the back of the room.

"As a Michigan grad, your Wolverines bit the dust Saturday, falling victim to Notre Dame."

"Ah, yes, they did! In Saturday's opener my Wolverines, ranked #9 in the pre-season polls, by the way – an interesting point to make after our focus on the number nine last week – fell to 13th ranked Notre Dame. It's a fair point, Jakob, but, truth be told, I was a grad student at Michigan, not an underclassman. As such, I never really got into the football craze of Ann Arbor. Besides, as I've told you, baseball is my sport."

"Right, nine Muses and all that!" Jakob laughed.

"Exactly," he said. "Football's eleven-man team is not nearly so mathematically interesting. I will make this prediction, though. Speaking of the diminutive underdog, the giant-killer, I like Notre Dame's coach, Lou Holtz. Standing at my height, only 5'10", his players on the sideline tower over him, like Goliath over David. Since today we are delving into the prophetic, let me now predict that he will guide the Fighting Irish to the National Championship this year."

His prediction came true. Notre Dame won the 1988 NCAA football championship, which made me happy. Coach Holtz had made a big impact in my home state of Arkansas, coaching the Razorbacks for seven seasons after being hired by Coach Frank Broyles eleven years earlier, in 1977, when I was eleven.

As a giant-killer, Holtz's most notable victory at Arkansas came in the Orange Bowl on January 2, 1978. I'll never forget it. Oklahoma was ranked #2 and a heavy favorite over #6 Arkansas, especially when Holtz suspended three of his best players prior to the game for a violation of team rules. A win would have secured the National Championship for Oklahoma, but Holtz led Arkansas to a stunning 31–6 victory, trampling the Sooners underfoot.

Holtz had crushed football's Goliath, leading to an appearance on *The Tonight Show* with Johnny Carson. Famous for his one-liners, he was a nationwide hit, but not so much with Arkansans, telling Carson that Fayetteville, where today I live and work, was not the end of the world, "but you can see it from there."

"The crushing of high hopes," Dr. Aaronson said, now ready to dive into the text, "such as the imminent disappointment of those who are today awaiting the Rapture, is the theme of Psalm 89. Ethan, its author, feels bitterly this disappointment. He had been so certain that he understood God's eternal plan that, when things didn't work out as expected, the logical conclusion was that God had turned his back on his own promise. Today, class, we arrive at a section known as the Oracle, in which the psalmist calls the name David for the second and the third times, first as the Oracle opens and then again as it closes. In this way, Ethan creates an envelope around this key section of the psalm."

"Why is it called the Oracle?" Michael asked.

"I'll answer your question with a question, Michael, which is this. Have any of you ever experienced a dream so unforgettable, so bursting with detail, so impactful that you immediately regarded it as more than a dream, imagining you had magically stepped out of one reality and into another? If asked to describe such an experience, feeling the word 'dream' to be inadequate to describe your experience, what word would you use instead?"

"Vision," I replied instantly, the posing of his question a perfect description of my two dreams.

"Precisely," Dr. Aaronson answered, snapping his fingers. "Vision is the word the psalmist uses as he opens this section, verses 19-20, 'Once you spoke in *chazon* (vision).' Ethan, you see, is quoting God back to God, reminding God of his own promise. God spoke these words, not in a mere *chalom* (dream), but in a *chazon* (vision). What David experienced, Ethan is claiming, was more than a dream. It was a vision, an oracle."

I closed my eyes to relish the remembrance of my own two

visions, seeing the *shemen kadosh* streaming down David's face, and his reach for me to dance just as my vision ended. Inhaling deeply in a vain effort to recover the oil's scent, I opened my eyes to see that Dr. Aaronson was looking at me, again. He seemed aware, as if somehow he knew I had just returned to his classroom from somewhere else.

"Let's get back to dancing with our text," he said, turning his attention from me to the class, "not losing sight of what we know is the psalmist's ultimate aim. While still tantalizingly hidden at this point in the progression of his argument, we know that his purpose is to blame God for abandoning his promise to David."

"Why couldn't he just get to it?" Jakob said.

"Well now, what fun would there be in that, and how depressingly devoid of the artistic? Ethan knows he is tiptoeing into dangerous territory. Think of him as a sharpshooter, perfecting his aim. Each element in this progression – the Hymn, then the Oracle – functions like a scope on a rifle. Having honed in on his vertical, north/south axis by sufficiently praising God in his hymn, now he turns his attention to his horizontal, east/west axis, reminding God of his own historical promises to David."

"Like the dervish dancer," I said, "one arm vertical, extended to God, the other horizontal and extended to the world."

"Very good, yes. In this section we have landed in David's world, which is why the Oracle begins and ends with David's name. If you recall my color scheme from our first class, I identified these two appearances of David as the Warrior, in blood red, and David the Monarch in royal purple. As for our dance steps, remember that our meter has shifted from the longer and more elegant 4-4 steps to a shorter, sprightlier moves of the 3-3 step."

I looked at the text as it was printed in *The Jerusalem Bible,* which showed clearly what he was talking about, the lines now clearly shorter.

"We will divide the Oracle into five sections of four lines each, called quatrains. I'll show you how the psalmist's choreography builds to a crescendo in the third section, the middle of the five, much as a novelist creates tension in order to resolve it. This precise scheme is a narrative device seen in, for example, the Book of Lamentations. Quickly now, without looking, can anyone tell me how many chapters there are in Lamentations?"

None gave an answer.

"Okay, let's turn to Lamentations, not to read it, but to observe its structure. How many chapters?"

"Five," I said, having found it.

"Good. Now, how many verses are there in Chapter One?"

"Twenty-two," I said.

"And in Chapter Two?"

"Twenty-two," virtually the entire class enjoined.

"Do you see a pattern?"

"Yes, but the pattern is broken in Chapter Three," Jakob said.

"Correct, Chapter Three has sixty-six verses, which is . . ."

"A tripling of twenty-two," I chimed in, "but Chapters Four and Five return to the pattern of twenty-two."

"Correct! And there's our structure, 22-22-66-22-22. What do think is going on here?"

"Well, the Hebrew alphabet has twenty-two letters, rather than twenty-six, as in English. Would that have anything to do with it?" I asked.

"It does. These chapters are structured as alphabetic acrostic compositions. Imagine each line of each chapter beginning with a successive letter in the Hebrew alphabet:

aleph, beth, gimel, dalet, he, vav, zayin, and so on. The third chapter alone triples that acrostic, so that the first three lines begin: aleph, aleph, aleph; beth, beth, beth; gimel, gimel, gimel; dalet, dalet, dalet; and so on until we reach 66."

Pausing to allow the pattern to sink in, he said, "I'm sure you all know the hymn, *Great Is Thy Faithfulness*?"

"Of course, one of my favorites," Jakob said.

Mine, as well. Jakob and I had sung it together many times during Sunday worship at Bellevue.

"Its refrain, 'Great is thy faithfulness, great is thy faithfulness, morning by morning new mercies I see,' comes from this middle, third chapter of Lamentations, verses 22 and 23, 'The *hesed* (covenant love) of the LORD never ceases, his mercies never end. They are new every morning. Great is your faithfulness.' I think it no accident that this highest hope is expressed in the middle chapter, like the middle finger rising higher than the others of your hand."

He held up his hand with fingers tight together, pointing to the height of the middle digit. Noticing the few giggles, he said, "Now, now, none of that, please. Let us be more mature. I speak of poetry and of style."

The giggles subsiding, he continued.

"In Lamentations, at the very peak of its five-point structure, we arrive at the author's pinnacle of hope, faith and optimism in the midst of dreadful lament. I want you to see how this narrative mechanism of intentionally breaking an established pattern heightens the impact at the very place of brokenness."

Dr. Aaronson's brief visit to Lamentations was the first time I had heard of intentionally breaking an established pattern for impact. Since that day I've sought to employ the mechanism in my own teaching, at times in obvious ways and, often, subtly.

"Intentionally breaking an established pattern is not merely a narrative device for literature. Let me show you how this same device is used effectively in comedy. One of my favorite artists is Gary Larson, who draws the *Far Side*. He uses this device often and expertly. For example, one *Far Side* frame has a group of ducks flying beside an airplane with five windows. Let's think of those five windows like the five chapters of Lamentations. In all but the middle window, Larson draws the caricature of a human face. In the third, however, the middle window standing out from the rest, a duck has taken its seat and is making a mocking face at the ducks in flight alongside the plane. In other words, the middle window is an opportunity for that one duck smart enough to have hitched a ride to say, 'Ha, ha! As you wing your way to work, flying in your V, I'm relaxing with a V-8!' Mr. Larson uses this same one, two, THREE, four, five scheme in many of his comedic panels. In another, we see five flowers. Four are giggling pranksters, the middle flower sporting a sign on the back of its stem reading, Weed Me!"

Dr. Aaronson's simple lesson from narrative structure has always stayed with me. I see it everywhere. Not only in literature and comedy, the venues he highlighted. I see it on Madison Avenue. For example, consider a *Wall Street Journal* full-page ad I saw in their Thursday, January 23, 2003 edition. I know the precise date because I kept the paper, the ad being such a fine example of this device that I've used it often in my teaching. The entire page is a sea of repetition of a simple four-letter word, Yada. Plastered over the entire page is the word Yada, eighteen rows, each filled with six Yadas. Now, I want to ask, who would pay to take out a full page in *The Wall Street Journal* to fill it with the word, Yada? No one would, of course. But when one looks closely, at one and only one spot on the page, the word Yada is replaced with "Standard and Poors

Equity Research." By establishing a pattern and then intentionally breaking it, "Standard and Poors" stands out. The point being, whether in literature, comedy, or commerce, this device of intentionally breaking an established pattern can impactfully make your point.

"Now," he said, "just as the third and middle chapter of Lamentations reaches the pinnacle of its expression, I see the same principle at work in the third and middle of the five quatrains of the Oracle, verses 26-29. Just as in Lamentations the lofty language of the middle chapter rises above the rest, so also the vocabulary of this middle section of the Oracle rises above the rest. Consider verse 26, which reads, 'He (that is, David) will invoke me, *Avi* (my father), *Eli* (My God), and *Tzur* (Rock) of my *Yeshuah* (salvation).' None of these words, exquisitely expressive of David's unique relationship to God, are found anywhere else in the psalm. They stand out, waving their arms, begging to be noticed."

The clock was nearing 3:30, but he pressed on for one more example.

"I want us quickly to observe this same narrative device in the four times David's name appears in Psalm 89. In three of the four, the governing verb is *shaba'*, meaning, 'to swear.' For example, verse 35, 'I have sworn on my holiness, once for all, and cannot turn liar to David.' The one outlier is verse 20, where the governing verb is not 'to swear' but 'to select.' It reads, 'I have selected my servant, David, and anointed him with my holy oil.'"

"So," I said, "the sequence is: God swore, God selected, God swore, God swore."

"God sure swears a lot," Jakob said.

"Right," I laughed, thinking of Sesame Street's jingle, "one of these things is not like the other."

"Well, it looks like you've all got it," Dr. Aaronson said,

picking up his books as a signal for the class to do the same.

"Class, we have arrived at the end. I hope not the end of the world, though we await tonight's conclusion of Rosh Hashana to see if Mr. Whisenant's prediction will pan out. In the likely event, though, that the world does not end tonight, our class on Thursday will resume with Psalm 89's Oracle section. See you then, and shalom.

Chapter 6

Dancing with David
in the Cave of Ein Gedi

WEDNESDAY, SEPTEMBER 14, 1988, 3:35 A.M.

Whether on September 13, 1988 Jesus would appear in the clouds to rescue his people from tribulation or not, the day held promise to be special for my family. It was my mom's fifty-fifth birthday, my age as I write now, looking back thirty-three years from 2021. Mom, the original Stella Maris, is still with us, eighty-eight years old and, thankfully, healthy.

Dad's birthday gift to mom in 1988 was a trip to Memphis to spend a couple of nights at the Peabody. The riverboat casinos had not yet been built in nearby Tunica, Mississippi. If in '88 the casinos had been there, I suspect Tunica would have been their destination, mom being one who enjoys playing the roulette wheel.

When dad called on Sunday afternoon to tell me they would be in Memphis on Tuesday, he listed a triad of destinations: the Peabody Hotel, Beale Street, and Mud Island.

Their primary goal, I knew, was so our family could celebrate mom's fifty-fifth together.

I had so wanted when class ended to walk again with Dr. Aaronson. Such walks would happen again and often during my last two semesters, but not today. Jakob and I left campus as quickly as possible after Dr. Aaronson dismissed class, arriving at the Peabody to join mom and dad in the lobby for a glass of wine before the march of the ducks. Since the 1930s the hotel had been famous for the daily 5:00 red carpet procession of ducks, set to the music of Sousa's King Cotton March.

After an hour of conversation and laughter, we watched as the ducks marched onto the red carpet from the ivory-carved fountain in the center of the lobby, disappearing into the elevator to be lifted to their rooftop penthouse.

"Think of it," Jakob said. "If Whisenant is right, soon we'll be like those ducks, disappearing as we go marching upward to Zion, to meet Jesus in the skies."

"What in the world are you talking about?" mom laughed.

After Jakob and I offered the capsule version of why millions believed Jesus would return before midnight, mom said, "Oh, yes, I've read about that. I suppose then, if this is that day and hour, it's even more important for our family to be together."

"I don't know, Mrs. Maris," Jakob laughed, "I'm not sure Beale Street is the best place for Jesus to find us when he returns."

Mom made the cutest I-don't-care face in response, having insisted that we have dinner on Beale Street, the birthplace of the Blues and only a block from the Peabody. While its reputation had fallen horribly in the 60s and 70s, by the late 80s its recovery was well underway.

Mom, a lifelong Elvis fan only a year older than the King

of Rock and Roll, joked that she was on a mission to see the bronze Elvis statue placed on Beale Street in 1980, three years after his death. When dad and I pointed out that she had seen it before, she replied that yes, she had, but that she wanted to see it on September 13, because it had been on that day – her 26th birthday in 1959 – that Elvis met Priscilla in Germany, putting an end to her young adult fantasy. With Elvis no longer available, she and dad married the following year, on June 5, 1960. I came along six years later.

One of my favorite family photographs is the one Jakob took of the three of us that night at the Elvis statue – mom, dad, and me imitating Elvis' iconic, guitar-playing pose. Looking at that photograph now, I can see how my fifty-five-year-old mom felt twenty-two again, just as I feel twenty-two now, rejuvenated by the Cave 53 discovery.

Dad wasn't the Elvis fan mom was, but he did love the Blues and, even more, New Orleans jazz. His favorite get-a-ways with mom were Beale Street and Bourbon Street. His first comment upon learning that I had earned a scholarship to C-cube was that he and mom would now have a four-year list of excuses to come to Memphis.

Two years earlier, during my sophomore year at C-cube, he surprised mom with a weekend trip to Memphis followed by a riverboat cruise down the Mississippi River to New Orleans. To this day mom speaks of that cruise as the best vacation she ever experienced with dad, surpassed only by our journey to the Holy Land the following year, which was, she rightly insisted, "not a vacation, but a spiritual pilgrimage."

Returning to the Peabody after dinner on Beale Street, dad asked us to come to the room before we headed out, saying he had a gift for me. Retrieving a record album from the dresser, he held it up so I could see it was a Miles Davis album, *Seven Steps to Heaven*.

"Stella, you're now a college senior and about to step into your future. Mom and I know you're still searching, struggling to make some decisions, which is why I want to give you this album, one of the greatest masterpieces of jazz from the 60s. It was recorded in 1963, just as the Miles Davis Quintet broke up, a time in his life when he needed to chart a new course, to put together a new future. I can't tell you how many hours I've sat and listened to its trumpet and piano, and how many revelations I've had while listening. It's time for you to have it."

"Dad, thank you, that means so much. I remember many nights coming into the den to kiss you goodnight, finding you with your eyes closed, listening."

"I fell in love with Miles Davis' music before you were born, but *Seven Steps to Heaven* is my favorite, coming to me at a time in my life, Vietnam, that was pretty scary. I hope it will mean as much to you as it has to me."

Jakob dropped me off at my apartment just after midnight. As he walked me to the door, I said, "Well, it looks like Mr. Whisenant was wrong. I guess the 100% failure record of every prediction of the return of Christ through the last two thousand years is still intact."

"Hold on. The world hasn't quite yet said goodbye to September 13. There are still some time zones that haven't flipped the calendar."

It was late, but going to sleep would not prove easy or instant, the music and sounds of Beale Street echoing in my head as I crafted memories from our family night of celebration. What was really keeping me up though, I knew, was my anticipation that today's third class would open a third portal to the biblical past.

Since Dr. Aaronson had mentioned Gary Larson's "The Far Side," I flipped through the collection of his work I had at home, Jakob having given me a collector's book the previous Christmas. I grabbed it and took it to bed with me to see if I could find other examples of Larson creating, then intentionally breaking, a pattern. It didn't take long.

"Dr. Aaronson needs to see this one," I thought, staring at a sea of identical black and white penguins on the shore. Talk about establishing a pattern! Here was repetitive sameness, all identical except for a single penguin who stood out, head and shoulders above the rest. Arms raised, that middle penguin was attracting attention, drawing all eyes to himself as he sang, "I gotta be me, oh I just gotta be me!"

Psalm 89, it occurred to me as I looked at that singing penguin, is Ethan's claim that David is the king standing out from all the rest. But what of Saul, Israel's king before David? Had he not also stood out? The Bible says he did, boasting that the Benjaminite stood "head and shoulders" above the crowd. If God lied to David, did he not lie to Saul first?

In politics there is always another seeking to stand taller than the one currently in power. No wonder King Saul viewed David's rise in popularity as a threat, his anger burning as the maidens sang, "Saul has slain his thousands and David his tens of thousands."

Gore Vidal, in a heap of cynicism, wrote, "Every time a friend succeeds, I die a little." I had seen Saul die a little in my last vision, trembling as David towered over Goliath.

Propping my mezuzah by the bedside clock, I recalled a story I once heard in a sermon, how in 1969 at the University of California Berkley a student under enormous stress, sensing he was falling behind, snapped. Berserk, he ran through the library shouting hysterically at the other students. "Stop working! Stop working! You're getting ahead of me!"

"How Saul-like," I thought as I leaned to turn off the lamp, wondering if my dreams might, tonight, bring me again to the young man David, his political fortunes on the rise and threatening to eclipse the glory of King Saul.

"Ellie!"
This time the voice was a barely audible whisper. The clock glowed its time, 3:35. Fitting that three's dance partner tonight would be five, our afternoon class having focused on the five quatrains of the Oracle.

"But why a whisper?" I wondered, turning away from the clock to close my eyes.

My dream awakening was in shadowy darkness. As my eyes adjusted to the absence of light, I heard the whispering of men I could not yet see.

"They're coming this way," one said with quiet urgency.

"Shhh!" said another. "Be still. *Hashem* will protect us. The cave is our refuge."

As my senses came back online, my skin shivered at the cave's coolness. I was sitting by a wall near an opening, close enough to lean and see that we were in a small recess in the back of a very large cave. The cave's main opening to the outside light was at least a hundred feet away.

As I pulled my head back, the outlines of four men came into view, their whispering now ceased. A fifth suddenly emerged from the opening, so abruptly appearing as to almost brush against me. I knew in an instant it was David, returning from his reconnaissance mission to spy on the activities outside, in the oasis.

"Saul approaches," he whispered, "to relieve himself."

These four were clearly David's chosen inner circle, his most trusted soldiers. While I had made no attempt to hide, no one had yet seen me in the darkness.

"*Hinei* (Behold!) my lord," one of them whispered, "*Hashem* has answered our prayers, delivering your enemy into your hand."

Seeing all four nod in agreement, I thought of Gary Larson's sea of penguins, gathered in black and white sameness.

"We must kill him! It is *Hashem's* will. Why else would Saul choose this cave for his toilet, unless God is directing him into your hands?"

David was now sitting in the midst of the four, the third of five. I caught a shadowy glimpse of another, lurking behind him. It was *Hakol*, but the cave's darkness hid all his features, even his jagged scar. In the stillness I heard *Hakol* whisper, "You have chosen to follow your *Kochav Hayam* into the peril of death, against my advice. Why not, then? Go for it, David. Kill Israel's anointed. Slay King Saul!"

"Then let it be so," David agreed, turning his ear away from *Hakol* to whisper to his four soldiers. Clutching his knife, he said, "But Saul's death must be at my hand only. Lay no hand on the Lord's anointed. The burden of assassination must be mine alone."

This was not, I knew, how it was to be.

"David," I said, not whispering.

Startled, knives were immediately, and incredibly quietly, drawn by all five, seeing me for the first time. Recognizing me, David reached out with both arms to create a wall, deflecting and aborting his men's defensive instincts.

"Eliana!" he said. "What word do you bring?"

"Take not Saul's life, David, for it is not God's will. Today, you must stand tall by standing down. You must show your worthiness by showing mercy. You must not crush the king's crown, but rather bruise the king's heel."

"How?"

"By stealth, clipping the ornamentation of the king's robe, humiliating Saul before the eyes of all Israel, and proving your faithfulness."

This was not only what David needed to hear, it was what he wanted to hear, mine the lone voice to contradict *Hakol*.

"*Eliana*, *Malaki* (My Angel/Muse), you have come to me this third time. Truly you are my *Kochav Hayam* (Star of the Sea). As *Yam Hamelach* (The Salt Sea) spreads its glory outside the cave, may Ein Gedi be forever remembered, not as the place of Saul's murder, but as the oasis of David's mercy."

One of David's men now alerted us with a wave of his arm to Saul's nearness. Only five feet from the rock wall's opening, Saul threw open his coat, squatting and groaning as he defecated. David wasted not a second, now confident of God's sovereign design. With but a single step and stretching to lie prostrate, he reached and lopped off the low hanging portion of Saul's outer robe.

Silently retreating as Saul continued to defile with his excrement this place made holy by the presence of the Lord's anointed, David remained quiet as Saul stood to go on his way, oblivious to the peril he had placed himself in, and to the mercy that had spared him.

David, confident he had listened to the right voice, went to the mouth of the cave and called after Saul. When the king looked back, David fell prostrate.

"My king, though I could have killed you, the Lord having delivered you into my hand, I have spared you, bringing no harm to God's anointed. Behold the corner of your robe in my hand as testimony to my loyalty, and may God judge between us."

I heard King Saul's loud weeping, calling David his son as he declared David more righteous than himself, affirming that he now knew it would be God's will for David to rule Israel, and appealing for David to spare his family when that day came.

When David promised he would spare the House of Saul, the king returned home.

As his four men joined him at the mouth of the cave to watch the retreat of Saul's regiment, I marveled at the sight of their five shapes, silhouetted against the light from the oasis. The scene made an image in my mind that has stayed with me ever since, how David's shape in the midst was not the tallest, but the shortest of these five.

As I pondered that image, I heard David's invitation. "We are now going to *Masada* (the stronghold). Please come with us."

I knew Masada well, the mountain thirteen miles south of Ein Gedi where King Herod, nearly a thousand years later, would build his southern fortress and where, during the time of the Roman assault in 70 CE, nearly a thousand Jews would hold out against Rome, committing mass suicide rather than allowing themselves to become Roman slaves.

"One day," I said to David, "Masada will be a place of great pride for all your people, a place symbolizing the courage of your people. In a day of wonders beyond your imagining, Israel's soldiers will one day come here to make their solemn vows, honoring and celebrating Israel's history, and especially you, their greatest king."

"Eliana, my *Kochav Hayam*, your words today have led me to stand tall by exalting mercy over anger. Will you not stay with me? Will you not accompany me to Masada?"

He couldn't have known how much I wanted to join him, but as he reached out to take my hand, I awoke in my Memphis bed.

Though I have often reflected upon my dream of guiding

David in Ein Gedi, telling the story in my teaching, Dr. Aaronson's translation of the third tablet brought the vision back in vivid detail. It is at this point that the two previously existing versions of Psalm 151, the Greek Septuagint and the Hebrew text from Cave 11, have nothing to offer. Tablets 3 - 6 from Cave 53 take the story of Israel's great king further along the trajectory of biblical history, and further into my own dreams of dancing with David.

David spares Saul at Ein Gedi
Psalm 151 – Qumran's Cave 53
Aaronson translation of Tablet 3
(No comparable version exists from either the Septuagint or
Qumran's Cave 11)

Yet my king took no glory in my glory,
the maidens' song stirring in him a soul-storm,
that the horn of David, mere minstrel,
is exalted above his own, as ten thousand overcomes a thousand.
Saul sought for my life, chasing me into the wilderness.
Searching for sanctuary, I entered a cave.
Overtaking me at Ein Gedi, spring where the young goats romp,
Hashem led Saul into my cave, seeking privacy to relieve himself.
My warriors whispered victory,
Hakol urging me to slay *Hashem's* anointed.
With assassination in my heart,
Malaki (My Angel/Muse) called out, "David!
Take not Saul's life, but only a corner of his robe.
Bruise the king's heel, not his crown.
Show mercy, so that tall you may stand before *Hashem*."
At *Yam Hamelach* (the Salt Sea) my God sent my *Kochav Hayam*,

Lighting the way to greater glory than that of vengeance.

By showing loyalty to *Hashem's* anointed,

My mercy revealed the king's shame.

Chapter 7

Fourth Aaronson Lecture – The Dance of Isadora Duncan

COVENANT CHRISTIAN COLLEGE, MEMPHIS, TENNESSEE

THURSDAY, SEPTEMBER 15, 1988, 2:00 P.M.

Dr. Aaronson's surprise entrances had become the topic of conversation among students gathering for class. His fourth lecture did not disappoint. Waiting for nearly a full minute after the bell, he appeared in the doorway wearing over his clothing a flowing sheer tunic and long white scarf. Barefooted! No other professor at C-cube would dare do such a thing. His moves were playfully sensuous. Once again, I was reminded of Johnny Castle dancing with Baby.

Swaying in mock seductiveness, he fully crossed the front of the classroom, wall to wall. Returning to the middle, he opened a guessing game as he continued to sway.

"I am often called the Mother of Modern Dance. It is

written of me that I was not merely the tenth Muse, but all nine Muses in one. My movements, it was said, were poetry personified."

Just then, quite the opposite of poetry personified, he stumped his toe on a leg of his desk and briefly stumbled, the class reacting to the incongruity with laughter.

"Can you guess who I am?" he said with a grimace, trying his best to ignore his pain and reengage the dance.

None hazarding a guess, he continued, "I was born in San Francisco, but I took my inspiration from ancient Greece, dancing barefooted wearing a white tunic. I combined Greek dancing tradition with the American love of freedom. I thought ballet rigid and unnatural, its costumes silly and its pointed shoes confining. The open sea was my inspiration. Its movements I found uniquely feminine, portraying the deepest yearnings of the body, worthy of imitation. Can you now guess who I am?"

Still, none offered a guess. I had no idea.

"I'm surprised you don't know me. Over forty books have been written about me, and countless drawings, paintings, and sculptures. Two major motion pictures have been made of my life, along with documentaries, plays, and poems. Do you not know me? I am hurt!"

His slow movements and soft voice holding the class hypnotized, we were shocked when suddenly all elegance vanished. Gathering the long scarf as a noose around his neck, he twisted himself into an unnatural position for his final clue.

"I died tragically, with a horrifying snap, the opposite of my dance. Yesterday, September 14, marked the 61st anniversary of my death, my scarf entangled in the axle of an open-air Bugatti motor car. This was long ago, before even your parents were born. Yet, in one of this year's greatest films my name was called, and not merely as a dancer, but as an object of worship. Now, can you guess my name?"

When none could guess, I blurted, "Don't leave us in suspense. Who are you?"

"Wrong question," the dancer quickly responded. "Ask me which of this summer's movies called my name."

"Okay, which?"

"*Bull Durham*, the perfect blend of baseball and dance. Did any of you see *Bull Durham*?"

I raised my hand and looked around to see that most in the class had also seen it. No surprise, it having been an enormous hit. I mentioned earlier how, when in his first lecture he spoke of baseball as the divine game, I thought he couldn't have seen *Bull Durham*, else surely he would have mentioned Susan Sarandon's line, "My church is baseball."

I knew now that I was wrong. Dr. Aaronson had been saving *Bull Durham* for this moment.

"This is going to be good," I thought.

"Susan Sarandon, in the role of Annie Savoy, said, 'I believe in the Church of Baseball. I've tried all the major religions and most of the minor ones. I've worshipped Buddha, Allah, Brahma, Vishnu, Siva, trees, mushrooms, and Isadora Duncan."

Jakob was first to jump in, saying, "Welcome, then, to C-cube, Isadora."

Her identity revealed, Dr. Aaronson laid aside his props and sat, putting on the socks and shoes he had placed under his desk before class.

"Since most of you saw *Bull Durham*, you heard Isadora Duncan's name but brushed it aside, her name heard and forgotten within the space of a few seconds. A haunting thought, if you ask me, knowing that when each of our dances through life end, the memory of us, even the most famous of us, is fleeting."

"Can you tell us more about Isadora?" I asked, intrigued.

Intrigued? Truth be told, I was enthralled. How would he relate Isadora to Psalm 89? I was learning to appreciate that one of the finest qualities of a good teacher is misdirection, the same quality that makes a magician magical. As a teacher, David Aaronson was a magician, artfully choreographing each illusion.

"Isadora, the Mother of Modern Dance, was born in San Francisco 111 years ago, in 1877. Sadly, her death was as dramatic as her life. Encountering a handsome young man in Nice, France, she suggested that he take her for a spin in his Bugatti. As they took off, she shouted to her friends, '*Adieu, mes amis, je vais a la gloire!*' It meant . . ."

"Farewell, my friends, I go to glory," I said.

While hardly fluent, I'd taken several years of French in high school and one in college. That sentence was easy, especially as slowly as he had spoken it.

"Exactly," he said, nodding to me and pacing to the other side of the classroom before continuing. "And so, she did, go to glory. Now, why would Annie Savoy and the fans of Isadora Duncan think of her as divine? Perhaps, I would like to think, because of the flowing of her dance. Verb-like, it moves. Like God. Should we not think of God as a verb, rather than as a noun? Yes, I think so, that God is a verb. Many theological arguments and, yes, many wars, could have been avoided had human concepts of the divine acknowledged this simple revelation."

That phrase, God is a verb, which I first heard from Professor Aaronson that day, stayed with me. Ten years later Rabbi David Cooper wrote a book with precisely that title, focusing on Kabbalah and mystical Judaism. Opening it, I was amazed to see that *God Is a Verb* had exactly 333 pages. "Surely no accident," I thought, recalling my professor's love of baseball's triple three.

"Looking ahead," Dr. Aaronson said, "when we are finished with our six classes on Psalm 89, our next focus will be the Song of Solomon. You will find the contrast in these two types of Hebrew poetry to be a shift from the highly structured, ballet-like dance of the psalms to the free-flowing style of Isadora Duncan, the Song of Solomon being exquisitely unstructured."

"Both forms of poetry exquisite, then, despite their differences?" I asked.

"Of course," he said, "just as different genres of music and dance can be equally enchanting, and just as wines are paired artfully with different meals. *Shir Ha-shirrim*, the Song of Songs, which is the title of the book in the Hebrew Bible, is as unstructured as falling in love. The most obvious thing with respect to its literary structure is the absence of its literary structure, the reader invited to follow the unpredictable give-and-take dialogue of lovers. The term 'falling in love' suggests something every lover knows, that there is an out-of-control element within the mystery of human attraction. The one in love finds himself, or herself, subject to outside forces, embracing the irrational in the quest for their beloved. One must read Song of Songs with that love-struck quality in mind. As is love, the song is untamed, uncontrolled. One cannot approach the Song of Songs as one might approach Psalm 89. The Song of Songs requires of the reader a willingness to enter the lover's state of emotional lostness."

He had been half-sitting on the corner of his desk, leaning really, as he talked about the Song of Songs. I won't deny that his relaxed pose, combined with his enthusiasm in talking about the Bible's most sensual poem, disrupted my ability fully to follow his words.

My wandering thoughts jerked back in line immediately,

though, when he stood to say, "Okay, enough about *Shir Ha-shirrim*. Before we launch head-over-heels into our next type of Hebrew poetry, let's return to the more elaborate structure of Psalm 89, our author choreographing our dance with the shifting cadences of Threes and Fours.

"Speaking of Threes and Fours. You may recall how my Red Sox lost to the Orioles last Wednesday by a score of 4-3, courtesy of Mighty Cal at the bat?"

"What, did Mighty Cal deal another blow to your Sox?" Michael laughed.

"No. In fact, we returned the favor last night, beating the Orioles by the identical score, 4-3. Mike Greenwell, our Red Sox "Gator" from Florida, our cleanup hitter, went 4 for 4 yesterday at the plate, hitting for the cycle, something as rare and heavenly for a batter as is a no-hitter for a pitcher – a single, a double, a triple, and a home run. It was Mike's 21st homer, a multiple of 3. Remember, baseball is all about numbers, about stats."

Walking to the whiteboard, he continued, "I find fascinating that a word for 'number' in Hebrew is *cheshbon*, meaning 'to think,' but also 'to reckon.' When you finish eating your meal at a restaurant in Israel, you ask for the *cheshbon*, the final 'reckoning,' the final 'count' of what you owe. The ancient mathematician Pythagoras would have loved this dual meaning of the Hebrew *cheshbon*, to 'think' by 'counting.' Pythagoras, you see, saw numbers not merely in their quantitative bulk, as mere instruments of accounting. He pointed to the qualitative value of numbers. In other words, numbers should make us think."

"About more than baseball scores, you mean?" Michael laughed.

"Oh yes, about much more than statistics. In fact, let's have some fun. Let's put our thinking caps on to imagine things that come in sets of three."

We jumped at that invitation, showering Dr. Aaronson with threes as he tried to keep up by writing them on the board. Three amigos. Three stooges. Three blind mice. Three musketeers. Three French hens.

Giving up trying to keep us with us, he turned to face the class just as Jakob said, "Three sheets to the wind," causing our professor to sway in mock drunkenness.

I decided to try some rudimentary Hebrew, saying, "This lecture is brought to you by the *Cheshbon Shalosh* (Number Three)."

"Well done!" he said. "Not quite how they would say it, but I get your drift. I have a good friend from Boston who moved to Israel a couple of years ago. He actually learned conversational Hebrew by daily watching the Hebrew version of Sesame Street. He lives there now as a guide, speaking Hebrew fluently."

Assuming a defensive posture like an infielder, he said, "Speaking of Boston, what about the triple play?"

"Back to baseball already?" I laughed.

He ignored me, forging ahead, "And what about sets of three," he said, "such as the patriarchs: Abraham, Isaac, and Jacob?"

"Father, Son, and Holy Spirit," Jakob chimed in, saying, "C-cube is a Christian school, so let's keep the New Testament represented, even in your class."

"Okay then," I added, "here's another: frankincense, gold, and myrrh."

"Enough New Testament," Dr. Aaronson laughed. "Let's move outside the Bible. How about Veni, vidi, vici?"

"A good one," I said, "and don't forget Winken, Blinken, and Nod."

"Rock, Paper, Scissors," someone shouted, adding the hand motions.

"Or," I said, remembering *Beetlejuice,* Michael Keaton's film released earlier that year. "How about 'Betelgeuse! Betelgeuse! Betelgeuse!' The magic formula for the poltergeist to appear."

"Perfect!" Dr. Aaronson said, rubbing his chin. "I wonder, then. If our class speaks her name – Isadora! – in unison three times."

He lowered his voice to a whisper, "Might our goddess of dance appear to us? If Isadora is all nine Muses together, do you think that she might travel through time and come to us?"

"And what would she be likely to say?" I asked.

"Get back to work!" Dr. Aaronson laughed, holding up his Bible as a signal that it was time for us to get back into the text.

"Students, today we finish our examination of the Oracle by looking at its last two quatrains, which is to say its last eight verses, 30 – 37. Here we see that our author, like Isadora, begins to move more seductively, stealthily. Now, rather than dancing, I want us to shift our metaphor for the remainder of today's class. Let's think of Ethan as a chess player on the verge of losing, the only strategy left to him being recklessly to expose his king, hoping to trick his opponent into making a mistake."

"Dr. Aaronson," I said, "if chess is going to be your analogy, Jakob is very good. Last year he won the C-cube chess tournament."

"Okay then, congratulations Jakob! We may lean on you a bit this afternoon. Since we're talking numbers, let me introduce you, in connection with chess, to the number eight. Thinking of chess basics, what is eight?"

"The most basic thing of all," Jakob replied, "since every chessboard has eight rows and eight columns, 8 x 8, sixty-four spaces on the chess grid."

"Right, so let's allow the last eight verses of the Oracle to be our field of play. What we find here is that Ethan's strategy has come to a perilous moment."

Dr. Aaronson's image of this portion of the psalm as a chessboard with opposing kings made me think of my last vision in Ein Gedi. It had been a chess match between two kings, David and Saul, with only one king left standing.

"Remember," Dr. Aaronson said, "the basic premise of the Oracle, that Ethan is using God's own words to remind him what he had promised to David. In the fourth quatrain, verses 30 – 33, Ethan appears to give God an out for reneging on his promise, affirming that there had been a conditional element to the promise. Would someone read them for us?"

As always, I was ready. "Should his descendants desert my Law and disregard my rulings, should they violate my statutes and not keep my commandments . . ."

"Stop there," he interrupted. "God has posed a potential scenario of David's progeny becoming unfaithful. What will be the result of unfaithfulness? That is now the question. Read on please, Stella."

"I will punish their sins with the rod, and their crimes with the whip . . ."

"Hold it," he interrupted me a second time. "Here, God declares punishment. What word begins the next line, I wonder? Read on, please."

"BUT," I emphasized the reading of the word Dr. Aaronson clearly wanted stressed, "never withdraw my love from him or fail in my faithfulness."

"Ah, so do you see," he said, "the game Ethan is playing? He may appear to have given God an out, but, like a chess player, Ethan is leading God into a trap, reminding God that his promise to David was never actually conditional, but always entirely unconditional."

After a pause, Dr. Aaronson continued. "In verses 34 – 37, the fifth and last quatrain, Ethan declares checkmate, quoting God to God as having promised, 'I will not break my covenant, I will not revoke my given word; I have sworn on my holiness, once for all, and cannot turn liar to David. His dynasty shall last forever, I see his throne like the sun, enduring forever like the moon, that faithful witness in the sky.' Then Ethan offers the Hebrew *Selah*, placed as if to declare checkmate."

"A brilliant chess move!" Jakob said. "Ethan has God completely cornered, using his own words against him."

"Well, at least he thinks he does," I said. "But what would happen if Ethan tried to reach across the board to topple God's king?"

"I don't think I would want to try that," Jakob agreed.

"It's a dangerous move," Dr. Aaronson said, "but we will see on Tuesday, with the next eight verses, 38 – 45, that Ethan does, in fact, declare checkmate."

"I think I'll break out the chessboard after class," Jakob said, looking at Dr. Aaronson. "Anybody wish to join me for a game?"

"Sorry, not I," Dr. Aaronson replied, "my birthday is tomorrow, and I have some special plans when we're done here."

Several chimed in to say, "Happy Birthday!"

"*Toda raba,*" he said. "I turn thirty-two tomorrow, born in 1956. I share my birthday, by the way, with David Copperfield, the magician who a few years ago made the Statue of Liberty disappear on live television. We, I David and he David, turn thirty-two tomorrow. While not a magician, it is my dream to make hidden things appear. That, in essence, is what teaching is all about, don't you think, to reveal what is hidden?"

"Abracadabra!" I said.

"Yes," he laughed, "and did you know that Abracadabra is

a Hebrew word? It means, 'I create what I speak.' After all, if David Copperfield can make things disappear, so that what actually is appears not to be, might I do the reverse, taking things that are not, and make them seem to appear? I leave that for you all to ponder. Have a great weekend, and I will see you at 2:00 on Tuesday."

Chapter 8

Dancing with David in the Wilderness of Paran

FRIDAY, SEPTEMBER 16, 1988, 3:38 A.M.

Promising to have me home by eight, Jakob picked me up at 6:00 and we headed to the Bombay Bicycle Club in Overton Square to grab a sandwich and a beer. I would have preferred to wait until Friday night for our date, but he needed to be in Helena over the weekend to meet with the King Biscuit planning committee. Helena, his hometown on the Arkansas side of the Mississippi River, was nearly a two-hour drive south of Memphis. The drive takes much less time today than in 1988, the 1980s being pre-Tunica-casino days, the roads still two-lane strips through cotton fields. Today an interstate quality road system rushes gamblers to their destination at much higher speeds.

Jakob, I could guess by his tone and body language, wanted me to tap the brakes on the speed of my enthusiasm for Dr. Aaronson and his Hebrew Poetry class. Since I was sure that he could see how taken I was with our new professor, I guided our conversation to avoid mentioning class. His trip to Helena the next morning provided the perfect topic for our date, the King Biscuit Blues Festival. The October festival was readying to launch its third edition, already drawing thousands of Blues fans to the historic river town that Mark Twain had said occupied one of the prettiest spots on the Mississippi River. Jakob was the youngest member on the planning team, and I knew he would eagerly talk about the festival, especially having only two nights earlier been with me on Beale Street.

My plan worked as we talked about the Blues and King Biscuit for the rest of our date until, as promised, we left Overton Square in time for him to deposit me at my apartment by eight. On the drive home, though, he surprised me.

"Should I see our professor as an adversary?"

"What?" I laughed, not convincingly.

"I think he has a thing for you. Worse, I'm wondering if you have a thing for him."

"That's silly. Jealousy is a dangerous thing. Remember how it drove Saul mad."

I had told David about my third vision, so the story of Ein Gedi was fresh. I realized, too late to make a different move, that Jakob would naturally see himself in the role of Saul. It was David, the newcomer, who was destined to become king. David Aaronson was, after all, the newcomer in our lives.

"You're right, of course," he said. "But if we're talking chess, remember that only one king survives. I intend to win this game."

"I would have it no other way," I said, unsure how completely my heart seconded my words.

Jakob kissed me goodnight exactly at 8:00 and headed to his car, turning back only to say, "Good luck with your fourth dream tonight. I can't wait to hear about it."

My dream wasn't at all what I expected. Unlike the first three, each real in the sense of being set in the geography of the Holy Land – the Shepherds' Fields, the Valley of Elah, the caves of Ein Gedi – this dream was unreal, cartoonish, set not in the Land but on a chessboard's 8 x 8 grid. It was as if I had floated into the animated scenes of Mary Poppins, chess pieces dancing like Bert the chimney sweep amid the gleeful laughter of the Banks children. Each figure in my dream was a chess piece, but with faces, voices, and silly movements propelled by short, unseen, legs.

Eight pawns on each side were facing off, each side protecting its king and queen. The white king clearly possessed David's face, but when I tried to make out his queen's face, it was obscured, unrecognizable. The black king's face was jolly and fat. The black queen at his side, though, was one of the most beautiful women I had ever seen.

I saw the black king, in defiance of his kingside knight's alarmed advice, expose himself needlessly, advancing forward past the pawns' protective line while hurling insults at the white king.

While this was going on, I saw the queenside black knight approach his queen with alarm, leaning to whisper a warning about her husband's bizarre conduct. She listened intently, her face registering shock. Suddenly she sprang into action, shouting a string of urgent commands to her queenside bishop, rook, and pawns. Each piece sprang into action, amassing materials to prepare for a journey.

When the black king, having finished his insults, withdrew into the safe circle of his kingside backline, it was now his queen's turn to move forward. With her knight at her side and followed by her pawns bearing gifts, she approached the white king, before whom she bowed. Then, standing erect, her entourage laid gifts at the white king's feet. The white king, absorbed by the black queen's beauty, listened as she castigated her own husband-king as a fool.

When the black queen at last finished and retreated, all the chess pieces relaxed. The stalemate over, all was calm. War, which seemed likely when the kings were facing off, had been averted.

Then, suddenly, an unexpected ending. The black king simply toppled, of its own accord. There had been no attack from the white king, nor any mutinous moves from his own men. It was as if the black king had been removed by a higher force.

The last thing I remember about the dream was the most remarkable of all, how the beautiful face of the black queen vanished, reappearing as the white queen. The queen had changed sides! The white king had taken the black queen as his own.

"Ellie!"

It was 3:38.

Eight. Of course, eight. After today's lecture, eight was the only possible number prepared to dance with three. Why, though, has the call awakened me after my dream, rather than before? Everything seemed upside down. The dream itself seemed upside down, a fantasy, an Alice in Wonderland animation, entirely unlike the realism of my previous visions. Had my dream been an animated version of David's rise to power over King Saul?

"What else could it be?" I thought, closing my eyes and hoping for more, that the call for Ellie would usher me to some interpretation of what I had just seen.

My vision's awakening was to a flurry of movement, soldiers reacting to orders being shouted. I immediately recognized David's voice, "Strap on your swords! This fool's insult will be rewarded with death! We came with *Shalom* upon our lips, and he has responded with evil. Nabal will die this day."

I recognized David's voice, but not this spirit of unhinged anger. Yes, he had been ready to take Saul's life in my last vision, but his actions were in no way unhinged or angry. In fact, they had been the opposite, a reluctant compliance with *Hakol's* urging. In Ein Gedi's cave, despite the dire drama of David potentially killing the king while defecating, David's spirit was kind, seizing with gratitude what my words offered, the opportunity to spare Saul. What I was now hearing bore no resemblance to the David of Ein Gedi.

"What has become of my David?" I wondered.

As a rebel, he had clearly amassed more strength since my last dream. I saw now not only four, but hundreds of armed men. These seemed to be acting as mafia, his rebels providing protection for Nabal's flocks and servants. If the bill for David's service had come due, Nabal was totally unfamiliar with the concept of being made an offer he couldn't refuse.

Would Don David really take this man's life, like a Mafioso? Had *Hakol*, in my absence, gained the upper hand in influencing David?

"David!" I said, roughly.

He turned to me, joy replacing the fury on his face, but only for a moment, his joy evaporating when he sensed my anger.

"Control yourself, David! Cease your anger! Trust God and show mercy."

Strange. While my three previous dreams had landed me in the midst of biblical stories I was familiar with, this was different. Who was this rich fool, Nabal, whom David had just ordered killed? Not knowing the story, I was on my own to guide David as his Muse. How was this supposed to end? I wasn't sure, but was following my instincts.

Clearly my earlier, animated chessboard dream of vying kings wasn't about Saul and David at all, but about David and Nabal. David was clearly the white king, but the black king with the fat and jolly face was none other than this wealthy landowner, Nabal.

"Eliana!" David said, "you have returned to me."

He bowed slightly and said, "*Malaki* (my Angel/Muse), what would you have me do?"

"Hold back your men, David! I have seen that Nabal's wife is coming to you even now, she in fear for her foolish husband's words and seeking forgiveness by bearing gifts. Show her mercy, David. Rise above your rage. Stand taller than revenge. God himself will right this wrong, and give you this woman as yours. I stood with you when the Lord delivered you from Goliath. Today, I will stand by you as he delivers you from an even greater enemy."

"A greater enemy? Nabal? This fool? He poses no threat!"

"No, he doesn't. You misunderstand. In this moment you are your greatest enemy."

His lack of response signaled understanding. At that very moment, the silence was broken by the approach of Nabal's wife.

Now, it was my turn to feel jealousy, seeing David's face light up when he looked upon her beautiful face. I heard her introduce herself as Abigail. She was the black queen of my fantasy chess match who would soon, after her husband's death, become one of David's wives.

My fourth dream was brief, ending when I saw David's gracious reception of Abigail. When I awoke, jealousy arising in my heart for what I now knew was Abigail's future as

David's lover, I found the story as the Bible relates it, in 1 Samuel 25, a chapter wedged between the two separate instances of David sparing Saul, in chapters 24 and 26.

I couldn't recall ever having read this story before. Now, though, after my vision, I read the relatively obscure biblical narrative of Nabal and Abigail with fascination.

Dr. Aaronson had labeled the Cave 53 tablet telling this story as Tablet 4, its position in the biblical sequence, but had wondered why David chose to tell this story at all, being relatively insignificant. He assumed its inclusion was because, once again, David stood tall in showing mercy. Yes, he did, thanks to my inspiration as his Muse.

Of course, I know that the real reason David included the story in his autobiographical Psalm 151 is that this was the moment providence Called me to appear to David. It's obvious that David's autobiography in Psalm 151 wasn't a random choosing of life events, but a telling of his encounters with his Eliana, his Angel/Muse, his *Kochav Hayam*. I was the common denominator for the six tablets.

David's future wife, Abigail, dissuades him from killing her husband, Nabal

Psalm 151 – Qumran's Cave 53

Aaronson transition of Tablet 4

(No comparable version exists from the Septuagint or Qumran's Cave 11)

Yea, mercy is greater than wrath.
After sparing Saul at Ein Gedi,
Samuel, prophet-anointer of Saul and David, died,
all Israel mourning together.
Then I came into the wilderness of Paran,

where lived the wealthy landowner, Nabal.

Three thousand sheep and a thousand goats belonged to this fool.

Beautiful was his wife, Abigail, and astute,

but stubborn was Nabal, lacking grace,

withholding hospitality in the festival of the sheep-shearing.

My warriors approached with kindness,

peaceful their requests, offering Shalom.

But Nabal spewed insult:

"Who is this David? Who is this son of Jesse?"

Filled with rage, I strapped on the sword,

intent on recompense for rewarding my kindness with evil.

Malaki (my Angel/Muse) called my name, "David!"

Her beauty shining through her anger, she said,

"Control yourself! Withhold your anger! Show mercy!

Heed the words of Nabal's wife, who approaches now

to plead for the life of her husband.

Have you not learned that you must rise above rage?

Have you not learned that you must stand taller than revenge?

Only trust, and God himself will right this wrong."

"Eliana," I said, "in you my God has answered me once more!

This fool shall live, and not die at my hand."

Then Abigail came to me,

not knowing that her pleas were already accepted,

because of the intervention of my *Kochav Hayam* (Star of the Sea).

After *Hashem* removed Nabal, Abigail became my wife.

Chapter 9

Fifth Aaronson Lecture – The Skydive Dance over Seoul

COVENANT CHRISTIAN COLLEGE, MEMPHIS, TENNESSEE

TUESDAY, SEPTEMBER 20, 1988, 2:00 P.M.

Dr. Aaronson included me in his classroom entrance for his fifth lecture, catching me in the cafeteria during lunch to tell me about the cassette player he had stashed in the classroom. It was pre-set, so my simple assignment was to hit Play after the bell had quieted the class. He would be outside waiting to hear the music for his entrance, which he warned me would be silly.

I doubt any of us had ever heard *The Hula Hoop Song* by Georgia Gibbs, but we would never forget it after Dr. Aaronson's Hula Hoop entrance. Once inside the door, he started the show, hilariously gyrating his hips, working in vain to keep a yellow Hula Hoop spiraling around his mid-section.

Elvis would have been proud.

Or not. It was a sad spectacle. While unable to keep the hoop on his hip up, he was faring much better with the two hoops on each arm. There were five hoops in all, each a different color. He was a hot mess, arms and hips wildly rotating in a not-at-all-synchronized attempt to keep the hoops spiraling.

After the laughter died down, he invited volunteers to show off their skills. I stayed seated, happy to miss that opportunity. Others, though, jumped at the chance to show themselves adept, enough for him to re-cue the Georgia Gibbs recording.

When the silliness drew to a close, he explained that *The Hula Hoop Song* had been a brief sensation in the Fifties, before any of us had been born, performed on *The Ed Sullivan Show* on September 6, 1958, exactly thirty years prior to our first Hebrew Poetry class.

While an interesting tidbit of music history, still I wondered how Dr. Aaronson would relate those five hoops to Hebrew Poetry. I knew he would, though. His gift was to take his students in seemingly irrelevant directions, never without purpose. If we had learned anything, it was that nothing in his presentation was extraneous to his theme, each smallest detail eventually connecting.

"Three days ago," he said, "on Saturday, September 17, the 1988 Summer Olympics began in Seoul, South Korea. How many of you watched the opening ceremony?"

I was surprised, turning around to look at the class, that only a few had seen it. I had not, but I saw Jakob and Michael both raise their hands.

"I'm sorry so many missed it," Dr. Aaronson continued. "It was beautiful, even magical, watching a skydiving team form the five-colored Olympic rings as they fell toward Olympiad

Stadium. The photography from above was as exquisite as the jump itself, a true sky dance."

Picking up the hoops to display the colors, he continued, "Do you recall, in my first lecture, how I assigned a different color to each of the four appearances of David in Psalm 89?"

"Of course," I said. "Green for David the Shepherd, Red for David the Warrior, Purple for David the King, and Black for David the Dead."

"Very good. Today I mean for the colored Hula Hoops – and by the way, I had a very, very difficult time finding them yesterday, toy store managers all across Memphis now knowing my name – to duplicate the five colors of the Olympic design. Yellow. Green. Red. Black. Blue. Does anyone know the story of these five colors as they relate to the Olympics?"

"I do," Jakob said. "They are the five colors found on all the flags of the countries participating in the Games."

"That's right. Did you tune in early enough to see the sky dive, Jakob?"

"I did."

"Wasn't it phenomenal? Thirty men forming five circles of six men each, all connected. Now, where else have we seen a circle of six men in this class?"

"In our first class," I said, "you formed the Star of David with six multi-colored whirling dervishes."

"Precisely! Six dervish figures, right arms extended to form the six-points of the Star of David. I saw that again in this sky dance, each circle formed by six divers with arms extended and connected, the circles linked to keep them from drifting apart. Watching that dive, I saw a powerful image of all nations coming together in good will for the Games."

His description of Saturday night's Olympic opening was so engaging that I found myself regretting I had missed it.

"Now," he said, holding up a hoop and running his hands

along the circumference, "these Hula Hoops are true circles. Those of the sky dance, however, while intended to represent the Olympic logo of circles, weren't actually circles."

"What were they?" Michael asked, "I saw it and they looked like circles to me."

"Yes, they did, but how many men made up each circle?"

"Six," I replied.

"So then, while it may have been intended as a circle, and seen as a circle, these were actually hexagons, six-sided figures. Keep that in mind as we come back to Psalm 89."

"Ah, here it comes," I thought. "Let's see what magic Dr. Aaronson will use to connect *The Hula Hoop Song*, the Olympic sky dive, and the hexagon. How will all this open up the meaning of Psalm 89?"

"The hexagon," he said, "is one of nature's favorite shapes. Can you think of some?"

"Yes, the pattern on the shell of my little sister's pet turtle is filled with hexagons," said one student from the back of the class, causing a ripple of laughter.

"I've heard snowflakes have six sides," said another.

"A fly's eyes," I said, "like Jeff Goldblum in *The Fly*."

Jakob and I had seen *The Fly* on our first date, Goldblum playing a scientist who, after a lab accident, becomes a fly-human hybrid.

"Wonderful," Dr. Aaronson said. "But I haven't heard yet the one I need, the most obvious of all."

"The honeycomb!" Jakob said. "My dad's hobby is beekeeping, and I've helped him at the hive enough to see countless hexagons filled with honey."

"Bingo!" Dr. Aaronson said. "Now, does anyone know where the honeycomb makes an appearance in the Hebrew Bible?"

When no one ventured a guess, he continued, "In Psalm

19, David says that the Torah is more to be desired than *zahav* (gold), is sweeter than *devash* (honey), and the drippings of the honeycomb. Now, each compartment of the honeycomb has six sides. I've always thought the honeybee to be exquisite evidence of the existence of God, its honeycomb a miracle of mathematics and geometry, an efficient architectural design to store honey."

"Okay," I said, "but that's Psalm 19. Aren't we seventy psalms off of our target?"

"Well, think. What did David say was like drippings of the honeycomb?"

"God's word," I said.

"Yes, and what did Ethan in Psalm 89 just take great pains to give us in the Oracle?"

"Oh, I see," Jakob said. "God's words. He was quoting God's words, God's promise to David, which should have been the gold standard, sweet as honey."

"Exactly! Ethan, though, having tasted God's honey, declared it rancid. Through the psalm's first thirty-seven verses, he has with great care set the table, using misdirection, diverting God's eyes from his true intention. Now he is ready to declare his intent. These eight verses (38 – 45) comprise a section I'm going to call the Blitz."

"So, we're shifting now from chess to football?" Jakob asked.

"We are," he laughed. "In this eight verse section Ethan charges at God, making accusations rapidly and recklessly, like a defensive coach releasing his entire squad to blitz the quarterback."

Taking his colored markers to the white board, he said, "Now, class, I want us to handle this section differently. We will read this section out of numerical sequence. We'll treat these eight verses as a block, a defensive unit having just come onto the field. If these eight are a team, let's ignore their verse numbers in the Bible and, instead, assign them jersey numbers: One thru Eight."

"Okay, why?" Jakob asked.

"Stay with me and you'll soon see. Now, instead of reading the verses consecutively, One thru Eight, we will read them from end to end, peeling off the outer edges of the envelope. We'll couple jersey One with jersey Eight, Two with Seven, Three with Six, and Four with Five."

"I like it," I said. "First with last and last with first. So, we just keep peeling the outer layers off, like an onion?"

"Hey, each couplet adds up to nine," Michael said.

"They do, don't they?" Dr. Aaronson said. "So then, let's call our little experiment, Peeling the Nines. Has a ring to it, doesn't it?"

Seeing our nods of affirmation, he said, "Okay then, let's Peel some Nines."

Dr. Aaronson took the colored markers and drew on the white board what looked like a football coach's diagram of Xs and Os. With Os he drew an eight-man offense, five blockers on the line and three in the backfield, marking the quarterback with an orange marker. With Xs he made an eight-man defense, numbering the Xs – X_1, X_2, X_3, etc. X_1 thru X_4 were on the line of scrimmage, facing the blockers on the offensive line. X_5 thru X_8 filled the role of linebackers and safeties.

After drawing the entire diagram, he circled X_1 and X_8 in red and said, "You begin, Jakob. Read for us, please, verses 38 and 45, the outer envelope of our eight-verse block. These wear the jerseys X_1 and X_8."

Dr. Aaronson's eager vibe made it clear he had some fascinating revelations to make, so I listened intently as Jakob read:

"And yet you have rejected, disowned;
And raged at your anointed . . .
You have aged him before his time
And covered him in shame."

"Thank-you, Jakob," Dr. Aaronson said. "Notice already, class, the rapid-fire accusations of the Blitz, Ethan in these two verses saying, over and over, 'You have. You have.' And what is it that he accuses God of doing? He's rejected and disowned David, covering him with shame."

Dr. Aaronson drew red lines from the outside X1 and X8 positions, forming arcs sweeping around the Os of the offensive line toward the quarterback. "Let's call these verses the Rush," writing the word Rush in red at the top of the board.

After taking a moment to check his diagram as it took shape, he said, "Now, since we've peeled off the outer envelope, let's proceed to verses 39 and 44, positioned in the X2 and X7 spots, the new outer layer of the envelope. Let's peel off that nine. Stella, would you read them for us?"

"I will," I said:

"You have repudiated the covenant with your servant;
And flung his crown dishonored to the ground . . .
You have stripped him of his glorious sceptre,
and toppled his throne to the ground."

"In this pairing," Dr. Aaronson said, "Ethan intensifies his blaming of God for the dynastic failure of the House of David, piling on yet more accusations.

Writing the word Swarm in blue, he said, "Let's call this pairing, the Swarm. Now that the quarterback can see that the Blitz is the obvious call from the defensive coach, the quarterback – meaning God, of course – knows he is exposed, seeing a swarm of defenders rushing at him."

Dr. Aaronson circled X2 and X7 with his blue marker, drawing straight lines through the offensive line, streaming past the blockers toward the quarterback.

"I want you to note something fascinating in this pairing, a match which indicates my scheme is not entirely my own invention, but perhaps our author's artistic intent. Stella, read again please, but this time read only the last half of each of your two verses, X2 and X7."

I read:

> "And flung his crown dishonored to the ground . . .
>   and toppled his throne to the ground."

"Do you see the match?" he asked. "I realize Hebrew language is not a prerequisite for this course, but I need to talk about these two half-verses as they appear in the Hebrew text. Were it literally translated to preserve the Hebrew word order, it would have read:

> "You have defiled / to the ground / his crown.
> His throne / to the ground / you have hurled."

Writing these words on the whiteboard, pausing long at each break to indicate a separate Hebrew word, he said, "Now, both of these phrases have three words in the Hebrew, the middle word of each being *le-eretz*, meaning, 'to the ground.'"

As he wrote *le-eretz* on the board in Hebrew, I asked, "Why do English translations prefer a different word order than the Hebrew?"

"Great question. Our English preference places the subject and verb before the object, obscuring the author's intent, his beautiful Hebrew chiasm. In Hebrew, the first phrase begins with the subject/verb, 'You have defiled,' and ends with the object, 'his crown.' Do you see?

You have defiled / to the ground / his crown.

"The second phrase flips that scheme, beginning with the object, 'his throne,' and ending with the subject/verb, 'you have hurled.'

His throne / to the ground / you have hurled.

"So, the original symmetry is lost?" I asked.

"Yes, unfortunately. English is an SVO language, meaning our preferred word order is Subject / Verb / Object. Translating in this way, though, tangles the author's delicate structure and muddies his design, which was to establish a perfect chiasm, allowing Verb/Object, then Object/Verb, to orbit around the common core of the word *le-eretz* (to the ground)."

He was on such a roll that none sought to slow him down by asking a question. We were mesmerized, not only by his enthusiasm, but by his ability to convey Hebrew poetic structure in such a clear way.

"Don't miss the truly amazing thing here. These two verse fragments alone, placed in this position, demonstrate that our Peeling the Nines exercise may, in fact, be an accurate deconstruction of Ethan's Blitz."

"In other words, you didn't just dream this up?" I asked.

"Exactly. We are, I believe, uncovering the artistic intent of the author. Only four years ago I was presenting this idea in a doctoral seminar in Ann Arbor led by the great Dead Sea Scroll scholar, Leon Friedman. Just when I thought he was drifting off to sleep, a sure indication of how off base and boring my analysis of the psalm was, he came alive as I described these two verse fragments, asking questions and complimenting the work. For me, it was an exhilarating moment inspiring confidence."

Readying himself with the next colored marker, he said, "Okay, Michael, it's your turn. Please read verses 40 and 43. Our Peeling of the Nines has now come to the X3 and X6 positions."

Michael read:

> "You have pierced all his defences,
> And laid his forts in ruins . . .
> You have snapped his sword on a rock;
> And failed to support him in battle."

Dr. Aaronson circled X3 and X6 in green, drawing a third set of lines, streaming through the blocking Os toward the quarterback. With now six arrows chasing the quarterback in the backfield, he showed the utter failure of the offensive line by allowing the green arrows to reach the quarterback, wrapping the orange-outlined quarterback in green.

"Thank-you Michael," he said, not looking up. "Read the first line again, please."

Michael read, "You have pierced all his defences."

"Ah, yes. The offensive line, you see, has totally collapsed. The wall protecting the quarterback has crumbled, which is why I call this pairing of jerseys the Sack."

Writing the word Sack in green, he said, "The quarterback is now *le-eretz*, on the ground. You see that I've shaded his circle in dark green to indicate he is eating grass, picking the turf out of his helmet."

Michael said, "As I read this, I noticed how different this

pair of nines is from the pair Stella read. She read about crowns, thrones, scepters – dynastic symbols. My pairing is oriented to the military – walls, forts, swords, and battle."

"Good eye, Michael! You may be sure I also pointed that out to Dr. Friedman, that the pairing of X2 and X7 pointed to Dynastic Failure, while the pairing of X3 and X6 points to Militaristic Failure."

With only one pairing of nine left, Dr. Aaronson said, "Okay, the Blitz section now has only two defenders left to join the action, verses 41 and 42, in the X4 and X5 positions. Let me read:

> Anyone may go and loot him,
> His neighbors treat him with scorn . . .
> You have let his opponents get the upper hand;
> And made all his enemies happy."

He circled the last two remaining Xs in black, drawing arcs that again reached the quarterback.

"Let's call this the Fumble," he said, writing the word in black.

"Ethan's Blitz was intended to so overwhelm the quarterback that he, God, fumbles. In this last pairing, he presents an argument that he hopes will cause God to reverse course, to reestablish the dynasty of David. The common theme is the shame and scorn of the dynasty's collapse. Ethan now turns his focus to the spectators in the stands, those who have just watched the collapse. The psalmist's message is clear. He's saying, 'It's embarrassing, God. The fans have nothing to cheer about. They are booing, and you are to blame.'"

Stepping back to admire his finished diagram of Xs and Os, he said, "So, our Blitz section is now complete – the Rush, the Swarm, the Sack and, at last, the Fumble."

"But let's remember," Jakob said, "that the quarterback is God. Getting the ball back, for him, should pose no problem."

"Excellent point, and one surely not missed by our author. He knows he's playing for the losing team every time he lines up against God, like the Washington Generals in every game they play against the Harlem Globetrotters. The loss is certain, which is why, on Thursday, perhaps we should call his final section, the Hail Mary, Ethan's desperate last appeal for God to remember his covenant."

Shifting the mood, he said, "Class, what we are reading in Psalm 89, and the Blitz in particular, is an example of a firm fixture of Jewish thought and faith, a willingness to ask uncomfortable questions, to be brutally honest even with God, despite knowing that, debating God, you're playing for the losing team."

Grabbing the remote, he said, "We began today by dancing to the Hula Hoop Song. Let's end it with another circling dance."

With a click of the remote the monitors lit up to show Danny Kaye and Harry Belafonte, on one side of the screen, and jubilant dancers forming circles on the other.

"Perhaps you've heard of *Hava Nagila*? Those words mean, 'Let us rejoice,' based on a passage from Psalm 118, which you all know, 'This is the day the LORD has made, let us rejoice and be glad in it.' *Hava Nagila* is sung at weddings, bar mitzvahs, bat mitzvahs. The song turned seventy years old this year, composed in 1918 to express rejoicing in the aftermath of the defeat of the Ottoman Turks. The Ottomans had ruled *ha-eretz* for exactly four hundred years, since 1517. On December 11, 1917, British General Edmund Allenby dismounted his steed and, in respect to Jesus who had entered Jerusalem on a donkey, entered the Holy City on foot through the Jaffa Gate, ending Ottoman rule and establishing a national home for the Jewish people.

"In this year of *Hava Nagila's* 70ᵗʰ birthday, I recall with rejoicing how my people were allowed to return to their homeland after the Babylonian captivity of seventy years, rebuilding the temple in the time of Ezra and Nehemiah. And, I rejoice in what happened forty years ago, in 1948, when Israel became a nation and my people again had a homeland after the horrors of the *Shoah*, the Holocaust, when six million Jews perished at the hands of Adolph Hitler."

The moment had turned solemn, our professor's mind now clearly in another place. His voice was different, almost shaking as tears formed in the corners of his eyes, which he quickly wiped away. The recording of *Hava Nagila* finished, he ran the tape forward, saying, "Now I want you to hear another song celebrating the moment of return. It was written in 1967 by Naomi Shermer, only weeks prior to the Six Day War."

"Jerusalem of Gold," I said, remembering hearing the song and its story when I attended a stage show featuring Hebrew and Arab folk songs and dances in Jerusalem.

"Yes, very good," he said. "*Yerushalayim shel Zahav* (Jerusalem of Gold) is so beloved in Israel that it has become the unofficial national anthem. When Shermer heard that the paratroopers sang the song when they reached the Western Wall on June 7, she wrote an additional verse about the *shofar*, the ram's horn, sounding from Temple Mount, the scene that actually unfolded on that day. The lamentation of her song was now, with the added stanza, gloriously balanced with the reality of Israel's return to the city. *Yerushalayim shel Zahav* was perfect to express the two-thousand-year yearning of the Jews to return home. Let's listen."

The monitors showed beautiful scenes of Jerusalem as we heard a version of the song performed by Shuli Nathan. This was not a song to dance to, as had been *Hava Nagila*, but a much more contemplative song.

After the music, he said, "*Hava nagilah*, students. Let us rejoice in our freedoms as Americans, this unique land that is in so many ways, a Promised Land. Our United States of America is, in a very real sense, a New Jerusalem. I'll see you Thursday."

I sat, mesmerized, as students filed out the door. Dr. Aaronson had, over the last ninety minutes, led us from the light laughter of The Hula Hoop Song to the intense sorrow of the Holocaust and then to the jubilation of Jewish reestablishment in the Land, and our own pride in the United States of America.

Watching wordlessly as he began to bundle his Hula Hoops, I blushed slightly as I imagined an entirely different scenario than football, wondering if he might ever be willing to Blitz past a different kind of line, that of decorum and ethics. Could a scholar like David Aaronson ever be attracted to a student like me? And, if so, would he dare tell me?

No, of course he wouldn't. Nor would I think of sharing with him my secret imaginings, how I relished the thought of David Aaronson's Rush. I might even, I mischievously thought, hope for a Sack, the thought of which made me whisper, "*Hava nagilah.*"

"Let me help you," I said, reaching to grab an uncooperative Hula Hoop.

"Thank you. Stella, if I may ask, do you think I should apologize to the class?"

"Apologize? For what?"

"For becoming perhaps too emotional."

"Emotional? Sir, that was the most impactful class I've ever experienced, period. Anywhere. Anytime. You have an incredible gift. Not only do you make the text come alive with your insights, you make me – I mean, you make my faith – come alive."

I had paused to adjust my wording in order to sound more appropriate, but he had to know that much more of me was coming alive than my faith. How could he not? I must have lit up like a Christmas tree when, finally, the last student exited the room, leaving us alone.

"I'm glad. Listen, I was hoping you would hang back again. I'd like to show you something if you have a moment. Would you walk with me to my office?"

To his office? Not stopping at the bottom of the steps, as in our previous walks?

"I do have time. Of course."

"Great," he said, stepping into the hallway. "You visited Israel last year, right?"

"Yes sir, with my parents."

"Do you recall if you visited Mt. Carmel?"

"Yes, I remember Mt. Carmel very well. While we were on the viewing platform at Mt. Carmel a string of Israeli fighters took off from a nearby military airbase. I recall the planes screaming over us, a deafening roar as we tried to hear our guide tell the story of Elijah and the prophets of Baal. Some were frustrated because of the noise interrupting the Bible lesson, but dad's face lit up with joy. My dad, Hans Maris, was a fighter pilot in Vietnam. I remember mom jabbing me in the side and pointing to dad with a smile, not wanting me to miss the happiness on his face. He may as well have been in that cockpit."

"Wow. I didn't expect such a precise memory."

"Well, dad's a very vocal supporter of Israel, and he talks about that site as being his favorite moment on the trip. I heard him teach his Sunday School class not long after our trip, telling how Elijah had seen a cloud the size of man's hand rising up out of the Mediterranean. At that same place, he told them, he had seen a fighter plane rising up from the sea. Just as with Elijah, dad saw this as a sign, a promise that God would defeat Israel's enemies."

"How good to know more about your father, especially his support of Israel. I like him already, and will look forward to meeting him at your graduation."

"Why do you ask about Mt. Carmel?" I asked as we neared the stairs. I paused there, waiting for an invitation to go beyond the spot where we had separated in our previous post-class walks. This time he motioned for me to continue walking. Rather than closing the door after we entered the office, he kept it open, following school policy for any professor visiting with a student, male or female. Not inviting me to sit, he continued to the corner behind his desk, where I saw a couple of frames leaning against the wall, which he picked up.

"As I was coming home from my Hula Hoop shopping excursion Friday, I was on Getwell Road and noticed a sign for an Estate Sale. I like Estate Sales, an opportunity to roam through other people's homes. I'm a treasure hunter at heart, I guess. You'd be surprised at some of the things I've found at Estate Sales. This home just off Getwell was stunning. The couple who had lived there were, as was obvious from their books and art, devout Roman Catholic. One section of items was filled with souvenirs from their trips to Israel."

Turning one of the framed photos to me, he said, "I saw this picture of a Carmelite Monastery, an aptly named Catholic order since it began with hermits living on Mt. Carmel as far

back as the 12th century. With magnificent views of the
Mediterranean, one of the landmarks of the monastery is its
lighthouse, guiding all the ships wandering lost upon the sea."

"Beautiful," I said, looking at the photo he was holding, his
left hand covering the bottom of the print in a way that looked
intentional.

"It is. But what struck me, the reason I purchased it, was
the name of the monastery."

He looked up to say, "Did your group, perhaps, visit this
place?"

"No, I don't think so."

"Well, look," he said, moving his hand to reveal the section
of the photo he had been covering. "It's the Stella Maris
Monastery."

"How about that?" I said, my excitement, if I am to be
honest, more about being with him in his office than about the
monastery. "I wish we had known. Maybe our guide could
have taken us by 'my' monastery."

"I know you said you didn't like sharing your name with
so many Catholic institutions, but I wanted you to see the
Stella Maris Monastery, and also the framed print that was
hanging next to it on the wall. It's a Catholic hymn I'd never
heard of, written in the 19th century by Father John Lingard."

As he turned the frame toward me, I could see that it was
a gorgeous print, its words presented in elegant calligraphy on
top of a deep blue background with white wisps to depict
foaming white caps. The Stella Maris Monastery's Lighthouse
was positioned to the right of the hymn. Leaning toward me
so our vantage point would be the same, and with our faces
closer than they had ever been, the excitement of which made
my face tingle, he read aloud its words:

"Hail, Queen of Heaven, the Ocean Star,
Guide of the wanderer here below,

Thrown on life's surge, we claim thy care,
Save us from peril and from woe.
Mother of Christ, Star of the Sea,
Pray for the wanderer, pray for me."

Pulling his face away and stepping back to a more respectable distance, he said, "Isn't that beautiful? A hymn petitioning Stella Maris, the Star of the Sea, to pray for the wanderer. And there you are," he said as he pointed to the lighthouse, "the Stella Maris Lighthouse, a guide to those wandering on life's rocky seas."

"Well," I laughed, "thankfully that's the job of that other Stella Maris. I don't think anyone would want me to guide them."

"Oh, I don't know. I think God has great plans for you."

"Thank you, sir. I have heard this hymn, by the way. My grandmother, Ursa Maris, a Catholic from Copenhagen, taught it to me as a child."

"Really? Why don't you sing it for me, so that I can hear the tune?"

"No, I don't think so," I said with a sheepish grin.

"Oh, come on. You can sing it softly, can't you?"

"No, sir," I persisted.

Stooping to lean the frames against his desk, he said, "Don't sell your skills short. I think you will be a lighthouse for many, a guide to many a wanderer. We are all wanderers, I suppose. How, for example, might a Jewish boy from Boston, beginning his teaching career, find his way to a Christian college in Memphis? I am a wanderer! But let us remember the words of Tolkien, 'Not all who wander are lost.'"

"Well, I must say I am glad you wandered this way, Dr. Aaronson."

"Have you read Tolkien? Perhaps *The Hobbit* or *The Lord of the Rings*?"

"Yes," I replied, "but it's been a while."

"I'm a Tolkien fanatic. As a Catholic, he was intensely devoted to Mary. The moment I saw this print I knew Tolkien must have had this hymn in mind, perhaps remembering it from his early childhood, when he wrote of Elbereth in *The Lord of the Rings*:

> O Queen beyond the Western seas,
> O light to us that wander here."

"Wow. I had no idea that a hymn I learned as a child was such an inspiration to Tolkien."

"Muses dance into our lives in many ways and at many times, don't they? When the student is ready, the teacher will appear."

Stepping toward the door to signal it was time for me to leave, he said, "I will pass these on to you someday, but for now, I need them. I'm already imagining how to use them in class."

"Thanks so much for inviting me to see them, professor," I said, stepping into the hallway, "and may the Star of the Sea guide you as you wander through the Estate Sales of Memphis."

Smiling at my cute comment, he closed the door, where I stood for a few seconds before turning to walk away, processing my feelings and acknowledging to myself how intensely I wanted him. Was he thinking of me in the same way? He had clearly been thinking of me this weekend as he shopped for an Estate Sale treasure. I was part of his treasure hunt.

By the time I reached the bottom of the steps, though, I felt foolish, sure that my desire would never be more than a student's infatuation. So, I thought, if this is all in my head, why not go all the way with my imagining? With Jakob, I had no problem waiting, successfully deflecting all his attempts to blitz through the line of my defenses. With David Aaronson, I imagined as I walked toward my car, it would be different. Since this exists only in my head, were he to attempt to penetrate my O-line, my attempt at blocking would be meager, at best.

I opened the car door and sat for a moment in the scorching seat, not much caring that my air conditioner wasn't up to the task of a Memphis September. I was thinking only about David. Driving off the lot, I looked up to Dr. Aaronson's office window, wondering if my imagining of being with him was mere fantasy, or if he was entertaining the same temptations.

Chapter 10

Dancing with David as the Ark enters Jerusalem

WEDNESDAY, SEPTEMBER 21, 1988, 3:36 A.M.

Home from campus and recalling the emotions Dr. Aaronson had exhibited in talking about the Jews return to the Land, I retrieved from the closet a small box of brochures and photos of my own intensely emotional visit the previous summer to Yad Vashem, the memorial to the six million Jews who perished in the Holocaust.

Opened in the 1950s, Yad Vashem is located on Mount Herzl outside Jerusalem. I recall especially being brought to tears at the then-recently-opened memorial to the estimated 1.5 million children who had been slain. It's a haunting memorial of light, candles reflecting in a dark space to create the impression of countless shining stars. The names of the children, along with their ages and countries of origin, are heard constantly, the list so long that the naming takes months before a new cycle begins.

I was contemplating the Shoah when I came across a photo that jolted me back in time. At Yad Vashem is a monument known as the Monument to Jewish Soldiers and Partisans Who Fought Against Nazi Germany 1939 – 1945. When I saw the picture of the monument with the three of us posed in front, I recalled how transfixed I had been by its message.

The memorial, designed by Bernard Fink, is formed with six huge oblong hexagonal blocks of granite laid in two haphazardly looking stacks of three to form the Star of David in the negative space between the stones, a blank Star of David against the Jerusalem sky. The six hexagonal blocks represent the six million Jews who perished.

Gazing at the image, I remembered how his lecture had featured the hexagonal chambers of the honeycomb. Looking at the harsh stacking of this monument, I could understand how those visiting Yad Vashem might question God, as did Ethan the psalmist, asking, "God, where are you? Why are you hiding when your people are in agony? Why do you allow evil to reign?"

One other feature of the monument stood out. The Star of David formed by the negative space between the blocks of granite is penetrated by a spearhead, a sword rising vertically through the entire star, meant to symbolize the Jewish soldier.

It had reminded me of a different Star of David, one mom was actually wearing in the photo that day, having purchased it in our hotel in Tiberias on the Sea of Galilee. It was a necklace of the Star of David with, not a spear, but a cross rising in the middle. Mom loves that necklace, often saying how, for her, it symbolized her Judeo-Christian faith.

As evening brought darkness, my anticipation of where tonight's dream might take me intensified. Where would I, tonight, be sent to wander? Into what part of David's life?

I picked up the Bible and began to read in 1 and 2 Samuel

the stories of David, beginning with my last dream of that fool, Nabal and his beautiful wife, Abigail. With David now married to Abigail, I wondered if I might ever see him again.

"Ellie! Ellie!"

I roused to look at the clock, which read 3:36. Of course it did, my Muse's game now obvious. The hexagonal honeycombs of Dr. Aaronson's lecture, along with the hexagons of Yad Vashem's memorial, had prepared me for Six as Three's dance partner tonight. I turned away and shut my eyes gently, readying myself for the adventure about to begin. Where would I wander tonight?

My fifth dream awakening was in the midst of raucous joy, people all around me dancing as in this afternoon's class video of *Hava Nagila*. Something exciting was happening. Priests were dressed in full and colorful regalia, lining up as if preparing for a parade.

I soon saw the focus of their attention. The Ark of the Covenant was in our midst. David, having now conquered Jerusalem from the Jebusites, had decreed that the ark be brought from the house of Obed-edom. Crowds were amassing for the spectacle, shouting and singing as wine and beer flowed, elevating yet more the spirits of the people.

With every sixth pace of the six who bore the ark, the train stopped, so that a sacrifice could be made. I saw David, reveling with abandon, leading this scene of bloody joy. Stripping off his outer garments, clothed now only in a linen ephod, he was close to exposing himself as he danced.

Unlike the quiet stealth I had witnessed from *Hakol* in my other visions, this time I heard him screaming. "David! Do not do this! Command your people to be quiet."

David had heard *Hakol*, surely, but this time I saw no

hesitation. His commitment to the joyous moment was abundantly clear. No voice of *Hakol* was going to deter him. I found myself suddenly close enough to whisper in his ear, "David!"

"Eliana," he said, clearly intoxicated. "My *Kochav Hayam*. It has been so long. Have you come to guide my parade?"

"Not to guide, but to participate," I said, lighting up with joy. "Rejoice this day! Rejoice, and do not hold back, for this is the day the Lord has made! If you are silent, Jerusalem's stones will take up your song. Rejoice, be glad! Call out to those in the city, '*Uru 'ahim*' (Arise, brothers!). Lead them in the dance, David, and I will dance with you."

David roared, "Then join my thirty-nine maidens! Let us dance!"

There were three concentric circles of women surrounding David, six in the interior circle, twelve in the middle circle, and twenty-one in the outer circle. The inner and outer circles danced around David in a clockwise rotation, while the middle circle danced counterclockwise. These rotating circles around David created a cushion around the king, reminding me of Secret Service agents creating space around the president.

David pulled one of the maidens out from the inner circle and whispered something in her ear, making her smile. Reaching toward me with a grin, she grabbed my hand and placed me in the ring at her place. And we danced.

I can affirm what the text of 2 Samuel 6 focuses on, the anger of David's wife, Michal, she the daughter of the same King Saul whose life I had saved by urging David to sheath his sword and spare his life. Michal's anger every reader of the Bible knows, but I will tell you what you won't know. After the dance, David patiently submitted to her screeching, giving her freedom to rant. Then, he simply left her, saying that no matter how much she might despise him for his dance, the young maidens of his kingdom would forever honor him for it.

I was among those thirty-nine dancing ladies driving Michal to fury that day. Surrounding the king in his gyrations, we created orbs. Our circles must have appeared, from her perch, a bit like the Olympic circles made by the skydivers descending to the '88 Summer Olympics.

Dancing in the first and tightest orb around David, he reached out and took my hand, inviting me to center stage in this epochal spectacle of Jewish history. While we could all see Michal when the parade passed under her window, the moment was too frenzied for me to make out the scowl that must have been on her face, her anger enshrined forever in scripture.

She had to see how her husband looked at me. That he had never looked at her in this way was a point she made abundantly clear in her tirade. The text is correct in saying that, after that day, David was finished with her, noting that she bore him no children to the day of her death. No, she couldn't, for after that day, he never laid with her again.

Before submitting himself to her wrath, he had asked me to wait. My suspicions about his intentions excited me, in the same way I had been excited by Dr. Aaronson's invitation to his office, but I wasn't sure the dream rules would allow me to wait. It was possible, I knew, that the moment would simply pass, that I would close my eyes and wake up in Memphis, starved for a touch from David that I would never experience.

One thing learned from the previous four visions is that I had no control over my return. The choice was not mine. In fact, I was surprised that my dream had continued this long, through the parade and David's confrontation with his wife.

I knew that David's asking me to wait was an invitation to intimacy in his private chambers, which I deeply desired.

When he returned, we spoke no words. There was no haste, though I'm sure we both expected, as each time before, that I would simply vanish.

The time elapsing in Memphis for my five visions had progressed only two weeks, but for David, fifteen years. I had first come to him as a teenager. Now he was thirty-three years old. And more beautiful than ever.

Drawing me close, our lips were so close that I could feel the warmth of his breath. I think we both knew that my transport away from him was happening but, unlike my previous visions, this time we were allowed a sweet lingering, as if the moment arrived in slow motion. My last sight of him, just as our lips brushed, was the pure joy on his face.

I don't know whether he could still see me or not, but I could hear his last words. "Go not away, my *Kochav Hayam*, for I love you. I grow older, yet you remain same. How is this possible? If it takes three years, three hundred years, or three thousand years, I will find you."

I awoke in my bed in Memphis, my lips moist in anticipation of David's kiss which, I feared, would never happen.

Not able to go back to sleep, I picked up a biblical commentary to read about David's dancing entrance into Jerusalem. Having just experienced the momentous event, I found the description depressingly bland. This dancing scene had occurred, the writer said, in 1012 BCE. This was 1988 CE, exactly three thousand years later. Seeing that, I remembered David's promise, "If it takes three thousand years, I will find you."

And so he has.

David dances in procession before the Ark entering Jerusalem
Psalm 151 – Qumran's Cave 53

Aaronson translation: Tablet 5
(No comparable version exists in the Septuagint or Qumran's Cave 11)

It had been through the water shaft
That I ascended, my spear rising to penetrate the Jebusite city.
Jerusalem was now, and forever will be,
'ir David (the City of David).
On the day I led the Ark into Yerushalayim,
I shouted, "This is the day Hashem has made!
Uru 'ahim, (Awake, my brothers), let us sing with joyful hearts,
For Hashem our God is with us!"
As Hakol pleaded for quiet,
I heard my name, "David!"
It was Malaki (my Angel/Muse),
my Kochav Hayam (Star of the Sea)
She said, "Rise and dance, David ben Jesse,
for even Yerusalayim's stones are singing for joy this day!"
Michal, my wife and daughter of Saul,
was filled with rage, angered at our dancing.
On that day I left Michal, Eliana now fully owning my heart,
but as our lips met, hungering for love,
my Kochav Hayam left me.
Though it be three thousand years, I will find her again.

Chapter 11

Sixth Aaronson Lecture – An Archaeologist's Dance of Discovery

COVENANT CHRISTIAN COLLEGE, MEMPHIS, TENNESSEE

THURSDAY, SEPTEMBER 22, 1988, 2:00 P.M.

Dr. Aaronson's props for the last of his six-lecture series on Psalm 89 were simple, a hard hat with attached headlamp and a garden trowel. My job was equally simple, he having found me in the cafeteria to ask me to flip off the lights off when the 2:00 bell sounded.

The unexpected darkness gathering everyone's attention, Dr. Aaronson entered the room crawling, headlamp shining. Spotlighting students one by one, every few feet he would look down, light spilling across the floor as he pretended to dig along the illuminated path.

He was whispering something, but his words were mumbled, intentionally inaudible. All strained to make out what he was saying, until we heard his punctuated, seven-word refrain: "Where / in God's name / is it hidden?"

Jakob was first to end the silence, saying, "Where is what hidden?"

The necessary question posed, Dr. Aaronson stood. I grinned, watching him easily rise to his feet, thinking how other C-cube profs would have needed assistance. Laying hardhat and trowel on his desk, he took the remote and aimed it at the monitor, which lit up with an image from the Dead Sea that I recognized immediately as Qumran Cave 4.

"This afternoon, class, we shall see as we complete our study of this extraordinary psalm of lament, that the psalmist was diligently searching for something hidden. 'Where in God's name is it hidden?' is the question he was asking throughout the psalm, but especially in this, his desperate and frantic finale. Aware that he must be blunt in his challenge to God's integrity, he has painstakingly built his argument in a way that would soften, as much as possible, his accusatory tone. The stage set, he now arrives at the rawest moment of his dangerous stratagem."

Teasing, I jumped in. "Perhaps, sir, if you'll extend our discussion to a seventh lecture, we might yet discover its hiding place. Isn't seven the number of completion in the Bible?"

"Ah, what a rare mood we are in today," Dr. Aaronson responded with a grin. "A superb proposition. In fact, I have been thinking since Tuesday night of a particular six that I desperately want to extend to seven."

"Really?" I asked. "You'll extend our study of Psalm 89?"

"No, I'm afraid we will today say goodbye to Psalm 89. Six will have to suffice. Next Tuesday we'll move on, leaving Ethan's bitter lament to engage a lustier bit of biblical poetry, *Shir ha-Shirrim*."

"I can't wait," I thought, knowing the theme of the Bible's most notorious love song to match my own emerging feelings. Romantic poetry will be the perfect follow-up to Psalm 89, especially since my fifth vision had already brought King David and me to the moment of our lips touching. As it turned out, though, my visions would end after tonight's sixth, leaving me yearning – for thirty-three years – for a seventh vision.

Jakob interrupted my thoughts. "I'm not sure love poetry will be an exit ramp from lament," he said. "It might be an entrance ramp. Love and lament, don't they carpool?"

"Indeed, they do. What an astute comment," Dr. Aaronson said. "It is the nature of love that the lover makes himself, or herself, willingly vulnerable, never far from hurt, nor a stranger to lament."

Walking toward the monitor and the image of Qumran's Cave 4, he said, "Class, let me explain my off-the-cuff remark. While this is my sixth and final lecture on Psalm 89, since Tuesday I have been hungry for a seventh, of a different sort. Not a seventh lecture, but a seventh record-setting moment for one of the greatest players ever to don a Red Sox uniform."

"Ah, here we go!" Michael jumped in. "Did the Sox lose 7–6 last night? Could they not get the seventh run?"

"No. In fact, we couldn't even get the first run! The Blue Jays shut us out to win, 1-0. What I am talking about is the great Wade Boggs. He went three for three, and with that production at the plate exceeded 200 hits for his sixth consecutive season, a feat unequaled by any major league player in baseball history. So, you see, the question now is, can he make it seven next year? I predict that he will, that his six will expand to seven."

"Gotta love those sevens!" Michael said.

"The number seven is, in fact, the number we will

highlight this afternoon. Hang on, though, as first I want to talk archaeology. The reason I crawled into class today, as if entering a dark cave, is that it was thirty-two years ago today – September 22, 1956 – that exploration began on Cave 4, the cave you see on the monitor. The most picturesque of the Dead Sea caves, its entrance is viewed today by thousands of tourists."

"You actually WERE crawling thirty-two years ago," I laughed. "Only six days old when archaeologists first crawled into that cave."

"Yes, so I guess you could say I was born for this, a crawler-in-training."

I remembered Cave 4 well, seeing it with mom and dad from the viewing area across the gorge. Our guide's voice could barely be heard over the clicking of our cameras as we snapped our photographs of the famous cave.

"Two caves – Cave 4 and Cave 11 – produced by far the most Dead Sea manuscripts. It's now been over three decades since any Dead Sea manuscript have been discovered. I believe with all my heart that there are more scrolls awaiting discovery by some intrepid explorer, future archaeological finds to fill in more of the gaps in our understanding of Jewish history."

"Would the scrolls necessarily offer knowledge of only Jewish history?" I asked. "What about other peoples who might have lived in the area? I recall from being there last year that Qumran is only a few miles from Jericho, the oldest city in the world. Might the Dead Sea caves offer discoveries from more ancient times than even Israel?"

"Excellent point. Yes, there is evidence of human occupation in that area both before and since the Jewish Essenes. It is entirely possible that texts could be discovered having nothing to do with the Qumran community. What if, long centuries before, there were others who ventured to these caves looking for shelter or, perhaps, to secure a hiding place for their sacred documents? The Dead Sea's mysteries, I believe, have not yet been exhausted."

Strolling away from the monitor, he continued, "While in Ann Arbor, I had the opportunity to participate in two summer digs, both in the north of Israel, one at Tel Dan and the other at Beth Shean. I hope someday to return to Israel to join archaeologists in other digs, perhaps near the Dead Sea. What a dream it would be to be a part of a Dead Sea discovery pre-dating the Dead Sea Scrolls. Something is yet hidden, awaiting discovery. I feel it."

"I can't wait to hear about your discovery," I said, a thought seconded by others with a scattering of "Amens."

"Getting back now to the text," he said, "there are six verses in this final section, the Hail Mary section. You will recall how we numbered the eight verses of the previous section, which I called the Blitz, One thru Eight, then began to Peel the Nines?"

"Yes, sir," Jakob said, "the Xs rushed through the Os, leading to a sack and fumble."

"Precisely. Let's imagine that Ethan's team has switched from defense to offense. So, our psalmist now has possession of the football, but it will take a Hail Mary pass to win. Since in this last section we're on offense, today let's place jersey numbers on the Os rather than Xs. By the way, does anyone know how many eligible receivers there are in football?"

"Five," Michael guessed.

"No, actually there are six eligible receivers, when you include the quarterback. That's perfect for my analogy, since our Hail Mary section has six verses, any one of whom may snag the pass to win the game. Let's give these six the jersey numbers O1 thru O6."

He wrote O1 thru O6 on the board, spacing O1, O2, O5, and O6 across the line, and setting the O3 and O4 positions in the backfield. Dr. Aaronson did love his colored markers, matching the O1 and O6 in red, the O2 and O5 in green, and the O3 and O4 in Orange.

"We'll do the same thing this time," he said, "except it will be a Peeling of the Sevens as we read O1 with O6, O2 with O5, and O3 with O4. All add to seven. Capiche?"

"Got it! Let's go grab that pass and score," Jakob said.

"Okay, Jakob, I want you to begin by reading verses 46 and 51, skipping everything in-between. These are our wide receivers in the O1 and O6 positions. Let's send them downfield."

Jakob read:

"Yahweh, how much longer will you hide? For ever?
How much longer must your anger smoulder like a fire? . . .
Insults, Yahweh, that your enemies have offered,
Insults to your anointed wherever he goes."

"Good, thank-you," Dr. Aaronson said as he drew elliptical paths from O1 and O6 toward the end zone. "Does anything at all stand out in this pairing?"

"It's trash talk," Michael said. "The defense is taunting the offense. You only throw a Hail Mary if you're behind and almost certainly you are going to lose. Doug Flutie's name isn't remembered because the Hail Mary works most of the time. It almost never works. The other team knows this and is trash talking the offense."

"Yes, very good. The enemy is spewing insults. Stella, let's peel another seven. Please read for us the O2 and O5 verses. We'll call these our tight ends."

I read verses 47 and 50:

"Remember me, the short time I have left
And the void to which you destine mankind . . .
Lord, do not forget how your servant was insulted,
How I take these pagans' taunts to heart."

"More trash talk, but is anything else here worthy of comment? Does anything match?"

"Well," I said, "O2 begins with the word 'remember' and O5 begins with 'Lord, do not forget.'"

"Exactly! In Hebrew both verses begin with the word *zakar*, meaning 'remember.' Those two words stand out on the page like the tall tight ends they are. Now, finally, let's send them all downfield and into the end zone. The verses wearing the O3 and O4 jerseys are verses 48 and 49. Michael, you're up. Peel that last seven, please."

Michael read:

"What man can cling to life and not see death?
Who can evade the clutches of Sheol? . . .
Lord, where are those earlier signs of your love?
You swore your oath to David on your faithfulness!"

"And there you have it! With Psalm 89's fourth and last mention of David, Ethan has thrown his Hail Mary pass."

"Was it an Immaculate Reception?" Jakob asked.

"Well, this is a Christian college, so the theologically correct answer to your question would be that the pass was, in fact, miraculously completed, since God answered Ethan's prayer by sending Jesus, born in the Davidic line, in David's city of Bethlehem, to rule Israel forever."

"Right," Jakob added, "so that when Jesus entered Jerusalem on Palm Sunday, they cried out, 'Hosanna to the Son of David.'"

Seeing our time was growing short, Dr. Aaronson said, "Class, I want to conclude our study of Psalm 89 by telling you about a very interesting accumulation of sevens. Seven days from today, September 29, the seventh flight of the Space Shuttle Discovery is slated to launch. This is NASA's Return to Flight mission, the first since the Challenger disaster nearly three years ago, on January 28, 1986, a tragedy claiming the lives of all seven crew members when it exploded 73 seconds into the flight, at 11:39 EST."

His recalling the Challenger disaster was met with solemn silence.

"I'm sure that you, as do I, remember exactly where you were when you heard the news. I was being led on a personal tour of First United Methodist Church in Ann Arbor, a church just off campus on State Street, across from the Frieze Building where our Near Eastern Studies Department was located. One of my fellow students worked as an administrator at the church. On that Tuesday, we were meeting in his office to work on a project for our Akkadian class, handling Babylonian cuneiform texts. We were finishing the tour of the church and about to walk across the street to Olga's for lunch when the halls filled with startled people sharing the news of the explosion. I remember well our shock, gathering around the television in one of the church's parlors, called Wesley Lounge. That's a lot of detail, I know, but that day is emblazoned in my memory."

Everything about him at that moment, his body language, his inflection, and the pace of his voice, demanded our attention.

"If you'll allow me, one of the few of your professors whose calling is manifestly not to preach, I want to say that I think next week's Return to Flight holds an important life lesson for each of us. To Ethan, all seemed lost. For him, the Babylonian destruction of the temple had forever scuttled the hopes and dreams of Israel. He craved a restoration, a Return to Flight moment, when Israel would again be given eagle's wings to soar. Perhaps we can end today by allowing Psalm 89 to be a lesson for living, that when life seems to ground us, we must never allow discouragement to evolve into despondency. I, with all Americans, will be watching the launch of Discovery with much prayer for success as America Returns to Flight."

I might as well have been the only student in the room. His words were meant for me. I was hearing his words as a spiritual Calling for me to Return to Flight. I had been ready, before I met Dr. Aaronson, to ground all my aspirations for ordained ministry. No more. With his classes and my visions, I felt the engines rumbling for a new lift-off of faith.

Glancing again at his watch, he said, "Now, class, thinking of sevens, I'm going to have to dismiss you seven minutes early, as I have a very special road trip embarking as soon as possible. Have a good weekend, and I'll see you Tuesday."

His announcement made clear that post-class questions would not today be welcome, so the class emptied quickly. I was last, of course, but rather than approaching him, I made sure he saw me turn to head for the door.

"Stella, I'm sorry we won't be able to visit today."

It was the opening I had hoped for. "You seem excited about your trip, Dr. Aaronson. I hope, wherever you're headed, that you have a great weekend."

"Thanks. Dr. Delk and Dr. Foley are waiting for me in the parking lot with the van loaded. We're leaving right now for New Orleans, and should be in the French Quarter by 10:00."

I was hustling beside him as he exited the classroom into the hallway, knowing our walk would be only a couple of minutes.

"Dr. Foley will have you all singing hymns on the road. You know that, right?"

Dr. Larry Foley was the head of C-cube's Music Department, one of the most highly regarded among four-year Christian colleges in the south.

"Not going to happen," he laughed. "We made him promise no hymns, only jazz. We're staying three nights at the Royal Sonesta on Bourbon Street, but the real reason for the trip is to attend Saturday's game at the Superdome between Memphis State and Tulane."

"Oh, I see," I said. "So, I guess that's why you've had football on your mind in both of our classes this week?"

"I hadn't thought of that, but maybe," he laughed.

He veered away from our usual path, heading down the shorter hall toward the parking lot. Like a defensive back outmaneuvered, I lost a step. Turning to recover, I must have looked like an X chasing the elusive O. My last words as he reached the door and stepped out toward the waiting van stopped him immediately.

"*Laissez les bon temps rouler*, Dr. Aaronson."

He turned, grinning ear to ear. "Very good! Let the good times roll, yourself. I'll see you Tuesday."

I watched that game, something I would not normally have done. I wasn't a Memphis State fan, but my Arkansas Razorbacks had an open date on that September 24 and the game from New Orleans was televised. Knowing Dr. Aaronson was at the game, I was more interested in the crowd shots than the action on the field, hoping to catch a glimpse of our three C-cube profs.

Though the Tigers lost to the Green Wave that day in a nail-biter, 20-19, our professors greatly enjoyed New Orleans. In class the following week Dr. Aaronson never said a word about the game, but he did bring the food and frolic of the

French Quarter into his lectures on the Song of Solomon. Evidently, risqué Hebrew poetry was well-suited to be opened up by the Big Easy experience.

If I was looking for Dr. Aaronson in the Superdome crowd that Saturday, it was to somehow, in some miraculous way, channel my thoughts to him. I needed him to understand what a miracle he had become in my life.

Though I had often craved to tell him, he still knew nothing of my dreams. My sixth vision, though, which I had received on Thursday night after his sixth lecture, had been so entirely different than my first five dreams that, had he been in town, I might have reached out to share them with him. That would have changed everything, so it was good that he wasn't in Memphis.

My sixth vision was the most powerful, the most transformational of all. Forever after, I have known with absolute certainty God's plan for my life, to give myself wholly to the church, as a wife pledging herself to her husband and a husband pledging himself to his wife, vowing to be faithful 'til death do us part.

My sixth vision was my ministerial Return to Flight.

Chapter 12

Dancing with the Son
of David in Jerusalem

FRIDAY, SEPTEMBER 23, 1988, 3:37 A.M.

With Dr. Aaronson on the way to New Orleans and Jakob again on the road to Helena, I opted for a quiet evening at home, knowing exactly how I wanted the afternoon and evening to unfold. After a brief visit to the library, I arrived home at 4:30, poured a glass of merlot, and put the Miles Davis album dad had given me, *Seven Steps to Heaven*, on the turntable. Dad had said the album was recorded at a time of transition in Miles Davis' career, having lost his quintet and needing to start all over. If this album had been his Return to Flight moment, I wanted to hear it.

Reflecting on Dr. Aaronson's comments on the Challenger disaster as I listened to the music, I remembered how I, then a freshman, had been in the cafeteria when, first hearing the news, we all rushed to gather around a television in the student lounge. My life has changed so much over these past three years. As a freshman, thrilled to be away from home and on my own, I had been certain of and excited about my Calling. Now a senior, my enthusiasm had waned to the point that not only my sense of a Call, but also my faith, had been grounded. Until David Aaronson showed up to pilot my Return to Flight.

Flipping the album, I poured a second glass of wine, wondering where my sixth vision would take me. The merlot and the music combining to make me drowsy, within a few minutes, I nodded off, and dreamed.

It was exactly what I had wished for, picking up where my fifth vision had ended, David's lips brushing my own. He was holding me tight, intending not to allow me to vanish, as I had in each previous rendezvous.

I signaled my willingness by returning his tight embrace, he leading our steps to move, awkwardly more than dancelike, toward the bed. He paused at the edge of the bed, lifting his head and taking a half step back, as if asking permission. My eyes conveying the permission he sought, he gently laid me back. Looking up at David in a moment of exquisite vulnerability, I abandoned myself to my desire.

I had appeared to David in my dreams throughout his public life, his Muse in critical moments of decision. This dream was different. No longer was I his Muse. I didn't know why I was here. I only knew this was the moment I had been hungering for.

When, in aroused passion, he finally spoke, I realized that I couldn't understand his Hebrew, as in my other dreams. Why? Where was my Other with whom I had shared my dreams?

In an instant, I realized this dream was not a vision like the previous five. I wasn't 'There' in the biblical past. I was nowhere else than 'Here.' This was an ordinary dream, a fact which didn't, I confess, in the least diminish my enjoyment of it. Arriving in my dream at a moment of intimacy I had never experienced in my waking life, I spoke the words I had spoken to Dr. Aaronson earlier, *"Laissez les bon temps rouler."*

As the last number on the album ended and the music stopped, I awoke, my first thoughts not of King David, but of David Aaronson, still on the road making his way to New Orleans. In my dream, oddly, the faces of these two Davids – king and professor – had blended. I so desperately wanted in that moment to tell David Aaronson about my dreams that I was glad he was in New Orleans, giving me time to steel my resolve to keep them private, so that our professor/student relationship might continue without further temptation to scandal.

After eating a sandwich, I sat outside on the balcony for about an hour. It had been a hot day in Memphis, reaching 93 degrees, but now was comfortable. I sat with my journal, remembering and recording the somewhat racy details of my merlot-napping-dream, a bit ashamed of the words I was using to record the experience.

When I finally went to bed, close to midnight, I held the mezuzah and kissed it. Wondering if my nap-dream was prelude to the real thing, I took the Bible and read again the story of David's dancing entrance into Jerusalem.

"Ellie! Ellie!"

It was 3:37 a.m., thrilling me at the mathematical symmetry of Three's now six dancing partners. My dream pairs had been a parade of thirteens, divine providence moving within my dreams in clockwork precision. Here are those partners lining up to dance with Three:

Vision One: 4
Vision Two: 9
Total: 13

Vision Three: 5
Vision Four: 8
Total: 13

Vision Five: 6
Vision Six: 7
Total: 13

Dr. Aaronson, bragging on Wade Boggs in class earlier today, craved for his record-breaking six seasons with 200 hits to stretch further, predicting Boggs would make it seven in 1989. And so he did. On September 25, 1989, Wade Boggs recorded four hits in five plate appearances against the Yankees, reaching 200 hits for the seventh consecutive season and breaking his own record. His streak, though, ended there.

My sixth vision began with my bedside clock's glowing seven. I kissed the mezuzah with a whispered prayer of thanksgiving, rolling over to seek sleep, wondering if my vision would be anything like my napping dream.

It wasn't. My sixth dream awakening was in Jerusalem amid jubilation, though I knew in an instant this wasn't David's Jerusalem. A greenish blur of color flashed, flapping back and forth. My eyes adjusting, I saw that these were palm branches, not blown in the wind, but being waved.

I knew in an instant where I was, my suspicions confirmed by the shouts, "Hosanna to the Son of David! Blessed is the One who comes in the name of the Lord!"

My sixth vision had brought me again to Jerusalem on Palm Sunday, the triumphant entrance of the Son of David. I couldn't see Jesus yet, the crowds being too large. We were still outside the walls of the city, ascending from the Kidron Valley toward Herod's glistening Temple Mount. The crowd was rapidly growing, people from within the city rushing out to accompany Jesus through its fabled gates.

I looked up at the Golden Gate, a sight so powerful that it drew to my lips the words of Psalm 24, "Lift up your heads, O you gates; be lifted up you ancient doors, that the King of glory may come in. Who is this King of glory? The LORD strong and mighty, the LORD mighty in battle!"

Our guide last year had timed his reading of that passage to match our motor coach cresting the Mount of Olives, the moment we caught our first glimpse of the Old City, its landscape dominated by the Dome of the Rock. After his reading, cued up was "The Holy City," leaving us all shedding tears of joy as we sang, "Jerusalem, Jerusalem, lift up your gates and sing!"

Jostled now in the melee, I felt something slam into the back of my legs. Able to keep myself from falling, I turned to see a young girl, six or seven years old, who had tripped into me. She was quickly back to her feet, giggling with glee.

"Isn't he wonderful, lady! It's Jesus the Galilean, King David's son, the Messiah. This is the day the LORD has made!"

Her enthusiasm was as contagious as it was funny. Laughing, I recited with her the rest of the verse, "Let us rejoice and be glad in it!"

Palm Sunday had, from my childhood, been my favorite day to attend church, children parading to the altar waving palms as the congregation sang, "All Glory, Laud, and Honor!"

Now, here I was, in Jerusalem on Palm Sunday. My excitement, though, was oddly muted, aware that my time with King David had passed. My sixth dance would not be with the one for whom my soul yearned.

Seeing the little girl on the ground after tripping into me, I thought of Dr. Aaronson's classroom entrance today on his knees, his slowly paced seven-word refrain, "Where / in God's name / is it hidden?" More than anything, I desired in that moment to share this experience with my Jewish professor, how God's promise to David had been fulfilled in Jesus, the Son of David.

Having been immersed for three weeks in Psalm 89's lament, I wanted to shout the answer to the question posed by its author: "Ethan, lament no more! God's promise to David is fulfilled in his Greater Son, born in David's own town of Bethlehem."

My first vision had been in Bethlehem with David the shepherd, I his Muse sent to counter the voice of *Hakol*. In each of my visions I steered David past *Hakol's* urgings. How, I wondered, if I am now sent to Jesus, could I possibly offer inspiration to the Son of God? Did Jesus, too, struggle with the Voice, with *Hakol*?

Working my way through the people, at last I saw Jesus. My last two visions had brought me to straddle two triumphant entrances into the Holy City, *Yerushalayim*. How alike and how un-alike these were. David entered the city to inaugurate his thirty-three-year reign from Jerusalem. Jesus' entrance would bring down the curtain down on his life of thirty-three years. I could not have suspected then, in 1988, that I was about to begin my own wait of thirty-three years, the parenthesis between my sixth and seventh visions.

Having experienced King David's wild dance of triumph, I now was witnessing how different it was for Jesus. If Jesus was joyous, it was in a sedated way. He sat on his mount as the people danced around him, unlike David, who had been the leader of his own parade, leaping and whirling.

I managed to work my way through the crowds so that I

was only a few yards from Jesus when he dismounted, now inside the gates. The man next to me shouted, *"Zeh hayom 'asah adonai, nagila ve-nishmeah bo!"* ("This is the day the LORD has made, let us rejoice and be glad in it!").

When Jesus, smiling broadly, turned to see who had shouted, he inadvertently made eye contact with me, losing expression as he gazed at me for a long moment. Suddenly, he broke out in laughter. *"Ken!* (Yes!)" he shouted to the man, *"Zeh hayom 'asah adonai, nagila ve-nishmeah bo!"*

The crowd heard Jesus' shout as a rally cry, all now joining the chorus of praise. Those surrounding Jesus gave way for a group of Jewish officials to approach Jesus as the crowd's "Hosannas!" grew louder.

Jesus leaned into the spokesman for the group, turning his ear to the man's mouth and straining to hear. At last, making out what the man said, he took a step back laughing, as if to say, "Are you kidding me?"

This was the moment which since childhood I've loved most about the Palm Sunday story. These religious leaders had asked Jesus to quiet the crowd's raucous display. Now I watched as a jubilant Jesus extended his arms to rotate full circle several times, saying loudly, "If all these were quiet, the rocks themselves would bellow their praise."

Drinking in the glory of this moment, I wondered again, why have I been sent here, to this man? How is it possible for me to be his *Malaki*, his Angel/Muse? What possibly could I, filled with doubt and sin, offer the Son of God?

I would soon discover what I, and what every sinner, has to offer Jesus. Just as the story of Holy Week moves quickly away from the Palm Sunday celebration to the much darker place of Gethsemane, so also did my vision. In an instant, the crowds vanished and I found myself alone in the darkness, in a cave outside the city.

Christians remember that day as Holy Thursday, recalling how in the Upper Room Jesus veered from the traditional Seder ritual to institute Holy Communion. My vision had not brought me to the Upper Room, but to the Cave of Gethsemane, the place to which Jesus and his disciples retired after the meal. I waited in the darkness for what seemed hours before I heard their approach, singing psalms as they walked. Finding a crevice in the back of the large cave, I hid and watched as the disciples guarded the entrance, Jesus venturing deeper into the interior to pray, very near where I was hiding.

One feature of the Gethsemane story has always amazed me, how his inner circle of disciples could fall asleep in that moment. Even Matthew, the gospel writer, pondered how they could sleep at such an earth-shattering moment. Was it merely the four glasses of wine they had imbibed at the Seder? No, but I think their sleep was divinely ordained to open a quiet space for me to inspire Jesus to follow destiny's path.

I stood in silence for a time, listening to Jesus plead for release from torture and death, the bitter cup he knew he was being called to drink.

When he finished his prayer, he looked up to me, unstartled, as if he had known the entire time that I was there. His forehead glistened with beads of sweat, scarlet streaks running down his face, a harsh contrast to the *shemen kadosh* (holy oil) I had seen streaming down David's face in my first vision. As tears welled in the corner of my eyes, I softly spoke his name, "Jesus."

"Eliana," he answered. "My father David named you in Bethlehem, when you first came in answer to his prayers. I wonder, has my Abba, through your dreams, answered your prayers? Will you return to me now, Stella?"

Shocked at this, the first time in any of my visions that my birth name had been called, I answered, "Has your Abba answered your prayers, Lord? Are you not praying for release from your destiny?"

"That is my prayer, yes. And, yes, he has answered me . . . by sending you."

"But how, my Lord, can I possibly be the answer to your prayers? I am not worthy to stand on this sacred ground with you."

"But you are, Stella. You are my father's *Kochav Hayam*, come now to guide me through the Via Dolorosa."

Calling my birth name for a second time, I recalled the Good Shepherd passage in John 10, how Jesus calls his sheep by name, and his sheep know his voice.

I knew his voice. This, I knew now, was the voice that had awakened me for each of my six visions. It had always been the voice of Jesus calling, and he smiled in knowing I finally recognized it.

"Ellie," he said, "like David, my father, I struggle with *Hakol*, the Voice of *diabolos*, with whom I battled forty days in the Judean wilderness. *Hakol* is present with me now, as with all flesh. For this reason I became flesh, so that I could hear *Hakol's* voice and, hearing him, understand the Tempter's power."

"And what does *Hakol* say to you now?"

"He urges me to call down legions of angels, to command them to rush to my defense."

"Why do you not?"

His answer wasn't immediate. He looked down, then back up to me. "I have called instead for you, my *Kochav Hayam*. You can do for me what legions of angels cannot."

"My Lord?"

"I need a star to guide me through these dark and turbulent seas, to choreograph my steps in this, redemption's bloody dance. Tell me, Stella. Tell me why I must not listen to

Hakol, why I must not abort my mission. I need to hear you say it."

My first impulse was to pose a theological argument for his suffering, recalling from my theology classes the many different views of the atonement. My more visceral answer, though, stripped away all theology, shrinking the entire cosmos to a single face. My own.

In that moment I knew my task was to guide Jesus' eyes to see into, not the mass of humanity as a whole, nor even the church for whom he was dying. He needed to see but one sinner in need of grace. Only one. Me.

"I am the reason, Jesus, that you must not listen to *Hakol*. I, lost in sin, can be redeemed only by your dying sacrifice. Without the shedding of the blood of the spotless Lamb of God, I have no hope."

Saying those words startled me with the blunt unfairness of what I was proposing. What sounded so solidly orthodox in college classes and pulpit sermons, when spoken to Jesus, one-on-one in Gethsemane, seemed naked selfishness, my utter greed heaping sin upon sin.

"Oh, child," he said, "surely my Abba would find another way to save you. Would he not spare his own Son the agony of the cross? *Hakol* claims it to be so."

"I don't think so. You are the Lamb of God, slain from the foundation of the world to pay the price for my sin – mine – and to provide for me a *sether* (hiding place). Remember how your father David prayed, '*Atah sether li*' (You, a hiding place, for me)? Jesus, I tremble knowing the awful price of my salvation, but I fear I am eternally damned without you as my *sether*."

How could I say such a thing? How could I be so selfish? How could I ask him to continue on this dark path to the cross? How could I ask him to die for me? I heard the words as I spoke them and was disgusted, however consistent with orthodoxy I knew my words to be.

I noticed how, as we spoke, his fingers ran up and down one of the four tassels at the corners of his robe known as *tzit-tzit*. Seeing my stare, he said, "Did you know, *Malaki*, that each *tzit-tzit* has thirty-nine windings?"

He lifted one corner of his robe to show me.

"Thirty-nine windings, the number of the divine name in the Shema, '*YHVH 'echad* (The LORD is one).' In my hands the threads dance, whirling through the thirty-nine windings as once you danced, thirty-nine maidens around my father as he entered *Yerushalayim's* gates. Your David did love the Three and the Nine, didn't he?"

His introduction of a light moment into a profoundly dire situation was unexpected and, oddly, unwelcome. I didn't need in that moment to think of David Aaronson, for whom I had entertained impure thoughts.

"We are Muses one to another, Eliana. I need you, as I engage my dance with death, its agony to begin with thirty-nine lashes."

"There it is again," I thought, "Thirty-nine. Three. Nine."

I knew that my answer, focusing not on the entire world but on a single sinner, was what Jesus needed to hear to stay on course with his destiny. I have wondered since if, in the mystery of God's sovereign will, he had allowed Jesus, all at once, to be visited by each and every sinner who would be saved by grace. Was I but one of millions visiting him this night? Billions? Was magic in the air, so that he spoke with each one of his redeemed, simultaneously? Was every sinner saved by grace his Angel/Muse in Gethsemane, helping him overcome *Hakol*? Was the miracle not that I was there with Jesus, since we were all there, but that I was given the gift of remembering?

I don't know. I only know that this moment was mine. Weeping at the thought of his agony, Jesus reached to my face, his fingertip touching a tear to wipe it away. Lost in the wrongness of that moment, touched by the Son of God, I was filled with shame that I was the cause of his suffering, yet also with joy that God loved me so perfectly.

The commotion in the garden arose suddenly. The sleeping disciples, jolted awake, rushed to Jesus' side. They must have wondered, seeing me, who I was and how I had been able to get past them, but there was no time to ask. The Roman soldiers, led by Judas, were approaching.

In that moment, the soldiers no more than ten feet away from Jesus, time slowed. Jesus turned to me and said, "Stella, it is time for you to serve me, as the bright star you are in the constellation of the redeemed. Your seventh vision will come, leading you to discover the seventh tablet, but you must wait."

"The seventh tablet?" I asked, not knowing then of any tablets whatsoever.

As he turned back toward the soldiers, he pointed upward.

"The seventh tablet will find you and your David at the place where my tears ascend."

With those words on his lips, and the sight of Judas stepping forward to identify Jesus with a kiss, my sixth dream ended and my long wait began, Gethsemane forever altering the course of my life.

I am not Roman Catholic but, like a celibate priest or cloistered nun, my vision of the Cave of Gethsemane had been my altar of commitment to the church of Jesus Christ. Marriage and childbearing, the things I had long imagined for my life, would no longer be possible.

With Jesus' promise of a seventh vision, I have kept my mezuzah at my bedside each night, prayerfully awaiting a seventh invitation to cross the threshold of time into the biblical past.

Until my professor's discovery in Cave 53, I had no idea what Jesus had meant about the seventh tablet finding me and my David.

I know now.

Shemaiah's Footnote
Qumran's Cave 53
Aaronson translation: Tablet 6
(No comparable version exists in the Septuagint or Qumran's Cave 11)

This song of David's exploits
is written by the hand of his scribe, Shemaiah ben Nethanel,
and dedicated, according to his wish,
to Eliana, David's *Kochav Hayam* (Star of the Sea).
More of David ben Jesse's final days and his final *deverim* (words)
will be revealed in an age to come,
when David's *Kochav Hayam* (Star of the Sea)
and the one she calls *Ishi* (my husband)
discover the seventh tablet,
which I, according to the will of the Lord,
have hidden until that day,
the day the Lord has made.
Let us rejoice and be glad in it.

Chapter 13

My Seventh Vision – The Impossible Dream

THE OLIVE TREE HOTEL, JERUSALEM

TUESDAY, JANUARY 18, 2022, 3:33 A.M.

Every minister has a Call story. Mine is how a twenty-two-year-old college senior's life was transformed by six Aaronson lectures on Psalm 89, each followed by a vision of being Sent, first to David and then to Jesus, David's Greater Son.

I've long intended to publish my story of *Dancing with David*, thinking it a rather remarkable Call story, standing out in so many ways from those I've heard other pastors share. It might be of interest someday, I thought, to some few, perhaps to my family and friends, church members past and present, and colleagues.

Perhaps not. I recall how, many years ago, one of my fellow pastors in Fayetteville, a Presbyterian, after hearing me share part of my story at a local ministerial alliance retreat on Mt. Sequoyah, an incredibly beautiful venue in the Boston Mountains overlooking downtown, was deeply offended.

Visibly shaking, he stood before the group after I told of my sixth dream in Gethsemane, to say, "Sister Maris, yours is not a Call story, but a Tall story!"

Other clergy at the retreat were kinder, understanding that I wasn't claiming the dreams to have been real, only that they had been real to me, sent to stir again my divine Call. I think though, that my Presbyterian colleague had detected something in my sharing that the others missed, that a part of me did, in fact, believe I had been with Jesus in Gethsemane.

That part of me, the believing part, re-emerged on September 6, with Dr. Aaronson's announcement of his Cave 53 English translation of the six tablets. I had fully expected on that night, having read and re-read with astonishment the Aaronson translation, to at last experience my long-awaited seventh vision.

It did not happen, though, not on September 6, nor since. Each evening since, I've immersed myself in David's last song, cherishing my role in it as David's Star of the Sea. When at last sleepy enough to turn off the lamp, I hold my mezuzah and whisper a prayer, craving that this night would be the night unlike every other night, opening a new portal into the biblical past.

Always, though – night after night after visionless night – nothing.

Until last night, my first night in Jerusalem.

Around Christmas, when I finished updating and editing my journals from 1988, I knew I could wait no longer. It was time for me to go to Jerusalem to find David Aaronson. I needed to hear his voice, the voice that once sent me as a wanderess through space and time.

I arranged my trip to Jerusalem so that I would arrive at the Mount Scopus campus of Hebrew University on January 18, the one-year anniversary of the Cave 53 discovery. That visit will occur later this morning, but since awakening, astonished by at last having received my seventh vision, I've been drinking coffee and writing furiously, seeking words to tell what has been revealed to me. I know myself now, my true identity, in ways I could never have imagined.

As the hotel's breakfast was yet hours from opening when I awoke from my vision, I began to write the story of my journey to the Holy Land, beginning with my late evening departure from Newark on January 16 and landing at Ben Gurion Airport in Tel Aviv yesterday afternoon.

I had checked with the university's administration to make sure Dr. Aaronson would be on campus. Naively, I suppose, I envisioned popping into his office and introducing myself, saying, "Shalom, Professor Aaronson, I'm a former student of yours from your first year of teaching in Memphis, Stella Maris."

Would he remember me? I couldn't be sure. My physical appearance is, obviously, very different. The journey from twenty-two to fifty-five is a long one.

Even if he doesn't remember me, I thought, surely his ears will perk up at the sound of my name, he having so recently identified David's Angel/Muse as his Star of the Sea. I wonder if he had thought of me at all when he first read those words on the Cave 53 tablets?

"That's it!" I thought, crossing the Atlantic. "I'll say, 'Shalom, Professor Aaronson, I'm your first *Kochav Hayam*, Stella Maris!'"

Not being one to watch movies or listen to music on long flights, preferring simply to sit and think, my mind wandered into half-a-dozen scenarios of how meeting David Aaronson might go, the common element in each being the fear of embarrassment should he not remember me.

If he did remember me, though, what would his hearing

of my name release in him? Nostalgic memories? Fondness? Perhaps a resurgence of youthful attraction?

What would be released is a fitting question, I think, since he had pointed out in his September 6 media conference that the very next day would be the start of the Jewish *Shmita* year, the Year of Release. He had said that his greatest hope is that what would be released in the coming year would be more information about the three-thousand-year-old skeletal grip that he had discovered embracing Cave 53's six tablets.

"Whose bones are these?" That was the question he had been asked in the news conference, only to say that the solution to that great mystery was, likely, the impossible dream.

"Well, Dr. Aaronson," I will be able to say to him this morning, "I am David's *Kochav Hayam*, and after last night's vision your impossible dream is no longer impossible. I know the identity of Cave 53's bones."

Will he believe me? It really doesn't matter. I know whose bones he discovered, and after I find the seventh tablet, the whole world will have all the proof needed.

At one point in the long flight, something else needed to be released. Drinking an abundance of water in flight, I was suddenly urgent. Sitting in one of the middle seats on our El Al flight, I had been reluctant to wake the man next to me in the aisle seat. Waiting was no longer an option. His perturbed look at my having awakened him made me want to say, "Look, jerk, if you want to sleep, I'll gladly switch seats with you."

It seemed to take him forever to get his things together and raise his tray table. When he at last stood, I scampered out of my seat and rushed down the aisle to the lavatory.

Sweet release.

I was in no hurry to get back to that middle seat, using the opportunity to walk and stretch my legs. Thinking about the

Shmita Year of Release, I took my phone and asked Google to search the number of days between September 7 (Day One of the *Shmita* year) to January 18 (my reunion with David Aaronson), discovering that January 18 would be the 133rd day of the current Sabbatical Year.

At the very moment my phone glowed with the numbers 133, one of the men in a seat near me stood to get into the overhead bin to retrieve his phylacteries for morning prayer. He was traveling with his wife and two young sons, the boys awake and incessantly bickering. Daylight was beginning to break and several of the orthodox had already found spaces to strap on their gear and begin their prayers. I knew that soon he would be rocking and swaying, dancing with God in his prayers.

Stepping aside to let him reach the bin, I heard him jokingly quote a very appropriate psalm to his two rowdy boys, *"Hinei mah tov u-mah na'im, shevet 'ahim gam yahad,"* ("Behold, how good and pleasant it is for brothers to dwell in unity"). He and his wife exchanged smiles as the boys, recognizing Psalm 133, calmed down.

Hearing the Hebrew opening to Psalm 133 – one of the fifteen Psalms of Ascent sung by ancient pilgrims as they approached Jerusalem's temple – my phone still glowing with the number 133 from my Google search, I took as a providential God wink.

The Psalms of Ascent were recited by pilgrims in ancient times as they approached Jerusalem and its temple. Psalm 133, then, was the perfect psalm for my own reflection as I winged my way toward Jerusalem.

Watching the man begin his prayers, a poem came to my mind that I had used in a Bible study class a few months earlier, "Prayers at the Broken Gate," by Lawrence Russ. He spoke of the men carefully strapping on the sacred words, describing them as elderly spacemen preparing for groundless voyaging.

"Exactly right," I thought as I watched the fringes of the prayer shawls shaking, remembering the poem's description of the ritual as soul-drunken swaying. Stepping aside to allow them space, I continued my stroll down the aisle with Psalm 133 on my mind, pondering its first word, *Hinei* ("Behold!").

That's the spirit, I thought, in which I want to arrive at Dr. Aaronson's door tomorrow. I want it to be a "Behold!" moment.

Goodness knows, I owe him one. How I had loved his unique entrances into the classroom, his *Hinei!* opening of each class, always calculated to get our attention and drive home his point. I remembered his twirling dervish dance, the sensuous swaying of Isadora Duncan, the crawling archaeologist. Soon, I thought, I'll have the opportunity to return the favor.

Thinking of the Psalms of Ascent, I reflected on the role of the pilgrim, wondering which of these passengers filling the seats of the El Al flight were mere tourists, and which will be pilgrims. Pilgrimage is different from tourism. The pilgrim's reason for travel is not merely distraction from work, relaxation, or finding new and exotic pleasures. Pilgrimage is a quest for self-discovery. One makes pilgrimage in order, not to discover the Land, but to discover something within themselves that can only be revealed by the Land. The true landscape the pilgrim traverses is that of the heart.

After fifteen minutes of walking and stretching, I arrived back at my seat to find my cramped-quarter seatmate refreshed, even pleasant. Awake now and talkative, he said, "I look forward to being home in Tel Aviv and seeing my wife and children. What brings you to Israel? Are you with a tour group?"

I told him I was alone, traveling to congratulate my former professor on tomorrow's anniversary of his archaeological discovery. He lit up with excitement, saying he had heard of the Cave 53 discovery and was fascinated by the new psalm and its mysteries, listing all three – the identity of the bones, the location of the lost seventh tablet, and the identity of this previously unknown woman, King David's Star of the Sea. I wondered, having introduced myself as Stella Maris, if he would make the connection between the Star of the Sea and my name's Latin meaning, but he did not. Still, our conversation from that point was most enjoyable.

After landing and gathering our luggage, before disappearing into the crowd, he turned back to me and said, "Welcome home, Stella Maris."

It seemed unusual to be welcomed home while landing in a foreign country on the other side of the globe from Arkansas, and yet there was something profoundly appropriate about the phrase. "Welcome home" is a greeting heard by pilgrims in Israel, no matter from what corner of the world they arrive. When pilgrims travel, they are always coming home.

After landing in Tel Aviv, I took an Uber from Ben Gurion to The Olive Tree Hotel in Jerusalem, a high-rise packed with busloads of tourists and located a short walk from the Old City's Damascus Gate. I chose it because I saw online that the olive tree around which the lobby was built had been a traditional resting spot for pilgrims making their way to Jerusalem. Legend has it that pilgrims in ancient times would rest sitting around this very tree, the website offering the absurd but delightful myth that at this spot they could still hear David playing his harp.

Ludicrous, yes, but it was the perfect hook for me. I

prayed, entering the lobby to admire the olive tree, that this hotel would be the place for my next dance with David.

After settling my luggage into my room, not wishing a large dinner buffet such as the hotel offered to the hundreds of Holy Land pilgrims returning hungry from their day's adventures, I opted to walk across the street and dine quietly at the American Colony Hotel. I had read about Horatio Spafford's 19th century purchase of this former Turkish palace for his American Colony mission, and how historic the hotel had become. My immediate interest in seeing the hotel was due to Spafford's writing of one of the best-known Christian hymns, "It Is Well with My Soul," after losing all four of his daughters in the sinking of Ville du Havre on November 22, 1873. Two hundred and twenty-two other souls, besides his daughters, lost their lives that day.

A glass of Cabernet with my meal, I thought, would supplement my jetlag and help me sleep soundly, relaxing my anxiety about taxiing the next morning to The Hebrew University's Mount Scopus campus to meet Dr. Aaronson. Scopus is a Greek name meaning "Lookout" but, it occurred to me, Professor Aaronson had no way to scope out my *Hinei!* arrival tomorrow.

Back at my hotel after dinner, I wanted to sit alone for a time beside the lobby's olive tree. My quiet meditation lasted only a few minutes, though, broken by a man emerging from the aptly named lounge, The Oasis Bar. The man was tall with silver hair, likely in his mid-60s, and wearing a lanyard with an orange nametag identifying him as traveling with EO, which he explained stood for Educational Opportunities Tours. Under his name, Nathan Wagner, were the highlighted words, "Bus Captain," he the leader of one of the groups of pilgrims staying at the hotel.

Approaching from behind, he had mistaken me for one of his own, calling me Abby as he approached, a strange coincidence for one who had arrived in Jerusalem craving to hear "Ellie" one more time.

Seeing my confusion as I looked up at him, he apologized, embarrassed, saying that since he had left the buffet an hour earlier, he had settled into the Biblical Archaeology Room. He responded to my annoyed silence with a grin, explaining the acronym to mean the B-A-R.

Despite my body language conveying obvious cues that I wanted to be alone, he asked me where I was from. When I told him I lived in Fayetteville, Arkansas, he turned almost jubilant.

"Small world!" he exclaimed, explaining that he was a pastor from Little Rock, leading a group of thirty-nine pilgrims in this, his fifteenth Holy Land journey. He seemed proud of those stats, reeling them off like Dr. Aaronson would reel off the batting averages of his Red Sox.

Asking if this was my first trip to the Holy Land, I told him it was my second, but that my first trip had been long ago, with my parents in 1987. My interest perked up when he said that at that time he had been a student at the University of Michigan, studying Hebrew.

"Really!" I said, now fully engaged. "I'm here to meet tomorrow at Hebrew University with Dr. David Aaronson, my former professor. He studied Hebrew at Michigan about that time."

"Oh yes, I recall David," he said. "I haven't spoken with him in many years. Decades, I suppose. I returned to parish ministry, while David chose to stay with academia. The last time we spoke, my Jewish friend was teaching at a Christian college, of all things, in Memphis."

"Right," I said. "I was one of his first students at Covenant Christian College. I've come to Jerusalem to see him and congratulate him on his archaeological discovery at Qumran. Tomorrow, you know, is the one-year anniversary of the discovery."

"Really?" he said. "I had forgotten. I took my group to Qumran and Masada today. What a missed opportunity! If only I had met you last night, I would have re-mapped our itinerary to be in Qumran for tomorrow's anniversary. How fantastic it would have been to have David join my group with a Zoom message to tell us about his discovery."

Reaching into his pocket to retrieve a card, he said, "Please give this to David and tell him Nathan Wagner is in Jerusalem and sends congratulations on his discovery. Tell him I'll be here a few more days and would love to re-connect to talk about old times in A-square."

Assuring him I would, I took Rev. Wagner's card and headed to the elevators. When readied for bed, I took my mezuzah and held it close, remembering that mom had purchased it right here in Jerusalem. My constant companion since my first vision, my mezuzah had finally come home. Placing it beside the clock, I breathed a bedtime prayer that this night would be different from every other night.

"So mote it be!" I surprised myself by saying, aloud.

Dad? Why had I suddenly recalled my dad, saying the Masonic Amen, as if dad had suddenly paid me a visit? I remembered that it was right here in Jerusalem, in a cave beneath the Old City, that he had taught me those words.

I quickly Googled – "Jerusalem, Masonic, Cave" – and saw that the cave we had visited in 1987 was called Zedekiah's Cave, also known as King Solomon's Quarries, where many of the great stones of ancient Jerusalem had been quarried. The legend that this was the place where Solomon's workers quarried the stones used in building the first temple made the mammoth cave of great interest to Freemasons, who have held annual gatherings there each year for over a hundred years. Its main hall, able to hold hundreds of people, spreads out under five city blocks of the Old City's Muslim Quarter.

My dad, proud of his having been raised to the third degree of masonry, that of a Master Mason, as well as being a Knight Templar in the York Rite and a 32nd Degree Mason in the Ancient and Accepted Scottish Rite (a degree he claimed made him, according the famous Arkansas Freemason, Albert Pike, a "Master of the Royal Secret"), had insisted that on our free day mom and I accompany him to visit the ancient quarry. Twenty-seven years after our Jerusalem visit, in 2014, dad was honored by the Supreme Council, which conferred upon him the esteemed 33rd Degree in recognition of his outstanding masonic work.

Off the usual tourist path, the cave was almost empty on the day we arrived. The thing I most remember is seeing the golden-hued limestone wall covered with half-quarried blocks of stone, rectangular shaped blocks once intended to end up above us in some royal building project or another. The most striking thing to me was that many stones-in-the-making, some massive, were simply left in situ, still attached to the wall. These stones, for some reason, had been rejected.

I hadn't thought of our visit to Zedekiah's Cave in years, but last night it all came back to me. I remembered how dad, standing near an enormous, half-quarried block of stone, took out his pocket New Testament and read 1 Peter 2:4-6, "As you come to him, the living Stone – rejected by men but chosen by God and precious to him – you also, like living stones, are being built into a spiritual house to be a holy priesthood."

It was at that moment that I had realized mom had been in on it the whole time. She put her arm around me as dad said, "Stella, your mother and I believe in our hearts that you are called to great things. You are a living stone being fashioned from God's quarry, chosen and precious. God has amazing plans for you. I don't believe that you, like these stones left useless on these cave walls, will allow your Calling to go unanswered."

It was obvious now why my parents had planned our Holy Land trip. This moment, deep in this cave, had brought us to the pinnacle of their plan. Seeing my emotions at the sudden awareness of their purpose, mom said, "Stella Ursa Maris, you are the SUM of joy for your dad and me. We have known from the day you were born that God had a special purpose for you."

Dad added, "I've known of this cave for years. Your mom and I wanted you to hear its message, the message in these unfinished blocks of stone."

As tears welled in my eyes, dad said, "May I offer a prayer of dedication as mom and I lay hands on you?"

We bowed our heads as dad prayed a short and simple prayer of thanksgiving for the opportunity to share this special moment with his wife and daughter. He committed us all to God's kingdom, ending his prayer with a loud, "So mote it be!"

On the way out of the cave several minutes later, I asked what he had said in the place of "Amen," and he explained how Masons end their prayers with these words. He felt especially inspired to do so, he said, while in Solomon's quarries.

Just then a large drop of water fell on my forehead from the cave's roof. As I wiped it away, dad said, "These drippings from the roof are called Zedekiah's Tears, remembering how the last king of David's dynasty tried unsuccessfully to use the cave as his escape route during Nebuchadnezzar's siege of Jerusalem and the destruction of Solomon's Temple. That temple had stood for four hundred years, perhaps some of its stones quarried from the very place where we are standing. As

Zedekiah ran for his life through this very cave, God's plan for Israel seemed ended, like this half-quarried stone, dead and useless."

"Until Jesus," mom added, "the Son of David, the chief cornerstone. Stella, we have been worried about you, but God has revealed to us that we need not worry, that his special plans for you will not be thwarted."

With such sweet memories conjured by the Masonic "Amen" that had risen to my lips unexpectedly, a quick search on Google Maps showed that Zedekiah's Cave was only a fifteen-minute walk from the hotel, near the Damascus Gate. I promised myself that before leaving Jerusalem I would make my way there to honor dad's memory. I felt him close to me, knowing I was so near the cave where he had preached the only sermon of his life. My last thoughts before falling asleep being of my father, I felt safe, certain that God was not finished with me yet.

"Abby! Abby!"

I jerked awake. It was 3:33 a.m.

My initial thrill at seeing the clock's line-up of Threes quickly vanished as I realized the name I had unmistakably heard was "Abby," not "Ellie."

No matter. My lobby encounter with Rev. Wagner had begun with his mistaking me for one of his pilgrims named Abby. Surely this was simply lingering in my sub-consciousness.

Three would need no dancing partner this night. Gazing at the perfect triad of Threes, I was filled with gratitude for what I knew was happening – my seventh vision.

I rolled away from the clock and closed my eyes, my last thought before drifting back to sleep being, "Who is Abby?"

My dream awakening was of my shoulder being shaken, and not gently, by the king's royal *sofer*, Shemaiah ben Nethanel.

"Abby! Abby!"

Though I had not met Shemaiah in my previous visions, I knew that this one shaking me was David's scribe, the sixth tablet having made clear his role in producing and hiding the tablets. I had come to imagine that the bones in Cave 53 were his, willingly dying beside his most precious work, David's last song. I envisioned him taking the tablets into the cave and positioning himself in precisely the posture he wanted his bones to be found. Like Elijah praying down fire from heaven, I imagined Shemaiah praying for the cave to collapse over him in an act of self-sacrifice, in full faith that God would reveal the tablets in his own timing.

Seeing I was now fully alert, Shemaiah stepped back to give me space. A glance at the room made it clear I was sitting by King David's deathbed, the air heavy with incense.

It occurred to me, seeing David, that not only had it been for me thirty-three years since my last vision, but for King David also it had been thirty-three years since my last visit, dancing in procession before the ark. I was with him at the beginning of his Jerusalem reign, and now again at the end.

There were two others in the room. The woman leaning over him and holding his hand was Queen Bathsheba, mother of Solomon. King Solomon stood behind his mother, his hands resting lightly on her shoulders.

Who am I, then? And why is Shemaiah calling me Abby, not Ellie?

"Abby," Shemaiah said, pulling my attention away from my scrambled mental assessment of the room, "King David has inquired of you, wishing for you to witness his final words, but he has already slipped back into unconsciousness. The time is near, you must now stay awake."

As I nodded assent, I realized that something different was happening in me, something very unlike my previous dreams. Though the vision had planted me abruptly into this moment, my mind was reconstructing memories of the last several hours in this room. It was as if a flash drive had been inserted into my brain, an entire set of memories repopulating in my head. These were my memories, no question about it. Yet, how could these be my memories if I, Stella Maris, had not lived them?

I had, from my very first vision, always sensed this Other with me, a companion whose knowledge of Hebrew had allowed me to share each experience in full awareness. My seventh vision completed my union with my Other. The memories flooding into my consciousness were of people and places I had not actually experienced. Yet, they were my own, undeniably.

I don't mean that I was reconstructing merely the memories of being in this room. I mean an entire lifetime of memories. I knew, at last, my Other's identity. I am Abishag, King David's concubine. I was, as David and Shemaiah called me, Abby. I am both Ellie and Abby, both Stella and Abishag.

From the very first time I read it, I've been strangely drawn to the opening of 1 Kings, the story of a beautiful young virgin, Abishag the Shunammite, being brought to an aged and bedridden King David. The text politely speaks of her as a human blanket, her presence intended only to warm an aging king for whom woolen blankets were insufficient. Of course, however uncomfortable to point out in a Sunday morning sermon, it is clear that the real reason for Abishag was to test his virility. If David was unable to have intercourse with Abishag, it would be time for a new king. His inability is acknowledged in an awkwardly phrased comment that the king did not have intercourse with her. The king's impotence set the stage for his son, Adonijah, to claim kingship, launching the contest he would lose to his half-brother, Solomon.

Sitting at David's bedside, I knew firsthand what I had always suspected, that Abishag was much more to David than a nurse's aide to a shriveling and shivering old king. David and Abishag were in love, despite his inability to consummate their – our – love.

"Where is everybody?" I asked Shemaiah, recalling how the room had been filled with officials of the kingdom before my weariness in watching over David had caught up to my body, sending me into a deep sleep.

Shemaiah answered, "In a moment of clarity, my lord ordered all officials and family from the room other than King Solomon, Queen Bathsheba and you. He asked only that I stay to bear witness to his last words."

Sighing heavily, he continued, "Which I am not sure now that he will be able to finish. The time draws near."

Still sweeping over me were memories of what I had not lived, yet which, I knew, were none other than my own. I am Abishag from Shulem. It wasn't that her memories were being poured into an empty vessel named Stella Maris. I wasn't assuming the identity of this other. I am this other, both Stella from Siloam, and Abishag from Shulem.

My knowing of King David was from dual perspectives. I could relive each time Eliana appeared to David as his Muse. Clear in my memory also were Abishag's, renowned in the Bible for her virginal beauty, falling in love with David while keeping him warm with love. He regaling her – regaling me – with stories of his adventurous life. He calling her – calling me – his *Kochav Hayam*.

David had known from the moment he saw Abishag that she was none other than his *Kochav Hayam*, the one who had been sent by God to him throughout his life, unchanged in beauty through the long years. Having at first protested his advisors' plan to bring a virgin to the palace as a concubine, his objections evaporated the moment he saw her, knowing it was me.

David ben Jesse's prayer, that his facing of death would not be without his *Kochav Hayam*, had been answered. The miracle of my visions was not that Stella of Siloam had been transported into the past, nor that Abishag of Shulem had been transported into the future. The miracle is that we two are mysteriously, magically one.

My seventh vision brought me again to David, even if in his dying moments, to witness his last words, the still hidden ending to Psalm 151, the seventh tablet. While the scene has occasionally been imagined by artists, I can tell you that Bathsheba and I stood at his two sides, she holding his left hand and I his right, both of us fighting to control our sobbing in order better to concentrate on his words. King Solomon stood over his mother, listening intently. Shemaiah sat next to me, near the foot of the bed with parchment on a small table, recording his words.

"Speak to him, Abby," Shemaiah said.

"David," I whispered.

I've always heard that hearing is the last sense to leave a dying person. It must be true. Hearing me whisper his name, David roused and, seeing me, his eyes flashed. Tightening his grip on my hand, he pulled me toward him.

"Eliana," he whispered, "you have always been the answer to my prayers. Long have I desired you, ashamed that we could not consummate our love. Hear these words that the Spirit of God has spoken to me."

Closing his eyes, his voice seemed stronger as he quoted the Spirit's revelation to him: "David ben Jesse, after wandering in Sheol for three thousand years, you will return to consummate your love for Abishag. In that day, David and Abishag will be one, husband and wife."

He opened his eyes and looked at me, making certain I had heard him. When I signaled that I had, he repeated as our eyes locked, "Three thousand years."

Looking to Shemaiah, he said, "I am ready."

As I moved back, allowing Shemaiah better to position himself to hear and record David's last words, I thought of David Aaronson. If I am both Stella and Abishag, could this David dying in front of me now be that David whom I will visit this morning in Jerusalem? Is David one with David, as I am one with Abishag?

These are King David's last words as I heard them spoken to Shemaiah in my seventh vision. I believe that these words, identifying the bones of Cave 53, will be found on the as-yet-unrecovered seventh tablet:

> Praise be to God, who does not abandon us
> even in regions of deep darkness,
> whose loyal love never fades,
> even in the valley of death's dark shadow.
> *Hashem* has answered my dying prayer,
> sending again *Malaki*, Eliana, my *Kochav Hayam*,
> unseen her beauty for thirty-three years,
> when last we danced as the ark entered *Yerushalayim*.
> Her comfort, now exceeding words, is fleshly warmth,
> and her true name revealed, Abishag.
> She it was who guided me as the scroll of my life unrolled:

Shepherd,
Warrior,
Refugee,
Rebel,
King.

Bathsheba, my love, mother of my son, the king,
While our beginning was in iniquity,
our sorrow profound in the death of our firstborn,
Hashem smiled upon our repentance,
blessing us with years of love, and with a son of great wisdom.

Solomon, my son the king, honor these my last words.
I was not reared in the palace,
with gold plates and silver goblets I did not dine.
In Shepherds' Fields I learned of *Hashem*,
in the wilderness I learned of kingship,
Hashem at my side.
You must make my end as my beginning.
I shall be gathered unto my fathers in the City of David,
but in *Yerushalayim* do not allow my bones to abide.
After nine months, secret my bones and my song
to my wilderness home.
Make the cave my hiding place.
There, embracing my song, I will sing in spirit dance,
I, the violin for Israel's song.

Abishag, my *Malaki*,
My bones will rest by the Salt Sea,
Until you, my *Kochav Hayam*,
return to guide the Wanderer home.
Our love, once consummated,
will bring healing to the Land.

Praise be to God,
the rock of my salvation, my strength always.
Shalom, Shalom, Shalom.

I don't know how many times David repeated Shalom. It was a holy moment, watching him draw his last breath, trying one last time to form the word Shalom, yet with no air in his lungs to make another sound.

I awoke in my bed at the Olive Tree, weeping, but at peace.

Chapter 14

Hebrew University

MOUNT SCOPUS CAMPUS, JERUSALEM

TUESDAY, JANUARY 18, 2022

If I had fallen asleep nervous, imagining Dr. Aaronson not believing, perhaps even scoffing at my story, my seventh dream had obliterated all such concerns. Awakening on January 18, I knew beyond any question that David Aaronson and I were, together, part of the divine plan. Would he know it, or would I need to convince him?

Waking early, I wrote on my laptop for nearly two hours, detailing my journey to Jerusalem and my seventh vision. Growing hungry around 7:00 and seeking a quiet dining area to enjoy breakfast, I would discover that the hotel offered no such venue, catering almost entirely to pilgrim groups. Instead, I was shuttled into the din of noise in the large dining hall's buffet, hundreds of eager pilgrims hustling to feed themselves so as not to be late for the departure of their motor coaches already lining up outside – cleaned, fueled, and ready to usher them to their next adventure.

The clamor of the dining hall matched the throbbing of my

heart, filled with joy after my seventh vision. I had an urge to stand on the table like a street preacher and declare to my breakfast audience how blessed they were to experience *HaEretz*, the Land. I would never have done that, of course, smiling to think how the hotel's doctor would surely diagnose me as having contracted "Jerusalem Fever," not an even-more-novel corona virus, but a mental phenomenon first described in the 1930s. Every year a few pilgrims experience Jerusalem as a psychotic trigger bringing on episodes of delusion and hysteria.

Returning to my room after breakfast to freshen up, I decided to delay my departure in order to avoid the pandemonium downstairs, pilgrims jamming the elevators and lobby, scurrying to join their drivers and guides while working their way through peddlers of ancient coins and personalized jewelry.

I began to regret my decision not to call ahead for an appointment with Dr. Aaronson. I had started to contact him several times, but keeping my visit a surprise seemed to me to be a sign of my trust in divine providence, a submission to the divine will.

By 10:00 the hotel was virtually empty, its tourists having scattered in different directions. I saw from my balcony what I thought surely was the last motor coach to exit, thinking how this late-to-start group was fortunate to have a guide able to convince pilgrims to take it easy and relax, that seeing less can be more meaningful than filling the day with non-stop action. It had not been that way with our guide in 1987, our tour leader herding us onto the bus at 7:30 each morning, my mom putting on her poutiest face as she boarded, jokingly grumbling, "Even the Holy Land isn't holy at this time of day! God himself doesn't get up this early!"

Like most groups, we crammed as much into each day as

we could, returning weary each night to the hotel. No wonder the Biblical Archaeology Room (the BAR) is so popular at day's end.

Watching the last coach pull away, I called the front desk to arrange for a taxi to the Mount Scopus campus, only two miles from the hotel. I held for only a few seconds before the concierge informed me that the driver said he would be at the hotel in exactly nine minutes, and that with current traffic, the drive to campus would take another nine minutes.

"How fitting," I thought, "on my first Jerusalem morning to be visited by two nines, a double triad of treys adding to eighteen on this 18th of January. David Aaronson, get ready!"

My driver, whose name was Hayim (a name derived from the Hebrew *Chaim*, meaning "life"), must have been an aspiring guide, chattering constantly and rarely falling silent. I don't mean that in a negative way. His English was perfect and, no doubt about it, Hayim lived up to his name, chock full of *Chaim*.

After entering the campus through the Buber Gate, Hayim began to rattle off landmarks, pointing to both the Faculty of Humanities and the Institute of Archaeology. I told him he could stop anywhere, saying it didn't matter since I wanted to wander through the campus for a bit on foot, the sun having now warmed the day sufficiently.

Thanking him for his expertise, I paid the fare, tipping 100%. He thanked me profusely, asking what time my appointment was and when I might need a ride back to the hotel. When I told him I didn't have an appointment, he looked up with a yikes expression and said, "No appointment? Good luck getting in to see your friend. Since Hamas detonated a bomb twenty years ago in the Sinatra Cafeteria that killed nine people, metal detectors and security are everywhere. Still, I have no doubt you'll find your way. I hope I'll see you again, and good luck."

Not remembering the bombing, as Hayim drove away I called it up and saw that the Hebrew University Massacre occurred on July 31, 2002. It had killed nine, five of whom were American students, and injured about a hundred others. While sparking vile celebrations in Gaza, the bombing was immediately condemned by world leaders such as President George Bush and U.N. General Secretary Kofi Annan.

"How," I wondered, "can people hate one another so much? Can the healing promised in my seventh vision really be possible?"

Looking back to the Buber Gate, I remembered one of my favorite quotes from the eminent Jewish philosopher for whom the gate was named, Martin Buber: "All journeys have secret destinations of which the traveler is unaware." I thought how perfectly Buber's words described my journey, having traveled from Fayetteville to Jerusalem with a specific destination in mind, my arrival timed to coincide with the anniversary of the Cave 53 discovery. As precise as were my plans, I could not have guessed what secret destinations awaited.

Admiring the façade of the Faculty of Humanities building, I found a bench and sat to offer one of my favorite prayers, written by another of my spiritual heroes, Thomas Merton: "My Lord God, I have no idea where I am going. I do not see the road ahead of me. I cannot know for certain where it will end. Nor do I really know myself, and the fact that I think I am following your will does not mean that I am actually doing so. But I believe that the desire to please you does in fact please you. And I hope that I have that desire in all that I am doing. And I know that if I do this, you will lead me by the right road, though I may know nothing about it. Therefore, I will trust you always."

Hayim was right. It had been naïve of me to think I could simply enter a Hebrew University complex to engage a professor without having made arrangements. While possible at home, on the Fayetteville campus of the University of Arkansas, I was now in Israel.

"I'm not in Ar-Kansas anymore," I thought, the place as strange as was Oz to Dorothy. "Lord, I have no idea where I am going! I do not see the road ahead of me, and I see no yellow bricks."

Entering the building, I passed through the metal detector easily. Seeing I wasn't wearing credentials to go further, a guard intercepted me, directing me to a security table to receive a Visitor's badge.

The young female security guard at the checkpoint asked which office I was visiting and what was my appointment time. Sheepishly confessing to not having made an appointment, her face relayed a clear message to this American tourist: "Don't you know this is 2022? No one has just walked off the street into a campus office or classroom building since the Second Intifada."

Apologizing, I handed her my passport, hoping I could convince her to call up to Dr. Aaronson and check on his availability and willingness to see me.

"I'm sorry," I said, "I wasn't thinking. Being in Israel for a week and having a free day, I had hoped to surprise my former professor, David Aaronson."

Upon hearing this, she closed my passport and asked, too enthusiastically to be merely a common courtesy, "You're Stella Maris?"

When I nodded, wondering how she knew my name and how she could have possibly been aware of my visit, she said, "Ms. Maris, welcome! Professor Aaronson called before his morning class to alert us to your arrival, asking that we treat you as a VIP."

Glancing up at the clock to see it was almost a quarter past eleven, she said, "His class should be finished by now."

I took the Visitor's badge she handed me and tried to concentrate on her directions to his third-floor office. It was difficult, my brain's electrical synapses firing nonstop trying to solve the mystery of how Dr. Aaronson could have anticipated my arrival.

"Of course!" it dawned on me as I reached the elevator. "His classmate from Ann Arbor, Rev. Wagner, from the lobby last night. He must have decided to call Dr. Aaronson to reconnect. There's no other way."

Stepping out of the elevator onto the third-floor hallway, I looked down at my feet to reflect upon the many steps I had taken on my journey to reunite with David Aaronson. I thought of the Irish Bull I'd used in one of my recent sermons, an oxymoron spoken by Sir Boyle Roche, an 18th century Irish politician famous for his "tips of the slung." Once, seeking to inspire Parliament to trust divine providence, he said, "All along the untrodden path of the future, I can see the footprints of an unseen hand." A double Irish Bull! Untrodden paths have no footprints at all, and footprints are not made by hands, seen or unseen.

At that moment, looking at my feet, I saw God's hand. Despite the uncertainty of how my meeting with Dr. Aaronson might go, I trusted divine providence.

God's timing was perfect. Rounding the corner to the long hallway where his office was located, I saw Dr. Aaronson walking toward me from the opposite end. He had entered the hallway at precisely the same moment as I, a delightful chiasm, an envelope structure like those he pointed out in the Hebrew Bible, the artistic mating of a story's beginning to its ending.

He wasn't alone, accompanied by an athletic looking,

black-haired, olive-skinned student in her early twenties. Aglow with an aura of youthful energy (I mean that he was aglow, not she, though, in fairness, she might have been – I don't know, since my eyes were fixed on David Aaronson), my heart beat faster.

Had he been alone, the game would have been over, but his being with a student gave me an opportunity to observe. My older professors in Memphis had oozed with ennui. Dr. Aaronson was now one of those older professors. If I had expected to see him today grown into that musty-professor mode, it was not to be. I could detect no weariness in David Aaronson. His features were those of a sixty-five-year-old, but as I looked at him, he was thirty-two again and I, at the sight of him, twenty-two.

When they paused in front of his office to continue their conversation, my mind traveled to the orb of faculty offices overlooking the cafeteria at C-cube. How like this one I must have looked in 1988, radiant with life on my walks with him to his office, hungry to hear more of his words, spellbound by his charm. Looking at him now, I saw sixty-five-year-old elegance.

I walked slowly past, careful not to make eye contact. Would he recognize me? He glanced up with a polite nod just as I passed, but with no detectable interruption in his conversation. I nearly laughed as I heard him say something about how he wished he could be in Beijing for the opening of the Winter Olympics.

"Classic Aaronson!" I thought, recalling how he had opened one of our classes with the five-colored skydive over South Korea to open the '88 Summer Olympics. How silly he had looked that day, entering class gyrating with five Hula Hoops spinning.

His glance at me now over his left shoulder made me think

of Michelangelo's statue of David in Florence, a 17-foot-tall sculpture capturing the young warrior's first recognition of impending danger, David's liminal moment prior to a battle whose outcome was as yet uncertain. The David Michelangelo gave to the world stands naked to the moment of action, just as he had been in my second vision, a hero struggling to overcome *Hakol*, the Voice of rationality urging him to quit the battle before the battle begins.

At the opposite end of the hallway I stopped, not wishing to pretend further that I had any other destination. Feeling his eyes following me, I pivoted. Despite his student companion still speaking, his attention shifted, now fully on me.

When with a grin I acknowledged his attention, he abruptly excused himself from his student, his right arm roiling in dervish-like coils as he called to me, "Stella! *Boker tov!* Good morning! Come! Come! We have much to talk about."

Vastly different had been all my imaginings of this moment. Something unexpected in me stirring, my face must have shone as I answered his call, my pace quickening with each step. Opening his arms for embrace, he fell silent, my speechlessness matching his, as if each of us knew something the other did not.

The hug lasted longer than what might be deemed appropriate for a professor and student, but not at all inappropriate for a professor and student reconnecting after thirty-three years. While I knew I had, and suspected that he had, experienced something bordering impropriety in 1988, our paths had crossed for only that single year, with no subsequent contact.

When we stepped back, I said, "I wasn't even sure you would remember me, Dr. Aaronson."

With a how-could-you-think-that look, he opened the door

and invited me to follow him in, saying, "Stella, please, please. Call me David. Not remember you? How could I forget my first Star of the Sea? You made it past security, so you must be wondering how I knew you would come today."

Walking into his office, I immediately noticed a print hanging on the opposite wall that was familiar. I had seen it before. David had shown it to me in his office after one of our classes. It was the Stella Maris Monastery and Lighthouse on Mount Carmel that he had picked up in a Memphis Estate Sale. He had been thinking of me when he purchased it, so obviously he had not forgotten me, keeping his Star of the Sea close, I suppose as a guiding Muse.

Once inside I returned to our conversation, handing him Rev. Wagner's card. "No sir, I think I figured out how you knew I was coming. I ran into Rev. Wagner at the hotel last night and he told me he had studied with you in Ann Arbor."

He looked baffled as he examined the business card.

"Ah, Nathaniel!" he said, looking at the card. "His name means 'God's gift,' and so he thought himself to be. I don't mean that in a bad way. I remember Nathaniel as a lover of life, able to laugh and feel no pressure as the rest of us struggled mightily to keep up. I think he always knew he would simply take what he could from Ann Arbor and return to ministry, having no taste for the publish-or-perish environment. I'll keep his card and give him a call."

"He didn't call you last night to tell you I was here?"

Seeing my confusion, he said, "No, I haven't spoken with Nathaniel, though you could say I received a call last night. As difficult as it will surely be to believe, I had a most amazing dream last night that told me you would arrive today. I awoke so certain of this that I called security. Honestly, though, I had convinced myself by mid-morning, in the light of day, that it had only been an extremely vivid dream sparked, likely, by the anniversary of my discovery of Psalm 151's Star of the Sea."

"Who was the man in your dream?"

"None other than the author, the etcher of the tablets himself, Shemaiah. He claimed to have summoned me to witness the king's last words, the seventh tablet."

"King David's last words?" I asked, anxious to hear his version of what I had also dreamed last night. Had we shared this dream?

David said, "Yes, David's last words. I heard him say to Solomon that he wanted his bones, after lying nine months in Jerusalem, to be escorted into the Judean Wilderness. It seems clear to me that last year's discovery of bones in Cave 53 inspired my dream."

I remained silent, waiting for him to go on.

"I saw Shemaiah near the foot of David's bed, recording the king's words."

"Were others in the room?" I asked.

"Yes. Queen Bathsheba and Solomon were by him, and the young nurse, whom the Bible calls Abishag. But the man identified her as . . ."

He paused, making certain our eyes were connected.

"As?"

"As you. Shemaiah told me that Abishag is David's *Kochav Hayam*."

In that moment my heart overflowed with gratitude, recognizing that God in his providence had taken care of all the details I had been fretting about, expending unnecessary time and energy trying to engineer what God had already engineered.

"Shemaiah told me that David's *Kochav Hayam* would arrive at my office this morning. He said, 'Her story you must hear, and your story she must hear.'"

"And you knew he was talking about me, how?"

"Stella, when I read *Kochav Hayam* on Cave 53's tablets last year, I immediately remembered you. It's no wonder that the woman I saw in my dream was as I remembered you, so that awakening from my dream, you were my first thought. I must have still been dreaming, though, and not yet fully awake, as I saw you on the beach, wearing a windblown white wedding dress with the Mediterranean Sea behind you."

I've often taught my congregation that God doesn't call anyone to a task without equipping them for that task. As I had many times before, I was now seeing the proof of that well-worn adage. David Aaronson, the professor who long ago invited me onto the Star of David dance floor, had joined the dance, and I had nothing to do with it. Divine providence had brought us together. I had imagined my greatest challenge as overcoming his visceral reaction of disbelief to the story of my dreams. Now I realized that the arguments I had spent countless hours crafting in my head, designed to convince him I wasn't a nutcase, would not be needed.

"I dreamed also last night of King David's death," I said, "but before I tell you about it you need to know that, for me, it was not my first, but my seventh dream."

Realizing it was now 12:00 and that he might have an afternoon class or need lunch, I asked, "Do you have time for me to tell my story?"

"*Ken! Ken!* Yes! Yes!"

"I need to begin at the beginning," I said, "so that you understand your own role in my story. I think when you hear it, you'll realize that your Cave 53 discovery of King David's song and of his bones was guided by divine providence."

I looked carefully to gauge his reaction. Detecting no skepticism, I continued.

"When I enrolled my senior year in your Hebrew Poetry class, I was ready to leave C-cube, my faith burned out. You began with Psalm 89, covering it in six sessions, inviting us onto the Star of David dance floor as our choreographer."

"Yes, I remember. I still use the six whirling dervishes to form David's star."

"On each night after those six lectures, I experienced a dream – a vision – of being sent to David as his Muse at key moments in his life's journey, beginning with Samuel's anointing and continuing through his dancing entrance into Jerusalem. I danced with David, leading the ark into *Yerushalayim*. My six dreams ended the night of your sixth lecture. I've waited thirty-three years for a seventh vision, which finally I experienced last night. I was, as you saw, at David's side as he died. Your first dream was my seventh. Welcome to my world."

Pausing to give him an opening to speak, he opted for silence, so I continued.

"My second vision was with David as he battled Goliath in the Valley of Elah. That's where he first called me his *Kochav Hayam*."

"Are you saying that your six dreams match the tablets?"

"Precisely, yes. I am."

"Don't think I'm doubting your story. After last night, I would be a fool not to believe. Surely, though, you see how others will claim your story to be fabricated to match my translation of the six tablets."

I smiled.

"Unless," he said, anticipating I had an answer.

"Unless," I finished his thought, "I had recorded my dreams."

"Did you?"

"I've always kept a daily journal. Then and now. I recorded all six of my visions thirty-three years ago, and they match your tablets. Since your translation was published, I've been busy editing and updating those journals, not only my six visions, but also my notes on your six lectures. I have the edited version with me on a flash drive, but I've kept all the hand-written originals also."

"Why didn't you tell me of your dreams back then?"

"You can't imagine how much I wanted to. I almost did, several times, on our walks back to your office. I was embarrassed, though, certain you would think me crazy. Truth is, as powerful and real as the dreams were, I myself had doubts. Over time, I began to regard them as private, miraculous only in the sense that I knew they were from God. I reasoned that they were sent to affirm my Call to ministry. Your discovery and translation changed all that."

"Forgive me for pressing this, but I'm just thinking about the path of convincing others. One's private journals can easily be faked."

"That's true. But in addition to my journals, over the years I've shared the story of my visions with many hundreds of people in my congregation."

"Really? Hundreds of witnesses?"

"Yes. Actually, my first confidant had been in real time, during the classes themselves. Jakob Rothman knew all about my dreams. Do you remember him?"

"Yes, he was your boyfriend, right?"

I noticed that, as he spoke, he glanced away. It was only for a second, but it broke our eye contact for the first time. He quickly recovered, though, so that I assumed his looking away was simply his trying to remember.

"Yes, my boyfriend. Actually, at the beginning of my senior year, my fiancé."

"Whatever became of him?"

"He became an attorney, but Jakob's real Mississippi River passion was music, especially Blues and jazz. I haven't spoken with him in over twenty years, not since he left his law practice to buy a restaurant on Beale Street. About a month after he opened it, he called to tell me about his decision to take a risk, to follow his calling so that he could be always near the music he loved. He invited me to come visit, but I never did."

"Why not?"

"Well," I said, ready to guide our conversation back to my visions, "I had broken off our engagement after my sixth vision, the only vision not aligning with your six tablets. In that vision, I met great David's Greater Son. You might have heard of him. His name is Jesus."

"Tell me, please."

"My sixth dream took me to Gethsemane, where I spoke to Jesus as he struggled with his decision to go through with dying on the cross. What he said to me led me to give my life to the church, completely."

"To marry the church instead of Jakob? Like a priest?"

"Well, I'm not Roman Catholic, but yes, exactly. I told Jakob about the vision the next day, insisting we could never be husband and wife."

"How did he handle that?"

"Honestly, I'm not sure. He seemed numb. I'm sure he had to be angry, though he didn't display anger. He just walked away."

"And you've remained unmarried?"

"Not at all. I've been married since that day, and happily. I married the church, my faith. I've pastored the same church for twenty-seven years, since 1994. I have often shared my Call story, which means they have heard me tell of my dreams. Hundreds of people have heard me share my story, including David's name for me, his Star of the Sea."

"I can only imagine how stunned you must have been to

read my translation."

"Astonished! Which is why, since the day I read your translation on September 6, I've been writing as Jehu drove his chariot."

"Furiously!"

"Exactly."

Growing serious, I added, "and not just writing furiously, but praying fervently for a seventh vision. After your discovery, I knew that if I were to discover the seventh tablet, I would need a seventh vision. But it never came, until last night in Jerusalem."

Allowing no pause, he said, "You must tell me about it."

"Last night at the Olive Tree Hotel – simultaneous to your dream, evidently – my vision taught me about myself. You called her Abishag, and so she was. And so I am, though I hadn't known that until last night."

"What do you mean?"

"I mean that I now, however strangely, possess memories of Abishag. During last night's dream we became one, however magical that sounds. I feel as sent to you as Abishag must have felt, being sent to King David."

"Sent to me?"

"Yes, sent to finish the task David gave me – gave us – on the night he died. I believe we are now sent to find the seventh tablet which Shemaiah separated from the other six tablets."

I was unprepared for what David said next.

"Well, the text is clear that you will discover the seventh tablet with your husband."

"Well, not exactly. It said, as you know, that it would be found by David's *Kochav Hayam* and the one she 'calls' *Ishi* (my husband). I have called my church 'My husband' for many years. In spirit, in prayers, in financial backing, my church is right beside me. We seek the seventh tablet together."

"You've given yourself completely to your church?"

"I have."

"Without regret?"

"None."

"And you've remained a virgin?"

Shocked by the question, I nonetheless nodded my affirmation.

"Then, truly, you are Abishag, and just as beautiful."

He turned away in a manner reminding me of the times in class when he had to break eye contact, as if on the verge of being inappropriate, walking away to the whiteboard as a distraction.

Turning back to face me, he said, "Suppose the text is to be taken literally? What if your husband need be at your side?"

"Well," I laughed, "then I'm in trouble."

"I told you," he said, reaching to take my hand, "that as my vision ended, I saw you in a windblown wedding dress by the Mediterranean. What I didn't tell you is that I was the groom, and that I knew exactly the spot, a wedding venue near Caesarea. You'll never believe the name of the place."

"I won't?"

"It's called *Kochav Hayam*, Star of the Sea. I attended the wedding of one of my TAs there two years ago. It's stunningly beautiful."

My silence doing nothing to deter him, he said, "Stella, I think it was obvious to both of us thirty-three years ago, however properly unspoken of then, that we had fallen in love. I didn't have the courage to speak it, even to myself. It was your last year of college and my first year of teaching. Becoming involved could have ruined my career, and our lives."

As his gaze held my eyes captive, his grip on my hand seemed to become both firmer and gentler at the same time.

How is that possible?

"For a long time after your graduation I regretted my caution. In 1988, it wasn't merely attraction that drew me to love you, but an eerie sense that we, together, were part of a divine plan. I'm not sure I can explain it. I only know I will not let another opportunity pass."

When he stepped out from behind his desk and knelt, knowing what was about to happen, I laughed. Laughed!

Quickly I explained, so that he wouldn't think I would refuse the proposal that I knew he was about to make.

"I'm so sorry, David. It is in joy that I laugh, believe me. I was just thinking that the last time I saw you on your knees was your sixth lecture. You were wearing a hardhat, searching for something hidden."

"Well then, I think I have, at long last, found my hidden treasure. Stella Maris, Star of the Sea, my courage failed me thirty-three years ago, so that I have been a wanderer since, never marrying, as if keeping myself for you without knowing it. Will you marry me?"

Chapter 15

The King David Hotel and Jerusalem YMCA

KING DAVID STREET, JERUSALEM

TUESDAY EVENING, JANUARY 18, 2022

There had been no hesitation in my reply, my "Yes!" bubbling up, ecstatically. How could we have been waiting for each other for so many years, neither seeking the other? God's providence, never at rest through these thirty-three years, had brought us to this moment.

Standing from his kneeling proposal, he apologized for not having an engagement ring to offer, promising to correct the omission as soon as possible.

"In lieu of a ring," he said as he opened a desk drawer, "I want to give you a necklace that will symbolize our union, a Jewish professor and a Christian pastor."

Reaching into the drawer, he produced a common piece of jewelry found in virtually every tourist shop, a Jewish Star of David with a cross rising in its heart.

"Perhaps our marriage," he said, "and, soon, our discovery

of the seventh tablet, will foster a unity, not just of Christians and Jews, but of all peoples."

Motioning for me to turn, he said, "May I?"

Clasping the gold chain at the back of my neck, he guided me back around so that he could admire how the necklace hung.

"Do you like it?"

"I love it," I said, taking it in my hand and lifting it to eye level. "Especially its symbolism of unity and of hope."

With his afternoon class looming, he arranged for a cab to take me back to the Olive Tree, saying that he would call after class with details for tonight's first date, promising he would make it special.

Back at the hotel, amazed at how manifestly my steps had been guided by God's hand, I headed for the lobby's olive tree to sit and give thanks. The hotel was quiet, its busloads of pilgrims still out on their itineraries.

"Can this be real?" I whispered.

My whisper must have been audible, as I was startled by a voice from behind.

"Yes dear, it is very real."

I turned to see an elderly woman, I would guess in her 80s, who had walked up behind me. Seeing the confused look on my face, she apologized.

"Oh, I'm sorry to interrupt your meditation, dear."

She turned to walk away, saying, "I hope you feel better soon."

"Feel better?" I asked.

She stopped and said, "Again, I'm sorry. I just assumed that you, like me, took today off from touring because you didn't feel well. I'm feeling much better now. I just needed to get out of my room and walk around a bit."

"Oh, I see. It's no problem. I'm glad you feel better."

For some inexplicable reason I wanted to talk to this woman whom I had never met. Having been surprised by every turn of providence in this day of wonders, I intended not to deny myself any providential encounter which might hold yet more wonders.

"What did you mean?" I asked.

"What do you mean what did I mean?" she replied, grinning.

"When you said that it is very real. What did you mean?"

"I just meant actually being in the Holy Land, in Jerusalem. Jerusalem has been in my heart since I was a child, my mother and father reading to me the stories of the Bible and of Jesus. For the last week I've been reliving childhood memories, making them real again. I wish my parents could be here with me, but they are long passed. I'm here with my son and daughter-in-law. My husband passed away last year, and my children invited me to join them in the Holy Land. It's magical here, don't you think? It's as if I feel my parents, the Holy Land connecting the generations."

"Very magical," I said, motioning for her to sit. "I know what you mean. I had the opportunity to be here with my mother and father, thirty-five years ago, when I was in college. I haven't been back since, so you can imagine how I, too, feel them with me, especially my dad, who passed away three years ago. Only this morning I was remembering dad taking me to Solomon's Quarries, not far from here. In that cave he prayed for God to use me as a living stone in his kingdom."

"And has God used you?"

"Well, I want to think so. I don't think, though, that God is finished using me. Not yet."

"You sound so joyful, dear. Even blissful. Something has

happened to you today, hasn't it?"

I was talking to this stranger as I might a long-time friend, refreshed by her companionship, as if she were a stand-in for my mother, who would be about the same age.

"Blissful? More than I could ever have possibly imagined. I said 'Yes' to a wedding proposal barely an hour ago, and we're about to go on our first date tonight."

Laughing with delight, she said, "Oh, my! Congratulations! You mean your first date as an engaged couple?"

"No, I mean our very first date, ever."

Wearing a "You're-kidding-me" face, likely wondering if I had been infected with Jerusalem Fever, she asked, "Isn't that a bit backwards?"

"It is, and exactly the response I would have expected from my mom!"

We spent the next thirty minutes by the olive tree, talking. If David was playing a tune on his harp by that olive tree, this woman was my listening companion.

My cell rang, and I saw it was David. Taking it as her cue to leave, she blew me a kiss for good luck and headed back toward the elevators.

Strange, I realized, that I never asked for her name, nor she mine. This nameless woman had been Sent as *Malaki*, my Angel/Muse.

"Stella," David said as I waved goodbye to my olive tree companion, "I've arranged transportation for you tonight at 7:40. The driver will take you to the King David Hotel. I'll be waiting for you in the lobby, and we'll dine overlooking the floodlit walls of the Old City at La Regence."

Unlike the loud buffet awaiting weary and hungry pilgrims, our first date would be in quiet elegance, enjoying delicious prime rib with an exquisite bottle of Cabernet. Around the time we poured the second glass, our conversation shifted from reminiscing about Memphis in 1988 – he wanting to know every detail of my six visions – to the six tablets of Cave 53.

When our server presented our options for dessert, David suggested that we not order, but instead walk across the street to have dessert at the Jerusalem YMCA.

Emerging from the King David Hotel, the YMCA's front façade was in full view. David explained that it had opened in 1933, designed by Arthur Loomis Harmon, the architect of the Empire State Building, which opened the same year.

"Clearly, Mr. Harmon was a very busy man," I marveled.

"The real reason I chose the King David for dinner tonight is so I could show you this building, my favorite in all of Jerusalem, and one of great importance in the history of the Dead Sea Scrolls. In its architecture, I think, you'll find many sermons."

"Really? And what is its message?"

"The Jerusalem Y's sermon in stone proclaims hope for unity. It houses the Three Arches Hotel. Do you see them there, the three arches?"

"I do," I replied, admiring the arches over the entrance.

"The YMCA focuses on the human triangle of spirit, mind, and body. That theme is paramount to the main areas of the building. The central tower, rising high for the ringing of its carillon bells, represents the spirit. The ornate auditorium represents the mind. And last, the gymnasium and pool focus on the physical body. Spirit, mind and body, all in unity."

"I think I was actually here in 1987, in the auditorium to see a group of singers and dancers performing, representing all the cultures living in the land."

"Yes, I've heard them also. Sad to say, they no longer have

that performance here, but I can think of no better place to sound forth a message of unity. Symbolized here are the three monotheistic faiths this land has known. The twelve cypress trees in the garden represent the twelve tribes of Israel, the twelve disciples of Jesus, and the twelve followers of Mohammed. There are three inscriptions on the façade: 'The Lord our God, the Lord is one,' in Hebrew; 'I am the Way,' in Aramaic, and 'There is no God but God,' in Arabic."

"How wonderful! It's like a temple."

"I'm glad you think so," he said, adding, "this building, by the way, is the only building ever nominated for a Nobel Peace Prize, in 1993."

Enjoying our dessert in the café, David having carrot cake while I enjoyed a scrumptious piece of cherry pie, he said, "So you recall being here in 1987?"

"I do. I recall cramming into the crowded buses at the Seven Arches Hotel on the Mount of Olives. There were many hundreds here that night, a packed house."

"And every night. Those dancers were amazing, weren't they? Blending the music of all the cultures of the Land fostered a hope, however elusive, of unity."

"I remember feeling exactly that as we watched the performance. And here now we are, you and I, instruments of God's plan. I believe that our quest to discover the seventh tablet holds forth the hope of peace."

"I believe that also, and can't wait to get our search underway."

Since we hadn't yet talked about a date for the wedding, his comment seemed the right time to bring it up.

"David, do you mind if I suggest a date for our wedding?"

"Of course. As soon as possible, I hope."

"I want to be married on March 9."

His face couldn't hide his disappointment.

"Not sooner? Not Valentine's Day, next month? Or even Groundhog Day, two weeks sooner?"

"No," I laughed. "Not Groundhog Day, for sure. No, I want the numbers Three-Nine in my anniversary date. You may think my reasoning silly, but I think of your love for baseball, the Three-Nine combination of three outs through nine innings that you emphasized on the day I met you. It's always stayed with me."

"You were listening!"

"I was, yes. At the end of your last lecture on Psalm 89, you won't recall, but you were rushed, trying to dismiss class early to get off to New Orleans."

"I recall it well, our stay on Bourbon Street."

"I'm sure you recall the trip to New Orleans, but what I meant is you won't recall how disappointed I was that your trip got in the way of what had become our post-class ritual, my walking with you back to your office."

"I think we both knew what those walks were. We were flirting, though neither of us would say it outright."

"I had planned that walk to be special. I was going to tell you about my dreams. I had experienced the fifth dream the day before, dancing with David in a way that brought us almost to intimacy. I knew what I really wanted was to pursue intimacy with you. I didn't care if you might have thought my story to be only a crazy student's crush on a professor. I wanted you, and had it not been for New Orleans, I think I would have told you."

"But you didn't tell me upon my return?"

"No, after my sixth dream, that night, I knew I could not."

"Gethsemane?"

"Yes. As I told you, I knew then that I couldn't marry Jakob. What I also knew, is that I could not pursue my feelings for you, or anyone else, ever."

"I still don't get the connection. How does all this lead you to select March 9?"

"Your lecture that day. This afternoon I re-read my journal entry on your sixth lecture. What I saw makes me want to be married on March 9."

"I can't wait to hear what I said."

"Concluding your lecture, you mentioned NASA's 'Return to Flight' with the Space Shuttle Discovery, which launched the following week. It was the first flight in nearly three years after the Challenger disaster."

"I remember."

"I wrote in my notes that you said the Challenger had exploded at 11:39 a.m."

"Already planning for our marriage to be a disaster?" he laughed.

"No, there's more. You used the 'Return to Flight' theme to challenge us to accept risk, to rise to our potential. You were speaking to me. You see, I had been ready, before your Hebrew Poetry class, to jettison all my plans for ministry."

"Okay, but that still doesn't tell me. Why March 9?"

"Well, after that class, the Space Shuttle Discovery became the symbol of my Return to Flight. I followed every launch, its exploits providing a tracking mechanism for my own ministry. I want it now, also, to be a symbol of my Return to Flight with you, which makes our wedding on Three-Nine perfect."

"I still don't understand the Three-Nine connection. Because it exploded at 11:39?"

"No," I laughed, "much more than that. Discovery, the third of the five shuttles built, set a record in how many times it was launched and returned to earth. Can you guess how many times."

"I'll guess, thirty-nine?"

"Yes, thirty-nine times. Now, guess on what day the

Discovery's adventures ended?"

"You're kidding! March 9?"

"Yes again. It landed for the last time on March 9, 2011, having served since 1984, an operational life of twenty-seven years."

"Three times nine!" we said, simultaneously.

"There's more. If you Google Discovery's total time in space, the answer is precise. Discovery was in space for 365 days, 22 hours and . . . wait for it . . . 39 minutes, and 33 seconds."

"Stop, stop, okay! No more convincing! March 9 it is, though I'm not sure I can wait fifty days!"

Walking out of the Y from under the triple arches, he turned around to admire the building again, pointing out the message written in three languages: Hebrew, English and Arabic: "Here is a place whose atmosphere is peace, where political and religious jealousies can be forgotten, and international unity be fostered and developed."

"That's beautiful, David, and we should adopt it as our core mission in finding the seventh tablet and making its message known the world."

He hailed a cab and got in with me, a pleasant surprise, since he lived in the opposite direction from the Olive Tree Hotel, near the Haas Promenade. He said he had never heard David play his harp, so he wanted to sit by that olive tree in the lobby with me.

With nightcaps ordered from the Oasis Bar, we talked and laughed for another hour. A few minutes before midnight, he took my hand to say, "Stella, a year ago today I made a remarkable discovery, but Cave 53 pales in significance to what I have re-discovered on this day, my love for you, and the destiny awaiting us."

"May I ask you to do something for our wedding?" I said.

"Anything."

"Let's both write our own vows."

"Okay," he said, hesitantly.

"With twenty-seven syllables."

"I don't know," he laughed. "I'm not sure I could say all I would want to say in twenty-seven syllables."

"Sorry, but it must be twenty-seven. I think I fell in love with you immediately, first class, a baseball fanatic pointing out the game's divine symmetry of three outs nine times. No game is complete without twenty-seven outs. And don't you recall Lennon's #9 Dream? His refrain of three lines, each line with nine syllables, for a total of twenty-seven?

"Of course, I do. I'm surprised you remember that bit of Lennon trivia."

"Oh, I remember. In your second lecture you told of Lennon's mysterious love for the number nine. My second dream awakening came that night at, believe it or not, 3:39."

"Well then, let's," he paused, eyes sparkling, "Let it be."

Chapter 16

Maranatha Assembly of the Blessed Hope

FAYETTEVILLE, ARKANSAS

SUNDAY, JANUARY 30, 2022

The sixth tablet prophecy made it clear that the seventh tablet could not be found without my having one to call 'ishi (my husband), so David and I agreed to delay beginning our quest until after the wedding. He had been disappointed, I knew, with my desire to set March 9 as our wedding date. Hungry to begin the quest, I'm sure he would have preferred to elope that day and put a spade in my hand the next morning.

If fifty days had been a long wait for him, it was barely enough time for me. The first eight days, prior to my return home to Arkansas, were spent in Israel, a head-spinning blend of a future bride's frazzled excitement in making wedding preparations with the relaxed wonder of a tourist privileged to have the famed archaeologist David Aaronson as a personal guide.

As the time neared for my departure from Tel Aviv, dread

set in as I pondered the difficult task before me, telling my congregation that my temporary leave of absence would now be a full resignation, a new and unfolding adventure forcing retirement from the congregation I had grown to love so deeply as their spiritual shepherd through twenty-seven years.

I had, of course, immediately called my mother from Jerusalem with the news of my engagement, but insisted she promise not to share it with anyone. I knew she would honor my wish, so that I could be present to lead the intensely emotional moment of my resignation at my beloved Maranatha Assembly.

The first Sunday after my return to Fayetteville fell on January 30. I decided, perhaps unwisely, to share the news early in the service, after our opening hymn. Our Minister of Music had chosen to welcome me home with our theme song, "How Great Thou Art," tears welling in my eyes as we sang:

> O Lord my God! When I in awesome wonder,
> Consider all the worlds thy hands have made,
> I see the stars, I hear the rolling thunder,
> Thy power throughout the universe displayed.
> Then sings my soul, my Savior God to thee;
> How great thou art, how great thou art!
> Then sings my soul, my Savior God to thee;
> How great thou art, how great thou art!

As my congregation always does when we sing that hymn, coming to the words, "I see the stars," their eyes connect with mine to offer gestures of acknowledgement of my Call to ministry, rejoicing in my vision of King David naming me his Star of the Sea.

Singing that line, some point at me, some raise their arms in praise to God, others reach out to me with palms up, as if to receive a blessing. Through twenty-seven years of my leadership and teaching, Maranatha Assembly has come to see me as their pastoral star, sent to guide them safely home through life's perils.

This odd custom during the singing of "How Great Thou Art" caught on many years ago. I was at first reluctant to allow it to continue, fearing visitors would be made uncomfortable, thinking they had stumbled into a cult. I was prepared one Sunday to instruct the congregation to cease and desist from the practice, but on that very morning, God told me to shut up.

A line of thunderstorms was making its way across northwest Arkansas that morning. Just as the congregation sang, "I see the stars, I hear the rolling thunder," a blinding lightning flash was followed by a boom that shook the building so hard I felt my legs tremble. I took that rolling thunder as a divine sign to abort my plan to chide the congregation, as if God had given divine assent to our little ritual.

I announced that "How Great Thou Art" would be our theme song. Should visitors be present, I would use the spectacle as an opportunity to explain that the congregation was not looking to me as a cult leader, but celebrating how God had, in a series of six amazing dreams, renewed my once-fading sense of a Call to ministry. The congregation was not worshiping me, but the God who Called me.

Knowing that my resignation would be utterly unexpected, I sat the assembly down after the hymn and veered away from the usual order of worship. I suppose I should have waited to the end to tell them, after the sermon. There would be no sermon this day, however. What followed was a love-saturated sacred moment between a departing pastor and her congregation, extending through the entire hour and beyond.

Tears flowed freely among the 339 worshippers who had

come that day to welcome me home from Israel, excited to hear news of my search for the seventh tablet. Looking over their faces from the pulpit, tears welled in my eyes as I thought how incredibly blessed I had been to share a twenty-seven year marriage with my Maranatha Assembly.

For Maranatha Assembly, the idea of marriage as a description of our pastor-congregation relationship was more than a mere analogy. Many times they had heard me describe my Gethsemane encounter with Jesus in my sixth dream, how Jesus' words had led me to abandon my plans to marry Jakob in order to give myself totally to his church.

For that reason, I had imagined they would hear the news of my engagement to David Aaronson as an angry spouse might hear their mate's confession of adultery, as if I were saying, "I don't love you anymore. I'm leaving you to live with another."

I was wrong. They listened intently, their joy increasing as I described how I had received my seventh vision on my first night in Jerusalem, a dream of being with King David in his dying moments. I didn't tell them everything, of course, withholding that I now knew my true identity to be Abishag. For now, that must remain unsaid, known only to David. Even my congregation would hear that claim with a high dose of incredulity, and who could blame them?

They marveled, though, as I described how God had providentially led my steps to David Aaronson at the very moment God had prepared him for my visit by giving him a simultaneous dream. As I described our meeting at Hebrew University, how at first sight I re-discovered my love for my former professor, any tears of disappointment for the loss of their pastor now became tears of joy for my gain of a husband.

Laughter erupted as I described David's proposal, how on his knees he professed his having loved me, in secret and in absentia, for thirty-three years. I proudly showed them the Star of David necklace I was wearing, pointing out the cross rising in the middle, the gift he had given me in lieu of a ring.

Sensing the service was nearing conclusion, I having answered all questions, one of our older men, Ray Fortson, a usually outspoken individual who had surprisingly not spoken through the entire service, stood and asked if he could offer the benediction. I feared he might ruin the mood of the service, his silence having suggested to me that he might be upset and angry.

Reluctantly, I called him to the front. I handed him a microphone and stepped aside, hoping for the best. A quick glance at some of my church leaders told me that they, also, were worried he might say something inappropriate.

What he did next, though, was exquisite, landing the congregation right where they needed to be to return to their homes confident of the church's future, and of mine. Reaching into his jacket, he produced a cigar, breaking the congregation up as his benediction became a George Peppard imitation of *The A-Team's* Hannibal Smith.

"I love it," he said, imitating Peppard's famous line with just the right smile, "when a plan comes together."

It was the perfect benediction.

As my congregation flocked around me after the service, several expressed a desire to come to Israel for the wedding. I had anticipated this, and decided to disallow it. While offering appreciation for their love and support, I told them our wedding would be private, that I had promised our venue that we would restrict the size of the wedding party to less than ten people in order to stay within their guidelines for what we call at Maranatha Assembly, "walk-in" weddings.

It was our willingness to restrict ourselves to a few people that allowed us to book *Kochav Hayam* on such short notice.

It helped, of course, that March 9 would fall mid-week, a Wednesday. Assuring them that we would have only two ministers and two witnesses in addition to the bride and groom, a total of six, they confirmed a 2:00 reservation. We must, however, have all our photographs taken and be entirely off the premises by 4:00.

Assuring them that it would be no problem for us to vacate the premises by 4:00, our venue was set. Our wedding would be on the beach, the Mediterranean's westward expanse filling our view as a symbol of promise.

Chapter 17

The Gai Beach Hotel on the Sea of Galilee

TIBERIAS, ISRAEL

WEDNESDAY, MARCH 3, 2022

Sleet was falling in Tel Aviv on the day I returned to Israel, Tuesday, February 22. David met me with an armful of roses when I emerged from the baggage area.

"Three bundles of nine roses," he laughed, releasing me from our embrace. "That's twenty-seven roses, one for each syllable of our wedding vows."

"How beautiful!" I said after we kissed, thankful the long flight was over and filled with joy in knowing I was now, truly, home. At that moment, it didn't matter how long our search would take. We were together. It was enough.

Shaking ice slivers out of my hair as we settled into our taxi, shivering from the cold, I said, "Thank God the wedding is still two weeks away!"

"*Ken!*" he laughed, "Yes! Today is no beach day. Fear not. In two weeks the weather will be splendid, no doubt. Were you able to finalize arrangements for your mom's flight?"

"I was. She and Hal will arrive next Tuesday afternoon, so I'll have to do this airport thing again. Hopefully in better weather!"

"Well, good news, you won't have to navigate it alone," I was happy to hear him say. "I've arranged to be away from the university beginning next Monday and through our wedding. I look forward to seeing your mom again, having only met her at your graduation."

"Forever ago! Mom was the exact age then that I am now, fifty-five. I thought she was ancient back then."

Now eighty-eight years old but still very active with no mobility issues, I chose mom to be my Maid of Honor. She would arrive in Tel Aviv on March 1, accompanied by her pastor from Siloam Springs, Rev. Harold "Hal" Chandler.

At seventy-two years old and a widower for three years, matching my mom's three-year widowhood, he and mom had been seeing each other for at least a year. I had known Hal for a dozen years, since he became mom's pastor in 2010. His wife, Karen, had become a good friend before we lost her in a tragic accident returning to Siloam from a shopping trip to Fayetteville.

My respect for Hal as a gentleman and a scholar made it easy for me to accept what was clearly growing into more than a casual relationship with mom. They were dating, I suspected, though mom had never described their relationship to me in that way.

My plan to arrange for their being at my wedding together worked perfectly. Not only was I honored to have Hal co-officiate the ceremony with David's rabbi, I was also relieved to know mom would have a traveling companion, not wishing for her to travel alone halfway around the globe.

It had been adorable how mom tried to hide her thrill

when I told her I had asked Hal to co-officiate.

"What did he say?" she asked.

"He said, 'No thanks, I'm afraid to travel on planes.'"

Her 'is-that-so?' reaction told me Hal had already called her with the news, I suspect as soon as he got in his car after we left Petra, a restaurant in downtown Fayetteville where I had invited him to lunch. Petra's Mediterranean fare, baklava being the perfect conclusion to delicious hummus and a pita pocket filled with falafels, was the perfect setting to ask him if he would accompany mom to Israel and co-officiate my wedding.

It wasn't difficult to coerce mom into admitting she already knew about my lunch with Hal. After only the slightest resistance, she told me what I already knew, that Hal was elated. Having never been to the Holy Land, the thought of walking where Jesus walked with mom, and meeting a famous archaeologist, amplified his excitement.

My home for the full week before mom's arrival would be The Three Arches Hotel at the Jerusalem YMCA. While David's classes kept him at the university each day, each evening was ours to be together and to get to know each other, David arranging dinner each night at a different Jerusalem restaurant.

The privacy of my daytime hours gave me time to focus on writing my story. At midday, typically, I would break and go out for a walk, heading to the shops and cafes of the Mamilla Mall, a pedestrian promenade near the Jaffa Gate, sometimes venturing on through the gate to explore the Old City.

Eager each evening to meet David for dinner, our conversations always began with Memphis remembrances. Having allowed him to take home and read my 1988 journal entries on his lectures, David arrived each evening armed with humorous observations about what I had chosen to record.

Eventually our conversations would turn from past to future, conjecturing on how to start our search for the seventh tablet and imagining what its discovery might mean.

The week flew by, our privacy ending when we met mom and Hal at the airport on Tuesday. We were all thrilled that David had been able to arrange to be away from the university, allowing him to lead us on a pre-wedding whirlwind tour of Israel, the trip giving mom an opportunity to know better her future son-in-law.

Mom and I would be roommates on the trip, as were David and Hal during our first three nights at the Gai Beach Hotel in Tiberias, on the Sea of Galilee. Before my return to Arkansas, David had brought me to this lovely hotel for two nights, so I was looking especially forward to sharing its amazing views of the Galilee with mom. Between the hotel and the sea is a spacious promenade area with an enormous pool, its inviting waters always bright blue.

A long fence barrier at the edge of the hotel's property runs along the Sea of Galilee, ten or twelve feet above the sea's edge, the walkway populating each morning with tourists readying their cameras to capture photos of sunrise over the Galilee. Others, like me, choose to ignore their cameras, seeking to forge impactful and lasting memories by silently drinking in the beauty the Galilean sunrise through meditation, wonder, and gratitude.

David's itinerary for our first day included important sites around the sea, including Capernaum, Jesus' center of operation during his Galilean ministry, and the recently excavated Magdala, an important ancient city on the Galilee only three miles north of Tiberias and likely the hometown of Mary Magdalene. By the end of the day we had driven completely around the sea, visiting places important to both Jewish and Christian history, breaking only for a meal of St.

Peter's fish (though I, not much of a fish person, opted for pizza).

My favorite site in the Galilee was the following day, traveling an hour north to the Tel Dan Nature Reserve. We began the morning on a warm and sunlit day, walking the paths alongside one of the headwaters of the Jordan River, its clear waters rushing past us in a roar as the snow melting on Mt. Hermon made its way to the Galilee, the lowest freshwater lake on earth.

David hadn't brought me this far north in our January trip, nor had we visited in 1987, so this was a first for me, and I found it stunning. We emerged from the nature trail at the entrance to Tel Dan, the ancient city where Israel's King Jeroboam built one of his two altars in an act of apostasy from Jerusalem. I marveled at the platform he built to erect his golden calves, an act rendering Jeroboam the most odious of all the kings of Israel.

I can't say why it impacted me so, standing at the altar and staring at the sin of Jeroboam ben Nebat, the king who turned his back on Jerusalem. I vowed to myself as I stood at that place of division that I would never turn my back on my Calling, which I knew now to be the discovery the seventh tablet.

Also at Tel Dan, David showed us the spot where in 1993 Avraham Biran's excavation uncovered the Tel Dan Stele, a Canaanite inscription of thirteen lines from the 9th century BCE, erected by the Syrian king, Hazael, claiming victory over King Ahaziah of the *Beit David* (the House of David). Our archaeologist guide explained the importance of the discovery, the only archaeological evidence outside the Bible of King David and his dynasty. Well, that is, until his own Cave 53 discovery on January 18, 2021.

When we returned to the Gai Beach, David wanted to relax on the balcony outside the lounge with a glass of wine, saying he needed to make some calls to the university. Seeing an opportunity to explore, I told him I would join him later, but that first I wanted to walk five minutes into Tiberias to pick up a few items at a pharmacy I had seen as we drove past. David thought that was a splendid idea and encouraged me to walk also on the promenade behind the high-rise hotels bordering the sea, a tourist area filled with cafes, ice cream and souvenir shops. Crowded with tourists on a beautiful afternoon, I walked along the boardwalk for several blocks, smiling at the cafe greeters positioned outside their entrances to urge tourists to enter their establishments. After the long covid shutdown, tourists were beginning to return in larger numbers, and these shops needed customers.

On the way back to the hotel, just as I was approaching the end of the promenade, I stopped cold as I saw a familiar looking man in the distance, smoking a cigarette as he leaned against the railing and gazed across the sea toward the Golan Heights. No happy tourist, I studied his angry profile for a full minute. When he jerked his stare to look at me, as if he had felt me observing him, he dropped his cigarette, a you-caught-me expression spreading over his face.

It was Jakob Rothman. Could it be a coincidence that my former fiancé was here, in the Galilee, less than a week before my wedding?

"Jakob?" I said, approaching closer.

"Stella," he replied, clearly shaken.

"What in the world are you doing here?"

"To see you, of course. I was hoping to surprise you tomorrow, on your fifty-sixth birthday. Surely you haven't forgotten our pledge to spend our fifty-sixth birthdays together. The Magic of the Cave at Fifty-Six, remember?"

I knew exactly what he was talking about but was too stunned to answer.

Pointing up to the hotel rising above us, he said, "I wasn't stalking you. I'm staying here, at the Caesar Tiberias."

"How did you know I would be here?"

"Well, it's not like you or your church has kept it a secret. Your church's website announced your retirement and your move to Israel to marry your former professor. Your mom's Facebook posts pretty much detailed your itinerary. Great photos, by the way. I especially enjoyed last night's post, you and your mom overlooking the sea. She looks very well, as do you."

My silence conveying to him that I didn't know what to think of his surprise appearance, he continued.

"Stella, what happened to marrying your church? You called off our engagement to marry your church. You've given up your vow for David Aaronson?"

"God is leading me in a different direction now. You wouldn't understand."

"I wouldn't understand? Truth is, it's you who need to understand something. After you hear what I have to say, I think you'll go back to your church and call the wedding off."

"Why are you doing this?"

"I didn't come here to proclaim my love for you. Although," he paused before going on with something between a grin and a grimace, "I suppose two failed marriages proves that, for me, no one could measure up to you. Truth is, I've come to protect you."

"Protect me?"

"Yes, and it won't be easy for me. To protect you, I have to confess. After you hear what I have to say, you'll see David Aaronson for the fraud that he is."

My disbelieving laughter was contrary to the emotions I felt surging.

"David? A fraud?"

"I'm going to assume he hasn't told you that he's known about your dreams all along, since the very beginning, since 1988."

I could offer no reply, though my stunned expression told him what he needed to know.

"No, I didn't think he had."

One of the greeters interrupted with an appeal for us to have a seat and look at the menu. Jakob looked at me and gestured, wondering if I might sit and talk.

"No," I said to Jakob sternly, then turned to offer a second, and more pleasant, "No, thank-you," to the greeter.

We moved away from the restaurant's front to stand further down the sea wall's railing.

"And you couldn't have just called to tell me this? You had to come to Israel?"

"Only last week I saw you were marrying Aaronson. I called your church and was told you were already in Israel. Believe me, I have no desire to come here, but what I have to tell you must be face-to-face. What other way is there to ask for your forgiveness?"

"Forgiveness? Jakob, you swore you wouldn't tell anyone. I trusted you."

"I know, and I failed you. But when you broke off our engagement, after your sixth vision..."

He stopped to choose his words carefully.

"I have no excuse for betraying you. I was angry and, frankly, I blamed Dr. Aaronson, even then. During that semester I watched as that man changed everything about you. I could feel you slipping away from me, one class at a time. When you told me our engagement was over, I was desperate. Going to Aaronson was my Hail Mary, hoping he would say something to you that might end your fascination with him."

"How much did you tell him?"

"Everything. I told him everything you had told me. All six dreams. And, oh my, was he ever eager to hear it all, pressing me for more details, even taking notes."

"Taking notes?"

"The man couldn't write fast enough."

"So," I started.

"So," he interrupted, "I suspect, and, honestly, I can't imagine you haven't suspected, that somehow he engineered his discovery to align with your dreams. You remember how he fantasized about sharing the magic of David Copperfield, born on the same day. He talked about it in class all the time, the magician's misdirection, wishing he could make something appear to be real, that isn't real. I think he has achieved his dream."

If Jakob was right, if I had ever suspected fraud, it was buried deep in my sub-conscious. At this moment my head, filling with questions, was ready to explode. Had my thrill at thinking my visions confirmed by the Cave 53 discovery kept me from asking the right questions? Had David really engineered all this? For what purpose? If the discovery was fraudulent, why weren't other scholars, or the Israel Antiquity Authority, questioning the discovery?

Despite my own questions, my defense mechanism kicked in.

"How do I know you're not the one who is lying?"

"Well, that's pretty simple," he laughed at the obvious. "Ask him."

"I will. I'm sorry for what my dreams did to us, but you need to know that I was falling in love with him then, and I love him now. If what you're saying is true, that he knew about my dreams, I believe he will have an explanation."

He looked at me silently for a long moment, slowly shaking

his head and saying with disgust, "I'm sure he will."

"So, was this your play? To meet me here, on the boardwalk?"

"No, but it's better this way. As I told you, I was hoping for something more public, to wish you a happy fifty-sixth birthday at breakfast tomorrow. I imagined it would have been my birthday present to you, saving you from making a huge mistake. After all, the Magic of the Cave at Fifty-six is too important to ignore."

"I remember. We celebrated your mom's fifty-sixth birthday together at Blanchard Springs."

Jakob's mother had been raised in Fifty-six, Arkansas, one of the strangest named towns in America, home to Blanchard Springs Caverns, a breathtaking example of a living cave system with stalactites, stalagmites, columns, and flowstones that are ever-changing, growing along the walls of the cavern. Many locals, as well as others throughout Arkansas and beyond, visit the caverns on their fifty-sixth birthday, searching for the Magic of the Cave at Fifty-six.

"We did, and we told each other that we would celebrate our fifty-sixth birthdays in Fifty-six, Arkansas, in the caverns. My birthday was last month, and I was there, missing you, dreaming you would come up and tap me on the shoulder. I wish we could be there tomorrow for your birthday."

When I didn't respond, he said, "Well, as I said, it's better this way. Tomorrow would have been an embarrassment for you. I thought I wanted that but, now that I've spoken with you, not so much. I can go home now. I'm truly sorry that I betrayed your trust."

I froze as he leaned toward me and kissed me on the cheek.

"I hope you can find a magical cave around here, Stella, for your birthday. I wish you a Happy Birthday, and a happy life, I truly do. I just hope it will be a life without David Aaronson."

As Jakob walked up the incline to the Caesar Hotel's entrance, my mind was busy pondering how to confront David. Jakob's words, "I'm going to assume David hasn't told you that he knew about your dreams from the beginning," were incessantly playing in my mind.

No, David hadn't told me he'd known about my dreams for thirty-three years, plenty of time to plan a Copperfield illusion.

"Jakob was right," I thought as I stepped through the front doors of the Gai Beach. "At the very least, David has lied to me."

I found him in a quiet corner of the lobby, having moved inside from the balcony where I had left him earlier, the air becoming cooler.

He seemed in a jovial mood, talking on the phone, but his happy expression instantly vanished when he saw my face. Excusing himself from his conversation, he rose to greet me.

"What's wrong?"

"I just ran into Jakob."

"Jakob? Rothman?"

His face showed none the shock I had expected it would, the look one gets in the moment they know that their lying has been discovered. This was quite the opposite. His expression seemed one of . . . excitement. How could that be? Is he this expert at lying?

"Yes, Jakob Rothman. He came all the way to Israel to warn me against marrying you, calling you a fraud. Is it true? Have you known all along about my six dreams? Did Jakob tell you in 1988?"

Not breaking eye contact with me, David said, "It is true."

"Then, is everything fake? Your love for me? The tablets? Was your discovery an illusion?"

"An illusion? Goodness no. It's all very real. My love for you is real, as is the Cave 53 discovery."

I was confused and angry. He knew he was caught, but I still registered excitement in his voice and on his face.

"Why, then, didn't you tell me you knew?"

"Because," he hesitated, smiling, "I was instructed not to tell you, until . . ."

"Instructed?"

"Please, let me finish. I'm excited because I've known this day was coming. Now, at long last, I can tell you the story I've been waiting all these years to tell you."

My anger was fading, not so much because of his words, but by his calmness, devoid of any sense of shame.

"Let's hear it, then," I said, trying my best to maintain an unbelieving expression, though in my heart I felt an odd enthusiasm matching what I was seeing in him.

"Stella, I told you the truth about my dream on the night before you arrived at my office. It wasn't, however, the entire truth. Now, at last, I can tell you about my first vision."

"Your first vision?"

He didn't answer, looking up to see several couples moving to the inside lobby from the balcony's chill.

"Yes, my first vision," he said, looking back to me. "I would invite you to my room, but Hal is there. Do you mind bundling up a bit to go outside and stand by the sea? Perhaps the Galilee will give up another of its miracles."

We stopped at the bar long enough for him to order two cups of hot chocolate, and when they were steaming in our hands, we walked past the pool to stand at the railing overlooking the Galilee. The glow on the mountains of the Golan Heights in the distance elegantly framed the scene, the colorful lights of several party boats dotting the surface of the lake.

Intent on not speaking first, I cupped my hot chocolate in silence.

"You see, when Jakob came to me to share your dreams, crushed by your breakup, it was confirmed to me, beyond any shadow of a doubt, that we were destined to be together."

"How can that be?"

"Because of my first vision."

"How many have you had?"

"Two."

"When was your first dream?"

"The night before we met."

"In 1988!" I blurted.

"Yes, in the early morning hours of September 6 I had my first vision. Unlike your dreams, which progressed through David's life, my two visions were of the exact same scene, King David's deathbed. All was the same, with Bathsheba, Solomon, Shemaiah and . . ."

"Me?"

"Yes, and you, Abishag."

He sipped his chocolate, then continued. "In my first vision, after David died, I saw his spirit lift from his body. It was eerie, to say the least, flipping from horizontal to vertical and floating directly toward me, to the place where I observed his dying in both of my visions. He greeted me with *Shalom Aleichem* and spoke."

"What did he say?"

"He said, 'David, my son, when you discover my song and my bones in the wilderness, my spirit will fill you. Soon, you will meet my Abishag, my *Kochav Hayam*. We were never able to consummate our love.' He looked back at the weeping Abishag, who was holding the dead king's hand tightly. Then, his voice grew stern. 'Tomorrow, you will meet the one in whom her spirit dwells, and you will love her. But you must have patience, for she will not yet know who she is. You must wait, even if for many years, until she learns for herself. Tell her of this vision only on the day she accuses you of betrayal.'"

"So," I interrupted, "you didn't tell me, because King David commanded you not to tell me?"

"Yes, until the day you accuse me of betrayal."

"And when you saw me the next day, on the front row in class, you knew it was me?"

"In the morning I had thought it only a vivid dream, but when you spoke your name and I recognized it as Star of the Sea, the equivalent of *Kochav Hayam* in Hebrew, I knew that the vision had been real, and that in you was the spirit of Abishag."

"I remember it well," I said, reaching to hold his hand, "how when you first heard my name, I sensed familiarity in your eyes, as if you were saying, 'Ah, there you are.'"

"Do you recall the reports that, when we first looked into the Cave 53 crevice on January 18 and saw the bones, I fainted?"

"Yes. You said that your students thought you had covid, quickly putting their masks on before you came to."

"What really happened, but what I couldn't have said to the media, is that when I saw the bones, I saw King David's spirit rising, just as he had in my vision thirty-three years earlier. That's when I passed out. I knew then that the time had come for God's final plan to play out. You can't imagine how difficult it was for me to wait, not to call you. To trust God's providential timing is so difficult, but I waited patiently for a full year, for my second vision to signal that you were on your way to me."

Hearing David, knowing in my heart that he was being truthful, my spirit calmed. Silently I turned to admire the darkening Sea of Galilee, marveling at God's providence which had directed our steps to this moment.

"Stella," he said, putting his arm around my shoulders and drawing me close, "Though I was falling in love with you in Memphis, I've been obedient to my first vision, waiting for the day when you would accuse me of fraud. God is sovereign, his timing perfect."

At that moment, one of the boats of partiers came close enough that its loud music reached us. "Listen to the music, David. How right you are! God's timing is absolutely perfect."

"What am I listening to?"

"Chicago, one of their greatest, 'I Don't Want to Live without Your Love.' Do you know what's special about that song?"

"I don't."

"It was released in our 1988. I still have the album. I played it all the time back then, background music for my studying. Before I met you, I heard those words thinking of Jakob but, as our Hebrew Poetry class went on, I realized I was thinking of you as I sang the words. I was falling in love, but also ashamed at how inappropriate it seemed."

"I understand. Truth be told, I would be utterly ashamed even now to tell you the thoughts I was having back then."

He listened for a moment and said, "Behold, God's engineering. Your song, accompanied by the gentle sound of the nighttime waves on the Sea of Galilee."

Filled now with a peace I knew Jakob's accusations could never take away from me, I said, "Let's just listen."

"No," he said, "let's dance."

And so we did. We slow-danced by the Sea of Galilee to the sounds of Chicago.

Walking back to the lobby when the song ended, it being time to meet mom and Hal for dinner, I was consumed with desire.

Never had I longed more to break my vow of celibacy-until-marriage than in this moment, wishing to hurry the path of God's sovereign design.

Sensing my yearning, he whispered, "A bit more patience, Abby. The time is near."

It didn't startle me at all that he had called me Abby. I knew now that this David who had spoken my name was both other and the same as my former professor and future husband.

Chapter 18

The Wedding at *Kochav Hayam*

NEAR CAESAREA ON THE MEDITERRANEAN COAST

WEDNESDAY, MARCH 9, 2022

I hadn't at all been disappointed the following morning – Friday, March 4 – that even my mom didn't think to wish me a Happy 56th Birthday. After all, it was to be a busy day of transition, the four of us packing up to leave the Gai Beach and set out for Jerusalem.

When mom and I arrived for breakfast, we saw Hal seated alone at a table next to the promenade with a gorgeous morning view of the sea. We joined him and ordered coffee, deciding to wait for David before we hit the buffet. Hal said David had left the room very early in the morning to go for a walk. When he joined us some ten minutes later, he looked incredibly refreshed.

My spirits were soaring, too, after the previous evening's dance by the sea. I was in love and my heart was fully at peace believing David's story. I had experienced too many miracles of providence not to believe.

I don't blame Jakob for imagining that David could have engineered the Cave 53 discovery to match my visions. The plausibility of the theory is sound. I simply choose to believe that the true engineer was not my David, but God.

Pulling away from the Gai Beach in our van after breakfast, David announced that our drive to Jerusalem would allow us plenty of time to visit a few important sites along the way. The first would be his personal favorite, the ruins of Beth Shean, where he had participated in a dig during college. Only thirty minutes south of the Gai Beach, Beth Shean (which in Greek and Roman times was called Scythopolis, the only Decapolis city west of the Jordan River) occupied a strategic location at the junction of the Jordan River Valley and the Jezreel Valley.

As he drove, David's persona took on his finest guiding mode, stressing how Beth Shean would provide a stark contrast to what we had seen thus far. Today we would see an urban site whose Cardo Maximus, lined with ornate columns, was more akin to Times Square than to the small Jewish villages around the Galilee.

Beth Shean did not disappoint. We marveled at the workings of the ancient Roman bathhouse, admired the partially restored theater which in ancient times had held seven thousand spectators, and laughed at David's explanations of the red-light district and his grimace-producing demonstration of how public toilets were used by the Romans.

David was a natural guide, his explanations brimming with pride in the Land and its history. At the end of the Cardo, he pointed out how some of the massive pillars had been left in situ, in contrast to those that had been re-erected along the Cardo so that modern tourists could gain a sense of what once was. These fallen pillars, he said, are reminders of the destruction of the devastating earthquake of January 18, 749 CE.

"January 18 is a most significant date for Stella and me," he said. "Remember, it was on January 18 last year that I discovered the six tablets of Cave 53 and," he paused to take my hand, "it was on January 18 this year that I discovered an even greater treasure."

"Aw," mom oozed, "how sweet!"

"I recall," Hal said, leaning hard against a massive fallen pillar as he pretended to try to dislodge it, "that your search of Cave 53 was intentionally planned for January 18, your timing having to do with the earthquake that brought this pillar down."

"It did, Hal, you've done your homework! On January 9 last year the area around Qumran, sixty miles south of us, experienced a cluster of minor quakes. I wondered if those quakes might have shaken some things up inside the cave which, four years earlier, had been determined to have once housed Dead Sea Scrolls, probably taken by looters and sold in the antiquities market. I chose January 18 for my search of Cave 53 in honor of the much larger quake that leveled this place."

Though David had countless times told this story in scholarly settings, he was clearly enjoying the opportunity to share once again the circumstances of his discovery with his rapt audience of three.

Turning away from the fallen pillars to face the *tel* rising at the end of the Cardo, David pointed out that this mound was the ancient Jewish city of Beth Shean, the place where the Philistines hung the decapitated bodies of Saul and Jonathan on the city wall, exposing Israel to shame after the royal family had been killed in battle on nearby Mount Gilboa.

I can still hear David's voice as he then quoted King David's lament upon hearing of Saul's death, a passage clearly meaning a lot to David who, with unique inflection and careful pacing, as if an actor on stage, quoted it from memory. Gazing up to the top, as if imagining where the walls once stood, he seemed to enter a mental zone in which he was alone with the ancient David as he recited the lament in King James English:

"The beauty of Israel is slain upon thy high places:
How are the mighty fallen!
Tell it not in Gath, publish it not in the streets of Ashkelon;
lest the daughters of the Philistines rejoice,
lest the daughters of the uncircumcised triumph.
Ye mountains of Gilboa, let there be no dew,
neither let there be rain, upon you, nor fields of offerings:
for there the shield of the mighty is vilely cast away,
the shield of Saul, as though he had not been anointed with oil.
Saul and Jonathan were lovely and pleasant in their lives,
and in their death, they were not divided:
they were swifter than eagles, they were stronger than lions.
Ye daughters of Israel, weep over Saul, who clothed you in scarlet,
who put ornaments of gold upon your apparel.
How are the mighty fallen in the midst of the battle!
O Jonathan, thou wast slain in thine high places.
I am distressed for thee, my brother Jonathan:
very pleasant hast thou been unto me:
thy love to me was wonderful, passing the love of women.
How are the mighty fallen, and the weapons of war perished!"

After the lengthy quotation, David paused for what seemed a full minute before he turned to acknowledge us. Mesmerized by the reading, we gave him that moment, remaining silent as we waited for him to rejoin us from wherever his soul had ventured.

We arrived at Jerusalem's Dan Panorama Hotel, only a block from the Jerusalem YMCA and the King David Hotel, just after 4:00. Hal would have the room all to himself for the next four nights, David looking forward to sleeping in his own bed.

He had made dinner reservations across the street at La Regence in the King David Hotel, where only two months earlier we had enjoyed our first date. After a delicious meal and before dessert had been ordered, Hal and mom excused themselves for a restroom break. Leaving the table at the same time should have made me suspicious. In only a couple of minutes, they re-entered with several servers and a birthday cake.

Watching mom with Hal as they wished me a Happy Birthday, I was glad that mom seemed so happy. Still, I closed my eyes and wished dad could be there. If he could only see me now, Stella Ursa Maris, the SUM of his joy.

I would soon see why no one had acknowledged my birthday. This moment had been planned by all three of my travel companions. David knelt and produced a beautiful diamond ring, placing it on my finger and saying, "Stella, my love, our engagement was so sudden that I had no ring. I am filled with joy that you said yes, and that in five days I will be able to call you my wife."

"It's beautiful, David," I said, as we embraced and kissed, mom crying as she took pictures with her phone. As David loosened his embrace, he whispered in my ear before he pulled completely away that he had another birthday gift for me, but that it must be revealed privately, after dinner.

When mom and Hal strolled off for some alone time to explore area shops and parks, David came with me back to my room. He must have arranged for a VIP suite, as the room opened to a massive balcony overlooking the city. The evening being pleasant, we sat on the balcony to talk. Not knowing how much time we had before mom and Hal returned, I wasted none. Wearing the cutest face I could muster, I said, "Your other gift, David?"

"Well, not a wrapped gift, but something you may like even more. I needed to tell you about something that happened early this morning on my pre-breakfast walk that, I believe, will provide a map for our search. It may be nothing but, on the other hand, I think it's everything."

"I can't wait. Tell me."

"Well, you know my love for numbers, how I think of numbers as not merely quantitative tools for counting, but also qualitative, bearers of messages. I think the Muses in our lives are not so much mystical as mathematical. That fascination has always served me well, opening my eyes to glimpses of divine order, nudging me into paths of providence. To see a number and allow that number to create a thought seems healthy to me."

"Until you enter a casino?"

"Yes," he laughed. "Maybe not so much in a casino."

"I do know this, of course. I've loved that about you since my first class when you spoke of baseball as the divine game – three by three by three through nine innings, like the Angelus bells. Don't forget, by the way, that our vows are to be no more and no less than twenty-seven syllables. Three times nine."

"Oh, believe me, I haven't forgotten."

"Get on with it then. What wonders did your mathematical Muse lead you to this morning?"

"Well, fascinated last night by your story of the Magic of the Cave at Fifty-six, I decided, in honor of your 56th birthday, to get up early and seek a cave, hoping for a miracle of enlightenment, since I have no idea where to begin our search for the seventh tablet. I couldn't think of a cave nearby, but many of the Holy Land's tombs are in caves, whether natural or man-made. Jesus himself was buried in such a place."

"And did you find such a cave-tomb?"

"Yes. Only a short walk south from the hotel, near the spa where tourists enjoy the hot springs of this area, is one of the most famous tombs in Tiberias, a rabbi from the 2nd century, Rabbi Meir Baal Haness, known as Rabbi Meir the Miracle Maker."

"Really? The Miracle Maker? And did Rabbi Meir make us a miracle?"

"I think he did. The name Meir is Hebrew for Enlightener, and I think I received enlightenment this morning. I know now where our search must begin."

"What! Are you kidding me?"

"I am not. As I prayed for a miracle at Rabbi Meir's tomb, thinking of the Magic of the Cave at Fifty-six, it occurred to me – a thought I believe was put in my head by Rabbi Meir – that there are only two chapters in the Hebrew Bible bearing the number 56. Only two, the Psalms and Isaiah, are sufficiently long to have 56 chapters. After calling up those two chapters on my phone and reading them, I now know that our search will not take us back into the desert. Instead, we will go . . . ."

"Yes?" I said as he paused, "where?"

"To the Mount of Olives."

"The Mount of Olives? You think the seventh tablet could really be that close to us? How could those two chapters be so specific?"

"I read Psalm 56 first, a rather odd psalm of David, set when the Philistines seized him in Gath, David pretending to be insane in order to appear to be no threat. Rabbi Meir's enlightenment came at verse nine in the Hebrew text."

"Of course, the power of nine!"

"It's as if, when David wrote it, he was talking directly to me."

"No more suspense, please."

"Praying in distress, David says to God, 'You have acted as a *sofer* (a scribe), recording my wanderings. You have put my tears into your bottle, recording them in your *sefer* (book).'"

"I don't understand. How do you see that as helpful?"

"In your sixth vision, you told me that Jesus spoke of your future discovery of the seventh tablet in the place where his tears ascend to heaven. That seems unusual, since tears don't ascend. Tears fall. I had thought, when you first told me about that, of the chapel on the Mount of Olives known as Dominus Flevit, a Latin term meaning . . ."

"The Lord wept! Yes, I remember it."

"Right, the Lord wept. It was built in 1955, over the site of a long-ruined Byzantine chapel, by the Italian architect, Antonio Barluzzi. The site is the traditional place of Jesus weeping over the city. The most prominent feature of the chapel is that it is built in the shape of an inverted teardrop, as if the tears of Jesus are," he paused and smiled, "ascending."

"The place where my tears ascend!"

"Exactly. I'm convinced our search must take us there. On each of the four exterior corners of the chapel, Barluzzi placed elongated jars to represent what is expressed in this passage, that God collects our tears in his bottle as an act of divine compassion, as if remembering our wanderings, our sufferings."

"You know," I said, remembering being with Jesus in Gethsemane, "now that you mention Dominus Flevit, I recall how Jesus, when he spoke of his tears, pointed up the hill in the direction of the chapel. Do you think he could he have known then the precise location of the seventh tablet, already buried for a thousand years before he was born?"

"If so," David said, "what if what prompted him to stop at that very spot and weep was more than the gospel accounts knew to tell us? What if he stopped at that spot, intentionally, to weep for his father David, knowing what was buried beneath his feet?"

"Amazing! And Isaiah 56?"

"Isaiah 56 was equally revealing, also pointing to the Mount of Olives as the place to begin our search. At the base of the Mount of Olives, in Gethsemane, Barluzzi had, much earlier in his career – in the 1920s – built another, much more famous church."

"The Church of All Nations."

"Right, which is why my eye stopped when I saw that Isaiah 56:7 tells of 'all nations' being gathered to the holy mountain."

"Isn't that the passage where *Yad Vashem* gets its name?"

"It is. To remember the six million Jews wiped out by the Nazis in the 1940s, the name *Yad Vashem* is lifted from verse five: 'I will give, in my house and within my walls, *yad vashem* (a monument and a name), better than sons and daughters. I will give them an everlasting name that will never be cut off.'"

David paused at that, I think in respect to the millions of sons and daughters who were lost during the Shoah, before he said, "I read the passage this morning as if it were describing us, you and me. It reads: 'Do not let the foreigner joined to *Hashem* say, '*Hashem* will surely separate me from his people,' and do not let the eunuch say, 'I am just a dry tree.' To them I will give *yad vashem* (a monument and a name) better than sons and daughters."

"And you see us in this passage, how?"

"Isaiah pictured the parents of these sons and daughters as two people – male and female, of course, but most surprisingly, Gentile and Jew. I see you as the foreigner in this passage. Though a Gentile, you are joined to God, so that Isaiah writes that you must not think God excludes you from his people. I see myself as the eunuch in the passage."

He ignored my smile, saying, "Well, while thankfully not literally a eunuch, I have certainly lived as one. To me, Isaiah says I must not think of myself as a dry tree, as childless."

Likely thankful for my silence, he said, "Rabbi Meir the Miracle Maker showed me that we, you and I, are the mother and father in Isaiah 56, the foreigner and the eunuch. While we are too old to bear our own children after we are married, God will give us something better than sons and daughters. So, I believe this passage, to which I was led at the cave-tomb of Rabbi Meir, is a promise that our discovery of the seventh tablet will gather all nations together."

"And make of them sons and daughters, I see. How beautiful! Can it really be that we are so blessed, chosen to play a role in bringing about God's eternal plan for the nations?"

"I believe that we are chosen for this purpose, and my birthday gift to you is that I won't be dragging you through the Judean wilderness to prove it. I think we'll discover the seventh tablet right here in Jerusalem. So, there you have it. Happy Birthday, Stella!"

"Aw," I joked, "I was looking forward to buying the appropriate wardrobe for spelunking."

Again, as a God wink, the timing was perfect. Mom and Hal returned to the room, eager to share what they had seen on their walking adventure around the Dan Panorama. They had walked to the nearby Yemin Moshe neighborhood, which they excitedly reported was established in 1891 by Moses Montefiore, the first Jewish neighborhood outside the walls. Handing us brochures of the Montefiore Windmill towering over the red roofed houses, they told how Montefiore used it to provide cheap flour for the residents.

Once the excitement of their Jerusalem discoveries was exhausted, David excused himself so that he could taxi home, ready to sleep in his own bed.

While the forecast didn't look good for next Wednesday's wedding on the beach, calling for rain to move in beginning Monday night and hang around for three days, it did mean we had three beautiful days of sightseeing left to enjoy. Since the next day was Shabbat, we decided to head out of Jerusalem, our itinerary taking us first to Qumran, then further south to Masada. Cresting the Mount of Olives near David's office at Hebrew University, the landscape transitioned into a dusty redness before our eyes as we headed into the desert toward Jericho and the Dead Sea.

Our Qumran visit began with a short 3D film on the history of the Dead Sea Scrolls and the Essene community, conjecturing how, during the frightening Roman approach after the destruction of Jerusalem, they had used caves to hide their most precious treasure, their library.

The film ended in a unique way. The entire back wall, which was the screen for the film, lifted to reveal what looked like the opening of a cave, an invitation for our brave band of explorers to step into the past. The faux cave we entered looped around like a horseshoe, pilgrims able to view numerous displays of actual Qumran discoveries before being at last spilled out onto the site of the ancient monastic community.

If there was any place in the Holy Land where David's expertise would shine, it would be here at Qumran. Recognized by a Qumran staff member, word spread quickly among the tourists that the archaeologist who had discovered the Cave 53 tablets was on site. People began to cluster around us as he guided us through the ruins toward the pinnacle moment of the Qumran visit, the pavilion overlooking Cave 4.

After David finished his explanation of Cave 4, he left us to take our photographs as he turned his attention to the tourists who had been following. Pointing in the direction of his discovery led to a string of people asking for selfies with David, their cameras pointed in the direction of the now famous Cave 53. David was clearly enjoying every minute of it, soaking up his Qumran stardom and autographing the tourists' brochures.

After David rejoined us, we enjoyed a delicious lunch at the Qumran Visitors Center. Mom wanted to spend some time shopping after lunch, purchasing beauty products made with the rich minerals of the Dead Sea before we headed south toward Masada, a drive offering extraordinary views of the sadly receding Dead Sea.

As we drove, David pointed out the wadis coming out of the hills to our right. At times of heavy rain, such as perhaps next week, he said, the wadis can suddenly fill with rushing water to create a torrent that can wash out roads and, sadly, take lives.

"Let me tell you a story," he said, "told by an old guide named Hillel, now retired. Once, a tourist asked Hillel who was the most famous person he had ever guided. He responded that many years earlier, as a young man, he had guided Frank Sinatra, and that one of his favorite stories from that trip happened right here in the Judean Wilderness. In his early days of guiding, he explained, there were far fewer restrooms available than today. On the day of Sinatra's visit, some on the bus were growing urgent, so Hillel asked the driver to stop near a wadi bed, allowing the pilgrims who couldn't wait another hour to walk out and relieve themselves."

We smiled at the thought, wondering why the distress of a busload of tourists would be so funny. He was, we would discover, setting up the punchline.

Growing serious, David said, "When the pilgrims asked Hillel the same question you are asking yourselves, how this unfortunate moment could create such a vivid memory, he beamed, saying that it was the most memorable moment of his career, he providing the inspiration for Sinatra's hit, 'Everybody Needs a Wadi Sometime.'"

David had timed the story perfectly, bringing us to the punchline just as we were coming into Ein Gedi, about halfway between Qumran and Masada.

"Remember," David reminded us, "that relieving oneself in this desert wilderness is the key element of a very important biblical story emerging from this spot, Ein Gedi. It was here that King Saul exposed himself, literally although unintentionally, to David, who graciously spared his life."

"Stella's third vision," mom said. "I can't wait to see it."

David pulled into Ein Gedi so that we could walk around the oasis. When Mom and Hal followed the sounds of laughing children playing near a waterfall, David pointed up to the cliffs at some cave openings.

"Do any of these caves look familiar from your vision?"

"No, not at all. Remember, I was on the inside of the cave, not out here. This was the perspective Saul and his army had as they searched for us in the caves."

"Shall we go up and explore a cave or two, then?" he said with a mischievous grin.

"Ha, ha. No, I think not. Let's push on to Masada, where David was headed after Saul returned to Jerusalem. I think he would have danced with me at Masada, had my vision not ended here. I intend today, though, to dance with my other David in Herod's palace, overlooking the Dead Sea."

After two more days of touring Jerusalem, the rains arrived on Monday night. On Tuesday we checked out of the Dan Panorama and made the hour drive in the pouring rain to The Seasons Hotel in Netanya, a high rise on the Mediterranean less than a thirty-minute drive up the coast to the *Kochav Hayam* wedding venue. David had chosen the hotel because his TA, whose wedding he had attended at *Kochav Hayam*, happened to have been the son of the hotel's manager. When David contacted him to inquire about rooms, we were promised many perks if we would stay there.

The heavy rains of Monday night and Tuesday cleared away at last, the sun bathing our wedding day with glistening warmth. Everything seemed to have fallen into place for our arrival at *Kochav Hayam*, so that we could exchange our vows on the beach.

Pastor Hal Chandler and Rabbi Rafi Rozen had connected weeks earlier through e-mail to ensure that the wedding would maintain elements of both Jewish and Christian ritual.

David stopped me just before we stepped under the chuppah. "Standing under the chuppah is more than merely a reminder that we will establish a home, a place having four corners and a roof over our head. When we step under this canopy, it's a most sacred moment. We will be stepping out of real time and into mythic time, as if entering a dream."

"That's beautiful, David."

"Shall we, then, step under the chuppah together?"

"Yes, with joy."

Rabbi Rafi opened the ceremony by saying to our two witnesses, my mother and David's sister, Eliana, who had flown in from Boston the previous day to join us in Netanya, "Your daughter and your brother seek your blessing as they have come to a threshold moment in their lives, two becoming one in the mystery of marriage. Will you offer them your blessing?"

Without hesitation, both responded, "We will."

Pastor Hal had prepared a homily based on the story of Jacob's ladder from Genesis. He had asked Rabbi Rafi if he would be willing to read the text in tandem with him, Hal reading the narrative from the New Revised Standard Version, Rabbi Rafi reading the quotations from God.

Rabbi Rafi had laughed when asked, saying, "As it should be! Of course, I'll play the role of God."

Pastor Hal began, "Jacob left Beersheba and went toward Haran. He came to a certain place and stayed there for the night, because the sun had set. Taking one of the stones of the place, he put it under his head and lay down in that place. And he dreamed that there was a ladder set up on the earth, the top of it reaching to heaven; and the angels of God were ascending and descending on it. And the LORD stood beside him and said . . ."

Rabbi Rafi then stepped into the role of God, saying, "I am the LORD, the God of Abraham your father and the God of Isaac; the land on which you lie I will give to you and to your offspring; and your offspring shall be like the dust of the earth, and you shall spread abroad to the west and to the east and to the north and to the south; and all the families of the earth shall be blessed in you and in your offspring. Know that I am with you and will keep you wherever you go, and will bring you back to this land; for I will not leave you until I have done what I have promised you."

Pastor Hal then finished the narrative. "Then Jacob woke from his sleep and said, 'Surely the LORD is in this place—and I did not know it!' And he was afraid, and said, 'How awesome is this place! This is none other than the house of God, and this is the gate of heaven.'"

Pastor Hal closed his Bible and turned 180 degrees to face the sea, breathing in deeply the fresh ocean air. Turning back to us with arms outstretched, he said, "Stella, David. How awesome is this place!"

We looked at each other, nodding our agreement.

He continued, "Thank you for the invitation to share this sublime moment with you in this awesome place. We are all here at your gracious invitation. May this beach be for you what Jacob experienced in our reading, a gateway to heaven."

Slowing his cadence and making eye contact with us, he said, "You, like Jacob, have dreamed dreams that have changed everything. Your dreams have brought us to this place. Like Jacob, you know your dreams to be heaven-sent."

Hal turned again toward the sea, pausing to draw a deep breath of the ocean air. Turning back to face us, he said, "The sight impacted Jacob so much that he wondered, 'Am I still on earth, or am I in heaven?' The two seemed linked, as if heaven and earth were embracing."

Stretching out his arms, he said, "On this beautiful beach, does it not seem that heaven and earth are kissing? Look to the westward horizon. Where does the sea end? Where does the sky begin? I can't tell. Perhaps you now, in this sacred moment, wonder as Jacob did, 'Am I still on earth? Or, in some mysterious way, am I in heaven?'"

I blurted out, "Heaven!"

My words caught us all, myself included, by surprise. I said again, blushing, "I'm in heaven," causing laughter to break out.

"As are we all!" mom said, proudly.

I turned to look at her, more radiant than I had ever seen my mother.

"Indeed," Rabbi Rafi laughed. "As are we all!"

Hal continued, "Your journey bringing you to this beach has been a long one of thirty-three years. May this day be for you a moment of sheer transcendence, calling you into a future brimming with promise, not only for you as husband and wife, but for what you, together, will bring to all the families of the world."

"So mote it be," I whispered, closing my eyes to remember my father's prayer in Solomon's Quarries, wishing he were here with us.

Mom reached out and gently touched my arm. "He is here, dear. This is the gate of heaven, remember? I can feel your dad, how he is so very proud of you. He stands at the gate, with tears of joy for you."

After reaching to wipe away my tears, she nodded to Hal that we were ready to continue.

Pastor Hal, changing his expression to one of seriousness, asked, "Are you ready now to exchange your vows?"

"Yes," we said, affirming our intent.

"Very well. Then turn now to face one another. I love it that you have written your vows in the mathematical structure of baseball, a formula taking you back to your first meeting as professor and student – three by three by three through nine innings. So, you've written your vows in three lines of nine syllables each. Do I have that right?"

"You do," I nodded.

Holding up an umpire's clicker, he said, "I assure you, by bringing to Israel this clicker from my days as a Babe Ruth and American Legion umpire, I will be counting to make certain each syllable is recorded. Be warned, I may make you start over if you miscount."

After a pause for our laughter to subside, he said, "Go for it, then. If our witnesses are ready with rings, David, you may go first."

David took the ring from Eliana and placed it on my ring finger. The ring in place, he looked into my eyes and spoke his vow, pausing between each line:

"Stella Maris, my Star of the Sea,
Kochav Hayam at *Kochav Hayam*.
Blissfully, I pledge my love to thee."

Hal looked at me and said, "He nailed it. Nine syllables three times. It's your turn, Stella."

I took the wedding band from mom and placed it on David's finger, saying:

"David, my teacher, my Muse, my guide,
'ishi, my husband, and I your bride.
With love, always, I'll stay by your side."

Wrapping a wine glass in a heavy velvet pouch, Rabbi Rafi informed his half-Christian congregation, "Jewish weddings end with a bang, the breaking of the glass. There are many things this act symbolizes. Most prominent is the destruction of the temple. Yet another is that marriage is a covenant. In the Hebrew Bible, to make a covenant something must be cut, so that covenant-making is symbolized by the broken shards. A third symbolism, my favorite, is that our human relationships know not only the heightened joy of a moment such as we are experiencing on this beach, but will also, over time, experience testing and sorrow. Love renders us vulnerable, the broken glass a reminder that our world is broken, in need of healing."

After pausing, he said, "Once Stella and David have crushed the glass, we bring to an end our mythic time under the chuppah. We have momentarily stepped out of this world of brokenness, into the presence of the Holy One, but we must now go back to live our lives, as best we can, to bring healing to our broken world."

We crushed that glass with style, all four in our wedding party shouting, "Mazel tov!"

With only six in our entire wedding party, our reception was simple, a delicious steak dinner in Netanya in a private room at the Rubinstein. David, tapping on his wine glass with a piece of silverware, gathered our attention.

"On the day I met Stella Maris, I invited her to dance on the Star of David dance floor. I showed the class how the Star of David had six points formed by two triangles, one upright and one inverted, male and female partners on the dance floor, each triangle having three points. As we stood under the chuppah this afternoon, it occurred to me that our wedding party had six points – three Christian and three Jewish, forming two triangles. At *Kochav Hayam* this afternoon, were we not all dancing on a Star of David dance floor? Thank you all, my dear friends, for joining us in today's amazing dance."

The Seasons Hotel had, as promised, offered many perks, mom and I having checked in on Tuesday to a top floor penthouse suite. The enormous penthouse was wrapped by a balcony so that we could step out to breathe in the invigorating air off the Mediterranean while enjoying an unobstructed view of the coastline stretching north toward Caesarea.

Mom had moved out of our room Wednesday morning before our departure for *Kochav Hayam*, after which David had the porters bring his luggage to the penthouse so that, returning to the hotel from our dinner reception, all would be ready for our first night as a married couple. We wanted it to be perfect since this one night, for now, would suffice as our honeymoon. After lunch the next day we would check out, take mom and Hal to the airport for their return flight and settle Eliana into a Tel Aviv hotel, she spending a few days visiting with Israeli friends before flying back to Boston on Sunday.

After providing taxi service, David and I would drive back

to his Jerusalem apartment, having decided to forego any more elaborate honeymoon until after we had discovered the seventh tablet. Having been absent from the university for over a week, he needed to catch up with his classes. He assured me, though, that once the semester was finished and the seventh tablet discovered, we would celebrate our wedding with an extravagant honeymoon, destination to be determined.

One would think, having waited thirty-three years for this moment, intimacy would be ravenously engaged. Instead, the nearer we came to privacy on our wedding night, my nervousness became increasingly apparent, making silly attempts to prolong our lobby conversation with our guests.

When our small talk over a long-lingering glass of wine in the lobby had become entirely inane, mom broke the ice by announcing she needed to retire. Her eye contact with me sent a very clear message to her fifty-six-year-old virgin daughter. "You will be okay, my child," are the reassuring words I heard through her silence.

Hal and Eliana picked up on mom's cue, excusing themselves and heading upstairs, saying how beautiful the wedding had been, thanking us for the dinner, and wishing us a good night.

As they disappeared into the elevator, David and I were alone. Strangely silent as we waited for the next elevator to take us to the penthouse, when its doors opened to receive us and we stepped in, I realized what a truly frightening threshold moment this was for me. Everything had changed when we spoke our vows, and now we were being called to live into that new reality.

While I had mentioned it often in sermons, I would now experience firsthand why the groom carries the bride across the threshold, to cushion her against the surging energy of the doorway that changes everything, the newlyweds leaving the past behind to embrace a new reality. I laughed with joy when David, opening the door to the penthouse, blocked my access. Holding out his arms, he swept me up and carried me inside.

Sensing I needed privacy to ready myself, David said, "I have a bit of a surprise for you, but I need to prepare it in the other bedroom. Would it be okay if I get ready for bed there and return in, say, fifteen minutes?"

"Of course, that would be perfect. A surprise?"

"Yes, and I think you'll like it."

Leaving the master bedroom, he turned at the door to say, "I love you."

"I love you, too, David."

When he tapped on the door at the appointed time and asked if I was ready, I invited him in, having already crawled under the covers.

I broke out in laughter as soon as I saw him. My professor was expert at making memorable entrances. David Aaronson knew how to break the ice with a class. My husband, I would now learn, would also be adept at taking the edge off the incredibly awkward moment of a sixty-five-year-old man and a fifty-six-year-old woman, both virgins and in love for thirty-three years, entering a bed together.

I had seen this entrance before, a repeat performance. It was his Isadora Duncan dance, introducing us to the famous dancer whose moves imitated the sea. The Mediterranean, just outside our window, provided all the music he needed. Floating barefoot across the room in a flowing sheer gown, I pulled myself up in bed to watch and laugh.

"What a perfect surprise," I said. "I remember how, the first time I saw you dance as Isadora Duncan, it reminded me of Johnny Castle and Baby, Dirty Dancing."

"Then come," he said, reaching for me. "Nobody keeps my Star of the Sea in the corner."

I shook my head and instead patted the covers beside me, all the invitation he needed to join me. Thanking him for his surprise entrance, silently we embraced, limiting ourselves to kissing, both forbidding our hands from any action that might suggest a desire to go further, each waiting for the other.

After several minutes of intimacy stalled, David sought again to lighten the mood, saying, "Well, I guess it's not true."

"What's not true?"

"I've heard that sex is better after forty. Or, was it fifty? Either way, we amply qualify."

"We do, don't we? I guess that maxim applies only the previously experienced."

David would be the first, after another few minutes, to move his hands in ways indicating a desire for deeper intimacy. I didn't think myself to be rejecting those advances, though he must have felt me tense at his touches. When he retreated from exploration, I didn't counter in any way to suggest I regretted his retreat, nor did my hands go on any adventures of their own.

At last, David lifted himself up with a smile.

"I'm sorry, David. I want to. I really do. It's just . . ."

"It's okay. I'm afraid, too. How about we just sleep beside each other tonight, and see what happens? Then, perhaps tomorrow?"

When I nodded my approval of the plan, he said, "Are you okay with me staying here, with you? Would you prefer privacy? I can sleep in the other room. We are alone and we are married. No one need know."

"No, David, I want you right here with me, please."

"Your wish is my command," he said, reaching to turn off the lamp.

Though the day had been emotionally thrilling, the now embarrassing ending kept me up for at least an hour, maybe more. David lay awake also, but for less time. I knew exactly when he fell asleep, for the first time hearing his snoring. It was very light, not at all like the horror stories I've heard from couples unable to sleep together.

My last glance at the clock that I can remember showed 11:11. Though our marriage had not yet been consummated, I felt completely safe, and utterly joyful.

I suddenly remembered that, in all the excitement, I had forgotten my mezuzah. Even after my seventh vision on January 18, I had kept my mezuzah by my bedside, a habit of thirty-three years.

As quietly as possible, so as not to awaken David, I slid out from under the covers and went to my bag, using my cell phone flashlight to open the bag and find it. Getting back into bed, I held the mezuzah tight, whispering a prayer, not my usual prayer for my dream to transport me into the past, but rather a prayer that God would give me the courage, here and now, to be the wife David desired and deserved.

I felt selfish as I quietly propped the mezuzah on the bedside table, remembering that the last journey into the past it had opened for me was to discover that I am Abishag. If I am Abishag, craving for three thousand years to consummate her love for her David, then who was I, Stella, to keep her from such joy? At last, with thoughts of having failed my Other, I slept.

If what happened next was a vision, it was different from all the others, my dream awakening being in the same bed in which I slept, with David having the simultaneous vision. I wasn't dreaming about him, nor he about me. We were in the dream world together, if a dream at all. I wasn't sure.

I saw David as the sixty-five-year-old man that he was, but as our now hungry and unobstructed advances heated, he was transforming into the David with whom I had danced, entering Jerusalem, the look in his eyes the same as on that day when we came so close to intimacy.

My two Davids were now both in their early thirties, King David's age when I had danced with him entering Jerusalem now matching David Aaronson's age when I first fell in love with him. The energies of my two Davids had merged. Though two, they were one.

If King David's spirit was one with my husband, Abishag's spirit was now fully within me. David was experiencing in me what I was experiencing in him, that in his mind I was blending with Abishag into the youthful form of a woman in her early twenties, as I had been when first we met in 1988.

With surging intimacy, harmonious with the waves of the Mediterranean below, at long last consummated were thirty-three years of my love for David Aaronson, and three thousand years of my love for David ben Jesse. That ours was no mere dream would soon be clear, our bodies upon awakening showing clear evidence that our experience had been real. David and Stella had been one with David and Abishag.

In the afterglow of our lovemaking David stood, completely naked and reaching for me to stand. Seeing my reluctance, he tore the blanket from the bed and wrapped it around me to help me stand. Taking one of the roses the hotel had left in the suite, he closed his eyes to relish its aroma, brought it to his lips to kiss it, then inserted the stem into my hair.

I balked when his dance brought us through the door and onto the balcony.

"David, no. We're naked."

"No, only I am naked," he said, "and we are on the top floor, in the penthouse, and away from all eyes. Let us dance to the nighttime sounds of the sea."

Chapter 19

The Church of All Nations and Dominus Flevit

THE MOUNT OF OLIVES

MARCH 17, 2022

Antonio Barluzzi, often called the Architect of the Holy Land, was born in Rome in 1884 with sacred architecture coursing through his veins, his maternal grandfather having been the architect responsible for the maintenance of St. Peter's Basilica. As a young man, Barluzzi felt a Call to ministry and considered entering seminary. He listened instead to another voice, that of his architect older brother, Giulio.

Barluzzi would never become a parish priest, yet he lived much as a Franciscan friar might. Though his building projects in the Holy Land gained renown, he never amassed the financial rewards one might expect to flow from such enormous success. No Holy Land pilgrim since the early 20th century has returned home un-touched by Barluzzi's vision, ambition, creativity, and energy. His twenty-four Holy Land projects – churches, hospitals, and schools – spanned four decades, from 1912 to 1955. Many of his projects were built on commission from the Franciscan Custody of the Holy Land, established in 1217 by St. Francis of Assisi to preserve sacred sites.

The Custody often commissioned Barluzzi to build churches atop the ruins of Byzantine and Crusader period churches that had fallen into disrepair during the four centuries of Ottoman rule from 1517 and 1917. Barluzzi was actually in the Holy Land to witness the end of the Ottoman period, entering the Jaffa Gate with General Edmund Allenby on December 11, 1917, that historic day marking the end of Istanbul's reign over Jerusalem. Allenby's was one of history's many triumphant entrances into the holy city.

In my visions, I had danced with David as he led the ark's procession into his new *'ir david* (City of David) and had also joined the Palm Sunday crowds witnessing Jesus enter the city. While I wasn't with General Allenby for his victorious entrance, I have seen the photographs of him walking through the Jaffa Gate after dismounting, a gesture of respect to Jesus. Somewhere in that parade was a thirty-three-year-old architect named Antonio Barluzzi.

My having been with David and Jesus in their moments of elation leads me to feel kinship with Barluzzi, two of whose churches David and I would visit on this momentous day, March 17, 2022, the day our search for the seventh tablet both commenced and ended.

David's early morning devotional at the tomb of Rabbi Meir two weeks ago, reading Isaiah 56 and Psalm 56 in honor of my 56th birthday, led us to these two churches on the Mount of Olives, both built by Barluzzi. The Church of All Nations is in Gethsemane, at the base of the Mount of Olives. Also known as the Basilica of the Agony, the church is the traditional site where Jesus prayed on the night of his betrayal and arrest.

Dominus Flevit, meaning "The Lord Wept," is a nearby chapel located up the Palm Sunday pathway. It commemorates Luke's description of Jesus weeping over Jerusalem: "As he approached Jerusalem and saw the city, he wept over it" (19:41).

These two churches provide a frame for Barluzzi's career. The Church of All Nations, so called because of the twelve nations funding its construction, was one of his earliest projects, begun in 1919 and finished in 1924. Dominus Flevit, consecrated in 1955, was at the very end of his career. Barluzzi would pass away five years later, on December 14, 1960.

David and I decided to begin our day at the Church of All Nations rather than fight the crush of motor coaches at the top of the Mount of Olives, the terraced pavilion where pilgrims cluster in their tour groups in front of the Seven Arches Hotel. Millions of pilgrims have created at that spot their most prized souvenir from their Holy Land journey, a group photo with the Old City's Dome of the Rock in the background. From there, pilgrims walk down the walled Palm Sunday path toward Gethsemane, usually stopping for a brief visit at Dominus Flevit.

Our day would take us the opposite direction. Beginning at the Church of All Nations, we would walk up the hill, rather than down, not an extremely difficult walk, Dominus Flevit being only a couple of hundred yards above Gethsemane.

Our search for the seventh tablet, we now suspected, would be very unlike last year's Cave 53 discovery of the six tablets. Ours would not be an archaeological project, but an investigative one. The place to begin our search, David had been convinced after his readings of "all nations" in Isaiah 56 and "tears in a bottle" in Psalm 56, would be these two churches. Today's plan would be simply to ask the caretakers about any known artifacts dating from the construction of the churches.

Isaiah 56, the passage leading us to the Church of All Nations, is most famous as the inspiration for the naming of Israel's museum of the Holocaust, *Yad Vashem*. Those two Hebrew words are found in verse 5, "To them I will give, within my temple and its walls, *yad vashem* (a monument and a name) better than sons and daughters."

David's interest, though, was focused on verse 7: "These (i.e., the sons and daughters) I will bring to my holy mountain and give them joy in my house of prayer . . . a house of prayer for all nations."

David felt that Rabbi Meir had led him to Isaiah 56, certain that God was speaking directly to us as a couple -- one a Gentile and the other a eunuch. He saw me as the foreigner, partaker of the divine promise despite being a Gentile and a Christian. He saw himself, unmarried and childless, as the dry-tree eunuch (though, thankfully, not literally).

It would be to us, David believed, a husband and wife too old to bear biological children, that God will give *yad vashem* (a monument and a name) better than sons and daughters.

"If our discovery of the seventh tablet is for the healing of all the nations," David had said, "what better place to begin our search than the Church of All Nations?"

The cab let us out in front of the church's glorious façade, one of the most memorable sights for any visitor to Jerusalem. Walking around to the north entrance of the church's grounds, we followed the path guiding guests around a small grove of ancient olive trees. The Basilica of the Agony was Barluzzi's grand project in his early career, its construction continuing for five years over the site of a 4th century church destroyed in an 8th century earthquake.

After entering the church, I told David I needed ten minutes alone, wishing to sit quietly to remember and reflect on my sixth vision with Jesus in Gethsemane. As I sat, David wandered. The dark quietness of the basilica was broken only by the hushed whispers of tour guides urging their groups toward the Rock of the Agony, a flat rock outcropping where tradition remembers Jesus praying on the night of his arrest. By leaving the interior of the basilica in semi-darkness, relieved only by subdued natural light, Barluzzi offered each pilgrim an opportunity to enter the dark anguish of Jesus.

I knew immediately that 4th century tradition had been wrong about this rock being the place of Jesus' agony. My vision had not been of an exposed flat outcropping of rock such as this, but of being in a cave with Jesus. For many years after my vision, I had wondered about that. Like most Christians, I assumed that Jesus prayed that holy night in a garden, not in a cave. It was in the summer of 1995, reading an article by biblical scholar Joan Taylor in the July/August issue of *Biblical Archaeology Review* ("The Garden of Gethsemane NOT the Place of Jesus' Arrest") that the accuracy of my vision was confirmed. I had been with Jesus in the Cave of Gethsemane, not in a garden. Though the cave is known as a holy site and near the church, not nearly so many pilgrims venture there as those coming to the famous basilica.

The cave, though, where was an olive press, is where Jesus prayed that night. He and his disciples frequented the place, perhaps even spent entire nights in the safety of its interior. It had been to this cave that Jesus and his disciples retired after their Seder meal in the Upper Room.

"I understand," David said, when I expressed misgivings about the church and its rock being the site of Jesus' arrest, "but let's remember that no matter which site is authentic, our reason for being here is guided by Isaiah 56's 'All Nations' prophecy. Regardless of which site is authentic, our search must begin here."

I stood near the Rock of the Agony and prayed, marveling

how it could be that I had been sent as a Muse to inspire Jesus to overcome *Hakol*, the Voice of his enemy calling for him to abort the redemptive plan, to instead call down legions of angels. David was right. It is of no consequence that this rock is not an X-marks-the-spot remembrance of Jesus' prayer. The prayers of millions of pilgrims pouring out their hearts at this place render it sacred.

Just as I closed my eyes to relish in this holy moment, a group sitting on the benches surrounding the rock began softly to sing a Lenten hymn I include every year in our Maundy Thursday worship at Maranatha Assembly:

Go to dark Gethsemane, all who feel the tempter's power;
 Your Redeemer's conflict see, watch with him one bitter hour;
Turn not from his griefs away, learn from Jesus Christ to pray.

As if a fountain had been opened, my tears flowed as I sang softly with them.

An elderly priest had been standing off to the side observing. I had seen the abundant joy on his face as he watched the pilgrims flow in and out, coming near the rock to pray and sing. Occasionally, if a group became a bit loud, he would appeal for quiet, but in a cheerful tone, never chiding as had the nun at the Church of the Beatitudes a few weeks earlier, scolding Pastor Hal for breaking some rule or another. We had laughed when David whispered, "Sorry, Hal, I should have warned you about Attila the Nun."

It must appear strange to the priest, I thought, to see my tears followed by a quirky smile as I recalled David's Attila remark. He had noticed something, that's for sure. My sense that he was watching me had not been imagined. As soon as I stepped away from the altar, ending my private time, he stepped toward me. Seeing this, David swooped in to join us and, grabbing my hand, introduced us to the priest. I had imagined, with the excitement that the new Dead Sea discovery had caused throughout the Holy Land, that the priest might have heard of David Aaronson, at least to recognize his name. This priest evidently had not, registering no recognition at all and making no mention of last year's discovery.

"Welcome, then, Stella and David, I am Father Jacques. Young lady, I saw you looking at the rock, as if it were a familiar place."

"Thank you, Father. I have been here before, many years ago. I visited with my parents as a college student."

"Oh, you misunderstand. I didn't mean that the place itself is familiar. I meant that familiar to you is that place in our hearts, often painful, where prayer is born from authentic spiritual experience. I see many tears in this holy place. Yours seem, somehow, different, as if you had been truly with Jesus."

Was Father Jacque's perceptiveness real, I wondered, or has he simply become adept at making pilgrims feel as if they had truly engaged with Jesus in his agony?

My silence, taking a moment to ponder what he had seen in me, was broken by David's mention of Barluzzi's architectural brilliance. Father Jacques' attention, though, remained focused on me for an awkward moment, as if ignoring David and waiting for me to reply.

At last, he broke eye contact with me and turned to David. "Yes, the church is stunning, but the most impressive thing about this place for pilgrims will not be its domes, or its lighting, or even this rock. What pilgrims will take home is their memory of praying here. In this place, one prays not only to Jesus, but with Jesus."

Father Jacque's words were entering my heart as a sermon. I could have listened to him more, but David sought again to press him into another mode, asking if he knew of any archaeological artifacts stored at the church, perhaps discovered during the church's construction.

At this, Father Jacques seemed irked. Shifting from architecture to archaeology, David had missed his point entirely, that the priest's domain was that of the soul, not of museum pieces of little interest to him, sitting and gathering dust. I could sense that he wanted to pin David down by asking a more searching personal question, "How is it with your soul?"

As moved as I was by the church and by Father Jacques, it was now time to ascend the Mount of Olives to Dominus Flevit. Exiting the basilica through the middle of its three grand outer arches, we paused on the steps to look across the Kidron Valley toward the walls of the Old City.

"David, we're looking for a tablet hidden three thousand years ago, a thousand years before Jesus prayed here. Do you think we really have a chance of finding it?"

"I do," he said. "We've seen miracles all along our journey. Rabbi Meir the Miracle Maker will not let us down."

Just then our attention was drawn to a group of children parading down the street in colorful costumes, their similarly dressed parents and teachers walking alongside, sounding noisemakers. The mini-festival of sight and sound was eliciting smiles from all onlookers.

"What's this?" I laughed, "a Jewish Halloween?"

"No, not Halloween, and while today is St. Patrick's Day, it isn't that, either."

"That's right, it is St. Patrick's Day! I've been so focused on our search that I forgot to wear green."

"Today is Purim, a day of celebration and revelry as we

remember the story of the Book of Esther, celebrating how God saved Mordechai and the Jews from Haman's anti-Semitic plot. Purim doesn't always fall on St. Patrick's Day, of course, but it does this year. I have a colleague at the university looking especially forward to today. Both Jewish and Irish, he'll double-down in his celebrating today, probably already drinking a Guinness at Dublin's Irish Pub here in Jerusalem."

Walking back through the garden of olive trees, we exited the church's grounds and, turning right, began our walk up the walled Palm Sunday path to Dominus Flevit. The path's ascent begins immediately behind the Church of All Nations. We paused our climb briefly at the entrance to the Church of Mary Magdalene, a Russian Orthodox Church predating both of Barluzzi's churches. Built by Tsar Alexander III in 1886, its seven gilded onion domes now gleamed in the early afternoon sunlight.

As we stood for a few seconds and rested, admiring the exterior of the church before resuming our ascent, David reached for my hand. I looked and saw he was wiping away tears.

"David, what's wrong?"

"The strangest feeling. We just left Gethsemane, the place of Jesus' betrayal by one of his disciples, Judas. I only now remembered that the first time the Bible ever calls this hill the Mount of Olives is in 2 Samuel 15, the story of David being betrayed by one even closer than a disciple. His own son, Absalom, betrayed him, a coup forcing David to flee Jerusalem. He came out of the city, across the Kidron Valley, and up this path toward the top of the Mount of Olives, weeping as he went. If this was a place of betrayal and weeping for Jesus, so it was also for David."

"We are one in so many ways, aren't we?" I said, squeezing his hand tightly.

In only a few more minutes our ascent brought us to Dominus Flevit. A small chapel very unlike the colossal Basilica of the Agony below, Barluzzi's creativity is nonetheless on full display, the chapel built in the shape of an inverted teardrop with four phials, bottles for tears, standing at the corners of the dome. Taller and more elongated than the jars in which were found the Dead Sea Scrolls, these phials were inspired by the passage David had read at Rabbi Meir's tomb, Psalm 56:8, God's promise to hold the tears of his people in a bottle.

A mass had begun in the chapel only a short time before our arrival, meaning we would have to wait thirty minutes or more before we could visit inside and, hopefully, speak to its Franciscan friar. The delay afforded us time to visit the courtyard's terraced overlook of Jerusalem and enjoy its spectacular vantage point of the Old City, traditionally the view that had moved Jesus to tears in the last days before his crucifixion.

David took on his guiding mode, pointing out several places of interest in the panoramic landscape spreading before us. Though the Dome of the Rock has dominated the view from this spot since the seventh century, vivid in the imagination of pilgrims is how the city might have looked in Jesus' time, the second temple prominent in the skyline.

Standing close to a small group of American pilgrims clustered around their unusually soft-spoken guide, I inched closer, better to hear him describe the necropolis of some 70,000 Jewish graves covering the western slope of the Mount of Olives, the largest and most important cemetery of Judaism. As I listened and looked, I marveled at the billions of tears shed on this mountain by those grieving the loss of loved ones.

Directing his group's eyes to a remnant of a Jewish cemetery below the overlook, he asked a pastor in the group to read a portion of Ezekiel 37, the prophet's vision of the Valley of Dry Bones. The pastor's voice being stronger than his guide's, I was easily able to hear his reading, God asking Ezekiel, "Son of man, can these bones live?" then saying, "Prophesy to these bones and say to them, 'Dry bones, hear the word of the LORD! I will make breath enter you, and you will come to life. I will attach tendons to you and make flesh come upon you and cover you with skin; I will put breath in you, and you will come to life. Then you will know that I am the LORD.'"

After the reading their guide, visibly emotional and speaking in almost a whisper so that I stepped closer again, straining to hear, completed the passage, reading, "I will bring you back to the land of Israel. Then you my people will know that I am the LORD. I will put my spirit in you and you will live, and I will settle you in your own land. Then you will know that I the LORD have spoken, and I have done it, declared the LORD."

Reverently closing his well-worn Bible held together with duct tape, the guide apologized for his emotion, explaining that his grandparents had immigrated to Israel after being liberated from Dachau in April of 1945. He said he couldn't read Ezekiel's words, God's promise of re-establishing Israel in the land, without becoming emotional, reflecting on how thankful to God he is for raising up the United States of America to defeat the Nazis.

"Adam," one woman said, clinging to the tissue with which she was wiping away her own tears, "there is no need to apologize. We are so thankful to have you as our guide. You have made us realize that we are at home here, that we are a part of the story of this land, and a part of your story. You have opened our eyes to the fact that we are family."

After thanking the woman for her kindness, he asked their group leader, "Pastor, would you lead us now in prayer, as we stand on this mountain of tears, to remember the goodness of God in bringing his people back to the Promised Land? And, would you pray especially for America's soldiers who may today be in harm's way, that God would keep them safe?"

"What is it about this mountain?" I thought, turning to see Dominus Flevit's inverted teardrop ascending to heaven, flanked by four jars filled with the tears of God's people. As Adam led his group back to the Palm Sunday path to continue their walk down to Gethsemane, I saw that David had been listening also, quietly. My personal guide, David Aaronson, had fallen silent, moved by the promise of Ezekiel's Valley of Dry Bones.

Hearing behind us a cluster of pilgrims leaving the chapel, their mass having concluded, we walked back to see a priest welcoming the pilgrims who had been patiently waiting to enter. Unlike Father Jacques, as soon as he made eye contact with us, we knew that no introduction of David Aaronson would be necessary.

"You're David Aaronson?" he asked with undisguised excitement.

"I am," David said, smiling broadly at having been recognized.

Reaching his arm around me, he added, "and with me is my new bride, Stella Maris."

"Stella Maris? Well, what a pleasure it is to meet you and your wife today, Professor Aaronson. I am Father Jerome, and I must tell you how thrilled I am to meet you. I've studied your translation of the six tablets with great interest."

"That's very kind, thank you," David said.

Tapping his cell phone, Father Jerome said, "You'll forgive me, but I have a rather urgent call I must make. Please stay, though, as this will take only a few minutes."

"Thank you, Father," I said. "We'll wait for you inside the chapel, if that's okay."

"Certainly," he said, stepping toward the vestry at the rear of the chapel and leaving us to admire the stunning view of Temple Mount through the domed-shaped window over the altar, its black ironwork elegantly framing the Dome of the Rock.

I pointed out to David a fascinating mosaic medallion at the altar, a hen with wings outspread, having gathered her brood of seven chicks. In red letters around the circumference of the medallion is the Latin text of Luke 13:34, "Jerusalem, Jerusalem, how often I would I have gathered thy children together, as a hen gathers her brood under her wings, but you were not willing."

"Magnificent!" David said. "A similar message, is it not, to the Church of All Nations? It's as if these seven chicks represent earth's seven continents, all nations – east, west, north, and south – coming together."

"Very perceptive, Dr. Aaronson," Father Jerome said, having walked up behind us unobserved. "The Apostle Paul wrote his letter to the Colossians that Christ is before all things, and that in him all things hold together, that all things on earth as well as heaven will be reconciled through the blood of the cross. This, Paul wrote, was a mystery kept for ages and generations."

"Thank you, Father," I said. "What beautiful thoughts."

"Speaking of mysteries being revealed," he said, now looking at me with a slight bow, "may I say that it is truly an honor to welcome the Star of the Sea to Dominus Flevit?"

Seeing our stunned response, he grinned proudly. "Remember, I am Catholic. Stella Maris is a name of the holy virgin that we revere. We Catholics sing a hymn, 'Hail, Queen of Heaven, the Ocean Star,' a prayer for Mary's guidance through life's storms. I love the hymn's refrain:

> Mother of Christ, Star of the Sea,
> pray for the wanderer, pray for me."

"I know the hymn," I said, liking Father Jerome more and more. "My grandmother, Ursa Maris, was a Roman Catholic from Copenhagen. She taught it to me as a child."

"How wonderful and very unusual that you know this beautiful prayer-song to Mary. I've always thought of her as the only Star of the Sea, but when first I read Dr. Aaronson's translation of the six tablets, I saw that King David had his own Star of the Sea, a thousand years before Mary was born."

I started to speak, but Father Jerome continued. "Is it not fascinating that the wife of the archaeologist who discovered the Cave 53 tablets actually bears the name of David's Muse?"

While his words might have conveyed a suspicion of fraud, I detected nothing in his tone or demeanor suggesting such. It seemed the opposite, in fact, as he laughed and said, "After your discovery last year, Professor Aaronson, did you go online to look for a woman named Stella Maris, searching for your own Star of the Sea?"

"Not at all," David said. "I knew exactly where to find her. Stella was my star student the very first year of my teaching career. Speaking of a mystery long hidden, I think we fell in love at the very first, but hid it, even from each other. Only two months ago did we fully realize it ourselves."

"Really? So, when you said new bride, you meant very new."

"Yes," I said. "We were married only last week, on March the 9th."

"March 9?" he laughed. "Now, that is truly fascinating."

"How so?" I asked.

"Ah, patience, you'll soon see."

Impishly, he added, "I need now confess that my call's urgency was that I had been instructed only yesterday to call the Custos when you arrived."

"The Custos?" David asked.

"Yes, the Chief Custodian of the Franciscan Custody of the Holy Land. He should be here soon. Our offices are very near, at the New Gate."

"But, how could anyone have known that we were coming today?" I asked, recalling how David had also known of my arrival at his office, prepared by a dream. Had the Custos received a vision?

"The Custos will answer that question, but I assure you March 9 is an interesting date," he said, just as he received a text and looked down at his phone.

"Ah, look now! They will be here in only ten more minutes. Now, Stella Maris, Star of the Sea, tell me, where are you from?"

"Arkansas, Father."

I hadn't expected him to know Arkansas, so was surprised when his eyes brightened and he said, "Really, a Razorback. What city?"

"I live in Fayetteville, but was born and raised in Siloam Springs. Do you know these places?"

"Of course, I do, yes. People visiting from the states are often surprised to discover that I am from Texas, Ft. Worth, a city with several Franciscan communities."

"A Horned Frog?"

"I am!" he laughed loudly. "Believe it or not, many years

ago I played tennis for the Horned Frogs of TCU."

Waving his right arm, he said, "Quickly, come with me."

He led us into the vestry and pointed to a hanging wall mural that was made, he explained, after the 1964 visit to the Holy Land by Pope Paul VI. Father Jerome pointed out a figure among the faces of the crowd in the mural.

"Who does that look like?" he asked.

"John F. Kennedy, no question," David said.

"Precisely! He couldn't, of course, have been here in the Holy Land with Pope Paul in 1964, having been assassinated the year before. The mural's artist, though, placed him here in spirit. I remember very well JFK's last day on earth. He awoke in my own city of Ft. Worth. I was in the third grade, nine years old, and my mom and dad took me to hear him speak that morning in a parking lot outside Hotel Texas, where he would later have breakfast with the elite of Ft. Worth society. Elite my parents were not, but proud they were, standing in the rain that morning and listening to our first Roman Catholic president."

Turning reflective, he added, "Who could have imagined the events of later that day? I actually saw John F. Kennedy on his last day on earth, and just before his last supper."

Looking at his watch, he said, "Now, they must be getting close, so let's walk outside and meet the Custos."

As we exited the chapel onto the path, he said, "Professor, you must know that your discovery is helping bring tourists back to the Holy Land after the pandemic has crippled tourism these last two years. I know your office is very near, on Mount Scopus. I've wondered since your discovery if I might ask the university if it's possible for me to pay a fee to monitor one of your classes."

"I'm sure I could help you make that happen," David said.

"Thank-you. I'm serious. I would love the opportunity to

sit under your teaching."

"Father, since you've read the six tablets, you know that the sixth tablet tells of a hidden seventh tablet, the finale to David's song. You surely have guessed that our being here today is no accident, but part of our search."

"I do, yes, of course."

"Are you aware, then, of any stories of archaeological finds during Barluzzi's construction of either the Church of All Nations or Dominus Flevit?"

"Not until last week, Dr. Aaronson. The Custos holds the answers you seek. Just a bit more patience, as . . ."

Looking down the path, he interrupted himself.

"Oh, good, here they are now."

David and I looked at each other, bewildered. Could the discovery of the seventh tablet be this easy? Has it discovered us? Is today another Purim, God's plan coming together in God's timing?

The Chief Custodian was followed by an entourage of three, two joining him in the traditional garb of their order and a third wearing a business suit and rolling a medium sized black suitcase.

Father Jerome eagerly stepped up to welcome the Custos and to make introductions, his excitement a contrast to the solemn face of the Custos, whom he introduced as Father Constantino, Chief Custodian of the Franciscan Custody of the Holy Land.

Father Constantino's stern expression remained unchanged during Father Jerome's introductions, punctuated only by an occasional lifting of his head to nod slight acknowledgement. I found his stare awkward, his eyes returning often to my mid-section. I don't suggest anything inappropriate, however socially inept it seemed, but I sensed that, if he could, he would have reached out to touch my belly.

After Father Jerome's welcome, Father Constantino motioned for us to exit the tourist area into a small room adjacent the vestry. Not yet having spoken a word, he motioned for us to have a seat at a small wooden table with room for only four chairs. He joined us at the table as his assistants stood along the wall behind him.

"Father Jerome, sit," he said a bit roughly as he nodded at the one empty chair, his invitation eagerly accepted.

David could wait no longer. "Father Constantino, we understand that you were expecting us to arrive today?"

With a sideways glance at me, he continued, "We wonder how that is possible, since we weren't ourselves sure, not until last night, that we would be here today. How could you have known?"

"Dr. Aaronson, to answer your question you need to know some of the history of the Franciscan Custody of the Holy Land, and of Antonio Barluzzi, the architect of the two churches you have visited today."

"You are aware that we were at the Church of All Nations earlier?"

"Well, we weren't certain, and we didn't know it would be you, specifically, but we did know that the search for the lost tablet would bring the Star of the Sea here, to Dominus Flevit."

"So then," I said, "our question not only stands but is all the more in need of an answer."

"If it seems miraculous to you, you are not alone in thinking so. You should know that until eight days ago I would not have believed possible what I am about to tell you. Still, I admit to having no other explanation than a miracle of divine providence."

David and I exchanged a gaze of astonishment.

"Father," I said, "David and I recently experienced a similar miracle of God's timing. Only two months ago, on

January 18, he had been made miraculously aware, through a dream, of my surprise visit that morning to his office."

"A dream? Really? On January 18?"

"Is that date significant?"

"As you will soon see, a January 18th dream makes what I have to tell you all the more interesting."

He nodded to the assistant handling the suitcase, who lifted it to the table and zipped it open, removing a wooden lockbox with three evenly spaced decorative brass straps. Lifting the box carefully, the man sat it on the table in front of us.

"The story of this lockbox," the Custos said, "and how it came into the possession of the Custody, began in this very room, sixty-six years ago today, March 17, 1956, which was Shabbat. Barluzzi had sent a message to the Custos of that time, Father Angelico Lasseri, to meet him here, privately. Since Dominus Flevit had been only recently finished, with Father Angelico not yet having led the chapel's first Mass, he assumed something was terribly wrong with the construction. Instead, Barluzzi presented Father Angelico with this box. Father Angelico wrote that, as he looked on, Barluzzi took a silver plaque and with two screws attached it to the front of the case."

Father Constantino turned the case so that we could see the plaque, which read, TO BE OPENED BY THE CUSTOS ON MARCH 9, 2022.

Seeing our wedding date on this mysterious box was stunning.

"Did Barluzzi give Father Constantino any idea what the box contained?" David asked.

"He was evasive, asking Father Angelico to think of it as a time capsule, remembrances of his long association with the Custody."

Holding up a key, the Custos said, "He gave Father Angelico this key which, along with the box, has been securely kept in the Chief Custodian's office. More than merely kept, honestly. Due to Barluzzi's prominence, it's fair to say this box and its key have been reverenced by every Custos since. Father Angelico wrote a message that has been passed down Custos to Custos until now, describing Barluzzi's demeanor as not consistent with that of merely placing a time capsule. Barluzzi's mood, he wrote, conveyed an unmistakable sense of mystery."

"Father," I said, "If this is a time capsule, why set the opening as March 9? Why not March 17, the anniversary of its placement in your care?"

"Father Angelico wondered the same. The answer to your question was made clear only when we opened it eight days ago. Thinking it might contain fascinating items of historical importance, a potential news event, I invited witnesses to the opening, including Father Jacques, whom you met earlier today, and Father Jerome, who recorded the opening on his phone."

"March 9 was an important date for these two, as well," Father Jerome broke in. "They were married on March 9."

"Married?" Father Constantino asked. "March 9 was your anniversary?"

"No," I said. "Well, yes. What I mean to say is that we haven't had an anniversary yet. We were actually married eight days ago, on March 9, the day you opened the box."

"I see," he said, nodding at Father Jerome, who was ready now to show us the recording. "This makes Barluzzi's message all the more miraculous, as you shall see."

Watching the recording of the March 9 opening, we saw the Custos holding up the key to the camera, smiling in expectation of at last discovering the contents of Barluzzi's box. After opening the box, he lifted a manila envelope, holding it up for the camera to show that, on the outside were large letters reading, 'TO THE CUSTOS.' As he pulled out its papers and began to read, the recording showed his expression gradually shift from excited expectation to confusion. After only a few more seconds, he stopped reading and asked all who were present to leave at once, at which point the recording ended.

"What did you read?" David asked.

"I'll show you," he said, lifting the envelope to expose a second box, metallic and firmly nested inside the larger wooden box. A second, smaller manilla envelope was wedged tightly between the metal and the wood. He lifted the envelope to show us the hand-written message on the outside:

THIS KEY TO BE USED ONLY BY THE STAR OF THE SEA AND HER HUSBAND, MARCH 17, 2022.

Seeing those words, I gasped, my heart pounding in my chest.

David exclaimed, "Baruch Hashem! Not only did Barluzzi know we would be at Dominus Flevit today, he knew about the Star of the Sea and her husband, a text which in 1956 was still buried, unmoved for three thousand years! How is this possible?"

"With God, my son," Father Constantino said, his cadence slow and deliberate, "all things are possible. The answer to your question, impossible as it will be to believe, is in Barluzzi's letter to the Custos. Holding up the document, he pointed to the large letters at the top. "As you can see, Barluzzi gave his letter a title, like a sermon: A Young Man's Vision and An Old Man's Dream."

"That's from Peter's sermon on the Day of Pentecost," I said.

"Quoting the prophet Joel," David added.

"Yes, and yes," Father Constantino said. "Barluzzi, as a young man, felt called to ministry, so it's not surprising that he would begin his message with a biblical reference. Beneath his title, he wrote the text from Peter's Pentecost sermon, preaching to pilgrims who had gathered in Jerusalem from all nations."

"I've been thinking," I said, "how, along with the theme of agony, tears being so prominent on the Mount of Olives, is also the theme of universality, of all nations. Tears of pain and division are, on the mountain, balanced by the joyful prospect of something universal happening here."

"Universal, indeed," Father Jerome jumped in. "Near here is the Church of the Ascension, a place remembering Jesus' ascent into heaven from the Mount of Olives. There he issued the Great Commission, sending the apostles out with marching orders to go into all the world and make disciples in . . ."

"All nations," I completed the verse in unison with him.

"And then," Father Constantino added, "after his ascension on the fortieth day after his resurrection, the disciples waited ten more days, until the fiftieth day, Pentecost. That's when the Holy Spirit fell on the disciples with tongues of fire so that they uttered unlearned languages, all nations now able to hear the message of our Lord's death and resurrection."

Hearing of the fifty days of Pentecost, it occurred to me that David and I had been engaged exactly fifty days, from January 18 to March 9, before the spirits of David and Abishag had fallen upon us on our wedding night, consummating their love.

Holding the document out for us to see, Father Constantino said, "Barluzzi wrote the text under his title."

Using his finger to trace line-by-line, he pointed out how Barluzzi had capitalized the words YOUNG MEN/VISIONS and OLD MEN/DREAMS:

"This is what was spoken of by the prophet Joel:
'And it shall come to pass in the last days, (saith the Lord),
I will pour out my Spirit upon all flesh:
and your sons and your daughters shall prophesy,
and your YOUNG MEN shall see VISIONS,
and your OLD MEN shall dream DREAMS.'"

He then turned the paper away from us to continue reading Barluzzi's words aloud: "To the Chief Custodian who opens this case on March 9, 2022, the 100th anniversary of the day that I, Antonio Barluzzi, became the seventy-seventh *Shomer* (Keeper) of King David's prophecy. On that day, in the Cave of Gethsemane, the limestone tablet protected within the metal box was placed in my care. I am the seventy-seventh in an unbroken, three-thousand-year chain of *Shomrim* (Keepers) dating from King Solomon's reign.

"The tablet was passed to me by Eliezer Ben Yehuda, the seventy-sixth *Shomer*. Ben Yehuda, who resurrected the Hebrew language for the modern era, died only nine months after he passed the tablet to me, in 1922.

"He told me that each *Shomer* before me had held the tablet – inscribed by King David's royal scribe, Shemaiah ben Nethanel – for thirty-nine years, a total of 2,964 years. I have possessed the prophecy of David for only 34 years, 1922 - 1956. Why my time was cut short, I do not know, but at the conclusion of my building of Dominus Flevit, I was instructed by Shemaiah in my second vision to convey the tablet to the Custos of the Holy Land, where it would remain for sixty-six years before being opened by the Star of the Sea."

Pausing to look at our faces, he found us spellbound. Nodding to acknowledge our amazement, he sipped a bottle of water before continuing Barluzzi's letter.

"The seventh tablet is the conclusion to King David's last

psalm, etched by Shemaiah's own hand. The first six tablets remain lost, hidden by Shemaiah in the Judean wilderness. Those six tablets, once discovered in God's providence, will initiate the search for the seventh tablet. As you read this on March 9, 2022, the Star of the Sea's discovery of the seventh tablet nears.

"My receiving of the seventh tablet happened during the construction of the Church of All Nations, when I was young man of only thirty-seven years. On the night before I received the tablet from Eliezer ben Yehuda I was visited in a vision by Shemaiah, who told me that I had been chosen as the next *Shomer*, a secret society of *Shomrim* stretching back three thousand years. He instructed me to go the Cave of Gethsemane at 2:00 in the afternoon the following day.

"Upon awakening, thinking it merely a vivid dream, I had no intention of leaving the construction site during the afternoon. After lunch, however, I felt mysteriously drawn to the cave, where the wonders of which you yourselves are now witnesses transpired."

The Custos paused and said, "Here's where your own January 18 dream becomes interesting."

He read, "Thirty-three years later, on Tuesday, January 18, 1955, I – now an old man of seventy years – received a second dream in which Shemaiah instructed me that my thirty-nine years as *Shomer* would not be completed. There would be no seventy-eighth *Shomer*. Instead, I was told to prepare the tablet for placement in the care of the Franciscan Custody."

Father Constantino stopped his reading, my gasp having made it clear that I wanted to say something.

"His two visions were in 1922 and 1955?" I said, looking at David. "A young man's vision and an old man's dream! When I received my first vision, I was twenty-two years old. When I received my last vision, only two months ago, I was fifty-five years old. And you, like Barluzzi, had dual visions, a young man and," I paused with a slight grin, "a somewhat older man. First, on the night before we met in 1988 . . ."

"And then thirty-three years later on the night before you arrived at my office. My old man's dream was on January 18th, just as was Barluzzi's."

Ready to continue Barluzzi's description of the miracle, the Custos continued. "At this point, Barluzzi divides the paper into two sections: The Young Man's Vision, 1922; and The Old Man's Dream, 1955."

"Organized as a sermon and equally repetitive," I said.

Father Constantino smiled, then continued the reading: "The Young Man's Vision, 1922: The morning after my vision – March 9, 1922 – was cool and rainy. I had no intention to follow through and go to the cave at 2:00, thinking my dream a fantasy. After lunch, though, the morning inspection of the basilica's progress finished, I felt drawn to the cave.

"Through most of Christian history, this cave has been considered a holy site, many regarding it, rather than the basilica's Rock of Agony, to be the actual spot of Jesus' arrest. This theory is compelling, and I admit to preferring it. There was no one in the cave on that chilly day, so I found a chair in which I sat to rest in the relative warmth, the cave sheltering me from wind and wet. Having waited until just after 2:30, weary from the responsibilities of the day, I closed my eyes, and fell asleep."

Father Constantino paused to shift in his chair before he continued.

"I was startled by a tapping on my shoulder and a voice calling, 'Antonio.' When the visitor was certain I was awake, he said, 'Shalom, Antonio. I am Eliezer ben Yehuda, seventy-sixth *Shomer* of David's Prophecy. That you are here tells me you have received your first vision as a young man, just as last night I received my second vision as an old man. Today, my thirty-nine years as Keeper will end, and yours begin.'

"Opening his case, he lifted the tablet, which was wrapped in several layers of cloth. Unraveling the cloth, he carefully handled several papers that had been placed between the layers of cloth. He showed me the tablet, pointing at the inscription. 'Antonio,' he said, 'You are chosen as the seventy-seventh Keeper of King David's prophecy. I have held the tablet, as have each of the seventy-five Keepers before me, for thirty-nine years. I received it in 1883, in this very cave, from the old man Moses Montefiore, who in 1860 built *Mishkenot Sha'ananim*, the Peaceful Dwellings, the first neighborhood outside the walls of Jerusalem. He met me in this cave two years before he passed away at the age of 100. As all the Keepers before me, Shemaiah has appeared to you in your first vision as a young man, bringing you here at the appointed time. Unless the prophesied time arrives while you hold the tablet, thirty-nine years from now, in 1961, Shemaiah will come to you in a second vision as an old man, with instructions on transferring the tablet to the seventy-eighth *Shomer*.'"

"Why, then, 1956?" I asked. "Why thirty-four, instead of thirty-nine years?"

"Let's read on for the answer," he said.

"There was one question I needed to ask Ben Yehuda. I wanted to know who was the Keeper of the prophecy when Jesus was alive, when my Lord prayed in agony in this very cave? Ben Yehuda smiled and said, 'I, too, asked Montefiore about the identity of previous *Shomrim*. He told me, as I now tell you, that the papers you have seen wrapped with the tablet list all of the *Shomrim*. I added my name to the list, as you will now add yours. To answer your specific question, the twenty-eighth Keeper, from 11 to 50 A.D., was Nicodemus, the

Pharisee who came to Jesus by night. Jesus told him that to enter the Kingdom of God, one must be born again. This much the gospel of John tells us, but what John didn't record is that Jesus, in response to Nicodemus' impertinent question of whether a man could enter his mother's womb a second time, called him aside to whisper, 'Is this so hard for you, *Shomer* of my father's prophecy, to believe? Have you not read in the tablet that David will yet return to father a child?' Nicodemus, having been true to his vow never to mention the tablet to anyone, was so shocked at Jesus' knowledge of the seventh tablet, that he could never doubt again that this was the Son of God.'"

It was now beginning fully to hit me that, if David were to father a child, I would be the child's mother, David's prophecy being fulfilled in my own womb. This is why Father Constantino had gazed so strangely at my belly, as if he had wanted to touch and bless my womb.

"Nicodemus," I said, "the Pharisee whose visit to Jesus gave us the phrase, born again, was a *Shomer*? Imagine, the names that will appear as *Shomrim* through three thousand years!"

"And each one faithful," the Custos agreed, "bringing the seventh tablet at long last, to you, David's Star of the Sea."

"Let's finish his first vision," he said. "There's only a bit more and a few of those names you are now wondering about are included."

He read: "Ben Yehuda then said, 'The first of the Keepers, the only *Shomer* knowing Shemaiah in the flesh, considered Shemaiah his teacher. 1 Kings 4:1 lists this man, Jehoshaphat ben Ahilud, among the important officials of King Solomon, the Bible describing him as Solomon's official recorder. When Shemaiah came back to Jerusalem from the desert, having deposited the six tablets along with David's bones in the cave, he asked Jehoshaphat to meet him secretly in the cave across the Kidron. At that time, before the olive press was installed in the cave, it was not yet known as Gethsemane.

"As I pass the tablet to you, the seventy-seventh *Shomer*, you are Called to continue the work of the society of *Shomrim*, inaugurated by Shemaiah in 1042 B.C. when he made his student, Jehoshaphat, the first *Shomer*. Jehoshaphat held the tablet until he received a vision from the then-deceased Shemaiah, thirty-nine years later, in 1003 B.C., in which he was instructed to go to the cave the next day and pass the tablet to the second *Shomer*. This man was a most interesting Keeper who, like you, Antonio, was a builder. Jeroboam ben Nebat was an important figure in Solomon's administration, the architect and builder of the wall called in the Bible the Millo. Jeroboam took the tablet with him into Egyptian exile after Solomon, hearing a prophecy that Jeroboam would one day ascend to the throne, sought unsuccessfully to have him assassinated. Indeed, Jeroboam did return from exile after Solomon's death to become the first king of the northern kingdom, ruling over Israel for forty years. In 964 B. C., the end of his thirty-nine years, Jeroboam was called back to the cave to pass the prophecy to the third *Shomer*. Considered at that time a traitor to Jerusalem, you can imagine that his return to the cave was daring, accomplished at great risk, in secret, and in disguise."

Father Constantino paused, looking up to say, "Barluzzi doesn't identify the third *Shomer*, nor any of the others. After Jeroboam, he changes the subject."

Reading on, he said: "Ben Yehuda then asked me if I had, in my vision, seen the bones. I affirmed that I had, that Shemaiah had taken me in my dream into a dark, cramped cave. I saw the stone tablets, but Shemaiah's focus was on the dry bones. He said, 'Antonio, can these bones live?' When I inquired whose bones these were, he said, 'These are the bones of David ben Jesse, King of Israel.' Upon hearing that, I saw sinew and flesh began to amass on the bones. I was witnessing King David's life in reverse, being restored. First, the cave's dry bones gathered into a complete skeleton, followed by muscle structure, then by flesh. At last, I saw David lying on his deathbed, his hand held by a young woman, sobbing. Time continued in reverse, until I saw this woman many days earlier lying beside him, as if a blanket of flesh for his warmth. I watched as his body continued to reverse in age, the beautiful woman staying the same age, perhaps twenty years old. When he became young enough, perhaps thirty, I saw David and the woman lying in the afterglow of lovemaking. I knew these two were David and Abishag when I heard him whisper, 'Abby, my Star of the Sea, our wandering is at last complete, our love consummated.' I saw them rise from the bed and dance, he naked, but wrapping her in a blanket. I saw behind them the waves of the sea as he picked up a rose, kissed it, and ran its long stem into her hair.

"Ben Yehuda, who had been listening with rapt attention to my description, said, 'I saw none of those things. I saw only dry bones. Surely, God has great plans for you, Antonio.'"

David and I had listened, stunned and speechless, to Barluzzi's description of our own wedding night. Both the Custos and Father Jerome noticed our astonishment and stared, waiting for comment. David said, "We hardly know what to say. As you were reading these words of Barluzzi for the first time on March 9, Stella and I were actually living them. You have described our wedding night."

"The scene was just as Barluzzi described it," I added, "the sea in the background, the dancing, the blanket, the rose."

After a time of reflection, the Custos said, "Perhaps we should continue," his tone suggesting yet more astonishing revelations to come. He read: "I then told Ben Yehuda that Shemaiah ended my vision by saying, 'Antonio, I will come to you again when you have built your last church on this holy mountain, at the place where the Lord wept.'"

Father Constantino looked up after that brief sentence to say, "And that is the end of Barluzzi's first section, his telling of his first vision, received as a young man in 1922."

Our silence offering no diversion, Father Constantino said, "Barluzzi is much briefer in describing his second vision, but it's revelations are equally astounding. Are you ready?"

"Yes," we said, in unison.

"The Old Man's Dream, 1955: The world changed much during my three decades as *Shomer*, especially during the forties. The War to End All Wars, raging when first I came to the Holy Land, could no longer be called by name, the world having been pulled into the horrors of the Second World War and the Holocaust, followed by the reestablishment of the nation of Israel in 1948. I, the seventy-seventh *Shomer* of King David's prophecy, witnessed all these things.

"As Shemaiah had predicted in my 1922 vision, my final project brought me back to the Mount of Olives. Nearing completion of the Dominus Flevit, on January 18, 1955, I received my second vision. Shemaiah told me in the dream, 'Antonio, sixty-six years from this day the six tablets of David's final song, along with his dry bones, will be discovered at the Salt Sea. The time is near for the faithful to know that my king will come back and, with his Star of the Sea, give birth to a child who will heal the nations.

"You, Antonio, are the last of the Keepers, the only *Shomer* not sent back to the Cave of Gethsemane to pass the seventh tablet to a successor. Instead, you will pass the tablet to the Chief Custodian of the Holy Land, not informing him of the treasure in his keeping. This must happen in God's timing, next year, on March 17, 1956. You will place the tablet in a secure box with instructions for only David's Star of the Sea to open it on March 17, 2022, the Feast of Purim. Place the tablet and its box into a larger container, with instructions for the Custos to open the outer box eight days earlier, on March 9, 2022, this holy day is the day the child to be born of David and his Star of the Sea will be conceived.'"

Father Constantino paused, letting Barluzzi's words sink in. Shemaiah's words to Barluzzi, recorded and passed on to Father Angelico sixty-six years earlier, and stored securely since, had pinpointed the day of our wedding. But how could I, at fifty-six years old, bear a child? This would be a miracle on the order of Abraham and Sarah bearing Isaac, or Zechariah and Elizabeth bearing John the Baptist, these the two most prominent miracles in the Bible of giving birth in old age.

After a moment of silence, I looked at David and we laughed. Laughed! We laughed, not in disbelief, but in joy.

"Do you recall, Stella, why Abraham and Sarah named their boy, Isaac?"

"I do. Isaac means 'he laughed,' Abraham and Sarah remembering how they laughed when they were told that they would bear a child in their old age."

"Or," David said, "perhaps God was the one who laughed, laughing to have brought such joy to his chosen."

"Oh, yes, I like that! God laughed! We are laughing with God!"

Father Constantino, reacting to our playfulness, said, "Shall I read on, children?"

"Please," I answered.

The Custos looked down to read Barluzzi's final words: "These instructions of Shemaiah, David's royal scribe, I have followed faithfully. Honored Custos, I wish I could be with you at Dominus Flevit to meet David's Star of the Sea, and to behold her wonder and joy as she first touches the seventh tablet."

Father Constantino sighed, dropped Barluzzi's letter to the desk, then leaned back in his chair.

David asked, "No more?"

"No more words," he said, turning the paper toward me, "only a drawing of a clock face, with the hands pointing to . . ."

"3:39," I said, seeing the paper.

Father Jerome gasped, pointing to the digital display on the wall. "Praise God!" he said, "Are we not bearing witness to the precision of divine providence?"

"We are, indeed," I replied. "It is 3:39 on the ninth day of our married life, begun on March 9th. Third month. Ninth day."

"Imagine," David whispered to me.

"Imagine?" I said, not looking at David but still staring at the wall clock's glowing numbers, 3:39.

"Yes. Imagine . . . what John Lennon would say about all these nines."

"Why should we be surprised?" I said, turning to David as the clock shifted to 3:40. "*Qoheleth*, the Teacher of Ecclesiastes, taught that there is a time – evidently a precise time – for every matter under heaven. The time for this matter, clearly, is 3:39. In God's sovereign timing, the seventh tablet has found us."

Father Constantino, his expression now one of sheer joy, drew from the second envelope a small key and a single sheet of paper with Barluzzi's handwriting. Rising to his feet and gesturing for me to likewise stand, his wording was made as an official presentation.

"Stella Maris, Star of the Sea, as Chief Custodian of the Franciscan Custody of the Holy Land, I am honored to present to you the contents of Antonio Barluzzi's box. I verify that it has been faithfully watched over by each Custos since it was placed in the possession of Father Angelico Lasseri on this very day sixty-six years ago."

My response was similarly official. "Father Constantino, on behalf of David's royal scribe and friend, Shemaiah, and of the seventy-seven *Shomrim* who have kept the seventh tablet safe for three thousand years, I extend my gratitude to you, and to all of your predecessors, for your diligent faithfulness in protecting the seventh tablet of King David's last song."

Looking down at the key and paper now in my hand, I continued, "May all the nations of the world be blessed by its reading."

Clutching the key in my right hand, I handed the paper to David and asked him to read Barluzzi's letter aloud.

"Are you sure?" he asked. "Shouldn't you read the letter?"

"I'm sure," I said. "You are the one I call *Ishi*, aren't you?"

Nodding, David looked down at the paper. As he read, I closed my eyes to imagine the words being spoken by Barluzzi himself: "To King David's Star of the Sea and her husband: David's royal *sopher*, Shemaiah ben Nethanel, during the nine months that the king's remains rested in Jerusalem, with great care inscribed David's final psalm on seven limestone tablets. Fulfilling the king's dying wish to be buried in the wilderness, after nine months and with King Solomon's assistance, Shemaiah transported his royal remains into the Judean Wilderness. There, near the Dead Sea, he hid them in a cave, along with the first six tablets.

"The seventh tablet now in your possession – David's dying prophecy – has been passed down at the Cave of Gethsemane by seventy-seven *Shomrim*. Each *Shomer* before me watched over the tablet for thirty-nine years, beginning and ending with a vision from Shemaiah – a Young Man's

Vision and an Old Man's Dream.

"On this 17th day of March – Year of our Lord 2022 – the seventh tablet is at last in your hands. With all my heart I wish I could meet you, but as I write these words in 1956 you are surely not yet born. Yet you, like Mary, the mother of my Lord, belong to the ages. I can't imagine the depths of your wonder and joy in knowing you are the Chosen One, that you have already conceived and will bear King David's daughter.

"While David's prophecy no doubt fills you with joy, with regret I say to you, as Simeon long ago announced to Mary, that a sword will one day pierce your own heart. Know that I, Antonio Barluzzi, seventy-seventh *Shomer*, pray for you and for your holy child, as with these final words I lock away the seventh tablet. Henceforth, it will be seen by no human eye, until the glorious day that it comes to you, David's *Kochav Hayam*."

David looked up from the paper. "That's it. That's all he wrote."

Prepping my phone, I handed it to Father Jerome, asking if he would record me opening the box. Eagerly he jumped to his feet to comply, recording as I placed the key in the lock, which worked as if new. What was immediately visible was cloth, and much of it, thickly wrapping a roughly rectangular tablet, similar in size to the six tablets of Cave 53. Slowly unwrapping the cloth to expose the tablet, an envelope fell from between the wrappings. Picking it up, we saw that Barluzzi had written the words, "The Seventy-seven *Shomrim*."

Shaking his head in disbelief, David said, "Imagine the names in this document, each with a unique story spanning thirty-nine years between their two visions."

Wordlessly, I laid the envelope to the side. Carefully, I reached for the tablet, gently peeling more than pulling the last layer of cloth away from the stone. When my fingers first came into contact with its surface, I was startled at what, to me, was a flash of light, as if someone had taken a photograph. I knew David had seen it also, his hand on my shoulder jerking in unison with my own recoil. The others in the room, though, seemed oblivious to what had happened. Father Jerome was still recording, unphased, and the Custos and his entourage were looking on with no sign of alarm.

"Did you see that?" I whispered to David.

"And felt it, yes."

"What was it?"

"I think it is David and Abishag, joining us for the dance, as they did on our wedding night."

I knew David was right when, looking at the tablet I could read its excellently preserved Paleo-Hebrew script as easily as if it were the morning English edition of *Israel Hayom*. My passenger, the one who had made me fluent in Hebrew during my visions, had returned.

Fully exposing the inscribed side of the tablet, I rested it on the table in front of David who, translating into English, read aloud:

"Praise be to God, who does not abandon us in regions of deep darkness.

Hashem has answered my dying prayer,

sending again Eliana, *Malaki*, my *Kochav Hayam*.

For thirty-three years I have longed to look again upon her beauty,

as when last we danced, leading the ark into *Yerushalayim*.

Her true name is now revealed, Abishag,

She who guided me as the scroll of my life unfurled:

I the shepherd, I the warrior,

I the refugee, I the rebel,

I the king.

331

Solomon, my son, king of all Israel:
I was not reared in the palace, upon gold plates I did not dine,
from silver goblets I did not drink.
In Shepherds' Fields I learned of *Hashem*, in the wilderness I
learned kingship.
So let my end be as my beginning.
In *Yerushalayim* do not allow my bones to abide.
After nine months, secret my bones and my song
into the wilderness, a cave my hiding place.
There, embracing my song,
my soul will wander in Sheol,
until my *Kochav Hayam* guides the wanderer home,
so that our love may be consummated,
bringing healing to the Land.

Our child, Malka bat David,
born on the Mount of Olives to wipe away its tear-flood,
will join her brother, the greater than Solomon,
the blessed Son of David yet to be born in my Bethlehem.
He will fulfill God's promise to me,
that the House of David will rule Israel
as long as sun and moon endure.
Selah.

On the day of their joining, sister and brother,
Female and male, both of the seed of David,
this troubled Land will be healed,
its peace spreading to all the earth."

I had imagined that my seventh vision had eliminated all
surprise from my reading of the seventh tablet. I was
mistaken. Shemaiah had withheld from my dream the most

wonderful revelation of all, that I would be, on the day the seventh tablet would be discovered and read, in the ninth day of a miraculous pregnancy, and that our child would be a girl, the daughter of David, and brother of Jesus.

Chapter 20

Augusta Victoria Hospital, Mount of Olives

NOVEMBER 26, 2022

Malka, the name King David had chosen for his daughter, is Hebrew for Queen. Since my own name, Stella, is the Latin equivalent of the Hebrew word for Star (*Kochav*), I asked David what he thought of naming our daughter Regina, the Latin equivalent of the Hebrew name, *Malka*.

He was enthusiastic, pointing out that the Regina Maris (Queen of the Sea) was the name of the schooner that had rescued Jews fleeing Denmark during the Nazi occupation, saving the life of his great uncle, Max Aaronson. Twenty-seven years old when rescued, Max was the first of the Aaronson clan to settle in Boston.

"That's beautiful, David. I hadn't realized that your ancestors, like mine, were Danes. Still, I want our daughter to bear her father's name, Regina Aaronson, not Regina Maris. Do you, perchance, know of any ships by that name?"

Laughingly assuring me that he did not, David countered

with a hybrid suggestion, that we use both the Latin and Hebrew for our daughter's given name (Regina Malka) followed by a hyphenated surname (Maris-Aaronson).

My OB/GYN, Deborah Stern (whom we chose from a list of doctors, David pointing out when he first saw her name that Stern is Yiddish for "Star"), got a kick out of the initials (RMMA) for Regina Malka Maris-Anderson. While in medical school, she explained, she worked part-time for a fertility clinic known by those very initials, RMMA standing for Reproductive Medical/Miracle Associates, a medical group devoted to helping women become pregnant.

"Well, we seem already to have taken care of that challenge, Dr. Stern," I laughed in our first meeting, "but we would love for you to walk with us the rest of the way."

My choice for where I wanted to give birth, Augusta Victoria Hospital on the Mount of Olives, surprised David and Dr. Stern, both immediately declaring it impossible. I heard their "No way!" as "Yes, sure!" How, I wondered, since in my womb was already the greatest miracle of all, could they imagine such a simple request unthinkable?

Augusta Victoria Hospital, a Lutheran hospital connected to the Evangelical Lutheran Church of the Ascension, is located on the northernmost part of the Mount of Olives at the point of Jerusalem's highest elevation. Near Hebrew University, the hospital is less than a mile from David's office, a fact having nothing to do with my request.

My choice had nothing to do with convenience, but rather that Augusta Victoria would fulfill the seventh tablet prophecy that Regina's advent be upon the Mount of Olives. Choosing Augusta Victoria in East Jerusalem would signal that Regina's birth held the promise of healing the rift between the two long-time adversarial families of the Holy Land, the Palestinians and the Jews.

The hospital was established after the 1898 visit to the Holy Land by Kaiser Wilhelm II. A momentous event heralded throughout the Holy Land, the visit of the Kaiser and his wife, Augusta Victoria, generated enormous excitement. The Ottoman Empire responded to the Kaiser's visit with a gift of land on the Mount of Olives. When the cornerstone for the church was laid nine years later, in 1907, construction began on what would become the first modern building in Jerusalem with electricity.

After sharing my vision while in the examination room David, with Dr. Stern's nodding agreement, sought to calm my excitement, reminding me that the hospital is devoted to serving the Palestinian population of the Holy Land. Dr. Stern added that the hospital has no labor and delivery area, but is a cancer center focusing on hematology, bone marrow, and dialysis, in addition to being a surgical center for cancer of the ear, nose, and throat. The hospital's focus, she said, was Palestinian children. Augusta Victoria, they agreed, would not be an option.

"David," I said, "has not our story from the beginning been a miracle? What small Christian college would hire a recently graduated Jewish professor to teach Old Testament, as C-cube did? Don't you remember the stir that caused, that a Jew who wouldn't even call the Hebrew Bible the 'Old' Testament would be allowed to teach Christian students? God's hand has guided this miracle from the very first day. He has shown me that he will clear the way for Regina to be born at Augusta Victoria."

At last nodding agreement, David noted that Augusta Victoria's 200-foot-tall bell tower was erected atop what was already the highest spot in Jerusalem, making it the perfect place to ring forth our daughter's birth.

"Let us then see if we can ring the bells," Dr. Stern chimed in, "for a reproductive medical miracle, Regina Malka Maris-Aaronson!"

I read later that when the four bells for the tower were delivered to the church from Hamburg in 1907, the road to Jerusalem from Jaffa had to be rebuilt to handle the enormous weight, the highways of that time inadequate to handle such a heavy load. I liked the symbolism of that bit of trivia, I told David, since all previous diplomatic efforts to pave the road to peace since Israel became a nation in 1948 had likewise proven incapable of bearing the load. As well-meaning as those efforts had been, the road to peace must now be completely rebuilt. Not by presidents and prime ministers, nor by ambassadors and diplomats, but by a newborn girl.

God did indeed clear the way for Regina to be born at Augusta Victoria. Father Constantino, a close friend of the hospital's CEO, privately verified to him the miracle of the seventh tablet's discovery at Dominus Flevit, and of how he had been the one, only nine days after our wedding, to inform me that I was carrying the child of promise – not only for Jews and Christians, but for all nations.

My due date, knowing my pregnancy had begun on our wedding day, March 9, would fall in early December. I fantasized at first that I might carry my baby all the way to December 25th, her Christmas Day birth declaring to the world that Regina was the twin sister of Jesus.

It was not to be, *Baruch Hashem*. At my age, carrying a baby beyond term would have been . . . well, miserable. Thankful I am now that my daughter's first blessing extended to her mother was to arrive early.

On Thanksgiving Day, November 24, David prepared a special meal of turkey and dressing to celebrate our homeland, the United States of America. Early the next afternoon, my water broke. David, having made special arrangements with the hospital to set up a small birthing center just for me, jumped into gear to rush me to Augusta Victoria.

After David called Dr. Stern, who assured him that she would be at the hospital when we arrived, he came to help me stand. I slowed his panicked urgency, saying, "Before we go, David, dance with me."

"You can't be serious!" he said, utterly annoyed.

"I am most serious."

And for a few precious moments, as if leading the way for Regina's entrance into *Yerushalayim*, I danced with David.

The delivery, though long, was not as difficult as I had expected. Dr. Stern and the hospital nursing staff, working together seamlessly, brought our miracle child into the world on Shabbat, Saturday, November 26, 2022, at 3:39 a.m.

Around nine o'clock on Sunday morning, David and I heard the laughter of children outside our hospital room window. Opening the blinds, we saw the thirty-nine children who had gathered. I stood, holding Regina up to the window for them to see, her first appearance to the world she was born to heal.

The jubilant children were guided by their chaperones to approach the window in groupings of three, reminiscent of the magi meeting the newborn Son of David in Bethlehem two thousand years earlier. It was a parade of joy, thirteen groupings of three children laying small gifts and flowers on the ground outside the window, then pecking on the glass to get her attention, hoping to elicit a smile. Adults were positioned at the window to hand the children leaves collected from nearby olive trees, which they held up and waved before dropping them to the ground.

We knew the story behind these children and their leaves. The children were from the church founded by Pastor Michael Tabash, a Palestinian Christian who named his new church after the congregation I pastored for twenty-seven years in Arkansas, calling it the Holy Land Maranatha Assembly of the Blessed Hope. The words Maranatha Assembly were on the front of the variously and brightly colored tee shirts worn by all the children.

Michael had formed his church the night of March 20, his immediate response of faith after hearing David's first media announcement of our having discovered the seventh tablet at Dominus Flevit three days earlier. David had taken three days to craft his announcement, knowing that the message of the seventh tablet would be earthshaking for Israel and the world. Over those three days, and with some difficulty, David had convinced the highly respected, but equally private, Father Constantino to join the Zoom call so that he might verify that the tablet had been in the possession of the Franciscan Custody for sixty-six years.

Opening the March 20 conference with the good news that we had discovered the seventh tablet and placed it in the possession of the IAA (Israel Antiquities Authority), David promised to publish very soon a full translation of the inscription. He knew, of course, that his announcement would damage his reputation as a scholar, placing at peril even his position at Hebrew University.

He began the conference by calling attention to the three mysteries posed by the Cave 53 tablets, mysteries he had listed at the conclusion of his September 6 media conference six months earlier: Where is the seventh tablet? Whose bones are these? Who is David's Star of the Sea?

After reminding the media of those three mysteries, David

made the startling claim that the newly discovered seventh tablet had answered them all:

(1) Where was the seventh tablet? Backed by the testimony of Father Constantino, he explained how the Franciscan Custody of the Holy Land had unknowingly possessed the tablet since 1956, deposited there as a time capsule by the famed Holy Land architect, Antonio Barluzzi, who claimed to be the last of seventy-seven *Shomrim* (Keepers) of the tablet. These *Shomrim*, Barluzzi claimed, had passed down the tablet for three millennia, since the death of King David. Incredulous, though stunned that such an extraordinary claim was verified by Father Constantino, the media attendees were then treated to an even more shocking claim.

(2) Whose bones were found in Cave 53? The seventh tablet, David claimed, had conclusively identified the bones as those of King David, his skeletal remains secretly relocated from Jerusalem nine months after his death and deposited in the desert in accordance with his wishes, at the command of his son, King Solomon. This revelation, David knew, would shock the Jewish world, offering yet another alternative to the long-disputed location of David's tomb.

(3) Who was King David's Star of the Sea? Knowing that his answer to this mystery would likely finish his career, David proudly proclaimed that Stella Maris, his former student and, since March 9, his wife, was none other than King David's Star of the Sea, the one whom the sixth tablet had prophesied would discover the seventh tablet.

The triad of mysteries solved, David's final revelation was the most startling of all, that the seventh tablet was King David's deathbed prophecy that he would return in spirit to father a daughter who, joining her Bethlehem-born brother, would bring healing to the Land and spread peace throughout the earth. Though David stopped short of claiming that he was himself the fulfillment of the prophecy, that the spirit of David ben Jesse had filled his body so that he would be the father of the coming miracle child, the inference was glaring, impossible to miss.

David concluded his March 20 video conference, "I met Stella Maris, David's Star of the Sea, in 1988, my first year of teaching in Memphis. Stella was enrolled in my class on Hebrew poetry, which I began with a study of Psalm 89, the psalmist's bitter complaint that God had abandoned his promise to David. 'Where is your promise to David?' was his question. 'Why have you turned your back on your anointed?' In God's timing, we now have the answer. God never for a second forgot his promise to the shepherd of Bethlehem."

David knew that after his video conference he would certainly be regarded as delusional, and likely terminated from his prestigious post at The Hebrew University. Our assumption was correct. Unlike the September 6 conference, which had been received and reported on by the media as the work of a respected archaeologist, the March 20 conference was declared bizarre and delusional. Despite tenure protection, David was terminated twelve days later, on April Fools' Day.

David used the April 1 date to declare as foolish the scholarly world in their inability to accept the miracle of the seventh tablet, a miracle supported by the testimony of Father Constantino. Still, the Custos' testimony, while unconvincing to the scholarly world, was sufficient to generate great excitement in the Holy Land and around the world, leaving the academic community scrambling to propose other viable explanations.

Favored among those explanations, of course, was fraud. Though remaining unexplained and unexposed, the theory that the Cave 53 discovery was an elaborate illusion was latched onto by the university's administration. The claim of fraud was, of course, bolstered by Jakob Rothman's coming forward to confess that he himself had planted the seed of delusion in 1988 by sharing his former fiancé's claim to have experienced six visions with their professor. It was that, he believed, that gave Aaronson the first inkling of an idea to create the massive deception, carefully constructing his illusion for thirty-three years. Jakob, of course, was quick to highlight David's classroom comments about being born on the same day as his hero of magic, David Copperfield. That calendar coincidence was enough for the media to sell the narrative that David Aaronson was nothing more than a conman.

The kindness toward me that Jakob had shown in Tiberias, assuming I had been duped and hoping I could be convinced to abandon my plans to marry David, had evaporated. Jakob's new claim was that I must have been in on the scam the entire time.

If the scholarly world was quick to claim that the new Psalm 151 discovery was fraudulent, Pastor Michael Tabash was the first and most enthusiastic believer. Calling family and a few friends together that night, he constituted his new church, eventually naming it the Holy Land Maranatha Assembly of the Blessed Hope.

While at first very small, consisting of only a handful of Palestinian Christians, Maranatha Assembly's rapid growth began after David published his full translation of the seventh tablet's text on May 19. The psalm's promise of a coming Daughter of David, and the undeniable miracle pregnancy of a post-menopausal Christian pastor who had claimed since 1988 to be King David's *Kochav Hayam*, spurred growth among their Palestinian Christian core, then spread to attract converts from Jewish communities and a growing mosaic of cultures.

David's choice of May 19 as his publication date was intentional, it being the Jewish holiday *Lag BaOmer* ("The 33rd Day of the Omer"). On *Lag BaOmer* bonfires are lit throughout Israel to celebrate the day that the deepest secrets of the Kabbalah were given in the *Zohar*, a Hebrew word meaning "radiance." In his preface to the translation, David said that he chose to reveal the message of the seventh tablet on *Lag BaOmer* so that the world might see, in each bonfire blazing throughout Israel, the radiance of the promise of the coming Daughter of David.

With the publication of the seventh tablet's prophecy, Pastor Tabash's Maranatha Assembly began its rapid growth, his preaching focusing on the three mysteries of the Cave 53 discovery, all now revealed to herald the imminent arrival of a newborn child, the Daughter of David. Central to his message was that Stella Maris was King David's *Kochav Hayam*, now miraculously pregnant.

David and I would become close friends with Michael and his wife, Tamara. I was often invited to visit the church and to preach as an honored guest, so that today, standing at our hospital window with Regina, David and I easily recognized many of the children's faces as they approached with glee, three by three by three, little gift-bearing magi.

We knew also the story of the olive leaves the children were waving and dropping outside our window. Eight hundred olive trees, many reported to be over a thousand years old, dot the landscape of the forty-six acres atop the Mount of Olives on land owned and operated by the Lutheran World Federation.

Every year, during the six weeks from mid-October to the end of November, Palestinian volunteers joined by tourists from around the world harvest those eight hundred trees. The nearly two tons of olives from the harvest are then pressed, the proceeds from the olive oil going to the hospital's Fund for the Poor, helping to cover the healthcare costs of patients unable to pay.

When I told Michael that Regina would be born at Augusta Victoria, he told me that he had volunteered in the olive harvest every year since 1994, working with other volunteers in an atmosphere of joy and laughter.

As it happened, this year's harvest ended on the day before Regina was born, November 25. Michael's message to his congregation that night, knowing that I had been taken to the hospital, claimed that the stage was now set for God to bring in the final harvest through *Kochav Hayam's* daughter, Regina. Taking his text from the last chapter of the Bible, Revelation 22, he declared that the tree whose leaves would be for the healing of the nations was none other than Regina Malka Maris-Aaronson, a seedling soon to be planted on the Mount of Olives and destined to be grafted into the family tree of her holy brother, Jesus, the Son of David.

Knowing I was already in labor, his sermon ended with a request for children volunteers to greet Regina the next morning with the healing leaves gathered from the olive trees atop the Mount of Olives. When thirty-nine children came forward to volunteer, Michael and Tamara decided to have them approach our window in a parade of threes.

After the parade of children, David and I enjoyed several hours of quiet rest, filled with thanksgiving for and marveling at the miracle of divine providence that brought us together in 1988, then again thirty-three years later, and now placing in our loving arms and joyful hearts our beautiful miracle.

Regina's dance with destiny has begun, the daughter of a Christian woman and a Jewish man – pastor and professor – who, in the mystery of God's will, became one with David and Abishag. Regina Malka Maris-Aaronson, the daughter of

David, has been born to accomplish what generations of politicians and diplomats have been powerless to achieve. I've seen too much not to believe the seventh tablet prophecy that Malka bat David will one day join her brother, Yeshua ben David, for the healing of the nations.

No voice of *Hakol* could convince me otherwise.

At 3:33 David's phone rang, just as we had planned, establishing a Facetime connection with our dear friend, Pastor Michael. During his early morning visit to the hospital with Tamara, we decided to make a public proclamation of Regina's birth at precisely 3:39 p.m., marking the beginning of the 13th hour of Regina's life. From our room, Michael had texted the entire membership of his church, calling an assembly at the Mount of Olives pavilion overlooking the Old City, only a mile south of the hospital. Now, David sat close by the bed as I held Regina, his phone at arm's length so we could view the spectacle.

Michael excitedly described the scene for us, turning the phone to show how the terraces had filled with people. Standing at street level, he was at the highest point, seen by all. After we shared our thanks and excitement, Michael handed his phone to Tamara, then stepped up onto a small platform to take the microphone from the portable public address system he had set up.

For a nearly a minute he stared at the large digital clock he had attached to the front of the podium, waiting for it to glow with the numbers, 3:39. His face breaking into a bright smile when he saw those numbers, he looked up to the crowd and shouted, "I bring you glad tidings of great joy!"

The crowd stirred with an excitement which quickly quieted, Michael making gestures for silence. He then proclaimed his Good News, crafted to replicate the angels announcing the birth of Jesus to the shepherds as they watched over their flocks by night. With exuberant joy he proclaimed Regina Malka Maris-Aaronson, born at 3:39 a.m. on the Mount of Olives, to be the fulfillment of King David's seventh tablet prophecy. Pointing down the hill, he reminded his church that the seventh tablet had been discovered just nine months earlier only a short distance away, at Dominus Flevit, where once Jesus wept.

Telling the biblical stories of both King David and Jesus weeping on this mountain, he proclaimed that now and forever the Mount of Olives would no longer be a place of tears, but a place of rejoicing. From our room, David and I laughingly joined Michael as he led the crowd in singing the chorus, "This is the day that the Lord has made, we will rejoice and be glad in it."

Several minutes later, as Michael continued his sermon, a nurse entered the room to check my vitals. Seeing him enter, David turned away from me toward the window, focusing his attention on his phone as he continued to watch and listen to the celebration.

"Oh, Stella, you should see the children! They are so beautiful, shining like stars."

These were the same thirty-nine children who had paraded past our window, now clustered around Michael, the different colors of their t-shirts spiraling around him. Michael wanted the spectacle to remind me of my dancing in circles around David, one of thirty-nine maidens surrounding the king as he led the ark into Jerusalem.

With David's attention fixed on his phone, he couldn't have seen how my expression had abruptly changed, terror seizing me as I sensed that evil had entered the room. The image in my head, hearing David speak of the children as shining like stars, was not one of bright colors dancing around Michael, but of the gloom of Yad Vashem's Children's Memorial, candles in a dark space reflecting like stars in remembrance of the one and half million Jewish children murdered during the Holocaust. How had such horrific thoughts intruded into my mind on this day of jubilation?

The nurse was silent as he wrapped the blood pressure cuff around my arm, turning his head in such a way, I'm sure intentionally, so that I couldn't miss seeing the top of the jagged scar extending from his blue mask toward his temple. This scar I had seen before.

Paralyzed with fear, I trembled when he reached out and patted my baby, whispering, "Queen Regina, for what purpose have you come to this mountain of tears?"

I had not heard that rasp since 1988, but it was unmistakable. This was *Hakol*, not in a dream or vision, but in the flesh.

Quickly he jerked his head to make eye contact with me. Seeing my fear, he pulled his mask down to expose a foul grin. Savoring my shock, he leaned close and whispered in derision the opening words of the Stella Maris hymn, snarling his mock-filled greeting, "Hail, Queen of Heaven! Welcome to hell."

Slowly lifting his now bare face away from my ear, it twisted into a horrifying rottenness, unmasking the essence of wickedness. Suddenly, he burst forth with loud laughter, at last alerting David. "Did you think peace would come this easy, Stella, without a fight?"

Turning to David, he roared, "You should have stayed in your father's fields, dancing with your filthy sheep!"

Hakol responded to our stunned silence by slowly and silently bowing, as an actor at the conclusion of a play. He stood, spread his arms wide, and said in a now calm voice, "Do you think, children, that your God has guided you? No, I alone have been the choreographer of your dance. I told you in Bethlehem, David, that if you followed this Queen of Heaven, she would lead you onto the dance floor of death."

His speaking of the word 'death' was slightly elongated, as if caressing its single syllable.

Before the word was completely out of his mouth, the air rippled with the shock of a massive explosion which seemed to shake the building to its foundations. The blast had been at the pavilion, so powerful as to be felt a mile away. An eerie calm followed, then chaos.

Hakol had vanished by the time our senses returned. Our hearts, filled with terror, were flooded with questions. Were Michael and Tamara okay? Had the children been shielded from the blast? We knew, of course, that they had not. Surely most, if not all, of the children had perished in the blast.

In an instant, weeping had returned to the Mount of Olives. I thought of Herod's slaughter of the innocent children of Bethlehem, stunned that the gospel record of the birth of the Son of David was repeating itself in the birth of the Daughter of David.

Barluzzi's prediction had swiftly come true, a sword piercing my heart just as Mary, the first Star of the Sea, had long ago experienced. I had always imagined that Mary's pierced heart was in watching her son suffer and die on the cross. Now, in the aftermath of the explosion, I realize that the first sword to pierce her heart had been much earlier when, fleeing with Joseph and Jesus for safety in Egypt, word reached them of Herod's slaughter. In the little town of Bethlehem, Mary would have known many of those children and their parents, just as David and I had come over the last nine months to know many of these now perished children and their families. Mary surely knew then, as I bitterly realize now, that the only reason for the bloody dying of these precious ones was that she had been chosen to give birth to a miracle child, and that it had been their unfortunate lot to be near the miracle.

"Where are you, God?" I wondered. "Why have you turned your back on your promise?" These, the very questions of Ethan's lament in Psalm 89, the text inspiring my Dancing with David so long ago in Memphis, seem as unanswered now as they were then.

I am no longer, though, a twenty-two-year-old novice. My answer to those questions is now one of faith. Yes, it is true that the children of Bethlehem would have been spared had Jesus never been born. But, if never born, he could not have died, paying the price for our sin. What then?

Flowing through the ages from Mary's pierced heart has been a healing river of love. I pray my own pierced heart will bear similar fruit to that of the first Star of the Sea, Regina's life bringing such immense blessing to the world that today's horrendous loss will someday be remembered as the church remembers the death of Bethlehem's children.

David's ancient enemy, *Hakol*, returned today, bringing horror and grief to the world. I believe, though, in the words of Martin Luther's greatest hymn, one my Arkansas congregation sang often at my Maranatha Assembly of the Blessed Hope:

And though this world with devils filled, should threaten to undo us,
we will not fear, for God has willed his truth to triumph through us.
The Prince of Darkness grim, we tremble not for him;
his rage we can endure, for lo, his doom is sure;
one little word shall fell him.

One little word? What single word could overcome the infinite stream of evil words spewed through the ages by

Hakol? His voice has been heard by every daughter and son of Adam and Eve, luring them into the pathways of sin and death with the same lie he once offered to Eve, "Thou shalt not surely die."

It had taken two words, *Kochav Hayam,* to frustrate *Hakol's* attempts to keep David from fulfilling his Calling. I am David's *Kochav Hayam,* his Star of the Sea, dancing with him toward a destiny even now unfolding.

And the "one little word" that will finally doom *Hakol?*

Regina.

ABOUT ATMOSPHERE PRESS

Atmosphere Press is an independent, full-service publisher for excellent books in all genres and for all audiences. Learn more about what we do at atmospherepress.com.

We encourage you to check out some of Atmosphere's latest releases, which are available at Amazon.com and via order from your local bookstore:

Twisted Silver Spoons, a novel by Karen M. Wicks

Queen of Crows, a novel by S.L. Wilton

The Summer Festival is Murder, a novel by Jill M. Lyon

The Past We Step Into, stories by Richard Scharine

Swimming with the Angels, a novel by Colin Kersey

Island of Dead Gods, a novel by Verena Mahlow

Cloakers, a novel by Alexandra Lapointe

Twins Daze, a novel by Jerry Petersen

Embargo on Hope, a novel by Justin Doyle

Abaddon Illusion, a novel by Lindsey Bakken

Blackland: A Utopian Novel, by Richard A. Jones

The Jesus Nut, a novel by John Prather

The Embers of Tradition, a novel by Chukwudum Okeke

Saints and Martyrs: A Novel, by Aaron Roe

When I Am Ashes, a novel by Amber Rose

The Recoleta Stories, by Bryon Esmond Butler

Voodoo Hideaway, a novel by Vance Cariaga

Hart Street and Main, a novel by Tabitha Sprunger

The Weed Lady, a novel by Shea R. Embry

ABOUT THE AUTHOR

A student of ancient Hebrew language and culture, Siegfried Johnson in 1990 earned a graduate degree in biblical Hebrew from the University of Michigan, after which he left Ann Arbor to enter ministry in the United Methodist Church, currently serving as Senior Pastor at Christ of the Hills in beautiful Hot Springs Village, Arkansas. He has continued to nurture his love for Hebrew studies by leading over thirty tours to the Holy Land and throughout the Mediterranean world, since 2010 serving as a Director of Travel Ministries for Educational Opportunities Tours, a faith-based travel company head-quartered in Lakeland, Florida.

Made in the USA
Coppell, TX
04 March 2022

74458675R00215